PATRICK A.
DAVIS

★ ★ ★ ★

A SLOW
WALK TO
HELL

POCKET BOOKS
New York   London   Toronto   Sydney

This book is a work of fiction. Names, characters, places and incidents are products of the author's imagination or are used fictitiously. Any resemblance to actual events or locales or persons, living or dead, is entirely coincidental.

An *Original* Publication of POCKET BOOKS

 POCKET BOOKS, a division of Simon & Schuster, Inc.
1230 Avenue of the Americas, New York, NY 10020

ISBN: 0-7434-7430-9

First Pocket Books printing March 2004

10 9 8 7 6 5 4 3 2 1

POCKET and colophon are registered trademarks of Simon & Schuster, Inc.

Cover design by Jessie Sanchez. Illustration by Ben Perini

Manufactured in the United States of America

For information regarding special discounts for bulk purchases, please contact Simon & Schuster Special Sales at 1-800-456-6798 or business@simonandschuster.com

Acknowledgments

No man is an island and that goes double for an author crafting a story. As always, I'd like to express my gratitude to my Air Force Academy classmates and pro-bono advisors: Colonel Dennis Hilley, Lieutenant Colonel (Ret) Michael Garber, and David Markl for their guidance and expertise on military issues. I'd also like to thank Lieutenant Colonel (Ret) James Hassall and his wife Cherie for going above and beyond the call of duty to provide crucial background information on Virginia Tech University. In addition, I'd like to express my appreciation to Dr. Bill Burke and Dr. Carey Page, for their ever-wise medical and forensic inputs.

Thanks also goes to my growing circle of unbiased proofreaders: My parents, Bill and Betty Davis; my wife, Helen; my brother-in-law, Michael Roche; my nephews, Eddie Coffin and Erik Olson; Chris Wells, Pat Dryke, Nate Green, Cecil Fuqua, Bobby and Kathy Baker, Eric Rush, and Connie and Mike Maloney.

Finally, I need to thank my publisher, Pocket Books, and my agent, Karen Solem, for their continuing faith in my ability to write stories that people might want to read.

To Bob and Katie Sessler,
for their patience, wisdom,
and most of all, friendship.

A SLOW
WALK TO
HELL

★ 1 ★

It was around 7 P.M. on a Friday evening and I was standing by the punch bowl in a drafty school gym, trying not to appear completely bored as I helped chaperone my daughter's formal middle school dance. I'd like to say that I volunteered for the duty out of a sense of parental obligation, but I hadn't. I'm Martin Collins, chief of police for Warrentown, Virginia, a small town seventy miles west of Washington, D.C., and babysitting three hundred adolescents came with the territory.

Understandably my thirteen-year-old daughter Emily wasn't exactly thrilled by my presence. She made me promise not to embarrass her in any way. By "embarrass," she meant I wasn't supposed to take photographs, talk to her or her friends, or come anywhere near her.

I tried to placate her by telling her I wasn't going to wear a uniform. "So you can chill. Your friends probably won't even notice me."

She gave me her patented "get real" look. "I think it's best if you pretend not to know me, Dad."

"Might be a little difficult," I said dryly. "I'm driving you to the dance. Remember?"

She stuck out her jaw at my logic. "You know what I mean."

"Honey, I'd like to at least take a few photos for your grandmother—"

"*Dad!*" She looked thoroughly horrified.

I gave up. After three books and a half dozen episodes of *Dr. Phil*, I still wasn't any closer to understanding the female teenage mind. My wife Nicole could have enlightened me, but she passed away from cancer when Emily was nine. My transition into the role of being a single parent hasn't been exactly smooth, but despite any mistakes I've made, Emily has turned out pretty well. She gets good grades, is popular at school, and usually does what I ask without copping an attitude.

"Fine," I told her. "I won't come within ten feet of you."

Actually, I thought it would be easy to keep up my end of the bargain, but it wasn't. At the moment, I was watching Emily slow-dance with a strapping blond kid who was already sprouting facial hair. Every so often he would casually slide a hand down her back and it was all I could do not to throw him through a wall.

I fought the impulse by draining a glass of punch, wishing it was a beer.

The song mercifully ended and the orange-haired DJ switched to a peppy Britney Spears tune. Emily and the boy reluctantly parted, but kept on dancing. I didn't like the predatory smile he was giving her and tried to intimidate him with a scowl. No dice. Raging hormone never looked my way.

I sighed. Maybe Emily was right. Maybe I shouldn't have come. Seeing her now, looking so beautiful in her long yellow dress, dancing with a boy, reminded me of how fast she was maturing. In the past year, she'd grown four inches and her figure was filling out. She wasn't my little girl any longer.

The thought of Emily growing up was difficult to accept, and not simply because she was my daughter and I loved her. Rather, it was because she looked so much like her mother. If you saw a photo of Nicole at thirteen, you'd swear that she and Emily were twins. They both had flowing auburn hair, wide cheekbones, and brilliant blue eyes that lit up when they laughed.

I felt a familiar tightness in my chest as I contemplated the wedding band I still wore. Nicole and I were married twenty years and when she died, part of me did, too. Since then, I've dreaded the day Emily would leave home to create her own life. Irrational as it might seem, I knew I would feel a sense of loss comparable to Nicole's passing.

I also wasn't looking forward to being alone.

As I watched the smiling young faces around me, I became irritated at how pathetic my life had become. If I *was* alone, I had only myself to blame. For a guy in his midforties, I was pretty well preserved. At six feet, I carried a trim 180 pounds, and my close-cropped blond hair had only a few flecks of gray. Over the years, I had opportunities for relationships. More than one woman had made her interest in me known.

But I'd always turned them away.

I recalled the one offer I wish I had accepted. She was someone I cared for deeply, but at the time, I still hadn't come anywhere close to shaking the ghost of Nicole. When I told this woman that I needed more time, she was understandably hurt. "Don't expect me to wait forever, Marty."

That conversation occurred eight months ago. We tried to continue as friends, but our relationship became increasingly strained. Even though we're neighbors, she began going out of her way to avoid me. It was almost comical. If I went outside to barbecue or mow the yard, she disappeared into her house, reappearing only when the coast was clear. Whenever I phoned her, she wouldn't pick up; if I stopped by, she wouldn't come to the door. On the occasions I managed to corner her, she was coolly distant and always seemed anxious to end our conversation. When I asked her about it, she said it was easier emotionally not to have any contact with me.

I almost told her what she wanted to hear then. Lord knows, I was tempted. In the end, I couldn't do it. She deserved a guy who would put her at the top of his list, who wasn't hung up on his dead wife.

So I backed off and gave her the space she wanted. It was one of the toughest things I've ever done, but at least it gave me the opportunity to see what life would be like without her.

I hated it.

Last week, I reached a decision and went by her place, ringing the bell until she finally opened the door. I told her I was ready to make a commitment.

I didn't get the reaction I expected. Instead of a big hug or a smile, I saw only an expression of sadness. She said quietly, "I told you I wouldn't wait forever."

Her tone more than her words told me what must have happened. I asked her if she was seeing someone else.

When she nodded, I felt like I'd been kicked in the stomach. I asked her if the relationship was serious and she said it was. After going oh-for-two, there wasn't anything left for me to say.

As I started to go, she said, "You're still not ready, you know."

It sounded like an accusation. I was about to argue when

I noticed her looking down at my left hand. I remained silent; in my heart, I knew she was probably right. When I left, I thought I noticed dampness in her eyes.

Probably wishful thinking.

The song ended and another began. A catchy hip-hop number, with the DJ rapping out the lyrics. The guy wasn't half bad. On the dance floor, the kids cheered him on and he rapped even louder.

But all I could hear was that damning phrase in my head: "You're still not ready."

A mixture of emotions swirled through me, punctuated by a profound sense of regret. I forced my eyes to my ring finger, knowing what I had to do. Slowly, I reached down and touched the gold band. As my fingers encircled it, they began to tremble.

You're not betraying Nicole's memory, Marty. You have to move on with your life.

Twenty years of history held me frozen. I was no longer aware of the pulsing music or the chatter of nearby voices. I was only aware of the ring and what it represented.

My fingers pulled and the ring started to slide—

I stopped. My belt was vibrating.

My relief over the interruption was palpable. Before I knew it, I'd thrown back my jacket and unhooked my cell phone. The caller ID read "U.S. Government," the number blanked out. On the other end, I could dimly make out someone saying my name. The music made conversation impossible. I shouted, "Hang on a minute."

Only one government agency ever called me, and when it did, it meant only one thing.

Someone was dead.

★

Ditching my cup by the punch bowl, I darted past a circle of scowling girls wearing Morticia Adams makeup, and hustled out the double doors into the quiet of the hallway. By the trophy case, I spotted Coach English chatting with the principal, Mrs. Roche. Ducking into a corner, I placed the phone to my ear. A tentative voice said, "Lieutenant Colonel Collins? Sir? You there?"

The use of my former rank confirmed he was with the Air Force OSI. Before becoming the Warrentown police chief, I'd served twenty years as an investigator with the Office of Special Investigations, the Air Force's criminal investigative branch. Upon my retirement, my old boss, in an effort to retain a cadre of experienced investigators, offered me a post as a civilian consultant, focusing exclusively on homicides. It was too good a deal to pass up. Since the military isn't exactly Murder Incorporated, the workload's light, rarely more than a couple of cases a year, and when I did work, I'd earn double my military salary. I also liked the idea of investigating an occasional homicide, since it provided a nice change of pace from the small-town cop routine.

"This is Lieutenant Colonel Collins," I said.

"Sir, hold for General Hinkle . . ."

There was a pause as the call was transferred. Brigadier General Charlie Hinkle was the OSI commander and an old friend. It was typical for Charlie to still be at work on a Friday night. After all, that's how he made general; he'd busted his ass by putting in years of sixteen-hour workdays. Frankly, that was a sacrifice I hadn't been willing to make, which explained why I topped out as light bird.

Was I envious that my old buddy Charlie was a general officer and I wasn't?

No way. That star on Charlie's shoulder had cost him. His second wife Mary walked out on him a several months back and I couldn't recall the last time he'd spoken with his two grown kids. But, hey, he made general.

Good for Charlie.

When Charlie came on the line, his words flew out in an excited Chicken Little falsetto. It didn't necessarily mean that the sky was falling, since Charlie tended to spin up easily. "Christ, oh Christ. We got a bad one, Marty. The heat I'm feeling is unbelievable. I just got off the horn with the SECDEF *and* the chairman of the Joint Chiefs. They want this thing treated with kid gloves. The word is that the White House will be monitoring the investigation. Right now, the game plan is to keep the killing quiet. I mean *quiet*. We're under orders to keep it from the press until at least twenty-two hundred hours—"

His words were all over the map and I had to cut in. "Slow down, Charlie. Take it from the beginning. Who the hell was murdered?"

"I'm getting to that. The victim's an Air Force major who worked at the Pentagon. A guy named Talbot." He paused, as if anticipating a response.

"Go on."

"You don't recognize the name, huh?"

Meaning I should. I searched my brain cells for a few moments. "Sorry. It doesn't ring any—"

When the bell suddenly chimed in my head, I gripped the phone hard. I now understood why everyone from the president on down was jumping through hoops. "*Franklin* Talbot? The guy who was all over the news last year, accused of being gay?"

"Yeah," Charlie said. "And if we're not careful, this thing could turn into a PR nightmare for the military. You remember much about Talbot's case?"

"As I recall, he supposedly confessed to . . ."

Charlie was already telling me. Last year Colonel Kelly, Major Talbot's boss, had met Talbot in a bar for a drink. Somewhere in the middle of Talbot's second Bloody Mary, Talbot casually dropped the bomb that he was gay. Since Talbot's admission had been entirely voluntary—Kelly had not questioned him on his sexuality or even brought up the topic—it met the tenets of the military's "Don't Ask, Don't Tell" policy, and Colonel Kelly could act upon the information. Kelly did so by formally levying a charge of homosexuality against Talbot, which, if proven, would lead to Talbot's discharge from the service.

As the Air Force's investigative arm, the OSI had the less-than-desirable job of determining whether Talbot was really gay. It shouldn't have been a big deal. After all, Talbot had confessed, right?

Not quite.

When the *The Washington Post* broke the story several days later, Major Talbot immediately went public and repudiated Colonel Kelly's statement that he was a homosexual, confessed or otherwise. I caught a clip on FOX News and recalled his expression of outraged innocence.

"Colonel Kelly is lying," he said flatly. "I never told him I was gay. *I am not gay.*"

"Why would Colonel Kelly fabricate the charge?" a reporter asked.

"You'll have to ask Colonel Kelly."

When the reporters did, Colonel Kelly had no comment. To the OSI and his superiors, Kelly stuck to his original statement. Without corroborating witnesses, it came down to a case of "he said, he said." After a week, the Air Force conveniently dropped the investigation, citing lack of evidence. Shortly thereafter, in an effort to escape the lime-light, Colonel Kelly requested a transfer to Germany.

This story should never have generated much press play. Other than briefly rekindling the continual debate about whether gays should serve in the military, it held little news value. In truth, the media's interest in Talbot can be summed up in two words: "celebrity" and "power."

Not Major Talbot's celebrity and power, but that of his uncle by marriage, the man who raised him after Talbot's parents were killed in a car accident and who sat to his right at the news conference.

The Honorable Garrison Harris, the charismatic congressman who chaired the powerful House Appropriations Committee and was everybody's odds-on favorite to become the next president of the United States.

★2★

After refreshing my memory about Major Talbot, Charlie filled me in on his murder. Since Talbot's body had only been discovered within the hour, Charlie didn't have much other than the how and where. Talbot's body had been found in his home by his housekeeper, a Mrs. Chang, who had called 911. From statements provided by the police who'd initially responded, there seemed little doubt as to the cause of death. "Someone really did a number on Talbot," Charlie said. "Multiple stab wounds and blood all over the place. And here's the kicker; the killer cut Talbot's dick off and jammed it in his mouth."

I winced. "Jesus . . ."

"Yeah. The press is going to *love* that angle. The SECDEF is concerned this could turn into a hate crime, with a military perp. If that happens, every pro-gay outfit and liberal politician will be screaming that the military promotes a climate of hate against gays."

"A hate crime?" I said. "I thought your investigation never uncovered evidence that Talbot was gay."

He snorted. "What investigation? We were ordered to go slow, so we did. Captain Hilley was the lead investigator, but he only got as far as interviewing Major Talbot and

Colonel Kelly before the case was shut down. Word was the SECDEF had no choice; Congressman Harris had him by the balls when he threatened to stall a couple of key defense bills."

Not exactly surprising news. Congressman Harris was an acknowledged master of political hardball. I pointed out to Charlie that by definition, a hate crime meant someone had killed Talbot specifically because he was gay. I added, "If his homosexuality was never proven—"

"The key is whether people *believed* he was gay. A lot of them did. When the story broke, Talbot received close to a hundred letters. Sick stuff. A dozen or so threatened his life if he didn't resign his commission. We managed to track down a few of the senders. Most were former military. One guy was a white supremacist from Alabama. Look, Marty, I want Talbot to be straight. I want the killer to be some pissed-off husband who found out Talbot was screwing his wife. But we both know someone stuck his dick in his mouth for a reason."

While I understood the symbolism of the act, I didn't consider it a slam dunk. I almost reminded Charlie about a similar killing where a colonel had lopped off the penis of his wife's lover. But instead of placing the appendage in the dead man's mouth, the colonel wrapped it in a box with a pretty bow and had it delivered to his wife.

I said, "Relax, Charlie. It shouldn't take long to determine if Talbot was straight. His housekeeper or friends will probably know. Hell, he might even have a subscription to *Playboy* or *Pent*—"

"Call as soon as you know." He rustled papers, getting impatient. "A couple of quick items. Congressman Harris is the reason we're keeping a lid on the story until twenty-two hundred. He was campaigning in Pennsylvania when they told him about his nephew. He's catching a charter flight back and doesn't want to be swarmed by reporters when he lands. He's scheduled into Reagan National at twenty-one thirty, give or take. He'll have questions, so get your ass over to Talbot's and find some answers. I got the address here someplace . . ." More papers rustling; Charlie wasn't what you would call organized. "What was that, Marty?"

"You order up a RIP?" I repeated. RIPs were computerized personnel printouts and would provide us Talbot's complete assignment histories.

"Chief Tisdale has a copy. He's en route to the Pentagon, to secure Talbot's office. You can swing by and pick it up from him. Anything else?"

Charlie had already briefed me that Talbot had worked in Air Force manpower, the directorate responsible for tracking the personnel authorizations mandated by congress. It was essentially a high-tech bean counting job. I said, "Those people you identified who wrote threatening letters—"

"Forget about them. There were only five and none live within five hundred miles of here. Captain Hilley's trying to contact them now. So far, he's spoken to three. A fourth is hospitalized and the fifth is working the night shift at a plant in Dallas. You got a pen handy?"

As I jotted down Talbot's address on the back of a business card, I was relieved to see that he lived in Arlington, Virginia.

Location of a crime determined jurisdiction. Since an Air Force member had been killed off a military reservation, the appropriate civilian authority—the Arlington County PD—would take the lead and I, as the OSI representative, would assist.

Don't misunderstand me; I had no qualms about running a high-visibility investigation. I'm a solid homicide investigator and was confident I could solve the crime. My concern was whether I could do so quickly enough to satisfy the media talking heads and various military and political heavyweights.

With luck, possibly.

But a man had to know his limitations and I knew mine. If anyone could solve this case in a rapid fashion, it would be the man who almost certainly would handle this investigation for the Arlington County PD.

Lieutenant Simon **Santos was** the department's homicide chief and a brilli**ant, instinc**tual investigator. Over the past decade, his successes had elevated him into a local law enforcement legend. Simon rarely took more than a few days to wrap up a murder. Often, he'd make an arrest within hours. How he did this, no one knew. After working with him on numerous cases over the years, I concluded there was one reason for his success: The guy was a genius, an investigative savant.

Of course, it didn't hurt that Simon was also worth a few hundred million dollars and could afford to keep an army of informants on his payroll.

"Yeah," Charlie said, when I asked, "Santos is going to be in charge. I spoke to Chief Novak; he's trying to hunt Santos down to break the news." His voice became apologetic. "You won't like this, but it comes straight from the SECDEF. Congressman Harris wants a daily update on the investigation—let me finish." He talked over me as I tried to cut in. "Anything Harris wants, you play along. He tells you to kiss his ass, you plant a wet one and smile. The SECDEF doesn't want to give Harris any reason to think the military is engaged in a coverup. You understand what I'm saying, Marty."

He was using his I'm-a-general-and-you're-not voice. I said calmly, "This is bullshit, Charlie."

"It's called *politics*. You seen the latest poll numbers? Harris is a lock to become the Democrats' presidential nominee. He's also holding a six-point lead over the president. Like it or not, the man's got a better than even chance to be sitting in the White House next January."

I bit my tongue to keep from saying something I might regret. "That it?"

"No." He waited a beat. "What's with you and Amanda?"

I tried not to sound surprised. "What do you mean?"

"I also assigned her to the case. She's at home, waiting for your call . . ."

"Okay—"

"When I told her that she'd be teaming with you, she said something mighty curious. She asked if I could find someone to take her place. What the hell is going on? Since when doesn't she want to work with you?"

"I don't know, Charlie."

"Don't give me that crap. If my two best homicide investigators can't work together, I've got a right to know."

"I don't know, Charlie," I said again.

"Fine. Play it cute. But there's a lot riding on this thing. You and Amanda have issues, it'd better not affect your goddamn job. Now call her and get down to Talbot's."

After he hung up, I stood there, staring at the phone. *She's at home, waiting for your call . . .*

But only because it was her job.

I punched in her number anyway.

Of course, Major Amanda Gardner was the woman I had strong feelings for. We'd met three years earlier, when she was assigned to assist me on a triple homicide. While I found her bright, competent, and attractive, I was initially put off by her Joan Wayne, supercop attitude. Whether we were crawling over the grisly crime scene or grilling an un-cooperative suspect, she felt compelled to prove that she was as tough as any male. If you acknowledged her femi-ninity, made allowances for it in any way, she became angry.

I didn't get it. She wasn't only a cop, she was a woman. A beautiful woman. Why deny it?

During our second case, I got the nerve to ask her this question, over a few beers. Instead of the telling me to mind my own business, she said, "You sure you want to know?"

When I nodded, she slipped back to her days as an Air Force Academy cadet and moved forward to the present, ex-plaining what it's like to be an attractive woman in a man's world. In a quietly reflective voice, she described a pattern of whispered sexual inferences and unwelcome amorous advances. The harassment had been constant and wearing, and Amanda grew to hate her appearance, hate the way men were attracted to her. When she became an officer, she considered bringing charges against some of the more blatant offenders, but knew that if she did, she would end her military career. In desperation, she decided to alter her image, create a persona that men would find intimidating and less appealing.

"So I cut my hair, quit wearing makeup, placed chips on both shoulders, and dared anyone to knock them off. I made it clear that I wasn't someone you messed with."

"And the men quit hitting on you?"

She nodded. "But there was a downside."

"They thought you were a dyke?"

"Yeah." She smiled. "I'm not, you know."

When her eyes lingered on mine, I had my first inkling

that she might have feelings for me. In the ensuing years, I tried not to reciprocate them. Looking back, I realized I'd made a mistake. But that's how it is with emotions; you don't control them, they control you. Now, when I'd finally reached a place where I could put Nicole's death behind me, it was too late.

I'm not naive; I never expected Amanda to wait forever. I'd only hoped she'd wait a few more months.

The phone was ringing in my ear. I pictured Amanda staring at the caller ID, trying to decide whether to answer. For the first time in months, she picked up. "Hello, Marty."

She didn't sound happy.

We conversed less than thirty seconds. Amanda kept her voice clipped and professional and never mentioned her aversion to working with me. Since the school was en route to Arlington, Amanda said she'd swing by and pick me up.

I asked her to stop by my place and retrieve my weapon, OSI credentials, latex gloves, and a notepad. "Mrs. Anuncio knows where they are." Mrs. Anuncio was my live-in house-keeper.

"Fifteen minutes."

After Amanda clicked off, I made two quick phone calls. The first was to Sara Winters, whose daughter was also at the dance. "Sure, Marty," Sara said, "I'll be glad to give Emily a ride home." Next, I phoned Mark Haney, my senior deputy, and told him that he'd be running the office, while I moonlighted with the OSI.

Clipping my phone to my belt, I swung over to Coach English and Mrs. Roche, and informed them that I had to bail out on chaperone duties. When I broke the news to Emily that I'd been called out on a case, she couldn't stop smiling. Walking away from her, it occurred to me that the two most important women in my life didn't want me around.

A guy could get a complex.

It was a cool spring night and I'd only been waiting on the sidewalk for a few minutes when I spotted the gold Saab turn into the parking lot. I walked toward it, waving my arms. As it rolled to a stop, I went over and got inside.

AC/DC played on the radio. Anything softer than heavy metal Amanda considered easy listening. I gave her a smile. She watched me for a moment and seemed about to say something. Instead, she bit her lip and nodded tersely toward the back seat. "Your stuff's in my briefcase."

"Thanks." Popping the latches to retrieve the items, I decided not to force the conversation. It was clear that my presence wasn't easy for her.

Five minutes later, we merged onto State Highway 26 for the hour drive to Arlington. Amanda never said a word and I could feel the tension between us. Easing back in my seat, I risked a glance and saw her fixated straight ahead. Under the flickering streetlights, I studied her profile and thought she'd never looked more beautiful. Over the past several months, she'd shifted away from the butch image that she'd crafted for herself. She was allowing her red hair to grow out and it now framed the perfect oval of her face. Her skin was tight, her complexion flawless, and she wore more makeup than usual. I also became aware of the scent of perfume, another recent concession to femininity.

My eyes drifted down to her suit. Another sign of the new Amanda. As long as I've known her, she's favored loose fitting and neutral colored clothing; this suit was an eye-catching red, stylishly cut, with a flared gold collar. In the OSI, we wore civilian clothing because we're more effective when no one knows our rank. Officers can be a pain in the ass when they're questioned by someone they outrank and enlisted personnel feel intimidated when grilled by someone they know is an officer.

I slowly faced front, troubled by a sudden realization.

When I'd first noticed Amanda's increasingly feminine makeover, I had enough ego to assume she'd made the changes for me. But thinking back, that conclusion didn't make sense. She'd been avoiding me for months. She made it clear that she didn't want me to see her.

So she must have made the changes for someone else.

By the time we reached I-395 twenty minutes later, Amanda was still giving me the silent treatment. This was ridiculous. Turning down the radio, I said, "Look, we're both professionals. We should be able to handle this situation."

She concentrated on her driving. "I am handling it."

"By not talking to me."

A shrug. "We're talking now."

"You know what I mean." I hesitated. "General Hinkle told me you wanted to be removed from the case."

"I thought it would be best."

"Why?"

"You have to ask?" Her eyes still focused on the road.

"Actually, I do. Any history between us shouldn't affect our ability to do our jobs. We should have enough self discipline to— What?" I caught a shake.

"Take my word for it. You don't want to get into this, Marty."

"Why not?"

The only response was the humming of the tires on the road.

"Amanda . . ."

Still nothing. She wasn't going to tell me. I was about to give up when she said softly. "You couldn't stand the answer."

The implication stung. I retreated, looking outside.

"Marty." Her voice was soft and sympathetic. "I didn't mean it that way. It's not what you're thinking."

I continued to gaze into the dark. "What? That you find my presence . . . offensive?"

"That's not it at all. I'm . . . I'm trying not to hurt you."

As the statement drifted toward me, I shifted toward her. She was finally looking at me. In the semidarkness, I sensed rather than saw her sadness. I said, "Hurt me?"

"Jesus . . ." She hunched forward and gripped the wheel hard. "I didn't want to get into this now. I wanted to wait. I wanted to a figure out a way to tell you."

"Tell me what?"

She struggled for a reply. "Last night, he asked me. Bob. He asked me to marry him."

I felt a sudden, stabbing sensation. Even though I knew the answer, I had to ask. "And?"

No response. She sat there with an anguished expression.

As if with great effort, she slowly lifted her left hand. In the glow of oncoming headlights, I caught the glint of a diamond.

"I'm so sorry, Marty," she whispered.

"I'm not," I heard myself say. "I think it's wonderful. Congratulations."

At that moment, my facade crumbled and I had to turn away.

★ 3 ★

The remainder of the drive was difficult for both of us. Amanda was wrapped up in self-recrimination for causing me pain and I was struggling to accept the reality that she would never become a part of my life. As a defense, we withdrew into our private worlds, to lick our emotional wounds. There was no eye contact and no conversation.

This couldn't go on. We had a job to do; we had to bridge our hurt and find a way to work together.

Could we?

I had my answer when Amanda turned into an upscale North Arlington neighborhood and simultaneously extended directions that she'd downloaded from the internet. "You mind?"

"No."

Flipping on the map light, I concentrated on the directions. At a four-way stop, we turned left and followed a winding street up a hill, passing increasingly larger homes, some that qualified as mansions.

"This explains why an Air Force major needed a housekeeper," Amanda said.

I nodded, glancing up from the paper. Here within the

Beltway, anyone from a lieutenant colonel on down usually resided in apartments or townhomes, since that was all they could afford.

"What do you think these places run?" Amanda said. "A couple million?"

"At least."

"So Congressman Harris must be footing the bill," she said. "Generous uncle."

"He can afford it." Congressman Harris had a fortune in the tens of millions, courtesy of his grandfather who'd founded a department store chain. I added, "Besides, Major Talbot was probably like a son to him."

"You know that Major Talbot is Mrs. Harris's sister's kid. He's not related by blood to the congressman."

"So what? The congressman raised Talbot. He obviously loved him—"

"That just it, Marty. They weren't close. Harris never even formally adopted him."

I gave her a look.

"I downloaded a couple articles on Talbot," she explained. "Got them in my briefcase. *The National Enquirer* had the most interesting account—" She caught my scowl. "Hey, a lot of what they write is true."

"Like J-Lo having an alien baby?"

"Look, you want to hear what I found out or not?"

"Can't wait."

She was glowering. It was an encouraging sign. Maybe we could quit walking on egg shells and resume a normal working relationship.

"According to the article," Amanda said, "Talbot moved in with the Harrises when he was eleven and had serious problems adjusting. He ran away constantly. When Talbot was twelve, he took off for an entire summer. Harris finally sent him to a military school and that apparently did the trick. Talbot got into the military lifestyle and has been a model citizen ever—" She stopped, frowning hard.

I waited. "Yes?"

"I think the article said . . . I'm sure that's where he went to college. Talbot's one of your fellow alums, Marty."

"He went to Virginia Tech?"

"Yeah. He was also in the corps."

This spoke well of Talbot. During my four years in the corp of cadets, I'd never met anyone who came from the kind of wealth or influence that Congressman Harris represented. As a rule, the rich and powerful don't fight wars; the poor and middle class do.

We crested the hill and turned left at another stop sign. Here the homes qualified as palatial, each nestled on several wooded acres and surrounded by an assortment of intimidating fences and walls.

"Jeez," Amanda said. "Look at the size of these places."

I was. Impressive.

"Doesn't figure, Marty. Even if the *Enquirer* article was wrong and Talbot and the congressman were close, what uncle shells out millions for his nephew's house?"

A valid question. Talbot was a bachelor and a relatively junior military officer. Why would he need to live in a mansion?

I sat up and pointed. "It should be the next house on the right. The one with the iron fence."

We rolled to a stop in front of an ornate wrought iron gate. A sign attached to it said in big black letters, PRIVATE PROPERTY. TRESPASSERS WILL BE PROSECUTED. And below: DANGER. ELECTRIC FENCE.

"Interesting," Amanda said.

I nodded. Another inconsistency. Why would an Air Force major feel the need to have an electrified fence?

Peering through the gate, we saw an elegant hacienda-style home, sitting at the end of a crescent drive lined by light poles. The grounds were expansive and immaculate, and included a guest house, a tennis court, and a small pond.

"You sure we're at the right place?" Amanda said.

I'd felt similarly perplexed and was comparing Amanda's downloaded address against the one I'd written down. I clicked off the map light with a nod. "They match."

"So where is everyone?"

It was a mystery. This was supposedly the scene of a brutal murder. There should be police vehicles and cops everywhere. But there was nothing—not a person or a vehicle of any kind.

I said, "Charlie Hinkle did say they're trying to keep the killing quiet."

"*This* quiet?"

I studied the main house. It was a sprawling, white adobe structure with a two-story center section and single-story wings fanning out on either side.

"A light just came on," I said. "Someone's home."

Exiting the car, I headed toward the intercom affixed to a gatepost. After a couple steps, I was suddenly bathed in a bright light. Glancing up, I saw that a spotlight attached to the top of the gatepost had come on.

"Video camera," Amanda called out. "Two o'clock."

I blinked, trying to focus through the light. I located the camera attached to the right gatepost, peering down on me. It moved fractionally.

Then from the intercom, I heard the crackle of a familiar voice.

"We're opening the gate now, Martin."

As I returned to the Saab, Amanda said, "That sounded like Simon."

"It was. He wants us to park around back."

She shifted into drive as the gate bumped against the stop. "You thinking what I'm thinking?"

"Yeah. This could be a short investigation if the killer is on videotape."

"Someone's coming," she said.

As we rolled through the gate, we watched the approaching car. It was a red BMW convertible and as it went by, I caught a flash of silver hair.

"Looked liked Harry," I said to Amanda.

"The guy who sometimes drives for Simon?"

I nodded.

"Wonder why he's leaving?"

Following the curve of the driveway, we swung around to the rear of the house and found it ablaze in light. Close to a dozen vehicles were parked against the fence that surrounded the pool. Except for the coroner's van and an ambulance, all the vehicles appeared unmarked, no doubt in an attempt to prevent the media from learning of the killing. This would prove to be a futile exercise. Police departments always had leaks. In a killing this big, someone would talk.

Amanda nosed in beside a gleaming black stretch limo that was parked at the end of the line of vehicles. Among the sedans and vans, it seemed glaringly out of place. It wasn't.

Some of Simon's fellow cops resented the fact that he

cruised around in a chauffeured limo; they assumed he did it to flaunt his wealth. Not true. Simon used a limo because he had pathological fear of driving. When he first told me this, I thought he was kidding.

Then I saw him drive. His hands shook and he broke out in a sweat. He was genuinely terrified.

They say geniuses tend to be eccentric and Simon is no exception. Included among his many idiosyncracies are an aversion to handshaking and a compulsion to wear the same suit. I don't mean the *exact* same suit, I'm actually talking about identical-looking suits. Specifically, Simon has a closet full of dark blue Brooks Brothers suits, which he wears with a razor-pressed white shirt, a red carnation in the lapel, and a wild bow tie. The only variation to his dress is the bow tie, which he cycles depending on the day of the week. Even though the ties are hideously ugly, they get your attention. That's the idea; no one forgot meeting Simon.

Amanda and I got out of the car and took in our surroundings. By the pool, we could see two burly men in suits—probably plainclothes cops—standing on the decking, smoking cigarettes. Neither looked familiar. Several uniformed officers armed with flashlights angled past us and disappeared down the slope of the hill.

"Neighbors probably didn't see much," Amanda said, pointing out the heavy woods on the property.

"No . . ."

She'd gestured with her left hand and I was staring at her ring. In the darkness of the car, I never had a chance to appreciate its size.

The diamond was huge. It was the biggest rock I'd ever seen. It had to be five or six carats.

Bob, it seemed, had money. A lot of money.

"Company," Amanda said.

I followed her gaze toward the pool. One of the cops had detached from his buddy and was walking toward us. His suspicious squint suggested he hadn't been briefed about our arrival. Leaning over the short fence, he casually fired his cigarette butt to the ground and not so casually asked, "Can I help you?"

When I told him we were with the OSI, nothing registered on his fleshy face. Obviously, he hadn't graduated at the top of detective school.

As Amanda and I passed him our credentials, a voice sang out, "They're okay, Richie. Simon's expecting them. We got the green light for you and Ben to interview the neighbors. Be cool. Don't let on that Major Talbot is dead until we get the okay."

Looking toward the rear of the house, Amanda and I saw a man emerge from the French doors and hurry toward us. He was slender, medium height, with wavy dark hair and movie-star good looks.

As usual Enrique Garza, Lieutenant Simon Santos's chauffeur, was dressed like a Vegas headliner. He wore a purple Armani suit, a dark blue shirt, and a purple tie. From his ears dangled looped gold earrings that had to be an inch in diameter. On anybody else, his flamboyant getup might look cartoonish, but Enrique could pull it off. He could wear a leisure suit to a biker convention and still exude cool.

"Okay, Enrique." Richie returned our credentials without bothering to look, then motioned to his friend and lumbered toward a gate at the back of the pool fence.

You wouldn't expect a homicide detective to take orders from a chauffeur, but then Enrique wasn't a typical chauffeur.

A former Navy SEAL, Enrique had been a homicide sergeant in the Arlington PD until last year, when he got canned because he almost killed a child killer during an arrest. In Enrique's defense, the other guy swung first and Enrique simply reacted. Normally, that shouldn't have been a problem, but Enrique used some kind of a ninja punch and drove the guy's nose cartilage into his brain, turning him into an eggplant.

Anywhere else, Enrique would have probably gotten a medal. But this is America, the most litigious country in the world.

The killer's family got a big-time lawyer and sued the city, claiming Enrique *intentionally* tried to kill the man. No one thought the family had a chance of winning the case, but the city decided they just might. After all, Enrique *was* a highly trained SEAL and should have been able to control his punch.

So the city settled the case out of court. In addition to whatever money they paid to the family, they also agreed to fire Enrique.

I'd once asked Enrique why he didn't sue the city for his job back. No jury in the world would punish him for turning a child-killer into a drooling slab of meat.

"It's not worth the hassle, Marty," Enrique said. "Besides, I got me too good a gig now. Simon pays me three times what I made as a detective and I get the added benny of assisting on his investigations. Hell, it's like still being on the force, only without having to put up with the horseshit."

He was lying. Later, Simon told me the real reason that Enrique never sued for reinstatement.

Enrique knew the trial would turn into a circus and had no desire to become a poster child for other people's agendas. He also didn't want to play the discrimination card. According to Simon, Enrique believed that his firing was justified; he'd made a mistake and lost control.

By discrimination, Enrique wasn't referring to bias against his Hispanic heritage. Rather he was talking about his sexuality.

Besides being a former SEAL and arguably the toughest cop in the Arlington PD, Enrique also happened to be gay.

I suspected that fact explained his presence here tonight.

*

Enrique waited for Amanda and me by the rear gate in the pool fence. He greeted us with a smile and we shook hands. As he turned away from Amanda, his eyes dropped to her ring. I expected him to offer his congratulations on her engagement, but he never did.

Curious.

When I mentioned we'd seen Harry leaving, Enrique confirmed that he'd had the day off.

"Simon called and said to meet him here ASAP. My place is over by Balston Mall, so I got here pretty quick. About the same time as Simon."

"Where was he tonight?" I remembered Charlie Hinkle's comment that the Arlington PD chief of police had been trying to locate Simon.

"At a Kennedy Center concert. The chief had an usher hunt him down." He nodded toward the cars parked along the fence. "Some response, huh, Marty? We've got twice the usual crime scene units. Forensics, CID, investigative support. Must be thirty people inside. Even the ME got here in under an hour. But, hey, it's not everyday the nephew of the next president gets knocked off." He turned and started across the decking toward the house.

As Amanda and I sidled up to him, she asked, "Who's the ME?"

"Who else? Cantrell."

Dr. Agatha Cantrell was the natural choice. A thirty-year

veteran, she was easily the most experienced ME in the coroner's office.

We skirted the edge of the pool. Amanda slipped me a glance which I interpreted and answered with a nod. Enrique wouldn't take offense. You can't be a gay cop and have thin skin.

Amanda still sounded like she had a mouthful of marbles when she said, "Ah, Enrique, there were some rumors about Major Talbot. The military is concerned whether he might be—"

"The answer is, we don't know," Enrique said, smiling at her awkwardness. "We haven't turned up anything which suggests Talbot was gay."

"You checked his computer?"

"Doing it now. The problem is Talbot had one of those programs that scrambled the internet addresses of sites he visited. That doesn't necessarily mean much. A lot of straight people cover their tracks on the net."

I said, "I don't."

He looked at me. "You've never visited a porn site?"

I hesitated. "Well . . ."

He winked. "Yeah, that's what I thought."

Amanda appraised me with an amused smile. I did my best to ignore it and her.

But she kept right on smiling at me.

"Anyway," Enrique said, thankfully changing the subject, "they're reading his emails. Might be something there. Simon asked if I'd seen Talbot at some of the clubs. To be honest, he looked a little familiar, but I can't swear to it. Could be I remembered him because his picture had been in the paper."

Amanda asked if Simon had questioned the housekeeper.

"He tried. Mrs. Chang's from China and her English is pretty poor. Finding the body also threw her for a loop. She was shaking so badly, she could barely talk. Simon had her driven home. He'll question her tomorrow, with an interpreter."

We were approaching the French doors and Amanda and I stopped to don latex gloves. Enrique was already wearing a pair.

"So," he said, eyeing us, "you figure out that Major Talbot was one paranoid man."

I said, "The electrified fence?"

"For starters. Notice that?" He pointed above our heads, to what looked like a light fixture. "That's a video camera. There are fourteen on this property. Eight monitor the fence, six the house. All computer controlled and linked to motion sensors. Simon and I were checking out the surveillance room when you drove up. It's a concrete box in the basement with a keypad entry system. The door's made of steel that has to be two inches thick. You should also see the alarm system. Infrared beams on all the windows and doors. It's even got a back-up power supply, in case the electricity was ever cut off." Enrique shook his head. "Major Talbot didn't screw around when it came to security. If someone did manage to get inside his house, Talbot was determined to preserve them on tape. Now the question is, what the hell was Talbot so afraid of?"

Amanda and I exchanged glances. I could tell she was getting excited and so was I.

Beating me to the punch line, she said, "With that many cameras, the killer must be on videotape."

"Depends. We need to review the remaining tapes. Could be the killer missed one."

Amanda and I were deflated by his response. She said, "Missed one?"

"Five tapes were removed from the video recorders. Had to be the killer. Billy Cromartie's in the surveillance room, checking out the ones that were left."

Amanda swore.

I was frowning, trying to understand. "But the surveillance room door. You said it had a secure entry system."

Enrique was reaching for one of the French doors, when he turned back to me. "Right. We had to call the security company to get inside."

"That must mean—"

"I know where you're going, Marty. You think the killer must be someone pretty damned close to Talbot for him to have entrusted that person with the entry code. Not necessarily. We figure the killer could have obtained the code from—"

At that instant, the door flew open, striking him hard. He spun. "Dammitt. Why don't you look where—"

A young woman rushed past us and ran over to a flowerbed at the edge of the decking. She bent over and began throwing up.

Enrique looked away from her, his annoyance fading. "Marva's new. Worked in CID less than a month."

Amanda said quietly, "That bad, huh?"

Enrique nodded. "That's why we figure Talbot told the killer the entry code to the surveillance room. He wouldn't have been able to help himself. Someone tortured the poor bastard before killing him." He motioned us through the door with a tight smile. "Welcome to church."

"Church?" Amanda said.

"You'll see."

★4★

Enrique had exaggerated; it wasn't a church.
   But it wasn't far off.

Amanda and I found ourselves in an open room of maroon tile and textured gold wallpaper. The proximity to the pool and the built-in wet bar suggested it was intended to be a family room, but it didn't look like any family room we'd ever seen.

The furnishings were Victorian, heavy and somber. The sitting area consisted of several ornately carved wingback chairs spaced across from a similarly intimidating couch. Heavy tapestries and formidable gilt-framed paintings lined the room. All depicted religious scenes. An enormous mahogany curio cabinet filled with icons and symbols of the Christian faith dominated an adjacent wall. In one corner sat a life-sized statue of Jesus; in another, a smaller one of Mary.

Amanda made a slow 360. "This is . . . amazing."

"Gets your attention, doesn't it?" Enrique said, coming forward. "Talbot was a big Catholic. Almost all the rooms are decorated like this. A spare bedroom upstairs even has an altar." He winked. "Simon must have felt right at home when he walked in."

He was only partially kidding. Before becoming a cop, Simon had attended seminary school. He never explained why he passed on becoming a priest, but I had a pretty good guess. His father, a big Miami real estate developer, got his rocks off by strangling young girls between business deals and dumping their bodies in Biscayne Bay. Simon learned the truth when he was something like ten or eleven. Since then, it's been the defining event in his life. He became a homicide cop not because he wanted to; he had to. In his mind, hunting down killers was the only way to atone for his father's sins.

Amanda said to Enrique, "*Almost* all the rooms . . ."

He shrugged. "Several are decorated with a single gold cross. Talbot's bedroom is the only place where I didn't notice anything religious. Just the opposite, in fact. It's pretty wild. C'mon. The body's in the west wing."

He led us through a door into a carpeted hallway. Large windows lined the left side, providing a view of the softly lit center courtyard. The hallway made a left and we passed a series of rooms: a spacious kitchen with dirty dishes in the sink, a formal dining area with a table that could seat a dozen, a music room complete with a grand piano. All contained a variety of religious images and icons. As we walked, Amanda said to me, "We can relax. Talbot's probably straight."

I tended to agree. Devout Catholicism and a gay lifestyle didn't strike me as compatible.

We entered a dramatic mosaic-tiled foyer designed to resemble a Mediterranean grotto. A tapestry depicting the crucifixion hung over a bubbling faux-stone pool. On either side of the foyer were marble hallways, leading to the two wings of the house. Amanda and I gazed up the staircase, which rose to a balconied landing. Several latent-print technicians were dusting the handrails. From the second floor rooms, we could hear the sounds of voices emanating down.

"Simon's got half the team searching Talbot's bedroom and his office," Enrique explained.

Amanda and I nodded; it was a given as to what Simon was hot to find.

Enrique swung toward the corridor on our right, then pulled up, frowning at Amanda. "Problem?"

She had stopped to study the oak front door. We could see the knob had already been dusted. Amanda looked at the nearest technician, a thin guy with tightly curled blond hair that looked suspiciously like Berber carpet.

"Did you dust the door knob?" she asked him.

"Yeah. Five prints. Three partials."

Amanda nodded slowly. Assuming the killer was moderately intelligent, the fact that he hadn't wiped the knob indicated he either hadn't entered through the front door or had worn gloves. Probably gloves.

She glanced at Enrique. "You find signs of forced entry on any doors or windows?"

"No."

"Major Talbot was home alone?"

"As far as we know."

"Do you know if he went into work today or—"

"The lunch plates in the kitchen suggest he took the day off. Either that or he came home early."

I scribbled a mental note to check with Talbot's co-workers.

Amanda's eyes went to an electronic keypad on the wall. "How about the alarm? Was it on or off?"

"What Simon got from Mrs. Chang was that it was off when she arrived. He couldn't confirm with her whether Talbot usually set the alarm when he was home. Odds are he did. We also can't rule out that the killer jumped him while he was outside."

Amanda and I were thoughtful at this possibility.

"Anyway," Enrique said, "Mrs. Johnson can probably tell us." He picked imaginary lint off his suit and turned to go.

Amanda said, "Mrs. Johnson?"

Enrique was disappearing down the corridor. Amanda and I trailed after him, our heels clicking on the marble floor. We came to a game room. In addition to a pool table and a dart board, I noticed a single gold cross on otherwise bare walls.

Amanda repeated her question about Mrs. Johnson. This time Enrique answered; she was another housekeeper.

"Works part-time. Simon tried calling her, but she's not home."

We passed a bathroom, then a well-equipped gym. Each contained a single cross on the walls and nothing else. Since we were obviously in the leisure section of the house, I finally deciphered Talbot's logic when it came to displaying religious symbols. In rooms that served a strictly functional or nonreligious purpose, he'd hung up a solitary gold cross and left it at that.

From a doorway at the far end, we heard a woman's voice. Her tone was soft and soothing, as if addressing a child. "It's okay, baby. I won't hurt you. I only want to turn your head a little. There. That wasn't so bad . . ."

"Dr. Cantrell," Amanda said.

To clarify something Enrique had mentioned, I said to him, "Earlier you indicated that Talbot wasn't necessarily close to his killer—"

"No, but he must have known him. Why else would he let him in the house?"

My point exactly.

We were almost to the end room. Dr. Cantrell was still talking. Enrique slowed to a stop and appraised me. "We're also pretty sure that the killer must have visited the house before."

"Why?"

"Because of *where* he chose to kill Talbot." Enrique nodded toward the open doorway just ahead. "It's a sound-proofed media room."

Amanda nodded grimly at the implication. I could only shake my head.

"Yeah," Enrique added, his voice hardening. "The cold-blooded bastard knew exactly where to take Talbot so he could work on him. He wanted a place where Talbot could scream his head off and no one would hear—"

He broke off, looking past us. Amanda and I turned at the sound of clicking heels.

A man in a long-tailed black tuxedo was entering the hallway, listening to a cell phone. His face was locked in a grimace. Moments later, he ended the call with a tight-lipped: "Yes, sir. We'll be expecting you."

Tucking his cell phone into his jacket, he continued toward us, his eyes shifting between Amanda and me as if confused by something. A hesitant smile played across his lips.

"I'm glad you could make it."

I had the distinct feeling Lieutenant Simon Santos wasn't talking to me.

Smoothly elegant.

Those two words fit Simon to a T, and not only because he happened to be wearing a tuxedo instead of his trade-mark dark blue Brooks Brothers suit. A youthful thirty-eight, he was tall and dark, with a gaunt, unlined face topped by longish black hair combed straight back. Most people who meet him for the first time are unsettled by his piercing black eyes, which seem to look right through you. As he approached, those eyes were focused on Amanda and I was getting a funny feeling why.

Stopping before Amanda, Simon squeezed her hand affectionately. This was an unexpected gesture and not only because he wasn't into touching. He and Amanda had never been particularly close. Both strong willed and outspoken, they had a history of butting heads over the nuances of a case. Amanda often initiated their disagreements; she had a hard time blindly accepting Simon's theories, even though he was usually proved right. That's not to say she didn't respect his opinions; she did. When Amanda agonized over whether to reveal how she felt toward me, Simon was the person she'd called for advice.

"He was the obvious choice," she said. "He's one of your closest friends and I knew he'd give me a straight answer."

An accurate assessment, which explained why I was bothered by what I'd witnessed.

Simon had squeezed Amanda's *left* hand. He must have felt her engagement ring through the latex glove. But as Enrique had done, he offered no congratulatory comment.

My earlier suspicion was reinforced and I tried to decide how I felt about it.

Was I angry that Simon had known and hadn't told me? Not really. Despite our friendship, I realized that if I'd been in his position, I'd probably have done the same thing.

Turning to me, Simon was all smiles as he asked about Emily. He wasn't simply making small talk; he genuinely wanted to know. Since Nicole's death, he'd appointed himself Emily's unofficial godfather.

I told him about the dance, how beautiful Emily looked.

As Simon listened, his mood became somber, his eyes going to the media room. From within, we heard Dr. Cantrell say, "I have to take your temperature, honey. Is that okay? Jerry, get some pictures before we cut the ropes. Maggie, hand me that knife—"

"It's a bad one, Martin," Simon said quietly.

Everyone in the world called me Marty, including my mother. Not Simon. "We've heard. Who was that on the phone?"

"Congressman Harris." He addressed Enrique, speaking quickly. "Pass the word that the congressman plans to arrive by nine-forty-five. Tell everyone I don't anticipate a disruption in our activities. Also have Teriko check Talbot's computer for a listing of his friends and acquaintances, including email contacts."

Enrique swung around to leave.

"Oh," Simon added, "and ask Richard to request printouts of phone calls that Talbot made over the past six months. From his home and his cell phones. Have the lists faxed to the car."

By car, he meant his limo, which had two satellite phone lines and all the high-tech communication equipment a millionaire homicide cop could ever want.

As Enrique hurried away, I checked my watch. It was only eight-fifteen. "Harris wasn't even supposed to land until nine-thirty."

"His flight departed early," Simon said. "He should land at Reagan National in less than an hour. There's a chance he could be delayed by en route weather, but for now, he wants us to assume that he will be on time. He's determined to view his nephew's body. I tried to advise him against it, but . . ." He shook his head.

Simon hated outsiders barging into a crime scene. But

he'd obviously gotten the word to handle Congressman Harris with kid gloves.

When I asked, he said he hadn't broached the topic of Talbot's sexuality with the congressman. "What's the point, Martin? Do you think he'd tell us the truth?"

"Probably not." Harris had spent political capital by publicly denying that his nephew was gay and odds were he wouldn't change his story now.

From the doorway, Cantrell said, "Take two more shots of his hands, Jerry. Zoom in close. Get the knot. That's it. Careful of the blood."

Simon removed rosary beads from his jacket and we filed into the media room to see the body.

★5★

It was a windowless room roughly twenty feet square. The walls were dark blue, almost black, and were made of a porous, sound-absorbing material. A stocky man and a petite blonde woman stood just inside the door, backs to us. The guy checked us out and drifted over to make room. Peering over Simon and Amanda's shoulders, I went clockwise and saw a refrigerator, a wet bar, a couple rows of plush theater chairs, and a wall-mounted movie screen. I could also make out the upper half of two people, a reed-thin man with a camera and a heavyset woman with short gray hair. They were standing in front of the screen, bending over something on the floor.

"All right, Jerry," Dr. Cantrell said to the photographer. "When I cut the rope, you shoot the ligature marks on the hands and the feet. Ready—"

The room was punctuated by a series of clicks and flashes.

I eased to the right. The chairs in the front row still blocked my view. I took another side step.

And saw him.

Christ—

I tried to prepare myself for what I would see. But nothing can prepare you for this.

Talbot was lying on his side, hands and feet bound behind him and secured to the legs of the theater chairs. His pullover shirt and jeans were stained dark red from numerous stab wounds to the torso and thighs. The zipper of his jeans was tented open and glistened with the tacky wetness of drying blood that had flowed down his right thigh and soaked into the carpet. From his televised press conference, I recalled Major Talbot had been an exceptionally handsome man, but he didn't look handsome now.

Kneeling, I forced myself to focus on his face. Talbot's eyes were locked wide, staring sightlessly in horror. Thin strips of duct tape covered much of his mouth, except for a slight opening above his lower lip.

That's where I was looking now. At the tip of a penis that was sticking out.

The camera stopped flashing and Dr. Cantrell and Jerry straightened. Cantrell held a surgical knife in one hand and two lengths of blood-stained rope in the other. As she passed them to the woman who was her assistant, Cantrell said to Jerry, "Get me prints as soon as you can."

"Sure, Doc." He gathered his equipment and left the room.

Cantrell stretched her ample frame. "Jesus, my back's killing me. I'm getting too old for this." She focused on Amanda and me. "Long time since I've seen the Air Force. What's it been? Couple years?"

Amanda nodded mutely. "About," I said.

"Do you have an estimate for the time of death, Doctor?" Simon asked.

"Give a girl a chance, huh?" Cantrell motioned to her assistant and the two women wormed Talbot's jeans below his buttocks. As they did this, Doctor Cantrell kept a running conversation with Talbot's body, saying things like, "I don't like this any more than you do, Franklin. But you heard the man, you've got to tell us when you died. It won't take long. We'll find who did this to you. I promise, honey."

Anyone who witnesses Cantrell talking to a corpse for the first time assumes that she has to be a little nuts. If she is, it's certainly understandable. Several years earlier, she got called out to process a young male who been killed in a car jacking. Since the victim's wallet was missing, no one knew who he was. When Cantrell arrived, she got the shock of her life.

The victim was her son.

Dr. Cantrell resisted all attempts to get her to leave. She was determined to process his body and by all accounts, did so in a calm, efficient manner. According to the cops on the scene, she gave no outward indication that she was working on her son, except for the loving way she spoke to his corpse.

She's continued the practice ever since.

Cantrell extended her hand. "Maggie. The thermometer—"

Her assistant produced a long rectal thermometer from a black case.

Two minutes later, Cantrell had her reading and passed the thermometer back to her assistant. Stepping around the bloodied carpet, she approached Simon and Amanda. "Between four-thirty and five-thirty P.M. I can narrow it down, if you can tell me when he last ate."

Simon said, "We're checking. It would have been lunch; the housekeeper had come to make dinner. How many wounds?"

"Fourteen."

"Including the fingers?"

"Fingers?" I said. Amanda and I swung around to look at Talbot's hands. Because they were tied behind his back, we'd missed seeing the injuries to his fingers.

"Yeah," Cantrell said to Simon. To us: "The tips of the index and forefinger on his left hand are crushed. Probably by pliers."

Amanda and I saw the tips of pulverized bone and flesh now. Enrique had called it. Whatever Talbot knew, he'd revealed to the killer.

Simon said to Cantrell, "You still conclude that the cause of death was cardiac arrest due to blood loss?"

A nod. "None of the other wounds are fatal, per se. Figured it took Talbot three, four minutes to expire, once his penis was severed." She sighed, looking down at Talbot. "Real shame. He was a good looking kid. For him to die like this . . ."

The room fell silent, all eyes on Talbot's corpse. We were picturing his final moments, as he lay there wracked with pain, swallowing and gagging as his life ebbed away.

"The sick son of bitch," Amanda muttered.

I had a theory about why the killer felt the need to stab the victim and also crush his fingers. When I mentioned it, I saw nods from both Simon and Cantrell. This was something they'd discussed.

"You're correct, Martin," Simon said. "The killer stabbed Talbot repeatedly, trying to make him reveal information. Talbot must have resisted, so the killer increased the pain level by crushing his fingers. When he got what he wanted, he finished Talbot off."

"It appears," Amanda said, "that there must have been more than one killer. It would take at least two people to tie up Talbot. One to hold a gun on him while the second person bound him."

"Could still be a single perp." Cantrell motioned to her assistant. "Maggie, be a dear and pass me the rope."

After Maggie handed over a plastic bag which contained

the bloodied rope, Cantrell held it up to us. "Slip knots. Easy enough for one person to keep a gun on Talbot while he slipped the loop over his wrists and cinched it tight." She passed the bag back to Maggie.

Of course this didn't prove there wasn't more than one killer, but only that one person was capable of securing and torturing Talbot.

Simon shrugged. "For now, we'll assume a single perpetrator."

"Information," I said suddenly.

All eyes went to me, but I was looking at Simon. He knew what I was asking.

"Assuming Talbot was killed for information," he said, "that would seem to rule out a hate crime. I understand Major Talbot worked in the Pentagon . . ."

I said, "Talbot's office served an administrative function. He wouldn't have been exposed to classified information. Certainly nothing anyone would kill him for."

"You're convinced the motive was unrelated to his military duties?"

"That's the most likely conclusion. Yes."

A faint smile. He'd already determined this. "Excuse me, Doctor."

When Cantrell moved aside, Simon knelt over Major Talbot, fingered his rosary beads, and began to pray.

Simon recited his two favorite Psalms dealing with death, the twenty-third and the thirtieth. This was another of his unique talents, an ability to accurately recall information stored in his mental Rolodex.

When he finished, Simon crossed himself and rose, looking down at Talbot. He took a couple of shallow breaths and seemed to struggle with his composure. "I want who did this," he said with feeling.

"Join the club," Amanda said.

His eyes sought hers and something unspoken passed between them. She placed a reassuring hand on his back and left it there. Another indication that their relationship had become much closer than I realized.

I told myself not to read to much into it. But I couldn't forget Amanda's ring and inference that came with it.

Bob had money.

As Amanda withdrew her hand, Simon said to Cantrell, "You appreciate the priority of this case?"

"Relax, Simon. I'll have the autopsy finished by tonight. Say around two." Addressing her assistant, Cantrell said, "Maggie, bag his hands and feet. Leave the duct tape on his mouth. I'll remove that when—problem, Simon?"

Moving toward her with an apologetic expression, Simon explained that Congressman Harris would arrive in a little over an hour to view his nephew.

"Aw, Christ." Cantrell threw up her hands and appeared really put out. "Why can't he come down to the morgue? We can be there in thirty minutes."

"I've explained that would be preferable. He insisted he wanted to view the body here."

Cantrell grimaced in frustration. "Fine. What do I care? So I've got to stay up half the night. It's not like someone my age needs beauty sleep. I assume it's okay to prep the body for transport and Nate here can still do his thing."

"Of course."

On cue, Maggie and the criminalist Nate went to work. Nate's job was to scour the room for trace evidence left behind by the killer.

To Simon, Cantrell said, "Let Maggie know when she can transport the body. Me, I'm going to get some dinner. Prima donna politicians give me a headache. The morgue is closer to the airport, but you know that. If I were you, I'd ask myself why the hell he really is coming here." She punctuated the comment with a knowing look, popped off her gloves, and walked out.

"She's right," Amanda said to Simon. "Harris would save fifteen minutes if he drove straight to the morgue. Why is he really coming here?"

He gave her a long look. "Don't you know?"

She started to shake her head, then stopped. "He's afraid we'll find something?"

"I don't think there's much doubt."

No one said what that something was; we all knew. After all, with a politician, image was everything.

Checking his watch, Simon said, "We don't have time. I want to determine the truth before Harris arrives. Let's see how the search is going upstairs."

As we retraced our steps down the hallway, Amanda and I tucked in on either side of Simon. I said to him, "You realize this might still be a hate crime."

He shook his head. "Talbot was killed for information."

"Unless the killer tortured Talbot to confuse the motive. Make us think it was a hate crime when it wasn't." My terminology sounded a little ridiculous in light of the horrific nature of the killing, but I was going by the legal definition of a hate crime, where the motive would have solely been based upon Talbot's sexuality.

"Why would he, Martin?"

"Try this. According to General Hinkle, Talbot received a lot of hate mail when he was accused of being gay, most from people with a military connection. It could be the killer was someone who wrote one of the letters. Hell, he could even be one of Talbot's co-workers. We know Talbot knew his killer, right?"

A skeptical look; he wasn't buying the hate crime angle. I wasn't either, but you never knew.

"Uh, guys," Amanda said. "Aren't you jumping the gun a little? For all we know, Talbot was straight."

I kept quiet, waiting for Simon to point out why this couldn't be true, but he never did. He just gave her a little smile. It was as if he didn't want to disagree with her and I tried not to dwell on the reason why.

As we entered the foyer and continued toward the staircase, I asked Amanda why Congressman Harris was coming here if not to suppress information that his nephew was gay.

"It could be something else he's worried about us finding."

"Such as . . ."

"How would I know?" She stopped at the staircase and circled a hand around the room. "Take a good look, Marty. This guy wasn't a Sunday Catholic; he was a *believer*." She glanced at Simon. "Your people have been searching for what? An hour? How come they haven't found anything suggesting Talbot might be gay?"

"The obvious reason," Simon said, finally speaking up, "was that Talbot was careful not to leave anything incriminating that his housekeepers might find. He was under investigation once before and knew he couldn't risk—"

"Simon!"

We looked up the stairs and saw Enrique standing on the railed balcony. "Simon, you better hear this!"

★ 6 ★

Talbot's office was the first door on the left. As with the family room, the furnishings were heavy and dark and included the requisite religious paintings on the walls. A formidable desk topped by a computer and a phone sat against a curtained window at the very back. A file cabinet with a couple of open drawers was tucked in the far right corner, a stack of files sitting on top. A pretty Asian woman and a short, muscular guy stood in the middle of the room, watching us as we entered. The guy was talking on a cell phone, asking someone to check a phone number.

"Yes, yes, I'll hold." He cupped the mouthpiece and announced, "It'll take a couple of minutes."

Nodding to the woman, Enrique said, "Teriko found the message on the answering machine and—"

"I thought you checked the messages, Enrique," Simon said.

"On the machine downstairs. This is the one for Talbot's second line."

He indicated the phone, which had a built-in answering machine, then appraised Teriko expectantly.

"It's the fourth message, Lieutenant," she said to Simon.

Without being asked, Teriko stepped around the desk to the phone and pressed play with a gloved finger. A metallic voice said, "Thursday, seven-twenty P.M. . . ."

She skipped it and the next two calls, then stood back.

"Thursday, nine-sixteen P.M." A pause, then a man with an extremely deep voice came on. His words were slurred, as if he'd been drinking. "Talbot? You there, Talbot? You fucking faggot. What the hell did you do? Go crying to your uncle? Jesus, you're one gutless son of a bitch, you know that. You'd better remember one thing, asshole; your uncle won't always be around to fight your fucking battles. Watch your back 'cause someday you'll turn around and I'll be there. You hear me, Talbot? *You hear me?* Goddamn fag."

A click.

The speaker hissed. Teriko punched it off and we all gave Enrique a sideways glance. If the vitriolic outburst bothered him, he gave no sign.

Simon said to Teriko, "Caller ID?"

"Only the number, Lieutenant. Richard's trying to get us a name."

Richard said, "Shouldn't be much longer. The phone company will fax out a printout of Major Talbot's calls—" He spoke into the phone, "Could you repeat that, Ma'am? Thanks."

He pocketed the phone, looking at Simon. "A pay phone at a bar in Crystal City, Lieutenant. Quigley's."

The bar's location was suggestive. A number of military lived in Crystal City because of its close proximity to the Pentagon. Enrique said, "That cinches it. The guy's got to be in the military. It's pretty clear that Talbot reserved this line for his work."

I said, "You listened to all the messages?"

"I did," Teriko said.

"And you're sure all the calls came from military personnel?"

"Pretty sure. Here. You can listen for yourself." She pressed the play button.

After the day and time, a woman said, "Major Talbot, Sergeant Crowley. You have a fifteen hundred meeting with Lieutenant Colonel Sanders on—"

I said, "Move on."

She went to the next message. "Hey, hey, Major Talbot, it's Captain Bingle. I won't be able to gin up numbers on the force structure allocations. I just got the word I'm being sent TDY to Barksdale—"

At my nod, Teriko skipped to the third message. "Franklin, Lowell Tenpas. Bad news. We'll need your talking paper on the POM by Tuesday morning. Sorry for the short notice. I've scheduled you to brief . . ."

Terkiko looked up at me. "There are eleven messages. All similar. Everyone who called made a reference to military rank or—did I say something?"

I didn't reply. The message had just ended and I was staring at the machine.

"My God," I murmured.

The words just came out. The instant I said them, I knew I'd made a mistake. Looking around the room, I saw everyone staring at me.

"What is it, Martin?" Simon asked. "What did you hear?"

My mind was spinning as I tried to figure out my next move. I asked Teriko to play the message again. After she did, I knew there'd been no mistake; I'd heard the name correctly.

"All right," Simon said, eyeing me. "What's so significant about the message?"

I shrugged. "Major Talbot was supposed to brief Major General Baldwin on Tuesday."

"No kidding," Amanda said dryly.

Simon said, "I assume you know this General Baldwin."

I hesitated. "I know him."

He waited for me to expand. I didn't.

He went on, "I recall a General Baldwin who ran the Air Force during the Gulf War?"

"An older brother. The Baldwins are a prominent military family."

Amanda nodded. Everyone in the military was familiar with the Baldwins, whose service to the country dated back to the Civil War.

Simon again contemplated me, expecting me to say more. He bluntly asked me how General Baldwin could be connected to the murder.

"I don't know that he is."

"I see." He seemed increasingly puzzled by my reluctant manner. "Could he have made the call threatening Talbot?"

"It wasn't his voice."

"But you still think the general could somehow be involved?"

"I have no reason to believe that." It was more of a quibble than an outright lie.

Simon's jaw tightened in exasperation. "Martin, please. If you know something pertinent—"

"I'm sure it's nothing."

"Oh, stop it, Marty," Amanda said. "You practically laid an egg on the floor. You think General Baldwin might be connected to the killing. Why?"

I felt her eyes cut through me. "I'm not allowed to say."

She was incredulous. "*Not allowed?* This is a homicide investigation."

Simon's face darkened. "Enough of this nonsense, Martin. I want you to tell us. *What are you doing?*"

The only thing I could.

I was walking out the door.

★ 7 ★

"**M**arty!"

As I hustled onto the balcony, I glanced behind and saw Amanda pop out from the office. "Dammit, Marty! Get back here."

I took the stairs two at a time, ignoring the curious stares from the fingerprint technicians.

"Marty, I swear to God I'll call General Hinkle. He'll order you to tell us."

I reached the foyer and looked back. Amanda was standing at the top of the stairs, her face tight with anger. "I'll do it. I'll call him. Don't think I won't."

I shrugged. "So call him. It won't change anything."

"Meaning you still won't tell us?"

"There's nothing to tell."

"You're such an ass." She spun on her heel and stormed back to the office.

By now the technicians were regarding me with crooked smiles. Berber hair grinned. "I'd say that's one pissed-off lady."

"What was your first clue?" I said dryly.

He laughed. "Kinda makes you feel sorry for the guy."

"Which guy?"

"The one who gave her that rock she's wearing. Poor bastard probably has no idea what's coming."

I was curious how he knew this. As big as Amanda's diamond was, he would still have to be damned observant to notice the protrusion through her gloved hand.

"I noticed it a couple days ago," he said, when I asked. "Musta been Wednesday. She dropped by the precinct to have lunch with Lieutenant Santos—say, you don't look so good. You okay, buddy?"

I wasn't, but managed a smile anyway. "I'm fine. How do I get to the basement?"

"Through the kitchen. Going to hide out there until she cools off, huh? I do the same thing with my old lady. Nine years we've been married and the only peace I get is when . . ."

I was walking away.

Simon and Amanda.

All I could think about was the possibility, just the possibility that it could be true. I kept telling myself Simon wouldn't move in on someone I cared about. He wouldn't.

By the time I reached the kitchen, I almost believed it.

I found the staircase at the rear, near a butler's pantry. Before heading down, I confirmed I was alone, freed my cell phone from my belt and punched in a number.

"General Baldwin's residence," a male with an Hispanic accent said.

I identified myself and ask to speak to the general. As I waited, I heard the faint sounds of conversation.

Major General Samuel T. Baldwin IV came on the line thirty seconds later. As usual, he sounded thrilled to hear from me. After exchanging pleasantries, I asked him if he had a recent change of assignment and he said he did.

"For the last two months," he said, "I've been the chief of Air Force Manpower."

As intimated in the message I'd heard. Consulting my watch, I calculated the time for what I needed to do. "Mind if I drop by in say . . . half an hour?"

A pause.

When he spoke, I sensed his suspicion. Despite our history, he knew I wouldn't pop by on such short notice without a good reason. "This a personal or professional visit?"

"Something's happened. We need to talk."

"I see." Another pause. Longer. "Tonight's not a good time. I've got a dinner party—"

"Thirty minutes." I ended the call before he could argue.

While I didn't seriously think he could be involved in the murder, there were too many connections for me to ignore. Not only was he Talbot's boss, but I knew he could be capable of extreme violence. Then there was his attitude toward gays and his link to the threatening call.

I hadn't lied to Simon; it hadn't been General Baldwin's voice on the message. But his Crystal City high-rise apartment was just down the street from the bar where the call had been made.

Another coincidence?

I went down the steps into the basement, worried about what I might see on the surveillance tapes.

The concrete box Enrique had described was wedged into a corner of the unfinished basement, not more than ten paces from the stairs. As I walked toward it, I realized Talbot could have locked himself in it, if he'd realized he was in danger.

Again, this reinforced the theory that Talbot knew his killer.

The steel door was open a sliver. I rapped once, got no

response. As I pushed through, a familiar voice said, "No, shit? That recent, huh?"

I eased into a cramped space not more than ten feet by six, packed with video equipment. Racks of video recorders lined much of two walls. Over to the right was a small control console with a desktop computer and a phone, two television monitors mounted above it. The monitor on the left was displaying a grid of images from various surveillance cameras. In the upper left rectangle, I saw the front gate; toward the bottom, cops walking up the hill toward the pool.

My eyes shifted to a graying, bespectacled black man in a dapper tweed blazer, who was seated at the console, talking into the phone, an unlit pipe clenched in his teeth. He held up a finger to me. "Just a sec, Marty."

Appearances can be deceiving, but not in Billy Cromaritie's case. He dressed like a professor at an Ivy League school and was easily as intelligent as one. While Billy analyzed evidence for a living, his passion was technology. Computers, digital cameras, flat-screen TVs, you name it, Billy always had to have the latest and greatest.

Which explained why Simon sent him down here.

Ending his call, Billy cocked an eyebrow. "Now *that* was interesting."

"What?"

He removed his pipe from his mouth and waved it around the cubicle. "Notice anything?"

"A boatload of VCRs."

"Look at the concrete *between* the cinder blocks."

I studied a portion of the wall, visible between the two TVs. "Concrete's dark. It's not close to being dry."

"That's because it was poured a little over a week ago."

I stared at him.

"Yeah. That was the security company on the line. I checked out two tapes and was wondering why they only had a couple days' worth of images on them. Ron, the guy I was talking to, told me that's because this thing was slapped together in four days. Talbot paid them double for a rush job. *Double*."

His meaning was clear. Whatever was the source of Talbot's fear, it hadn't manifested itself until last week.

Two VHS tapes were stacked on the console. I asked if those were the ones he'd checked out.

"Right. Both from cameras at the back of the house."

"And?"

He looked longingly at his pipe before reluctantly sliding it into his blazer. "Saw the maid, Mrs. Chang. Also a gardener. Oh, and another lady. Kind of looked like my grandmother. She was here quite a bit over the last couple days. Probably Mrs. Johnson, the other housekeeper."

It made sense that the images on the tapes went back several days. Because the video recorders were motion activated, a single tape could last a week or longer before being recycled. "No one else?"

"Not yet. We won't find anything. You heard that the tapes from the front of the house and the gate are missing?"

"Yeah . . ." I was frowning quizzically at the television monitors.

"Let me guess," Billy said. "You're thinking it'd be a pain in the ass if Talbot had to come down here, whenever someone came to the gate."

I nodded. "I'm also wondering how Talbot would even know if a camera had been activated by a motion sensor. He sure wouldn't be sitting here, watching the whole time."

"Damn right he wouldn't. A tone sounds whenever a camera comes on. Like a doorbell. When it goes off, Talbot can call up the cameras from any TV in the house. Sweet, huh?"

"I didn't hear the tone when I came up."

"Simon had me kill it. It was driving everyone nuts. It only took me a couple minutes to figure out how." He tapped the computer, pleased with himself.

I asked him how Talbot knew which camera picked up motion.

"A menu pops up on the TV. It shows which cameras are active. It's similar to this."

He clicked the mouse and swung the computer screen toward me. I saw a listing of the cameras, each with a corresponding number and a cryptic description of its location.

"See the numbered boxes?" Billy said. "Notice how some are red but most are green?"

"Green means active."

"Right. Most of the cameras are operating because of the people we got crawling around. Normally, they'd be red. With his fence, Talbot wouldn't even have animals setting off the motion detectors."

I'd seen enough. With the missing tapes and the newness of the system, the odds were General Baldwin was in the clear. "You going to be around for a while, Billy?"

"Most of the damned night. Once I wrap up in here, I've got to get my ass upstairs. The chief wants the house completely processed before we leave." He shook his head gloomily. "Jesus, I hate celebrity killings. Everyone jumping through their ass. Give me a dead gangbanger anytime. You're in and out, and home in time for Leno."

I grinned. Billy liked to bitch. But after twenty years on the job, he'd earned the right. "Mind if I borrow your car for about an hour?"

"Sure. Toby's got the keys. He drove. You know Toby

Chandler? Big, bald guy. I think he's upstairs in the master bedroom." His eyes flickered past me to the door. "Is that you, Carolyn? How's the prettiest officer on the force?"

Turning, I saw an attractive uniformed cop with curly blond hair walking toward the cubicle, a cell phone in her hand.

Carolyn stopped just outside the door, blushing. "Hi, Billy. I was told a cell phone won't work inside there."

"It won't."

She glanced at me. "Agent Collins?"

"Yes."

"This call is for you, sir." She offered me the cell phone.

I realized at once who it probably was. "Looks like I'm in trouble, Billy."

He laughed. "Better you than me."

As I stepped from the cubicle and took the phone, I was thinking Amanda really had called General Hinkle.

I was mistaken.

Simon was on the other end. Instead of pressuring me about General Baldwin, he said simply, "I thought you might need a car, Martin."

I hesitated, instantly wary. "Why?"

"Do you?"

"I might."

"Fine. Tell the officer."

"Simon, why are you doing—"

A click. He was gone.

I passed back the phone to the cop. "You have a car for me?"

From her shirt pocket, she produced a set of keys. The key chain was made of leather, with the initials A.G. embossed on it.

Amanda Gardner.

As I went up the stairs, I was thinking hard. Because of my reaction to hearing Baldwin's name on the tape, I wasn't surprised that Simon had deduced I might come down to the surveillance room or might need a car. What *did* surprise me was that he'd offer me the use of a vehicle, especially Amanda's.

I knew how Simon's mind worked. He wouldn't give up this easily on finding out what I knew about General Baldwin.

He was up to something.

My hunch proved right.

The moment I passed through the pool gate, I spotted the figure sitting in the passenger seat of the Saab. As I came closer, the silhouette tipped me off to the person's identity.

Opening the passenger door, I said, "Out, Amanda. I'm going alone."

She shot me a frosty glare. "Then you'd better start walking."

"I'm the one with the car keys."

"I'd like to see you get me out of the seat."

"Don't tempt me."

"Don't make me kick your ass."

She probably could. She was a third degree black belt in Tae Kwon Do and I'd seen her reduce a weightlifter into a whimpering mound of flesh with a flick of her wrist.

We stood there, eyeing each other. Her perfectly formed face was defiant, all trace of her earlier emotional turmoil toward me long gone. She was now a hard-nosed cop, working a case.

"Have it your way. Catch." I tossed her the car keys and started walking toward the house.

"Where the hell are you going?"

I kept walking.

"Oh, for—will you chill out? I'm not going tag along when you talk to General Baldwin. That's where your going, right? To his apartment in Crystal City?"

I slowed to a stop, watching as she unfolded herself from the Saab. She'd obviously checked Baldwin out. "I'm supposed to believe that?"

"Cross my heart."

"Why are you coming, then? You enjoy my company?"

She snorted. "Don't flatter yourself. Chief Tisdale is waiting for me at the Pentagon. We're going to search Talbot's office." She shot me a disparaging look. "After all, *one* of us should try to solve this murder."

I let the dig pass. "I'm not going to talk about General Baldwin."

"Oh, goodee."

"I'm serious, Amanda. I won't discuss him."

She sighed. "Tell you what, Marty, I'll make you a deal. You keep your mouth shut and so will I. Now quit screwing around and let's get going."

Of course I didn't believe her.

But by the time we turned into the Pentagon's cavernous south parking ten minutes later, she hadn't made a peep. I didn't get it. This had to be the reason why Simon had arranged for Amanda and me to ride together. He wanted her to grill me about General Baldwin. Yet she never asked a single question.

All's fair in love and homicide investigations, and I knew Amanda hadn't remained silent because she'd given her word. That told me there had to be another reason. Could she and Simon have guessed the answer?

Some of it.

★

I rolled to a stop by the pedestrian bridge which led to the Corridor Two entrance. The Pentagon's massive limestone walls loomed dark and ominous against the moonlit sky. Despite the late hour, the parking lot was moderately full, reflecting the heightened demands on the military since 911. In order to support the war on terrorism and Iraqi occupation, a number of offices were forced to burn the midnight oil.

Amanda stepped from the car and paused, looking at me with a strangely amused expression.

Here it comes.

But when she spoke, she said, "There's something I forgot to mention, Marty. Chief Tisdale and I are going to search *two* offices."

"Oh?"

"Simon phoned Congressman Harris, asked him about the message. You remember the part where the caller said Harris screwed him over . . ."

"Yeah, sure."

"Harris said the accusation was absurd. When Simon pressed him, he did mention someone who'd threatened Talbot recently."

I waited for her to say the name. She didn't. She just kept looking at me with that amused expression.

I sighed. "You're not going to tell me who it is, are you?"

"It's a name you're familiar with."

I squinted at her. "What? Are you trying to say it's General Baldwin?"

She batted her eyes innocently. "I don't know. Am I?"

Christ. "Amanda, knock off the games. This is important. I need to know if—"

"Gee, not much fun, is it?" With a sardonic smile, she shut the door and walked away.

★ 8 ★

The Mayflower Towers apartment building was one of a line of seemingly identical glass and chrome high-rises that defined Crystal City. Ten minutes after leaving the Pentagon, I swung under the entrance's concrete awning and parked in a space reserved for guests. Going up the steps to the glass doors, I thumbed the intercom button and peered into a marble lobby, focusing on the security desk. A large black man in a guard's uniform was seated at it, flipping through a magazine. He looked over with disinterest before reaching to his desk.

"Help you?" the speaker cracked.

After I gave him my name, there was an extended pause and I thought maybe General Baldwin had conveniently forgotten to pass on my name.

Finally, the door buzzed and I entered the lobby, heading for a bank of elevators at the back. General Baldwin lived on the thirty-second floor, where the penthouses were located.

Not many two-stars could afford a Crystal City penthouse apartment, but Baldwin had the benefit of a trust fund established by his father, a retired full general. As I intimated, the military was the Baldwin family business.

Every Baldwin male was expected to join either the Army or Air Force—for some reason, none had ever served in the Navy or Marines—put in a career, then retire with their pre-ordained one to four stars. Occasionally, a Baldwin topped out at full colonel, but that was rare. As with a civilian organization, the military's promotion system was predicated upon connections and the Baldwins had those in spades. While they didn't get rich during their active duty tenure, they made up for it later, usually by sliding into high paying management or lobbyist positions in a variety of defense-related industries.

The elevator deposited me into a quiet hallway with pile carpeting. General Baldwin's apartment was the third one on the right, and as I approached the twin oak doors, I detected faint music and the murmur of conversation. Someone laughed out loud.

I rang the bell.

Baldwin had always been big on entertaining. Like the rest of his family, he considered cocktail or dinner parties crucial to fortifying relationships. He approached golf and bridge similarly. As long as I've known him, he's played both regularly, but rarely with people he considered friends.

"What you have to understand, Marty," he once told me, "is that competency in your job is only part of the promotion equation. The rest comes down to the social game. Not only how well you play it, but if you even want to play at all. A lot of guys don't and I don't blame them. Sucking up to people is a pain in the ass."

"I don't want to play."

Disappointed, he shook his head. "You'll never get a star, Marty."

Tell me something I didn't know.

The door opened and a slight Hispanic man in a tux

peered out. Since General Baldwin didn't have hired help other than maid service, I concluded the guy was associated with a catering company. "Mr. Collins?" His accent confirmed he'd answered the phone when I'd called.

I nodded and eased inside.

"The general asked that you wait in the study, sir."

"I know the way."

I cut across a large living room done all in pale cream. The furnishings were minimalist and elegant, modern art work on the walls adding splashes of color. Several Asian artifacts tastefully accented the decor, softening the sterile feel. From hidden speakers came the sound of soft classical music.

As I angled toward a hallway, more laughter erupted and I glanced past a Chinese screen into the dining room.

A full house.

Ten people, six men and four women, spaced around a stunning glass table that appeared to be suspended in midair. A blond man in a tux hovered over them, refilling coffee cups from a silver decanter. General Baldwin was seated at the head, his back to me. Since this was a social gathering, he had on a dark suit instead of his medaled Air Force uniform. I recognized two of his guests. The red-faced man doing all the laughing was a former Virginia congressman with a reputation as a military hawk. The severe looking woman across from him was the secretary of the Air Force.

General Baldwin said promotions came down to how well you played the social game. He played it well.

He glanced over and we exchanged a look.

Continuing down the hallway, I entered a masculine study lined with floor-to-ceiling bookshelves. Most senior officers had an I-love-me wall and Baldwin was no exception. His was filled with plaques and photographs highlighting his career as a fighter pilot and military stud. Several Civil War–era rifles also were mounted above his desk. They were part of the general's impressive collection of military guns, many of which had been used by his predecessors in war.

My eyes fell on a picture on the wall, which was larger than the rest. It showed General Baldwin as a young major, receiving a silver star for his heroics during the first Gulf War. The beaming full general who was pinning the medal to his chest was Baldwin's father.

"My second favorite photograph," a deep voice said behind me.

Sam Baldwin entered the room, drawing the door closed behind him. Even in a suit, he still resembled the college basketball player he once was. At forty-six, his six-five frame was spare and hard, and his close-cut brown hair showed no signs of gray. Only his facial lines reflected his age. Numerous and deeply etched, they hinted of a life filled with more than its share of stress.

It wasn't easy, making general.

"Is that your favorite, Sam?" I nodded to a silver-framed photograph sitting on his desk. An attractive woman in her late thirties stood beside a teenage boy with a remarkable resemblance to Baldwin.

"Yeah." Sam walked over to the desk and stared at the picture, smiling faintly. "Ryan just got accepted to the academy. Class of 2007."

I heard the pride in his voice. The legacy was continuing and another Baldwin would serve his country. "Congratulations." I added, "How's Ann?"

"She remarried last month. Even sent me an invitation to the wedding."

"You didn't go?"

"No. It would be . . . awkward."

It didn't surprise me his ex-wife had invited him to her wedding. Even though they had divorced ten years ago, they'd remained very close.

"Ann's one in a million," I said.

"Don't remind me. You know we spoke at least once a week. It's true." He was quiet, a suggestion of sadness moving across his face. "I'll miss our talks."

A reference to the fact that Ann now belonged to someone else.

With a sigh, he eased down behind his desk. I settled into an armchair across from him. After contemplating me for a beat, he said, "I wish I could say I'm glad you're here, Marty."

"So do I, Sam."

"I assume there's been a murder . . ."

I nodded. He knew I worked homicides for the OSI.

"With some connection to me?"

"The victim worked in Manpower."

He waited for me to say the name. When I didn't, he said irritably, "You going to tell me who it is?"

I intended to, but at the moment I was reminding myself I had to ignore our friendship. I was a cop with a job to do.

I said, "The name won't be released for another hour, so I'll need you to keep it under your hat . . ."

"Give me the fucking name, Marty."

"Major Talbot."

"My God." He popped upright. "When? How?"

As I recounted the details, Sam progressed from a series of disbelieving head shakes to open-mouthed shock, finally settling on tight-lipped anger at the suggestion that someone who worked with Talbot might be responsible. By the time I finished my account, I concluded that his reactions communicated the appropriate levels of surprise and disgust.

Still, something about them bothered me.

"Who?" he demanded. "Who do you think is responsible?"

"Don't know. There was a threatening call on Talbot's answering machine. It came from a male. We're trying to ID him."

"Hell," he grunted. "That could be anybody. You must have a reason to believe the caller worked in Manpower."

"Major Talbot had two phone lines in his house. The message was on the one that he reserved for his work."

Sam shook his head. "I can't fucking believe this. I really can't. I suppose you want to know if I'm aware of anyone who might have hated Talbot enough to kill him."

"Yes."

"The answer is no. If Talbot had problems with someone, I wasn't aware of it. Nobody reported anything to me."

"So you're not aware of anyone who might have threatened Talbot?"

He blinked at me. "Of course not."

It wasn't unusual that Sam would be in the dark about personal conflicts among the people in his directorate. As a general, he wouldn't be privy to worker-bee gossip.

I asked him if Talbot might have been working on a classified project. Something which could have led to his killing.

Baldwin snorted even before I finished. "Get real, Marty. We're not talking about the National Security Agency here. Manpower is full of bean counters."

Essentially what I'd told Simon.

Now came the hard part and I braced myself for his response. I'd run across people with a shorter fuse than Sam, but not many. Keeping my voice casual, I said, "How well did you know Major Talbot?"

"Not very. I got over two hundred people in the direc-torate. Most I still don't know. Like I said, I've only been the chief for a couple months. I'm familiar with Talbot because he's briefed me several times." He shrugged.

"I need you to be more specific on your contacts with him, Sam."

He frowned. "More specific?"

There didn't seem any way to sugarcoat the question, so I asked him straight out. "Have you ever had a personal con-versation with Major Talbot?"

"A personal conversation? Why would you care—"

He stopped. It dawned on him what I was really asking. In an instant, his jaw muscles knotted and his nostrils flared. I knew what was coming and tried to head it off by saying, "Easy, Sam. I had to ask because—"

Too late.

At that instant, he erupted in a dramatic fashion. He shot forward in his chair, his face twisted in rage. "You fucking son of bitch. You're disgusting, Marty. You really are. You think you can walk in here and accuse me without cause. Just because of something that happened twenty-five years ago. Well, fuck you. Of all people, I can't believe that you . . ."

His voice rose with every word. He wasn't shouting, but he was close. I said, "Sam, take it easy. Your guests might overhear—"

"*Screw easy.* After all I've been through. After all it's cost me. You think I would . . . that I actually could . . ." He struggled, trying to form the words.

In the end, he couldn't bring himself to do so and slumped back into his chair. He sat there, panting like he'd run a race, eyes fixed blankly on his desk.

"Sam," I said quietly. "I had to ask. It's my job."

No response. He wouldn't look at me. His breathing rate slowed and he continued to sit like a mannequin. I knew better than to say anything else.

His eyes crawled up and I saw his hurt. "We were good friends once, Marty."

"We still are."

He seemed about to respond, then reconsidered. In a thick voice, he said, "You'd better leave."

"I still need answers, Sam."

His jaw hardened again and I anticipated another explosion.

Instead, he regained control with a deep breath. "I didn't have anything to do with Talbot's death."

I produced my notepad, saw him tense. "Relax. No one will see your comments but me."

He eyed me sullenly, unconvinced.

"Where were you between four-thirty and five-thirty this afternoon?" I asked.

"My office till four. I slipped out to the POAC for a workout. I was back before five. You can check with my exec, Major Tenpas." The Pentagon Officer Athletic Club was located on the east side of the building.

I made a note, feeling a twinge of hope. While this wasn't an ironclad alibi, it was close. It would take Sam ten minutes to walk to his car and another ten to fifteen to drive to Talbot's. Round trip, we're talking forty to fifty minutes.

And the killer took a lot more than twenty minutes, torturing and murdering Talbot.

"Can anyone verify seeing you at the POAC?"

He shrugged. "It's not very crowded then. The guy who checks IDs might remember me. There were also a couple men in the locker room. I don't know who they were."

"You got Major Tenpas's home number?"

He opened a desk drawer and produced a Palm Pilot. After I jotted down the number, I asked him when he last saw Major Talbot.

"Hell, I don't know. His office is only two doors down from mine. The last time he briefed me was over a week ago, if that's what you're asking."

It sorta was.

I said, "And that's the last time you spoke with him at any length?"

He glowered in disgust.

I took that as a yes and moved on, asking him if he'd ever visited Talbot at his home.

"No."

"Did you ever call him at home?"

"Never." He paused. "He did phone me here on Tuesday evening. He had a question about a talking paper he was putting together on the POM. I'm using it to brief the Air Force Council next week."

The Program Objective Memorandum was the military's budgetary wish list and the Air Force Council was a group of three-star generals who oversaw its formulation. The talking paper had been mentioned in one of the messages on Talbot's answering machine.

"Is that the only time he called you at home?"

A nod.

I jotted a note to check Talbot's phone records and shut my notepad. "All right, Sam. We'll need to question Talbot's co-workers tomorrow."

"Call Major Tenpas. He'll make the arrangements."

As I rose to leave, Sam remained seated. He was slumped back against his chair, staring at the photograph on his desk. I said, "I'm sorry about this, Sam. I really am."

He didn't seem to hear me. I turned for the door.

"Marty."

I glanced back.

When Sam spoke, his voice was quiet, but contained an undercurrent of emotion. "It's coincidence. That's all. I wouldn't jeopardize Ryan's future or my family's name. You know I wouldn't."

"I know."

"This investigation. Who knows what might come out. If something does, I could lose everything." His gaze hardened. "I trusted you. You gave me your word. Remember?"

The guilt floated toward me. "I remember."

He eased forward, eyes fixated on me in anticipation. I knew what he was waiting to hear.

"I want the truth, Sam," I said quietly. "Did you have any contact with Talbot other than what you told me or any knowledge of what's behind his death?"

"No, Marty. I swear to God."

"Sam, if you're lying, you realize I can't—"

"Have I *ever* lied to you?"

He had me. As far as I knew, I was the one person he'd always told the truth to, except for possibly his ex-wife.

I was torn. As I cop I was supposed to maintain my objectivity. But all I could think about was what would happen to Sam if the truth came out.

"All right. I'll do what I can to cover for you."

He sagged back with obvious relief. "Thanks, Marty."

As I left the room, he was again staring at the photograph of his son and ex-wife.

★9★

As I crossed the living room toward the door, the eyes of Sam's guests followed me, indicating they'd at least caught the volume of his tirade, if not the words. For any other host, this would lead to an awkward scene. In Sam's case, he'd smoothly dispel their concerns with a beaming smile and a plausible explanation. Before they could assimilate what he'd said, he'd hit them with a series of one-liners that would have them in stitches. By the time the guests departed, the argument they'd overheard would be long forgotten.

In the end, this was why Sam excelled socially. He had an innate charm that allowed him to manipulate people without them being aware of it. Or if they did catch on to what he was doing, they didn't give a damn. They enjoyed the ride too much.

A mutual acquaintance once called Sam the best bullshit artist he'd ever seen, and I agreed. That's why, as I waited for the elevator, I had to ask myself if he'd been bullshitting me.

I replayed his reaction to Talbot's death, trying to understand what had troubled me. I recalled his horror and revulsion . . .

And then I remembered his eyes.

Just now, they'd been filled with desperation as he practically begged me to cover for him. Yet earlier, when he'd listened to the grisly details of Talbot's murder, they'd been curiously flat and unresponsive.

Had Sam been putting on an act? Could he already have known Talbot was dead?

Impossible.

Sam was a dedicated professional soldier and a good man. Sure he had a temper which could lead him to harm someone in a fit of rage. But we're talking about a methodical, sadistic killing. No way could Sam be capable of something as horrific as that.

Still . . .

I recalled the specific phrases he used moments earlier.

I wouldn't jeopardize Ryan's future or my family's name. Dammit, you know I wouldn't.

He thought those words would enhance his innocence, but they had the opposite effect. They gave him a motive.

I shook my head. I had to know if he'd only left his office for an hour.

The elevator dinged and the doors opened. By then I was already thumbing in the number for Major Tenpas.

The elevator descended toward the lobby.

In my ear, the ringing stopped and a woman with a tired voice answered. When I asked for Major Tenpas, she shouted. "Lowell! For you."

I heard a TV playing loudly. A Bugs Bunny cartoon. A girl shrieked, "Mommy, Davy hit me. Mommy!"

A boy said, "I didn't. She's lying. I didn't."

"*In the face,*" the girl wailed. "He hit me in the face."

"Davy," the woman said, sounding more exasperated

than angry, "how many times have I told you not to hit your sister? Lowell, do something about your son."

"Upstairs to your room, young man," a man growled. "Now."

"But, Dad—"

"You heard me."

Into the phone, the man said wearily, "Major Tenpas."

After I identified myself, I immediately noted his suspicious tone. For anyone in the military, receiving a call from the OSI was like hearing from the IRS. Whatever the news was, it could only be bad.

"Sounds like you've got a war going on, Major," I said.

He forced a laugh, sounding only slightly more relaxed. "Yeah, and we're losing. What can I do for the OSI, Agent Collins?"

Once I told him, he said, "That's about right. The general went to the POAC around sixteen-hundred and returned an hour later."

"Can you be more specific on when he returned?"

"Only when he left. We had a staff meeting which broke up a little before sixteen-hundred. I know the general was back before the secretary Mrs. Lopez left for the day, at seventeen-fifteen. He signed a couple letters she'd typed up."

"So he was back by seventeen-ten?"

"A few minutes earlier."

"How long did the general remain in his office?"

"Until he went home at eighteen hundred."

"You were at work until then?"

"You know any execs who leave before the boss?"

It was a silly question. An exec's job was to be at his boss's beck and call. I asked him if Major Talbot had gone to work today.

He sounded puzzled by the topic change. "No. He took a day of leave."

"He say why he needed the day off?"

"Not to me."

"Do you know if Major Talbot had any conflicts with his co-workers?"

"Not to my knowledge. Franklin . . . Major Talbot . . . can be a pain in the ass. He's meticulous as hell, always rechecking his figures and everybody else's." He hesitated. "Look, I don't suppose it would do any good to ask what this is all about."

The elevator chimed and I stepped into the lobby. The guard was still at his desk, looking bored out of his mind. "You'll know tomorrow, Major."

"Know what exactly?"

This guy was smooth. No wonder he was a general's exec. "Nice try, Major."

After I asked him to arrange for Major Talbot's co-workers to be available for interviews tomorrow, I thanked him for his help and hung up, feeling a palpable sense of relief.

Sam had an alibi.

Tucking away my phone, I checked my watch. A quarter after nine. Amanda would need at least an hour to search the offices, so that left me plenty of time.

"Quigley's," the guard said. "Sure, I know where it is."

★10★

All I had to do was head south for a few blocks and hang a right into the strip mall across from a Days Inn. Quigley's was tucked into the northwest corner, a green neon sign flashing its name.

After I walked inside, I hung out by the door, checking out the interior. As the name suggested, it was a cozy, English-style pub, complete with burnished wooden floors and wainscoted walls. A long bar ran the length of the room, a chalk board mounted behind it, listing a variety of beers and ales. Comfortable booths lined the right side, tables spaced out on the main floor. A juke box at the back played an old Rolling Stones tune, a dartboard affixed on the wall beside it. Over to the left, I located the pay phone, wedged into a tiny alcove beside the restrooms.

My eyes drifted over the predominately male patrons. Because it was a Friday night, the place was crowded. Most wore civilian attire, but there were a number of military uniforms. People who had just gotten off work from the Pentagon or one of the other DoD offices in the area.

Two attractive waitresses in short Union Jack skirts shuttled between the tables, occasionally barking out orders to the bartenders, a balding guy with Popeye forearms and a buxom brunette wearing a low-cut peasant blouse.

As a waitress scurried by with a tray of beers, I said, "Oh, Miss—"

She never broke stride.

Bellying up to the bar, I waited for one of the bartenders to notice me. "What'll you have, Mister?" the woman asked.

I produced my credentials, trying to keep my eyes above her impressive cleavage.

As I asked her about the phone call last night, she said, "You want Joseph. He talked to the other cop."

"What other cop?"

She hurried over to her partner. After a whispered conversation, Joseph came up to me, placing his massive forearms on the counter. In a conspiratorial voice, he said, "You're fast. I didn't expect you for another fifteen minutes." He glanced down at my credentials, which I was holding open. "Hey, you're not Lieutenant Santos."

By now I figured it must have been Simon whom he'd spoken with. "I'm a military investigator, working with him."

He still seemed perplexed. "You *are* here about the phone call, right? The one Santos said was made from the pay phone last night?"

"Yeah, but I didn't know he'd contacted you."

"Not more 'n five minutes ago. Do your thing, but be cool, huh? I run a nice, clean place. Mostly government and military types. That's how come I knew who made the call. I'm not sure of his name, but he told me he was military. Air Force. Staying across the street at the Days Inn. He's been coming in regular for about a month. Never made any trouble except for last night. He was one pissed-off camper from the minute he came in. Kept going on about how he'd been

fucked over to anybody who'd listen. Something about a pro-
motion. Man, he pounded them down. Whiskey straight up.
Really got hammered. I had to ask him to keep it down.
Before he left, I saw him make the phone call."

I was frowning, struck by something he'd first said. "You
want me to do my thing and be cool?"

"If you're going to arrest him, do it outside. I don't want
you spooking the customers. Like I said, this is a reputable
place."

It hit me then. "You mean the man is here now?"

"Sure. That's why Lieutenant Santos was coming out.
The guy shows up almost every night at nine and never stays
more 'n an hour. Like clockwork." He glanced past me.
"That's him, sitting in the back corner. He's starting off like
he did last night. Knockin' down the booze."

I found myself following his gaze. Through the dim light
I saw a table full of Yuppie thirty-somethings, flirting with a
waitress. I saw a woman and a man with their heads bent together, cooing intimately. I saw several young Army officers,
playing darts and trash-talking drunkenly. And just past
them, in a booth near the jukebox, I saw a large man with
close-cropped red hair, sipping a drink.

The last thing I expected was to recognize him.

"I'll be damned," I said.

It's someone you're familiar with.

Those are the words Amanda had said to me in the car.
At the time I thought she was referring to General Baldwin,
but she wasn't.

The reason I hadn't considered this man a suspect was
because he was supposed to be out of the country. If anyone
had a grudge against Talbot, it would be him.

When I asked Joseph if there was someplace where I

could talk to the man in private, he looked decidedly un-comfortable.

I said, "Up to you. I can do it in here, but it could get ugly . . ." I didn't have to say anymore. Joseph indicated a door behind the bar.

"Use my office in the back."

"Thanks. How much has he had to drink?"

"Three or four whiskeys."

Nothing like questioning a pickled full colonel about a murder. I dug out a twenty from my wallet and held it up to Joseph. "I need another favor."

"What?"

When I told him, he looked even less thrilled. "Make it fifty."

All I had left was seventeen dollars. When I offered it to him, he reluctantly pocketed the money. "What if he won't come?"

"He'll come. Just give him the name I told you."

"He doesn't, I still keep the money."

Another concerned citizen. "Fine. Keep the money."

He started out from behind the bar. I was about to head for the office when my phone rang. I checked the caller ID; it was Simon.

"I need to take this, Joseph."

He shrugged and wheeled around back to the bar.

Into the phone, I said, "Hello, Simon—"

That was as far as I got before he went off on me. At first, I thought it was because I wouldn't tell him about General Baldwin. Then I realized it was something else entirely.

Someone had talked.

Simon spoke for a full minute without seeming to take a breath. He was furious. As I listened, I pushed through the door behind the bar, entering a darkened hallway that reeked of stale smoke. Continuing past a storeroom, I turned into a cluttered office that contained a battered desk strewn with papers, a couple of rickety chairs, and little else.

Settling behind the desk, I pushed aside an overflowing ashtray. In my ear, I noticed a silence and realized Simon had finished talking.

I said, "It's not like this is a surprise."

"It is a surprise, Martin. It shouldn't have happened."

"Simon, your department leaks like a sieve. This isn't the first time you've been burned."

"Exactly. That's why Chief Novak and I were so careful. Only people whom we trusted were told of the murder."

"One of them must have talked."

"They didn't."

"What about your investigating team?"

"No."

I decided not to argue. Simon didn't have many weaknesses, but one was loyalty to the people who worked under him. Frankly, that's the reason I didn't think he'd make a play for Amanda. Out of loyalty to me.

"It wasn't the OSI," I said. "We can keep our mouths shut." I wasn't being defensive, but stating a fact. Unlike civilian cops, military ones never leaked.

"It must be someone on the mayor's staff. Perhaps one of Congressman Harris's political enemies." Simon sighed unhappily. "Not that it really matters who talked. The damage is done. Congressman Harris will be angry and I'm forced to address the situation. Are you in Crystal City?"

"You know I am."

He ignored my comment. "Listen carefully. I want you to go to Quigley's bar. According to the bartender, the person who made the call is—"

"I'm about to question him now."

"You're *at* the bar?"

"Yeah."

A silence. He wouldn't say it, but I could tell he was impressed. "Call when you're finished."

"Give me about fifteen—"

A dial tone. Typical. Simon had enough ego to assume that when he was finished talking, you were to.

As I put my phone away, I heard the sound of a door open. Then Joseph's voice: "Second room on your left, sir. Yes, sir, that's the name I was given."

Heavy footsteps came toward me. I quickly uncradled the desk phone, laid the receiver aside, then attempted to look busy by shuffling papers. When the footsteps stopped, I glanced up. There in the doorway stood the man who a year earlier had generated headlines by accusing Major Talbot of being gay.

Colonel Brian Kelly.

★11★

Colonel Kelly was a big, heavy-framed man, with a rugged face and the misshapen nose of a boxer who'd caught one punch too many. Even though he was dressed in a tan sports coat and yellow golf shirt, no one familiar with the military would mistake him for a civilian. Not with his see-through haircut or tiny colonel's insignia pinned to the lapel of his coat.

His face knitted into a frown. "Who the hell are you?" he demanded. His diction was clear and there was no sway in his stance. Not bad for a guy with four ounces of booze in him.

"I handle accounting for the bar." I glanced at the receiver. "I took the call."

He still appeared suspicious. Either I didn't look like an accountant or he wasn't buying the phone call, or perhaps both. He said sarcastically, "The guy said his name was Talbot, huh?"

"Yeah. Right." My attention on the papers in my hand.

"How the hell would Talbot know I was here?"

My head shot up in annoyance. "Look, fella, you don't want to talk to him, fine. I got work to do." I started to hang up the phone.

"Wait."

I froze, watching him. His face contained a hint of doubt. Could the call be on the level?

The seconds passed as he tried to decide.

"You better not be bullshitting me," he grunted, coming over and taking the phone.

"Hello, Talbot? Talbot?"

Kelly slammed down the phone. "I fucking knew it. What the hell is this? Some kind of a joke?"

"No joke, Colonel Kelly." I held up my credentials.

As he scrutinized them I prepared myself for another angry outburst. Instead, he said, "The OSI? Hell, I was wondering when you guys were going to show. The little prick must be shitting in his pants, huh? Good. Nice to know I got to him."

Just like that.

After Kelly eased into the chair across from me, I said, "So you admit making a threatening phone call to Major Talbot last night?"

"It wasn't a threat. It was a promise." He said it with a wink and a smile.

I couldn't understand why he was being so candid. When I started to remind him that a threatening phone call was a court martial offense, he cut me off with a dismissive wave.

"Save it. I know I shouldn't have done it. But, hell, it was worth it. Besides, what's the Air Force gonna do to me? Slap my knuckles and force me to retire? You think I give a damn? The cocksucking fag already ruined my career."

"Colonel, if you don't mind, I'd appreciate it if you—"

"What?" He puffed up in annoyance. "My language offend your sensibilities? Let me tell you something, Collins. What I'm saying is true. Major Talbot is a fag."

I caught his use of the present tense. An effort to throw me off? "How can you be so certain he's gay?"

"Don't you read the papers? *He told me.*"

"He denied it."

He rubbed his face. "Yeah, yeah. Look, in case you haven't figured it out, it was a setup. The bastard set me up. He wanted me to turn him in, so he could deny it. Make me look like a homophobic asshole."

I resisted the obvious comeback. "In your message, you referred to Congressman Harris as being responsible for—"

"It had to be him who pulled the strings, got me passed over for a star." He eyed me darkly. "The brigadier list came out yesterday."

I'd deduced this much from Joseph's comment about a promotion. "You might have been passed over anyway."

His head gave a jerk; I'd touched a nerve. "Collins," he said icily, "I was two years early to light bird and two years early to full bull. I've been an aide to a four-star and a military assistant to the secretary of the Air Force. I attended the National War College and earned two masters degrees. I had every square filled and outstanding ratings. *I should have gotten my fucking star.*"

He sat back, his face flushed with the outrage of the wronged.

I didn't say anything. I focused on his eyes and found what I expected. Hate.

We played the stare game for several seconds. He blinked first, his anger ebbing. "Look, I'll admit I've got strong feelings against Talbot . . ."

I almost made a gagging sound.

"But if you were in my shoes, you'd feel the same way. I told you I made the call. Now you do what you have to do and I'll get back to enjoying my evening."

"I still need answers for my report, Colonel."

"Fine. Make it quick, huh? I got some serious drinking to do." He said it with a wry smile as if he was kidding. We both knew he wasn't.

I had to ask myself if he was drinking only to soothe his disappointment over a failed promotion, or if there was another more ominous reason.

Producing my notepad, I asked him when he'd returned from Europe.

"Last month. I'm the deputy chief of Air Force Personnel at the Pentagon."

This explained why Sam and Major Tenpas had denied that anyone in Manpower held deep resentment toward Major Talbot. Even though I knew the answer, I asked Kelly why he hadn't been reassigned to Manpower upon his return, since that was his area of expertise.

"Why the hell do you think?" he grunted. "The brass wanted to keep Talbot and me separated."

"Did it work?"

"You mean have I seen Talbot since I got back?"

"Yes."

"Sure. Several times. The Pentagon's a big place, but not that big." He flashed a cocky grin. "I ran into him in the john only last week. He practically pissed on himself when he saw me standing next to him."

"Did you confront or threaten him in any way?"

The grin chilled. "Did he say I did?"

"I'm asking you, Colonel."

He hesitated, then shook his head. "No. I never said a word to the fucking fairy."

Let it go, Marty.

I couldn't. The man had been brutally murdered. It

didn't seem right. "Colonel, please. Call Major Talbot by his name, huh?"

"Aw, for the love of—" He glowered at me in disgust "Let me guess. You're a bleeding heart lefty, right? You believe it's wrong to judge people. Figure it will *offend* them. Hurt their *feelings*. Here's a news flash, Collins. There is such a thing as right and wrong. Standards of behavior that are unacceptable. That's what the military is all about, enforcing those standards. Or didn't you read the fine print when you signed on?"

He was trying to push my buttons and it was working. It was all I could do to keep from telling him to kiss my ass. "Colonel, you're out of line."

"*I'm* out of line? Let me ask you something. You think gays should serve in the military?"

Brother. I didn't want to go anywhere near this. "Colonel, I'm a criminal investigator. I'm not here to express my opinion."

"You better damn well start. I've got a right to know if your biased."

I met his hard gaze with one of my own. "I'm not."

"Like hell. I can see it on your face. Those reporters who hounded me looked at me the same way. Like I was a bigoted piece of shit. Well, I got news for you and them. What I am is a soldier and a patriot. Those words probably don't mean jack to you—"

"Colonel—"

"I swore to protect this country and I mean to do just that. America is surrounded by crazies who want to do her harm. Any minute we could be hit with another nine-eleven or worse. The only way America will survive is for our military to be strong. *Strong.* Root out the bastards where they live—"

"Colonel, please—"

"We can't afford to be part of some feel-good social experiment. In any other profession, I could give a shit about someone being gay. But the military is different. We can't allow gays to serve openly. It effects unit cohesion, our capability to fight. You ever been a grunt, Collins?"

I was caught off guard by the question. "No."

"I have. I was an Army Ranger before I joined the Air Force. I can tell you unit cohesion was everything. You eat, sleep, train, and crap together. The men in your unit become closer than your own family. Look at what happened during the last Gulf War. When the bullets started flying, those kids weren't fighting for God and country. They were fighting to protect their buddy's ass. Any one of them would take a bullet for their platoon mates and never think twice. You believe those young soldiers would feel the same way if the guy sitting beside him in the next foxhole was gay? Not a chance. Right or wrong, someone who's gay will be looked at as different. He'll never fit in or be completely trusted. You know what I'm saying is true. Dammit, you know." He punctuated the comment with a glare, daring me to respond.

I said quietly, "You through, Colonel?"

He thought for a moment, then nodded. "I guess I am."

He rose from the chair and headed for the door.

"Colonel Kelly, we're not finished!"

He continued out into the hallway.

I swore and sprang after him. "Sir, I'm not here only because of your threatening call."

He kept walking. He was almost to the door, leading into the bar. I said, "Colonel, Major Talbot was murdered this afternoon."

That got him. He went still, his hand on the knob.

Slowly, he faced me and I was struck by his expression. It was calm, showing no hint of surprise. His eyes met mine and I saw a flicker of understanding.

"The phone call," he said. "That's why you said it was from Talbot. You wanted to see if I'd answer it?"

I nodded.

"I did. That should prove something."

"You made it clear you believed it couldn't have been from him."

"Not because I thought he was dead. Talbot hated me. He'd never call."

I motioned him toward the office. "Let's finish this discussion inside, Colonel. Please."

A look of resignation crossed his face. "Give me a minute."

"A minute for what?"

He opened the door and entered the bar.

★ 12 ★

*D*ammit.

The door was closing behind him. I hurried over, yanked it open—

And stopped short.

Colonel Kelly wasn't taking a powder; he was ordering another drink.

From the doorway, I watched as Joseph poured him a double whiskey, neat. After fortifying himself with a swallow, Kelly walked back toward me.

"I didn't kill him, Collins."

"But you wanted to?"

"Would you believe me if I said no?"

"I might."

He smiled pleasantly. "You're a goddamn liar, Collins."

He casually strolled down the hallway toward the office.

We'd returned to our previous seats. After jotting down his statement, I contemplated him across the desk. "So you don't have an alibi?"

He swirled his whiskey glass which was already half empty. "Guess not. I was house hunting this afternoon. My family will be flying out next month. They remained in Germany, to finish out the school year."

Referring to my notepad, I said, "At seventeen-thirty, you met with a realtor to tour a home in Arlington. . . ."

"Yeah."

"The address is less than three miles from Talbot's home."

"If you say so."

"Two hours before that, you drove around several Arlington neighborhoods, but never spoke to anyone."

"No." He paused. "I checked out a house around seventeen hundred or so. No one was in, but as I left, I noticed a woman gardening next door. She might remember me."

I asked him for the address. He recalled the street, but not the house number. "Can't miss it. It's at the end of a cul-de-sac and has one of those yellow Buy Owner signs out front."

"And your car?"

"A two thousand Explorer. Tan."

After marking this down, I asked him if there was any particular reason why he concentrated on Arlington neighborhoods?

"I don't like long commutes."

"I see. And not because you wanted to live near Major Talbot?"

"Now why would I want to do that?" His face the picture of innocence.

He was going to make me say it, so I obliged. "Because it would make it much easier for you to harass him, Colonel."

He dismissed my accusation with a laugh. "You've some imagination, Collins. I got better things to do than to go around stalking Talbot."

"Your phone message suggested otherwise."

A shrug. "I was drunk. People say a lot of things when

they're drunk. Doesn't mean shit." He flashed a tight smile as if to say, prove different.

I couldn't . . . yet.

Changing the subject, I asked him to expand on a topic he'd alluded to earlier.

"Why'd Major Talbot set me up?" Kelly said. "Hell, that's easy. It was a preemptive strike."

"Meaning . . ."

He swallowed more booze before replying. For the first time, I noticed a glow in his cheeks and a slight slurring in his speech. The man was human after all.

"Talbot," he said, "knew I knew he was gay. He figured I was going to eventually get him, so he'd decided to beat me to the punch. Admit his homosexuality to me in private, then deny it after I formally leveled the charge. You don't believe me, huh?" He read my skepticism.

"What I don't understand," I said, "is why you would think Talbot was gay in the first place? Did he give you any reason?"

"I could just tell. He was single. Never dated and hated sports. Had a lot of guy friends and—"

He was ticking off stereotypes. I countered with: "He was also a devout Catholic."

"So what? He could be gay *and* religious. Or maybe he was using religion as a cover."

"You really believe that?"

"Listen," he said, eyeing me. "All I know is that he and Major Coller hung out together."

I said, "Coller?"

"Lyle Coller. He's a computer analyst assigned to Manpower. Coller's a real pretty boy. Effeminate as hell."

I got it now. "So you assumed Coller was gay and by extension—"

"Assume, hell. I *knew* he was gay. I knew they were both gay. Everyone knew it. I was the only one with the balls to say so."

The picture was almost complete. I squeezed in the last piece, saying, "So you confronted them about being gay?"

"In a manner of speaking. I told them that I knew what was going on and ordered them to cool it, or I'd be on them like stink on shit."

This was a violation of the Don't Ask, Don't Tell policy, which prohibited senior officers from ferreting out suspected homosexuals without cause. Not that Kelly would care.

He killed off his drink and leaned back in his chair. "Anything else you want to know?"

His face was very red, eyes glassy. I went for it and asked him if he had anything to do with Talbot's death.

"Fuck, no."

His gaze was steady and there was no hesitation in his response.

Truthful, I reluctantly wrote down.

After getting Kelly's office and hotel room number—he was residing at the Days Inn across the street—I told him he could go.

As I rose to follow him out, I noticed Kelly pause in the doorway, watching me.

"Something on your mind, Colonel?"

"You never answered my question about your possible bias against me. How do I know you're not out to screw me like those reporters?"

"I'm not."

"That's not good enough. We're talking about the murder of the nephew of the next president. Congressman Harris will squeeze the brass hard for answers and the brass will come down on you. I'll bet they're already pressuring you now. Am I right?"

I hesitated.

"That's what I thought. So you see I've got a major problem. I know I'm the easy choice. What I don't know is whether you'll take it."

"You'll have to trust me, Colonel."

"Wrong answer. From where I sit, you're looking like some closet lefty. Now maybe that won't influence your decision, but I'm thinking . . . you know . . . it just might."

He spread his feet wide, looking at me accusingly.

I wasn't under any obligation answer to him. I'm not sure why I did. In the end, I suppose I felt he had a right to know whether I could be objective.

"For what it's worth, I don't believe gays should serve openly in the military."

His eyes widened in surprise. "Well, hell, why didn't you say so. Jeez, you had me going. You and me think alike, huh?"

"Apparently. Excuse me, Colonel."

I stepped past him and went down the hall.

It was true.

My views toward gays in the military were similar to Colonel Kelly's. Did I believe they should be ferreted out and prosecuted? Of course not.

But I did believe that gays couldn't serve openly without undermining the military's combat effectiveness. As Colonel Kelly intimated, the esprit de corps which binds soldiers together is a fragile thing. Anything which disrupts their unique camaraderie and creates tension would significantly reduce their ability to operate as a single entity, a crucial requirement in battle.

Did I wish this wasn't the case? Yes.

But the reality was that homosexuals were looked upon as different, not only in the military, but also in society as a whole. Until that stigma was gone, gays would never be accepted in such inherently macho organizations like the military. Anyone who believes otherwise is fooling themselves.

That's why I'd supported the Don't Ask, Don't Tell policy as an acceptable compromise. It allowed gays to serve as long as they kept their sexuality to themselves.

Sure, there were problems with the policy, the most serious being the fairness with which it was implemented. On one end of the spectrum, you had guys like Kelly, who ignored the guidelines and conducted their own witch hunts. On the other end, you had people like me and General Baldwin and countless other professional soldiers who supported the policy in theory, but found it impossible to enforce in practice.

You think like me, Colonel Kelly had said.

If he only knew . . .

★ 13 ★

Driving from the bar, I called Simon to brief him on Kelly. When he answered, he told me to wait. In the background, there was a jumble of voices. A woman said excitedly, "The camera's in the air-conditioning vent, Lieutenant. I can see the lens."

"Don't disturb it, Cherie," Simon said. "Larry, get Billy Cromartie."

"On the way, Lieutenant," a man said.

Simon returned to me, his tone clipped and anxious. "Things are progressing rapidly. We discovered another surveillance camera that wasn't tied into the central system. We also found several videotapes which are illuminating."

I said, "By illuminating—"

"There's not time to discuss them now. Can you pick up Amanda and return here? It would be better if you saw the tapes for yourselves."

If Simon wanted us to see the tapes this badly, he must have a good reason. "All right, I'll call her."

"Good. Now quickly, your impressions of Colonel Kelly."

"On paper, he's a prime suspect. He's a big guy and a former Army Ranger. He could have controlled Talbot and stomached torturing him. He also blames Talbot for getting him passed over for general and doesn't have an alibi for the time of the killing." I paused, then added, "But the message he left bothers me. Why make a threatening call to Talbot the day before murdering him? It doesn't figure."

"I agree." Simon said. "Frankly, I'd be surprised if he was the killer."

A conclusion he'd reached separate from my input. It had to be because of the videotapes. I was tempted to ask him what they revealed, but just then, Enrique called out, "Simon, the natives are getting restless. If you want to talk to them, you'd better do it now, before Congressman Harris arrives."

"All right." To me: "Get here as soon as you can. I need your assistance on establishing motive."

"You do? Why?"

But Simon had turned away from the phone, issuing orders. "Enrique, don't let those tapes out of your sight. If anyone asks, they do not exist. Cherie, when Billy arrives, tell him to check the camera—"

A click. Simon had finally remembered to disconnect the call.

I was frowning as I lowered the phone. While I had a good idea whom Simon was going to talk to, I was puzzled by his comment to me. Why would he need my help establishing motive?

One possibility came to mind and as I stopped at a red light, I speed-dialed Amanda's number, hoping Simon hadn't told her to search a third office.

As I pulled up to the Pentagon's Corridor Two pedestrian bridge, I spotted Amanda's familiar silhouette coming down the steps. In her left hand, she carried a folder—Talbot's

RIP that she'd received from Chief Tisdale. When she emerged into the glow of nearby streetlights, two Army officers turned to look at her as she went by. A natural reaction for heterosexual males. After all, this was the new, repackaged Amanda, the kind of woman who could make men walk into walls.

Including me.

As she came toward me, I couldn't take my eyes off of her. Her tailored suit clung to her curves, accenting the swell of her breasts and the thinness of her waist. As I watched her, I felt a stirring. I knew what I was feeling was wrong and waited for the guilt to come. For the first time since I could remember, it never did.

When Amanda crawled into the seat beside me, I caught the scent of her perfume. It was almost too much and I wanted to tell her not to marry Bob. To give me one more chance.

But the emotion of the moment gave way to reality. If I surrendered to my impulse, I would come across as needy and desperate. She'd made her decision and I had to accept it.

Jesus, it was difficult.

Tossing the folder in the back, she frowned at me. "You okay?"

I realized I was still staring at her. Trying to keep my voice casual, I said, "Sure. Why?"

Something in my voice must have given me away. Her sudden pitying expression suggested she knew what I was thinking. She abruptly turned and gazed out the window.

I felt embarrassed. Several cars were approaching behind us, so we had to sit in an uncomfortable silence, waiting for them to pass. I decided I had two choices. Either I could pretend nothing happened, or—

"Look, Amanda, I'd like to explain—"

"It's not necessary." She turned toward me, her eyes soft and sympathetic. "We knew it wouldn't be easy."

"No . . ."

"I never intended to hurt you. I want you to know that."

I nodded, not trusting myself to speak.

She gave me a smile. It was a nice smile. "If it helps, this is also hard on me. I still sometimes wonder if I'm doing the right thing."

My heart thumped hard. Could she be giving me an opening? It almost sounded as if she wanted me to ask her not to—

"Coast is clear, Marty."

Amanda was looking back at the last car as it went by. When she faced front, her expression was all business and I realized the opportunity was gone.

If it had ever existed in the first place.

As we zigzagged our way around to the north side of the Pentagon, Amanda summed up the results of her search of the offices of Colonel Kelly and Major Talbot.

"Nothing," she said. "Chief Tisdale and I went through their file cabinets and desks and didn't find anything that came close to giving us a motive. The chief's waiting for the SAs, so he can access their computers."

Each Pentagon office had a security administrator who troubleshot computer problems, and handled the passwords. Sometimes the SAs were contract civilians but more often than not, they were junior officers who got stuck with the job as an additional duty.

I said, "Colonel Kelly's computer shouldn't take long. He can't have much on it. He's only been in town for a month."

She shrugged. "Either way, it'll be a waste of time. If Colonel Kelly is the killer, he's too smart to keep an incriminating email. Same thing with Talbot. Why would the killer send a threatening email that could be traced?"

I reminded her of Kelly's phone message.

"I'm still trying to figure that one out." She glanced over. "It seems to me there are three possible answers. One, Kelly is innocent like you and Simon seem to think, but has terrible timing . . ."

I was nodding. When I'd phoned, I'd told her about my interview with Colonel Kelly and my conversation with Simon.

"Or two, Kelly was so drunk, he completely forgot about making the call until after the killing."

I gave her a look.

"Easy, Tiger. I'm not buying that one either. The third possibility is that when Kelly made the call, he never intended to kill Talbot. But something happened and he changed his mind."

"And left the message on the machine for us to find?"

"Kelly would have to assume that Talbot would tell someone about the threatening call. He couldn't delete the message without appearing more guilty."

Thin, but Amanda realized this. She was only brainstorming, considering all possibilities, no matter how unlikely.

"So," she said, watching me, "you going to tell me how you figured out Kelly was going to be at Quigley's?"

"Brilliant detective work and insightful mind."

"Brother. It's getting deep." But there were the beginnings of another smile.

As we worked our way around the edge of the parking area, she brought up the tapes that Simon wanted us to see.

"Let me get this straight," she said. "These are from a *new* surveillance camera. . . ."

"Yes."

"And Simon never said what was on them, but you're pretty sure that whatever it is, it clears Colonel Kelly?"

"Apparently."

She tapped her tooth with a nail, digesting this. At a four-way stop, I hung a right toward Glebe Road. She said, "You do realize what this means, Marty. If Colonel Kelly isn't on those tapes, that leaves open another troubling possibility . . ."

She trailed off, letting me fill in the blanks. I dismissed her inference with a head shake. "General Baldwin won't be on those tapes."

"The general told you that?"

"Yes."

"He specifically said that he never visited Talbot's home."

"Yes."

"And you believe him?"

"Yes."

Her mouth opened and closed. She wasn't going to let this go. The best defense is an offense and I reminded her how she'd responded to the question I'd asked over the phone.

"You told me you weren't searching General Baldwin's office," I said.

"I couldn't without probable cause." Her tone wary, wondering where I was going with this.

"Before we left Talbot's," I continued, "you checked out General Baldwin, right? That's how you knew his address?" At her nod, I went on. "Simon also probably asked you to download his photograph from the Pentagon database. He would have wanted a picture for comparison in case Billy Cromartie found someone on those surveillance tapes—"

"Shit," she said.

I nodded.

"Okay, okay," she said grudgingly, "you're right. If Simon had seen Baldwin on a tape, he would have asked me to search Baldwin's office. Since he never did . . ."

"It's not Baldwin on the tape."

We rode without speaking for a while. Out of the corner of my eye, I noticed Amanda shooting me glances and I realized she was gearing up for another attempt.

"Forget it," I said. "I'm not going to tell you anything about General Baldwin."

"Why not? If he's not on the surveillance tapes, what does it matter?"

"No."

"You know they were both stationed together five years ago?"

My head snapped around.

"Oops. Guess not." She grinned, nodding to the folder in the back seat. "I had General Hinkle fax out the RIPs on Colonel Kelly and Baldwin, so I could compare it to Talbot's. General Baldwin and Major Talbot were both stationed at San Antonio in ninety-nine. And now Talbot is . . . was . . . working for Baldwin. Interesting, huh?"

"Is it?"

"Sure. They've got a history together."

"Not necessarily. San Antonio's a big base."

"Enough's enough, Marty. I know why you're doing this."

"Doing what?"

"Have it your way." She clicked on the map light, then reached around and plucked up the folder from the rear seat. Casually flipping it open, she said, "Amazing what you can pick up from a RIP. Take where someone went to school. General Baldwin, for instance. Imagine my surprise when I saw where he went to college." She looked at me expectantly.

I was silent.

"Small world. First you and Talbot. Now General Baldwin. You all went to Virginia Tech."

I still didn't reply. There was nothing I could say.

"Out with it, Marty. Admit you knew General Baldwin from college. That's why you initially suspected him, isn't it? You know something about him that made you—"

I flipped on the radio and cranked up the volume.

She immediately clicked it off. "Dammit, we're supposed to work together. You said so yourself."

"Not on this."

"Why the hell not?"

I concentrated on my driving.

"Jesus, you're impossible." She sat back in a huff.

Another silence followed, which was fine with me. We made a left at a light. In the distance, I could make out the hill where Talbot resided.

Amanda began drumming the dash. I risked a look. The drumming stopped and she shot me a glare. "You think you're smart, but you're not fooling anyone. You really aren't."

I didn't take the bait. With Amanda, it was easier to let her have the last word.

The only problem was, this wasn't it.

"You had us going," she went on. "Simon and I couldn't figure out what you were hiding from us. He came up with this theory. I thought he was crazy, but now—"

"He's wrong."

"You don't even know what it is."

"He's still wrong."

"What's the matter with you? We have a man who was butchered. *Butchered.* I understand Baldwin is a friend—what?"

I was pointing her attention to a large vehicle with a familiar logo, sitting at a stop sign ahead of us. Amanda bent forward, squinting. "Isn't that a Channel Five news van?"

★14★

A ZOO.
   That's the only way to describe the scene outside Talbot's home. As we followed the antennaed press van with the WTTG logo toward the front gate, I counted over a dozen media vehicles and five satellite trucks camped along the road. Most were local, but a number represented national and international news services. A large semicircle of reporters, photographers, and TV cameramen were crowded by the gate, their backs to us. To their left, more TV crews were setting up and a Farrah Fawcett clone was peering into a television camera, engaged in a somber play-by-play.

   "Great," Amanda said. "What the hell do we do now?"

   "Drive through. They'll move out of the way."

   She glanced over dubiously.

   Thirty yards from the gate, the van pulled over to the side. I slowly cruised past it, riding the horn. The crowd parted to look back at us, and as they did, Amanda and I spotted a familiar figure standing before them, framed in a portable spotlight.

   "You called it," Amanda said. "Simon's giving a press conference. Looks like he wants us to stop."

Simon was holding up a hand toward us. I responded by flashing my lights, then parked at the edge of the driveway.

As the crowd re-formed around him, Amanda and I lowered our windows to listen. From Simon's cryptic account, it was clear he was summarizing what he'd told them earlier. In a slow, measured voice, he confirmed that Major Talbot had been murdered at his home in the late afternoon and that there were no suspects. He reminded everyone that this was a joint investigation between the Air Force—he plugged me as the senior OSI agent—and the Arlington PD, and emphasized that both organizations would not rest until Major Talbot's killer or killers were apprehended. After expressing his condolences to Congressman Harris and his wife, Simon wrapped up his summation by holding up a framed photograph of Talbot and requesting that anyone with knowledge of the crime to notify the Arlington PD.

The moment he stopped talking, Simon pushed through the crowd toward the Saab. His movement generated instant chaos. Reporters and TV news people scurried after him, fighting to shove microphones up to his face as they hollered out questions.

"Lieutenant, if you'll just give us a minute . . ."

"Lieutenant Santos, what was the cause of death?"

"Is this a hate crime, Lieutenant? Was Major Talbot gay?"

I had to admire Simon's self-control. Even though it had to be driving him nuts to be constantly touched and jostled, he gave no outward sign. His expression remained completely calm, almost serene, as he walked toward the—

And then it happened.

Five yards from the car, Simon suddenly spun toward a female reporter who was holding a cassette recorder. In a loud, harsh voice, he said, "What did you say?"

The reporter was a matronly woman in her fifties. She recoiled, flustered by his sudden anger. "I . . . uh . . . well . . . I was wondering . . ."

Simon turned away in disgust and continued toward the Saab. For an instant, the reporters were too stunned to react. Then, as if one, they banked after him like a swarm of bees in flight, shouting more questions. One man ran up to Simon and jammed a mike into his face. He knocked it angrily away.

"He's really ticked," Amanda said. "I've never seen him lose his cool like this."

"You hear what the woman asked him?"

"Something about torture. Here they come. Better get our windows up."

Simon yanked open a rear door, clambered inside, and slammed it shut. I thumbed the automatic locks, looking at him. I had to shake my head at his appearance. His tie was askew and his hair mussed. This for a guy who freaked out from too much human contact.

Simon laid Talbot's photo on the seat. "Drive, Martin," he growled.

Easier said than done.

We were surrounded. Photographers continued to press their cameras against the windows, blinding us with flashes. I honked the horn and motioned people out of the way. No one moved. I cracked my window and shouted angrily. All I got was the bright light from a TV camera in my eyes.

"News at eleven," Amanda said sarcastically.

I was down to my last option. With car in park, I floored the gas. At the sudden roar of the engine, the bodies literally flew out of the way.

We slowly continued toward the gate. It was already beginning to open.

Once we passed through, Amanda said to Simon, "You going to tell us why that reporter's question about torture upset you?"

He still looked upset. He'd straightened his tie and was combing his hair. With a last swipe, he said, "There's only one way she could have known Talbot was tortured."

Amanda's brow furrowed. "*One* way? Simon, a lot of people knew Talbot was tortured. Half your department—no?"

In the rearview mirror, I caught Simon's head shake. He said, "I explained to Martin that Chief Novak and I were very careful whom we told of the murder. We were even more discriminating on the aspect of the torture. We wanted to prevent people from leaping to the conclusion that this was a hate crime. Only the immediate investigating team was aware he'd been tortured. No one else knew. Not even the mayor. Even you weren't aware of the torture before you arrived."

A statement we couldn't argue. I said, "You still believe no one on your team could have—"

"Absolutely not."

This was a question I had to ask because of his comment to Amanda. As we circled around the house toward the back, I went with the followup.

"Simon, you said there was only *one* way the reporter could have known about the leak . . ."

"Yes."

Amanda and I waited for him to elaborate. Nothing. Simon adjusted the carnation pinned to his lapel. Stalling.

Amanda said, "You're not going to tell us, are you?"

"It's only a suspicion."

The magic words. Simon had an aversion to guessing wrong. If he had doubts about a theory, he rarely voiced it until he was sure he'd be proved right. I said rarely because

Simon occasionally broke this informal rule. But the odds were slim and I wasn't holding—

And then he said it. So quietly, I almost didn't hear.

"It was me," he said.

I was pulling into the parking space Amanda and I had vacated earlier. I put on the brakes and shifted around to face Simon. Amanda said to him, "*You* were the leak."

"I'm afraid so."

"Why? Why would you tell the press?"

"I didn't. I told someone else. Someone who I thought would be the last person to contact the media. Even now, I can't believe he did. But it had to be him."

"His name?" Amanda said.

A silence. Simon grimaced angrily.

"Harris," he said finally. "I told Congressman Harris."

★15★

A second stunning revelation. Amanda immediately dismissed it, saying, "No way, Simon. You're wrong. It can't be Harris. He's the one who insisted this be kept from the press. I suppose the leak could have come from one of Harris's staffers—"

"It wasn't a staffer," Simon announced flatly.

"You can't possibly know—"

"I know. It wasn't a staffer."

I saw Amanda tense up. Despite their apparent truce, the one thing she couldn't stand was Simon's arrogance. The way he was always so sure of himself.

"Simon," she flung back sarcastically, "a staffer is a helluva lot more likely to be the leak than Harris. A lot of these people work for the highest bidder and it's certainly possible that one of them sold out Harris—"

She broke off. Simon was giving her that vague smile of his, the one that told her he knew something that we didn't.

Acceptance crossed her face. She knew better than to fight it. She sighed. "Okay, okay. Let's have the rest of it."

"I called the congressman to warn him about the press," he said. "He should have been furious over the leak, but he wasn't. He told me not to concern myself about what had transpired. I couldn't understand his shift in mood. Earlier he'd been difficult and confrontational and now he was suddenly agreeable." He gave Amanda and me a long look. "I think we know why."

There was a brief pause as Amanda and I tried to explain away the facts Simon had described. When I asked, Simon confirmed that Harris still intended to come here tonight, but would not arrive until ten-thirty. The congressman gave no reason for the delay.

This seemed to counter Simon's conclusion and I told him so. I added, "By leaking the killing to the press, Harris is insuring they'll be present when he arrives. Why would he do that? The reason we've kept this quiet was so he *wouldn't* be grilled by the press."

"I don't know, Martin." He fingered his bow tie uneasily. "It can't be for publicity. As a leading candidate, he has more publicity than he could ever want. We've also assumed his purpose for coming here was to suppress the truth about his nephew. Obviously, that can't be the case or else why would he leak the killing to the press?" He shook his head. "No, I don't understand it. Unless . . . could he be unaware of . . ."

He was gone for several seconds. Abruptly, he said, "Impossible. Harris has to know about Talbot. He has to."

His eyes came back into focus.

Amanda and I realized what he must be talking about. She said to him, "You found it, didn't you? You found proof that Talbot was gay?" She sounded disappointed.

"It's why I wanted you to come here. See the tapes for yourselves."

I was confused by his last remark. "You aren't talking about tapes from the surveillance camera you discovered, right?" It seemed unlikely that surveillance tapes would yield evidence of homosexuality, unless maybe Talbot had engaged in a tryst in his pool.

Simon's voice turned apologetic. "I misled you, Martin. These aren't surveillance tapes."

Confirming they were porn videos.

I felt myself getting angry. I was used to Simon's I-got-a-secret games, but he'd told me a straight-out lie about the videos. I asked him why.

"I thought it was best, Martin."

In other words, payback. He was paying me back for withholding information on General Baldwin. I almost fired off a disparaging remark, but realized it wouldn't do any good.

"We need to hurry," he said, unlatching his door. "I want you to view the tapes before Congressman Harris arrives."

"Don't put yourself out on our account."

A wasted comment. Simon had stepped from the car. Amanda cracked her door, eying me skeptically. "We're supposed to believe he called us here to watch porn?"

It did sound a little ridiculous.

As I killed the engine, I wondered if I was mistaken. Perhaps Simon hadn't misled me, to get even. Perhaps he had a specific reason for—

My hand froze on the ignition key. The words I'd over-heard on the phone had come back to me. What the female cop had said to Simon.

The camera's in the air-conditioning vent, Lieutenant. I can see the lens.

Son of a bitch. He'd lied to me again. Simon *had* found another camera. A camera located in the house. And if it hadn't been installed for surveillance . . .

That had to be it. That's why Simon wanted me here and why he wouldn't tell me—

"Marty," Amanda called out, "you going to take all day or what?"

She was waiting beside Simon. I got out and tossed her the keys. As we crossed the pool decking toward the house, I casually asked Simon where we were going.

"Talbot's bedroom."

Surprise, surprise.

The forensic processing had spread to the rest of the house. As we passed the various rooms, we saw technicians methodically searching drawers and closets. Berber-hair was in the kitchen, lifting a print from a phone. He flashed me a toothy grin. We were buddies now.

Approaching the staircase I noticed Simon and Amanda were lagging behind, speaking in low tones. When they saw me watching, they fell silent.

"A guy might get the idea you were talking about him," I said, as they walked up.

No response. Neither one even glanced at me as they continued up the stairs. I took the hint. It was back to two against one again.

I was tempted to take my ball and go home. Until I came clean about General Baldwin, they'd always be suspicious of me. Wonder what I was hiding.

"Coming, Marty?" Amanda said.

She and Simon were halfway up the staircase, gazing down on me. As I looked at them, I became aware of how attractive they appeared together. Two beautiful people.

"I'm considering withdrawing from the case."

Surprise flew across their faces. Simon looked pained. "Don't do anything rash, Martin."

"I'm not. I've decided it might be better for everyone concerned if I recuse myself."

"Especially General Baldwin?"

I said nothing.

Simon's eyes narrowed. "Loyalty to a friend can be misplaced. In this case, it is."

I stiffened at the inference. "You found something on General Baldwin?"

A flat smile. "Come on up, Martin. We need your assistance."

They stood there, waiting to see how I would respond. Of course there was only one thing I could do. They knew it and so did I.

As I went up the stairs, I wondered if my good friend General Sam Baldwin had also lied to me tonight.

★ 16 ★

Amanda said, "Think bed and red, Marty."

"A red bed?"

"Not exactly."

When I followed her into Talbot's master bedroom, I understood her comment.

We were standing in a sprawling split-level room that was easily twice the size of my living room. The lower level was toward the front and contained a sitting area with a leather couch, a couple recliners, and a coffee table. Midway across an expanse of carpet was a short staircase that led to a balconied raised section, dominated by a sleigh-style bed. The bed was huge, half again as wide as a standard king. For a bachelor, it seemed pretentious and unnecessary.

I looked to the ceiling above the bed. The air vent was there.

The remaining furnishings consisted of two intricately carved dressers, a wardrobe fully seven feet high, and a massive entertainment unit. Through open double doors beyond the bed, I could make out the tiled walls of a bathroom. Unlike the rest of the house, the room's decor was antiseptically bare. Not only didn't you see anything remotely religious, but there weren't even any personal pictures or mementos on display. All you saw was the color red.

The walls, the furniture, the drapes, the carpeting—everything was a mind-numbing blood red.

Except for the bed.

From the bedframe to the bedding and pillows, the most dominant object in the room was completely white. While I had no idea what reason Talbot must have had for this dramatic contrast of colors, I did know one thing.

"Major Talbot," I said with feeling, "was one very strange guy."

No reaction from Amanda. Her attention was on Simon, who stood at the far side of the room, conversing quietly with Enrique and Billy Cromartie. A plump woman in a gray suit waited off to the side, following their conversation. Billy stepped over to the entertainment unit and opened a panel, revealing a DVD player and a VCR. Next to the VCR, I noticed a small black electronic box. Simon joined Billy and they continued speaking in earnest tones, looking at the box. They were a good thirty feet away and I couldn't quite make out their words.

As I was about to walk over, Amanda pointed my attention to the only other person in the room —a burly man camped on the couch in the sitting area. He was holding up a wicked looking automatic. After popping out the clip, he removed the bullets, placing them in a glassine bag.

Amanda asked him where he found the pistol.

"Under the pillow," the man said. "The second one was in the top drawer of the nightstand, by the bed."

We moved closer to him and spied another automatic lying on the coffee table. A brown folder sat next to it.

"You find any more weapons in the house?" she asked.

"Not yet, but I'll bet a month's pay we will." He shrugged, inserting the empty clip into the automatic.

"The safety wasn't set on either gun and there was a round in the chamber. Talbot wanted to be able to grab the damn things and fire. Wonder what the hell he was so damned afraid of?"

The singular question we were trying to answer.

As we stepped away from him, we saw Billy coming toward us, looking tense. He nodded wordlessly and hurried out the door. Simon was still by the entertainment unit, talking with Enrique and the woman. Like Billy, their expressions were also grim. The woman picked up a cardboard evidence box from the floor and held it up to them. Simon plucked out a tape, inspected it briefly, then returned it and picked up another.

"Like it makes any damned difference what we watch," Amanda said.

"Let's get this over with," I said.

After a couple steps, I realized Amanda wasn't with me. Glancing back, I saw her shaking her head.

"I don't feel right about this, Marty. Peering into Talbot's private life."

"We're cops. It's what we do."

"So to solve his murder, we destroy his reputation?"

I shrugged. "We might be able to keep it from the press."

"You're dreaming. You saw the crowd outside. Someone in the department will leak this to them. It's too damn big."

She looked thoroughly angry and disgusted. I said, "This bothers you that much, huh?"

"Damn right, it does. Major Talbot doesn't deserve to be humiliated like this."

A rare display of empathy from the woman who was known around the OSI as the Ice Princess. It seemed that not all the recent changes in Amanda's life were cosmetic.

She scowled at me. "What are you smiling at?"

I hadn't realized I was. I shrugged. "I was just thinking it's a good thing."

"What's a good thing?"

"The new you."

"Oh, for—" She reddened and turned away. She quickly switched the subject, announcing, "Enrique was wrong about this room."

I frowned. "Okay . . ."

She made a circle with her arm. "He said there's nothing religious in here. He missed the point about the color. The red in itself has religious connotations."

I was nodding my agreement when another explanation came to mind. I don't know why I thought of it. Possibly it was because of what we would soon see on the tapes. Or perhaps it was because I remembered what someone had once told me long ago.

"Hell," I said. "I think Talbot was saying he was going to Hell."

She regarded me with suspicion. "You get that from Simon?"

"No. Is that what he said?"

"Yes."

This response came from Simon, who was coming over, carrying a video. Behind him, Enrique was inserting another tape into the VCR.

"Before we view the tapes," Simon said, "there's something I need to tell you about them. They actually came from—"

"The video camera you found," I finished.

Simon made an exaggerated blink, which was how he reacted when surprised by something.

"Camera?" Amanda said. "I thought there *wasn't* any camera."

Simon stopped before me and I detected something unexpected in his eyes. Regret. He asked, "How did you know, Martin?"

"Know what?" Amanda said. "One of you want to tell me what we're talking about here?"

I said to Simon, "You told me you needed me to establish motive. I wondered why." I looked at the woman holding the evidence box. "Then I remembered hearing her on the phone, talking about a camera in an air-conditioning vent."

Simon shook his head. "I didn't want to deceive you about any of this. But after your reaction this evening, I felt I had no choice. I was afraid you might not come if you knew the truth."

Another indication he had something on General Baldwin or was at least trying to make me think he did. Knowing Simon liked getting into people's heads, I decided to see if he was bluffing.

"Cut it out, Simon. We both know you don't have Baldwin on tape."

He shrugged. "I never said I did."

"That does it," Amanda said. "Someone better start talking. *Fast.*"

We found ourselves confronted by two irritated green eyes. She said to Simon, "Start at the beginning. Are you saying you *did* find another surveillance camera and these tapes are from—"

"No."

She frowned. "But Marty just said—"

"Technically," I said, "it's not a surveillance camera." To Simon, I said, "I assume it's in the vent above Talbot's bed?"

"Yes."

"And that box you and Billy were looking at?"

"A wireless infrared receiver to receive the video signal."

Amanda said, "Oh, hell—" Her eyes dropped to the tape Simon was holding against his side. "So that porn video—"

"Homemade." I answered. I reached down to take the tape from Simon. As I grasped the box, I realized it was empty. Turning it over, I saw that it was a studio release, a popular action picture. Now it was my turn to be confused and I looked at Simon.

"That's what took us so long to find them," he said. "Talbot hid them in commercial video sleeves."

Just then we heard loud, tinny laughter. Facing the TV, we saw a *Seinfeld* rerun on the screen. Enrique lowered the volume with a remote and looked to us.

"Anytime you're ready," he said.

As we walked over to the TV, Enrique said to Simon, "Okay, if I miss the show?"

"Of course."

He handed Simon the remote. "It's all set. Coming, Cherie?"

"Right behind you. Once is all I can take." Cherie placed the evidence box on the floor beside the entertainment cabinet and hurried over to Enrique who was waiting by the door.

Simon said to him, "Tell everyone not to disturb us for the next few minutes."

"Sure, boss." As Enrique reached around to pull the door shut, he noticed John, the guy on the couch, giving him a wiseass grin.

"Something funny, John?"

Enrique said it casually, but his words had an instantaneous effect. John's smile disappeared and he swallowed hard. "Uh, no, Enrique. Nothing."

"You sure? Because it looked like you thought something was pretty damned funny."

"It's nothing, Enrique. I swear." John concentrated on the gun in his hand as if it was the most important thing in the world.

Enrique made no move to leave. He remained at the door, gazing coolly at John. Behind him, we saw Cherie taking everything in with an amused smile.

"Leave us, John," Simon ordered.

John's eyes darted to Simon. He licked his lips nervously. "Ah, Lieutenant, I'm not quite finished—"

"Please," Simon said firmly.

John reluctantly packed up the guns and went toward the door. Enrique stepped aside and as John squeezed past, he whispered into his ear. John went pale. He nodded dumbly, mumbling under his breath.

"What was that, John?"

"I said I'm sorry."

Enrique gave us a knowing wink and as he closed the door, we could hear Cherie laughing.

"Teach him to screw with Enrique," Amanda said.

This was how Enrique had learned to make it as a gay cop. By making it clear he wasn't going to tolerate being demeaned.

On the TV, a car commercial was playing. Simon pointed the remote and the commercial was replaced by an image of two nude men lying on an enormous bed.

One was Major Franklin Talbot.

★ 17 ★

The angle was taken from above, indicating it was the camera in the vent. The zoom had been set to perfectly frame the center of the bed and there was no sound. Talbot's partner was a dark complected man with black hair. They began to kiss and I instantly felt physically repulsed. It was all I could do to make myself watch.

Frowning, I realized something was missing from the screen. When I mentioned it, Simon explained, "Billy said the camera is little more than a lens with a transmitter. Unlike a camcorder, it doesn't record the time and date automatically. That would have to be done through the VCR."

Which obviously hadn't been set up to do so.

We kept watching. The action was picking up. Amanda turned away from the TV.

I said, "I think we've seen enough, Simon."

"Not yet. I want you to see the second man's face. There."

The black-haired man had been lying on his side and we'd only seen him in profile. At that moment he'd rolled on his back and Simon had frozen the tape.

Amanda inhaled sharply while I stared in amazement.

"My God," she said. "It's Benny Rider."

For almost five years, Benny Rider had been the weatherman at the highest rated evening news show in Virginia. Handsome, glib, and charming, Benny had also filled in for Al Roker on *The Today Show* and many people figured it was only a matter of time before he was signed on full-time by a network.

And possibly he would have been, except that Benny decided to come out of the closet. He justified his decision at a news conference, saying it was the new millennium and he didn't think Americans would care about his sexuality.

Bad move, Benny.

A majority of his fans had been women. When their fantasy died, so did Benny's ratings and his future with NBC. After a year, his station let him go and Benny took solace in booze and drugs. Last month, I read in *The Washington Times* that he'd decided to clean up his act and enter rehab the following week.

I suppose that's what made Benny's story so tragic. He was so close to getting himself clean and turning his life around. All he had to do was keep straight for another week. Just one more week.

But it turned out Benny didn't have another week. The night before he was supposed to enter rehab, Benny went on a final drug binge and ingested one speedball too many. His body was found the next morning by—

"Get me another tape, Martin," Simon said.

As Simon ejected the tape from the VCR, I knelt beside the evidence box. "There are only two tapes?" Since Talbot had gone to the trouble to install a video camera in his bedroom, I'd assumed he'd have a library of videos.

Simon held up the video we'd just seen. "For a total of three. Including this one, we know that Talbot recorded at least one more. If you notice, there are numbers written on the labels . . ."

I plucked out a tape from the box and slipped off the sleeve of another popular studio release. On the label affixed to the side, I saw nothing except the printed number 2. I checked the second tape; number 1.

When I glanced up, Simon and Amanda were standing over me. "Good," he said. "That's the one I want to view next."

As we exchanged videos, he said, "That's number four. Number three is missing." He reinforced the comment with a knowing look, making it clear what he suspected.

The missing tape was the motive for the killing.

I felt a sinking sensation. It was clear why Simon wanted me here, but there was nothing I could do about it.

As I rose, Simon inserted the video into the VCR. Amanda asked him if he thought Talbot might have been engaged in blackmail. A logical question since we'd only assumed that Congressman Harris had been the source of Talbot's money.

"No, for two reasons," Simon said. "First, Teriko found records of Talbot's trust fund, established by Congressman Harris. Talbot receives one-point-two million dollars annually. Second, as a military officer, Talbot would have no credibility as a blackmailer. Any potential victims would know he couldn't reveal his homosexuality without ending his career."

Amanda nodded; she'd never seriously considered the blackmail angle. She said, "So Talbot just got off on secretly taping his lovers. One of them found out about his kinky practice and decided to get the tape back. Only problem was, Talbot wouldn't give it to him. Or maybe the killer didn't ask. Maybe he just decided that Talbot was too much of a risk and had to go. That how you see it?"

She was addressing Simon. He said, "Your first scenario is

the most likely. We know Talbot realized he was in danger."

"That's what I don't get," she said. "If Talbot was scared of this guy, why didn't he give him the tape?"

"Perhaps he did and the person killed him anyway." Simon thought, then shook his head. "But the torture seems to rule out this possibility. What other information could the killer have been trying to extract, if not the location of the tape?"

"Punishment," Amanda said. "The killer might have tortured Talbot to punish him."

I raised my eyebrows at her.

"Hey," she said, noticing. "It's a *theory*, not the gospel. Before you dismiss it, ask yourself if Talbot would have held out once the guy started cutting on him."

"Probably not."

"*Probably*? We both know Talbot would have spilled his guts the moment the guy started cutting him. But the sick bastard kept on torturing him. You ask me, there's only one reason. He wanted Talbot to suffer. Period."

I had to admit her logic was sound. "Okay."

But she was looking quizzically at Simon who'd gone still, eyes fixed into space. He murmured, "Perhaps . . ."

Then he trailed off, lost in his thoughts.

Amanda cocked an eyebrow at me. I shook my head. I had no idea what triggered this. Odds are it was something Amanda had said.

After a few seconds, Simon slowly nodded, coming back. She said to him, "Well?"

He hesitated; his initial impulse was always to keep his theories to himself. "Perhaps it wasn't the tape."

Her face went blank. "Sorry."

"What the killer wanted. Perhaps it was something else he was after."

Now she appeared completely mystified, as did I. She said, "But he *took* it. We know at least one tape is missing."

"Precisely. But we don't know that the killer has it."

Amanda and I considered this new wrinkle. Could the killer have murdered Talbot for some *other* reason we had yet to understand?

"Your thoughts, Martin."

On rare occasions, Simon used me as a sounding board. I said, "Logic tells me the tape had to be what the killer was after . . ." I saw him nod. "And that once he obtained it, he killed Talbot to prevent him from revealing their affair. But this last point bothers me. Why did he feel Talbot was a danger to him? Talbot couldn't kiss and tell without ruining his own career. Then there's the effect on his uncle. It certainly wouldn't help the congressman's campaign to have his nephew publicly admit—go ahead." He was about to interrupt me anyway.

"I doubt Major Talbot was concerned about costing his uncle votes. Not with the resentment he felt for him."

"Well, well," Amanda said, swinging around to me. "Now where have I heard that before? Hmm?"

I ignored her and asked Simon how he knew this. I was damn sure he'd never read a scandal mag in his life.

He shrugged. "It's common knowledge that the two men didn't get along. That's why you've never seen a photograph of Major Talbot accompanying his uncle to a campaign rally or a speech."

As if anyone except Simon would have noticed. I said, "So when the congressman defended his nephew against the homosexual charge—"

"A political calculation. As you've concluded, it doesn't enhance a politician's popularity to have a homosexual in the family."

"And Talbot's million-dollar trust fund?"

"It's a curiosity. But Talbot is family and the Harrises don't have any children of their own. In any event . . ." He faced the television and raised the remote.

Amanda made a face. "We really have to watch them all?"

He glanced at her, his tone sympathetic. "Bear with me. It suggests a pattern."

"Beyond the fact that we've got a couple of guys who were lovers and are dead?"

"Actually," Simon said, "I was alluding to something else. But we still have to consider that the two deaths could be related."

She squinted at the remark. "You got any evidence that Benny's death was anything but an accidental drug overdose?"

"No."

"But you're going to check with the ME who made that determination?"

"Of course. We have to be certain. As before, focus on Talbot's partner in this tape. The pattern I was referring to will become apparent."

And seconds after he pressed "play," it was.

★ 18 ★

The pattern was fame.

On screen, we saw Talbot lying beside an older man in his fifties. Amanda and I immediately recognized him as Ross Pelman, the star of a long-running sitcom back in the eighties. Like Benny Rider, Pelman had come out of the closet. Unlike Benny, it hadn't hurt his career. Over the years, Pelman had been a popular pitchman and hosted several game shows.

There was also another notable difference between Rider and Pellman, but I had to ask to be sure. "Pelman's still alive, right?"

"Yes," Simon said. "We checked."

He ejected the tape, slipped it into its sleeve, and passed it to me as I handed him the third video from the evidence box.

This time when the tape began playing, Amanda and I didn't recognize Talbot's partner, who was a slender blond man of approximately the same age.

Simon paused the tape so we could study his face.

"He's good looking," Amanda murmured.

I had to agree. He was almost pretty, with fine, effeminately delicate features.

"Notice his hair?" Simon said.

"Short," Amanda said. "Well above the ears. Run the tape a little—freeze it. Hair's tapered in the back. He could be military . . ." She paused, thinking. "We could make a print from the video. Show it around Talbot's office—"

I said, "Major Lyle Coller."

They both looked at me.

"Colonel Kelly," I said, "described Major Coller as an effeminate officer who worked with Talbot in Manpower. Kelly was convinced they had a thing going."

"You got an address or phone number? No?" She reached for her phone, to have the duty officer at the OSI desk run Coller down.

Simon shook her off. "Teriko printed out a list of Major Talbot's acquaintances from the computer. It's rather extensive. Coller is almost certainly on it. Martin, would you mind getting it from her?"

Amanda had already started toward the door, but for some reason, Simon wanted me to do this. "Sure. Okay."

"Put the list in the folder on the coffee table."

I went over and picked up the folder. I felt several pages inside and was about to open it when Simon said, "Martin, it would helpful to obtain Coller's description, to confirm whether he is the man on the tape."

I told him I'd planned to do this.

"If the description matches," he continued, "call Coller and advise him that someone from the police will be arriving to interview him this evening. Make sure he understands not to open his door to anyone else. Only the police."

"You think he's in danger?" I asked.

"Possibly. If he knows the identity of Talbot's other lovers."

Confirming he still believed the missing tape was behind the murder. "What about Ross Pelman?"

"He's vacationing in Europe."

Lucky Ross.

At the door, I glanced back and saw Simon lean close to Amanda and whisper something to her. She responded with a hesitant smile and began fingering her engagement ring through her latex glove. "It's beautiful," she said, loud enough for me to hear. Simon beamed and for the second time this evening, squeezed her shoulder affectionately.

Only friends.

I sighed and went into the hall. Just before I entered Talbot's office, I opened the folder and found myself looking at a picture of Sam in his uniform—the one Amanda had downloaded from the Pentagon Web site. With the two stars on his shoulders and the fruit salad on his chest, Sam looked like a general straight out of central casting. It was an ability he'd always possessed, to look the part of the perfect soldier.

I flipped the photo and saw faxed copies of Talbot's phone records. I studied the first page which depicted the calls Talbot had made this month, from his home lines. Close to a dozen of the entries were highlighted in yellow and I focused on the first one. The previous evening, Talbot had placed a call to an Arlington—

My eyes widened. I scanned the highlights. All were to the same number. I turned the page. More highlights—

I shook my head and closed the folder. It was clear why Simon had wanted me to see this. He was subtly cranking up the pressure, trying to squeeze me to the point of cracking.

So much for my theory that he was bluffing.

"Major Coller?" Major Tenpas said. "Sure I can describe him."

I was sitting in an armchair in Talbot's office, talking to

him on my cellular. Teriko was camped behind the big desk, stacks of colored folders from Talbot's file cabinet spread out before her. Every criminalist had a specialty and hers was financial and accounting matters. She flashed a friendly smile. This was a notable change from the chilly reception she'd given me when I first walked in, requesting the list of Talbot's acquaintances.

"The lieutenant knows about this?" Her tone dripped suspicion. Understandable. She'd seen me get into a hissy fit with her boss and walk out on him.

"He sent me to get it."

Her hand reached for a thin sheaf of pages, then paused.

"It's okay," I said. "Simon and I kissed and made up. Ask him if you want."

"That you kissed him?"

Her deadpan delivery threw me. I couldn't tell if she was joking. "Uh, it's a figure of speech."

"Not a Freudian slip brought on by this case?"

I rolled with it and said, "Never can tell."

She smiled and handed me the pages.

On the phone, Major Tenpas said, "I don't suppose you'll tell me why you're interested in Major Coller." He'd provided Coller's description; it matched the man in the video.

"You suppose right, Major. I understand Coller and Talbot were quite close."

A long pause. You didn't become a general's exec unless you were an up-and-comer. You didn't survive the job unless you were discreet. Tenpas coughed, sounding uncomfortable. "I can tell you they were friendly enough for Major Talbot to pull some strings and get him a good job."

"What job?"

"With his uncle's campaign. Major Coller's starting at

the top. He's going to work as an administrative assistant for Mrs. Harris."

"Coller is separating from the Air Force?"

"Turned his papers in last week. Kind of short notice, but he figured this was too big an opportunity to pass up."

Especially if Harris won the election. "Anything else about Coller's relationship to Talbot you can tell me?"

He hesitated. "I'd rather not say."

"I think you just did, Major." As I hung up, I realized that Colonel Kelly hadn't fed me a line. Others in Manpower *had* suspected that Coller and Talbot were an item.

As I glanced down at the list of Talbot's acquaintances on my lap, Teriko said, "I'd say Major Talbot was pretty well connected."

I nodded.

The list was seven pages long and contained over a hundred names, all with phone numbers, most with home and e-mail addresses. Teriko's comment was directed at the third or so who could be classified as either minor or major celebrities. The majority were politicians, but there were several film and TV stars, a couple of sports figures, and three general officers. Being the nephew of a powerful congressman and potential president obviously had its bennies.

Turning to Coller's name, I thumbed his number into my phone. Teriko said, "Before I forget, I need you to pass on to the lieutenant—"

I held up a finger. A softly precise voice on an answering machine said, "This is Major Lyle Coller. I'm sorry I missed you . . ."

I checked my watch. Ten-twenty, but it was Friday night. At the beep, I left a message, stuck the list into the folder, and rose to my feet. "Pass on what?" I asked Teriko.

"Sergeant Fuqua dropped by to talk to Lieutenant

Santos earlier. But you were watching those . . . videos." She said it like a dirty word, which, in this case, it was. Her eyes sought out an opened notepad on the desk. "Fuqua says to tell the lieutenant that all the sheets for Talbot's bed are white."

"Okay . . ."

She shrugged. "All I know is that the lieutenant asked Sergeant Fuqua to go through the hall closets, see what color the oversized sheets were. So far all the ones Fuqua found are white. Now the sheets for the guest beds are a variety of colors and patterns."

"I'll tell him. Thanks for the help."

I walked out, shaking my head. *Sheets?*

★ 19 ★

They're making their move.

Upon entering Talbot's bedroom, I saw Simon and Amanda waiting for me on the couch in the sitting area. Unlike when I'd left, their faces were tight and somber. It occurred to me that this could be the primary reason Simon had asked me to leave. So he and Amanda could coordinate the full press they were about to give me.

"Close the door, Martin."

I did and walked over to them, stopping at the edge of the coffee table. Simon waved me to a recliner across from him and Amanda.

"I'll stand." Simon was a master of intimidation. He wanted to put me into a position where I'd be looking directly at the two of them.

He shrugged. "As you wish, Martin."

My eyes went to Amanda. Her face was stone, but I thought I detected a crack of sympathy. Maybe I just wanted it to be there.

Simon said, "Coller's description matched the man in the video?"

"Yeah." I followed up by relating that Talbot had gotten

his buddy Major Coller a plum job, working for Mrs. Harris.

Simon digested this thoughtfully, eying the folder in my hand. "I assume he's listed?"

"Yes, but he's not in." I told him about the message I'd left.

"I'd like to be there when you question him."

"Fine." Simon usually didn't tag along when Amanda and I interviewed military suspects. By indicating he wanted to do so, he was emphasizing Coller's importance.

"His address?"

"Seven, eight minutes from here. A townhouse near Silas Park."

"Convenient," Amanda said.

"Read it to me," Simon said.

After I gave him Coller's address, he placed a call to an Arlington PD dispatcher, relayed a description of Coller, and requested a patrol car be sent to his residence. "Have the officer phone me the moment Major Coller arrives, Dee Dee. No matter how late. Thank you."

He slipped his phone in his jacket, appraising me with the piercing gaze he usually reserved for potential suspects. It was a strange sensation. I'd seen him question dozens of people over the years, but never figured that one day I'd be on the hot seat.

"You saw the phone calls that I highlighted?" he said suddenly.

"Yes."

"Rather numerous."

I nodded.

Simon anticipated a response. When I remained silent, he said, "Martin, please. Don't make this any harder than it is."

I heard the reluctance in his voice. He didn't want to do

this any more than I did. But we both knew we had to play it out.

"General Baldwin didn't kill anyone, Simon."

"He had motive. He's a man with a family reputation and a career to protect."

"You're making assumptions you can't prove."

"So you still deny—"

"Yes."

His smooth face tightened, but when he spoke his voice remained calm. "General Baldwin's name is on Major Talbot's address list."

"So what? Talbot worked for him. You probably noticed there were two other general officers listed. My guess is they were also former bosses—"

"Talbot," he interrupted, "only had their office numbers. In Baldwin's case, he had office, home, and cellular numbers."

"Simon, you're reaching big-time. You really are. Major Talbot prepared briefings for General Baldwin. Some were completed at the last minute, well after duty hours. On those occasions, he would need to call General Baldwin to clear up any final additions—"

"Twenty-three times in the past two months?"

Simon thought he had me and I considered playing my trump. But that wouldn't guarantee he'd tell me what else he had and I wanted to know.

I gazed back coolly.

He said, "We still haven't received the printout of the calls Talbot made on his cell phone. When we do, I anticipate even more. Now, do you have any reason to explain the frequency of the calls?"

"I told you. Major Talbot worked on briefings—"

"Oh, stop it, Marty," Amanda said. "You know damn well

no major calls a two-star that many times. We're talking about two to three calls a week *to Baldwin's home*."

Her eyes matched the hard set of her jaw, any suggestion of her earlier empathy gone. She was a cop grilling an uncooperative witness now.

I said, "Those calls could be work related—"

"Right. And I believe in the tooth fairy." She looked to Simon. "Let's quit screwing around and finish this."

He nodded.

I knew what this meant; they also had trump.

Amanda fished her notepad from her jacket and opened it with a flourish. Referring to it, she said, "Two neighbors drove by Talbot's at around four-twenty this afternoon. Mrs. Imelda Stefanski and her teenage daughter Becky. They remembered seeing a green sedan sitting at Talbot's front gate, waiting to go in. Mrs. Stefanski thought it might have been a Lincoln or Caddy. We ran a check with the DMV—" She saw me tense up. "Well, well. Guess you know General Baldwin owns a green Caddy."

"It doesn't prove anything. A lot of people own green Cadillacs. Unless they can identify the driver . . ." I trailed off; she was smiling at me.

"The *driver*," she said, "was getting into the car as if he'd just buzzed the intercom. The Stefanskis only glimpsed him from the back . . ."

I felt myself relax. Then she slammed me with the kicker.

"A white male, dark brown or black hair. They had the impression he was tall. They were certain he had on a military uniform." She paused for effect. "A blue uniform with two stars. Mrs. Stefanski's husband's a retired colonel and she notices rank—" She practically came out of her seat. "For crying out loud, Marty, who else could it be? It had to be Baldwin."

I continued to shake my head, trying to understand how this could be possible. "It can't be Sam. He has an alibi. I checked with his executive officer, Major Tenpas. He verified that Sam was only gone from his office for about an hour—"

I stopped; I'd heard my own words.

Sam's executive officer, Major Tenpas.

"Ah, hell," I said.

Simon seem puzzled by my reaction, but Amanda sat back with a look of satisfaction. Like me, she knew that the singular trait an exec possessed above all else was loyalty.

I felt foolish. I'd taken Tenpas at his word because I wanted to believe him. I wanted Sam to have an alibi. But after I left Sam, he had at least three minutes to call Tenpas, tell him to—

"Should be easy enough to check, Marty," Amanda said.

When Major Tenpas answered my call, I tore into him, reminding him that lying to an OSI investigator was a court-martial offense. Then I told him that Major Talbot had been murdered and that General Baldwin was a suspect. I summed up by telling him that we had eyewitnesses who could place Baldwin at Talbot's home at the time he was supposed to be in the POAC.

"Now," I said, "when the hell did General Baldwin really return this afternoon?"

There was a long pause. When he replied, I expected him to sound rattled. Instead his voice was completely calm.

"You understand," I said, at the conclusion of his statement, "that I will personally bring you up on charges if you're lying."

"I understand."

"You could go to jail."

"I told you the truth. I know what I saw."

I hung up, shaking my head at Simon and Amanda. "He still insists Sam was back in the office by seventeen hundred."

Simon and Amanda had no comment. There wasn't any need. Since we believed the two female witness, we knew Tenpas had to be lying.

"No bullshit, Sam. I want the truth. Did you have any contact with Talbot other than what you told me or have any knowledge of what's behind his death?"

"No, Marty. I swear to God."

I sagged into one of the recliners. Amanda and Simon continued to watch me in silence. From their sober expressions, it was clear that they took no pleasure in the fact that I'd been so wrong.

"Martin," Simon said softly. "I'm sorry."

I forced a smile. "You called it. You said my loyalty was misplaced."

"Is it still?"

Even now, it was hard to give him what he wanted. "Simon, I know how it looks. But if it turns out Sam is innocent and this gets out . . ."

"No one will know." He looked at Amanda. She nodded.

I knew they would keep their word or at least try. But the reality was that this was a high-visibility murder investigation and Sam was the prime suspect. Once that fact became known, every media outlet would scrutinize his past. Eventually, someone seeking their fifteen minutes of fame would come forward.

I told myself I was doing the right thing. The only thing I could. Still, a hollow sensation welled up inside me.

Guilt.

★20★

Twenty-five years was a long time. I closed my eyes, speaking as the memories came back.

"In college, everyone has a best friend and Sam was mine. We'd roomed together since our freshman year and by the time we were seniors, we were as close as brothers. I'm not sure what drew us together. Other than being in ROTC and members of the cadet corps, we had no real shared interest. As a Baldwin, Sam was born into military aristocracy and constantly worked to live up to that legacy. Sports, grades, climbing up the cadet pecking order, you name it, Sam was driven . . . bred . . . to be the best. I was just the opposite. I was a laid back, small town kid from Warrentown. I didn't possess Sam's pedigree or ambition. My goals were to survive college and cadet life, get an officer's commission so I wouldn't have to fly crop dusters like my dad.

"Maybe that's why Sam and I hit it off. We each got something positive from the relationship. Whenever he got too intense, I could get him to relax. Talk him into kicking back with a few beers, maybe play some touch football or go waterskiing at Clayter Lake. Sam had the tougher role. He took it upon himself to get into my face whenever I kissed things off too much. I used to resent it, but the truth was I probably would have flunked out if it hadn't been for him. I can't tell you how many nights he stayed up, helped me cram for one exam or another.

"Friends like Sam are rare. I thought we'd remain close forever. But then I never envisioned what would happen on our last trip to Clayter Lake.

"The lake's close to the school. It's only thirty minutes from Blacksburg, the town where the college is. Whenever we had a free weekend, a group of us would camp out, get a little waterskiing in and drink some beer. Just relax and chill out. Forget about the chickenshit of being a cadet.

"Anyway, the trip was Sam's idea. It surprised us because it was a couple weeks before we graduated and with finals coming up, we figured he'd want to study. But he loved hanging out at the lake. It was the one place where he could completely relax, escape the pressure of being a Baldwin. So we talked Jimmy and Hank into it. Convinced them they had to party with us one last time.

"It was Jimmy who told Randy he could come along. Why Jimmy agreed, I'm not sure. All I can figure is Randy must have heard about the trip and asked him. None of us knew Randy well. He was a regular student, not a member of the corps. I'd had him in a few classes. He was a quiet guy who kept to himself. I always thought he was a little strange. But if Jimmy said he could ski with us, we weren't going to argue. Jimmy was from Blacksburg and it was his father's boat.

"We got to the campground around five that Friday. School hadn't let out for the summer, so we had the place pretty much to ourselves. We skied for a couple hours, until it got dark. Then we sat around the campfire, grilling burgers and drinking beer. And talking about our futures as commissioned officers. What kind of career we hoped for, who was going to stay in for the full twenty, that kind of thing.

"Randy sat there and didn't say much. Since he wasn't a cadet, I guess he felt a little out of place. I know I would have, if I'd been him.

"It was well after dark when it happened. Probably around ten. By then, we were all pretty loaded. We'd finished up one case and were working on the second. Sam was the most wasted. You could always tell when he'd had too much because his personality changed. Normally, he was mellow, low keyed. But pour enough booze in him and he'd get defensive as hell, blow up at the slightest thing. A couple times, he and Hank almost got into a fight. Hank was going to be a Marine. He enjoyed riding Sam about being a pampered Baldwin, of having his future handed to him without having to work for it.

"I remembered Jimmy had gone into the woods to take a leak. And Hank was . . . I'm not sure where Hank went. Scrounging firewood, I think. Me, I was beat and had decided to turn in. I'd just crawled into the tent when I heard Sam shout, 'You motherfucker!'

"Right away, I thought Hank must have come back and said something to him. But when I looked out the tent, I saw Sam standing toe to toe with Randy. Sam looked as mad as I'd ever seen him. His eyes were wild, crazed. I knew what was going to happen next. I shouted, 'Sam, don't do it!'

"I was too late. Sam tackled Randy and knocked him to the ground. He sat on top of his chest and began punching the hell out of him. Randy screamed, tried to fend off the blows. It didn't do any good. Randy was a little guy and Sam was too damned big.

"I ran from the tent, hollering at the top of my lungs for Jimmy and Hank. When I reached Sam, I tried to pull him off of Randy, but couldn't do it. He fought me off with one hand and kept punching Randy with the other. He was out of control. Every time he hit Randy, he yelled, 'It's not true. It's not true.'

"Jimmy and Hank showed up and we managed to wrestle Sam off of Randy. We had to hold him for what seemed like forever before he calmed down. Randy lay there whimpering and spitting up blood. He was a mess. Sam had really done a number on him. Split lip, busted teeth, blackened eyes. We were going to call for an ambulance from a pay phone, but realized it'd be quicker to drive him to the hospital. There was one twenty minutes away.

"During the ride, Sam sat in the back seat and never said a word. Never explained what Randy had said to set him off.

"When we got Randy to the hospital, the doc took one look at him and called the cops. They showed up and we all gave statements. We thought they were going to arrest Sam and they probably would have, if he hadn't been a Baldwin. His name carries a lot of weight in that part of Virginia. A lot of the Baldwin men graduated from Virginia Tech and after their military and business careers, returned to the area to live. One of his uncles had been the school president and a cousin had been a state senator.

"It was around three in the morning when Sam and I got back to our room. Up to then, he'd shown no emotion. None. He was completely withdrawn, almost catatonic. But the moment we went inside, that all changed. He broke down and began to cry. I thought it was because he'd sobered up enough to understand what he'd done and how much trouble he was in. Baldwin or not, he'd hurt Randy bad. At the least, he'd get booted from the corps of cadets and ROTC, ending any hope of a military career. At the worst, he could get jail time.

"But it turned out Sam wasn't crying about those things. Rather, it was something else that I never saw coming. By now, you've guessed what it was. What it had to be. There, I've said it. I've told you the truth. All of it."

I sat up and opened my eyes.

Simon and Amanda were watching me. She said, "So General Baldwin really is gay?"

"Yes."

"He was married, had a child. Was that a cover?"

"Yes . . . and no. He loved Ann, his wife. He thought being with her might change his . . . feelings. It didn't."

She shook her head, having difficulty comprehending this.

Simon said to me, "And Randy's remark to General Baldwin?"

"Sam had gone to a gay bar in Dupont Circle. He'd never been to one before. He got paranoid and left almost immediately, scared that someone he knew might see him. It turned out someone did. Randy was in the bar."

"So that's what set General Baldwin off? When Randy said he knew the general was a homosexual?"

"Yes."

"Did General Baldwin tell anyone else he was gay?"

"Only me. He knew he could trust . . . me." I had to will out the last word.

"Even though you know the military regulations expressly forbade gays from serving?"

This question came from Amanda. She was referring to the policy in place before Don't Ask, Don't Tell, which prohibited even closeted homosexuals from being in the military.

I said, "He was my friend. I didn't give a damn what the regs said. I couldn't turn him in. I . . . couldn't."

She sat there, looking at me. I waited for her to criticize

my decision. To characterize her politics as conservative was an understatement.

She smiled faintly.

Simon said to me, "I take it General Baldwin was never arrested or removed from the school?"

"I underestimated his family's influence. His uncle and grandfather were major financial donors to the school. They pressured the administration and got the incident shelved. They also paid Randy a substantial sum to drop the assault charges."

"Does General Baldwin's family know he is gay?"

I shook my head. "He told them he'd walked into the bar by mistake. They believed him . . . or wanted to."

"And the general explained away his rage by . . ."

"Telling them he was drunk and lost it, when Randy insinuated he was gay." I shrugged.

Simon's expression softened. "I know this isn't easy for you, Martin . . ."

"No . . ."

"So I hesitate to ask my next question. It will be particularly difficult. It requires you to be completely objective. Forget that General Baldwin is a close friend—"

"He isn't anymore."

His eyebrows went up. So did Amanda's.

"It's what I was alluding to earlier. Ever since he told me he was gay, our relationship has never been the same. Sam's a proud man. He was raised to be proud. He couldn't handle the shame that he felt being around me, knowing I was aware of his secret. He believed it made him a lesser person in my eyes. It didn't, but I could never convince him of that." I shrugged. "It was easier for him to pull back, stay away. So that's what happened. He stayed away."

Nods of understanding. Amanda bit her lip, seeming to fight her emotions. If she kept this up, she was going to lose her ice-princess title.

Her eyes drifted to the red walls and remained there with a quizzical frown. I knew what was bugging her and answered her question before she could voice it. Yes, I said, General Baldwin was also a Catholic and, yes, I had made the remark about the red color suggesting hell because of something he once told me. "It's a long story."

"We've got time."

I hesitated because this was again something I'd promised never to tell anyone. Of course, it didn't matter anymore. I'd already broken my word.

So I told her and Simon about the turmoil Sam experienced when he first realized he was gay. He was only sixteen at the time and desperate to talk to someone about it. Knowing he couldn't risk confiding in family or friends, he went to the one person he could trust—his priest. According to Sam, his priest listened sympathetically, but regretfully informed him that the church was quite clear about his fate if he ever acted upon his urges.

He would go to Hell.

Since then, Sam has lived with the certainty that he was a spiritual time bomb. That's one reason he tried so hard to change, got married, all the rest of it. He was determined to save his soul. His efforts failed because he couldn't deny his biological reality and he has accepted the fact that he's damned. The realization terrifies him. He doesn't want to go to Hell.

"Anyway," I said, "I'm pretty certain we're dealing with a similar fear in Talbot's case. As religious as he was, it's not beyond reason to believe he painted his bedroom red as a reminder of the consequences for engaging in homosexual sex." I shrugged. "Maybe he thought it might stop him from acting upon his urges. Who knows?"

Amanda nodded slowly. "Perceptive, Martin." Simon said quietly.

He agreed with me because his experiences as a seminary student had probably led him to conclude much of what I said.

Amanda said, "And the white bed?"

I shook my head; I didn't even have a guess.

"Purify," Simon said. "At some level, I suspect he was trying to purify what he was doing. Hoping to forestall or possibly alter a damnation that he believed was inevitable."

This could be psychobabble bullshit, not that we'd ever know. What we *did* know, however, was that Major Talbot was a troubled gay man.

For several moments, we were quiet, staring at the stark whiteness of the bed.

Simon changed the subject and addressed me apologetically. "Ah, Martin, with regard to General Baldwin, I have to know whether—"

"I believe Sam could have killed Major Talbot."

"Yes."

I measured my response. Simon wanted me to be objective and I was trying to do my best. I knew that Sam was capable of rages and would do almost anything to protect his family's name.

And yet . . .

"No," I said. "My instinct says no. If Talbot had been beaten to death in a drunken rage, that would be one thing. But we're talking about a calculated, cold-blooded murder. Sam doesn't have that in him. He's not capable of—"

At that moment, the door flew open and Enrique barged into the room. He was breathing hard as if he'd been running. "You better come on down, Simon. It's almost here. It surprised the hell out of us when we saw it. We thought he was driving. How come you didn't tell us? We barely have time to organize a security perimeter."

"Tell you what?" Simon asked.

Before Enrique could reply, we heard a rhythmic beating sound. It was faint, barely audible. Still we recognized it immediately.

It was a helicopter.

★21★

Simon sprang from his chair and followed Enrique out the door. I started to go after them when I felt a hand on my arm.

Amanda's big eyes were focused on me. Releasing her grip, she said, "Some of the things I said to get you to talk about Baldwin. They were out of line. If I'd known—"

"You were doing your job. You had a right to question what I was hiding."

A tiny, relieved smile. "If it helps, I think you did the right thing. Keeping the general's secret."

"You'd have made the same decision?" It was important for me to know that she wasn't just talking.

She answered slowly, thinking as she spoke. "Call it my academy upbringing or my Midwest convictions, but I don't support gays in the military. Never have. That said, I also know I couldn't turn in a friend." She grimaced wryly. "I guess that makes me a hypocrite. How can you support a policy and not have courage to enforce it when it affects you personally."

"It's called being human," I said.

She smiled again and squeezed my hand. I tensed at her touch and she jerked away as if she'd been scalded. Her eyes searched mine for an explanation and I knew better than to even try.

"We'd better get going." I started to leave, walking quickly. I only managed to make it a couple steps before—

"*Marty.*"

Shit.

I stopped and reluctantly about-faced. Amanda was giving me *the* look. She said, "Mind telling me what that was all about just now?"

"It's nothing. You surprised me. That's all." I tried to come off as completely sincere.

"Like hell," she snapped.

I sighed. "Look, can we talk about this later?"

"What do you think?"

"Amanda, it would be better—"

"No."

I saw the stubborn set of her beautiful jaw. No way would she let this go. I gave in, saying, "It's us. It's the relationship that we have now."

"What relationship?"

"That's just it. We don't have one. You're engaged. I have to accept that fact. But it's difficult when . . . when you do things, say things that make me believe there's a chance—"

She cut me off with a look of incredulity. "*It was a gesture.*"

"I know, but—"

"*Between friends.*"

"Amanda, please. Consider it from my perspective—"

She interrupted me again. She was really pissed off. "I *am*. You want a purely professional relationship, you got it. From now on, it's strictly business between us. When this investigation is finished, I'll ask General Hinkle not to assign us to work together again. *Ever.* You happy now?"

Now I was getting angry. "*Me* happy? You wanted this, remember?"

She addressed me in a patronizing tone as if I were a child. "You really don't understand, do you? Some fucking cop you are."

"Get what? What are you talking about?"

"Forget it, Marty. It doesn't matter. It was a crazy idea. I'm not sure why I even agreed to try. Serves me right. Let's just finish this damn case, so we can each get on with our lives." She brushed past me and walked out the door.

I stared after her, feeling stunned and confused. She said she wanted me to make the right decision and I thought I had. What the hell did she want from me?

Exiting the house, I nodded to a uniformed cop by the door and crossed the Spanish tile porch. Amanda and Simon were standing on the stone walkway that wound past the flower beds toward the driveway. I strolled up to them, stopping near Amanda. She immediately sidestepped around Simon, placing him between us. Simon watched this little display with a wry smile. He was enjoying this.

With a sigh, I focused on winking lights hovering in the moonlit sky. The silhouette of a corporate helicopter was visible several hundred feet up. As it descended toward the sprawling lawn, I shifted my gaze toward the gate. The crowd of media had grown, almost doubling in size. Amid the camera flashes and glare of TV lights, I could make out more uniformed police officers who'd been deployed to insure that no one tried to enter the grounds. You can't be too careful where the security of the leading presidential contender was concerned.

I said to Simon, "You didn't know the congressman was flying in?" Because he might have simply neglected to tell us.

"No."

I shrugged. "Guess this tells us why Harris wasn't worried about the press being here."

"Does it?"

A comment which generated glances from Amanda and me. For an instant, our eyes locked. She severed the link with a frosty look and turned away.

Seconds later, the helo touched down, rocking gently on its skids. The rotors slowed as the engine was shut off. A small door opened and the figures of two men hopped out, their heads bent to avoid the still spinning rotor blades. After carefully surveying their surroundings, the men assisted the other occupants from the helicopter.

"Secret Service," Amanda said, proving she could still talk, just not to me.

As a presidential front-runner, Congressman Harris was entitled to Secret Service protection.

Four additional figures emerged from the chopper. Three men and a woman. Their faces were difficult to distinguish in the dim light, but we knew that the couple walking hand-in-hand must be the congressman and his wife.

"I was afraid of this," Simon said. "He stopped to pick up his wife. He shouldn't have done so. Particularly in her condition. It's unwise."

He sounded irritated. Apparently, this was another little detail that Congressman Harris had conveniently forgotten to mention to him.

I said, "Her condition? Is she ill?"

"She's being treated for exhaustion. It's why she didn't accompany him to Pennsylvania."

The group started across the lawn toward us. Simon automatically straightened his tie and adjusted his cuffs. Amanda ran a hand over her hair and smoothed her suit. I just stood there with my hands to my side. When you're sporting a borderline crew cut and wearing an off-the-rack suit, there wasn't any point in primping.

I began humming a tune.

There was no reaction from Simon, but then his interest in music began and ended with classical. Amanda eyed me sourly. "Not funny."

I looked back innocently. "Excuse me?"

"You know what I mean."

"Know what?"

"Act your age for once." She pivoted and headed down the walkway. As Simon and I followed her, he gave me a questioning look. I explained I was humming, "You're So Vain." He grinned. I knew it was funny.

"Simon!"

We stopped about halfway down the walkway, looking back. Enrique was bounding down the front steps.

"Okay," he said, jogging up to Simon. "I gave Dr. Cantrell's assistant Maggie a heads-up. Everyone else knows to be cool. I told them not to do anything stupid, like ask for autographs. Here." He handed Simon a packet of latex gloves.

Pocketing it, Simon said, "And Mrs. Johnson?"

The part-time maid; Simon must have asked Enrique to try contacting her again.

"Still not in," Enrique said, "but her husband swears she'll be home any minute. I'll give her another shout pretty soon and ask her about the sheets."

The comment jogged my memory. I said, "Simon, I forgot to mention—"

He'd resumed his trek down the walkway. By the time I turned around, Enrique was going back up the stairs.

Amanda said, "You wondering about the sheets?"

I blinked, surprised she'd actually spoken to me. "You know what Simon's after?"

"I can guess. It's pretty obvious if you'd paid attention to the videos."

Then she flashed a mocking smile and promptly departed after Simon.

I almost called out who was being immature now. The reason I held off was because I realized she'd provided a clue to Simon's interest. I thought hard, trying to remember. No good. I've have to see the videos again to be certain.

Obvious my ass.

We waited under a lamp at the edge of the driveway, as the group approached. The small procession moved slowly, every face leaden. No one spoke or attempted conversation. They were treating this like a funeral procession, which, in reality, it was.

Congressman Harris and his wife led the way, their hands still clasped together. In person, they looked much more striking than they did on TV. Even though Harris was well over fifty, he easily passed for someone a decade younger. His blow-dried hair was thick and brown, and his face possessed a boyish charm that the camera and the voters loved. In her early forties, Teresa Harris looked more like a former beauty queen than the Olympic athlete she once was. Blonde and blue-eyed, she had a long, willowy frame and despite the exhaustion that Simon had mentioned, moved with an athletic grace honed by years of dedicated training. Her sport had been skiing and in an interview with Barbara Walters, she said that missing out on an Olympic medal — she'd placed something like fifth or six in her event — was the one failure which still haunted her.

I doubt if she's failed at anything since.

"She's really stunning, isn't she?" Amanda said. "No wonder they're leading the polls."

She said they, not he. It wasn't a misstatement. In addition to her beauty and athletic prowess, Teresa Harris had been blessed with exceptional intellect and ambition. In her own right, she'd been a senior partner at a prominent DC Law firm, had served as an undersecretary of the treasury and more recently, as the head of the U.S. Olympic committee. The latter position had heightened her national visibility and early on, the campaign decided to emphasize her credentials as much as her husband's. Posters, TV spots, pins, bumper stickers—you name it—her smiling image was always visible beside his. According to a recent editorial, Teresa had suggested this two-for-one strategy in an attempt to attract the female vote. So far, it was proving wildly successful. In four short months, Harris had risen from the back of the pack to become his party's nominee because of one reason—his wife.

Focusing on the two people bracketing the Harrises, I realized I'd made an error in my previous assessment. The person hovering next to Mrs. Harris was actually a black woman. Her size had thrown me. She was well over six feet, solidly built, with close-cut hair and shoulders that were easily as wide as mine. Her Amazonian appearance ended at her face which was finely chiseled and attractive. As I looked at her, I knew I'd seen her before, but couldn't place her. I didn't have that trouble with the graying, barrel-chested man walking beside Congressman Harris. He was Roland Slater, the shrill voiced, fire-and-brimstone campaign manager.

The two Secret Service agents brought up the rear, walking in a stiff cadence that reminded me of toy soldiers. The agent on the left was pushing forty, medium height and weight, with a square jaw and an even squarer flat-top hair-cut. His sandy-haired partner mirrored his height and looked about ten years younger. I kept waiting for them to blink. They never did.

As the entourage came to a stop, Simon initiated the in-troductions. If he was nervous about meeting someone of Harris's stature, he gave no sign. His diction was smooth, his manner attentive and sympathetic. The black woman was Abigail Gillette, a personal assistant to Mrs. Harris. Her name awakened my memory. She'd been a star college basketball player and a former Olympian. The latter con-nection explained how she'd got the job working for Mrs. Harris.

No one introduced the Secret Service men, but then they wouldn't. Everyone had perfunctory handshakes ex-cept for Slater, who had a viselike grip which he squeezed hard in an attempt at intimidation. *Prick*.

"My deepest condolences for your loss," Simon said.

The congressman and his wife nodded. Mrs. Harris's grief was clearly evident. Her eyes were dull and unfocused, and her lower lip trembled. She transferred her grip to her husband's arm as if on the brink of collapse. If Harris felt a similar sense of loss, he was certainly doing a good job of hiding it. His expression was coolly regal, devoid of any emotion.

"We'd like to see the body, Lieutenant," Harris said. His baritone voice indicated it wasn't a request, but a command.

Simon's eyes sought out Mrs. Harris. Gently, he said, "Mrs. Harris, if I might suggest, it might be better if you re-main—"

"No," she said, with surprising force. "I . . . I have to do this. I have to see Franklin."

Simon raised an eyebrow at Harris. The congressman

patted his wife's hand. "Teresa understands it will be . . . un-pleasant."

"Of course." Simon still appeared reluctant. "It is a crime scene, Mr. Congressman. I'm afraid I have to restrict access to the minimum." He looked at Slater and Gillette.

Slater said, "Now just a damned minute—"

"The lieutenant's right, Rolly," Harris said smoothly. "We certainly don't want to compromise the crime scene."

"We're accompanying the congressman, Lieutenant."

This came from the flattop who stepped forward with his Secret Service sidekick. Flattop planted his feet wide, eying Simon. "Where the congressman goes, we go."

Simon never intended to exclude the agents, but Flattop blew it by his arrogant manner. Simon would not allow himself to be bullied.

"No," he said.

Flattop looked as if he'd been slapped. "We're federal agents. You can't prevent us from—"

Simon said, "Congressman."

Harris appeared amused as he addressed Flattop. "Wait out here, Agent Hassall."

"But, sir—"

"*Wait.* You people have already screwed up enough for one day. Right, Coleman?" Harris glanced pointedly at the younger agent.

Agent Coleman immediately looked to the ground, embarrassed. Resentment flashed in Hassall's eyes, but he wasn't stupid enough to reply.

Both men drifted back.

"Lieutenant," Mrs. Harris said. "If I could see Franklin now."

After Simon passed them each a pair of latex gloves, he led them up the walkway. Amanda and I brought up the rear, watching Mrs. Harris with concern. As she approached the house, her cadence slowed and she clutched her husband's arm even harder.

"She doesn't look like Superwoman now," Amanda said softly.

This was a name some political pundits had taken to calling her. I'd seen editorial cartoons, where she'd been pictured wearing a cape with a big S.

"Simon's right," I said. "She shouldn't have come."

★22★

Dr. Cantrell's assistant Maggie and two white-jacketed EMTs were waiting in the hallway with Enrique. They watched with a mixture of respect and awe as Simon escorted Congressman Harris and his wife into the media room. Talbot's body had been prepped for transport and was lying on a gurney, encased inside a neoprene body bag. Simon pulled the zipper down only far enough to reveal Talbot's face. His penis had been removed from his mouth, but you could still see the mass of coagulated blood crusted to his lips and chin. Mrs. Harris fell upon his body and began to cry. Loud, shrieking sobs. She wailed, "My boy . . . my boy . . ." Her husband tried to comfort her, but she kept pushing him away. Even though we witnessed her devastation, it didn't mesh with our mental image of her. In public, she was always so supremely confident and in control. Yet here she was, reacting not as some distant aunt or a detached political superstar, but as a very human mother who had lost a child. I knew only too well this kind of emotional pain. When Nicole had passed away, I'd wanted to die too.

"Explains about the trust fund," Amanda whispered.

"And something else."

Her eyes followed mine to Harris. Simon was watching him, too. Even now, as the congressman gazed upon his distraught wife hugging the corpse of his nephew, his expression remained blank and unresponsive.

"Cold," Amanda said.

After a minute, Congressman Harris pulled his wife off Talbot's corpse. She struggled briefly; she didn't want to go. In the hallway, she collapsed again and I came forward to assist Harris. Simon caught my eye and shook me off. It was the correct call; it wasn't my place. Harris guided his wife down the tiled corridor and out the front door, where his entourage was waiting. The personal assistant, Abigail Gillette, immediately rushed forward.

"Wait, Abbie," the press secretary Slater said sharply.

Gillette froze, her expression quizzical.

"You," he said to Simon, Amanda, and me. "Over there." He jabbed a thumb at the edge of the porch.

We looked at him as if he was certifiable.

He clapped his hands impatiently. "*Now*, people. We haven't got all night."

Simon bristled; he wasn't going to comply. I wasn't either. Who the hell did this pompous jerk think he was. This was a crime scene and—

"Do it, Lieutenant."

We glanced over to the steps, where Harris stood with his wife. He was glowering at us. "Move."

Simon's jaw muscles flexed, but he eased over. Amanda and I followed.

"*Thank you*," Roland Slater said.

He turned his stocky frame and fixated on the front gate. Flashes continued to pop off at a dizzying rate. Slater spun back to the Harrises, contemplating them from several angles. Harris had an arm around his wife's waist, hugging her close. Slater made a twisting motion with his hand. On cue, the congressman turned his body, until he and his wife were lined up the with gate. "Perfect, Garrison," Slater said, grinning. "Absolutely frigging perfect. Now give me sad."

Harris's facial muscles relaxed.

Slater paced before him, chattering instructions. "Not too much. We talked about this. I'm looking for an *impression*. You're trying to be strong in the face of adversity. Better, better. Hand higher on her a back. Pillar of strength. That's it. Jesus, this is going to be good. We're talking another ten million votes easy." He stepped off to the side, beaming.

"I think," Amanda said, "I'm going to puke."

Simon and I nodded, similarly sickened.

This was hardball politics taken to the nth degree. By tomorrow, the image of Harris comforting his grief stricken wife would be plastered across the front page of every paper in the country. Something told me that the congressman's poll numbers were about to rocket out of sight.

For a full minute, the congressman and his wife remained on the steps, so every photographer with a telephoto lens could shoot off a roll. The entire time, Mrs. Harris remained pressed up against her husband. She seemed completely out of it. I don't think she was even aware of this impromptu photo shoot.

"Okay," Slater announced, rubbing his hands. "That's a wrap." He winked at Harris. "We got a winner, boss, believe me. Start practicing your inauguration speech, Mr. President. What are you waiting for, Abbie? Take Mrs. Harris to the helicopter. Chop, chop."

Gillette hurried forward, tenderly took Mrs. Harris from

her husband, and led her away. After a few steps, Mrs. Harris shook off her hand and turned to look back toward Simon. Her grief had disappeared, replaced by a look of quiet anger.

"Find the bastard who did this, Lieutenant," she said.

"We will, Mrs. Harris," Simon said.

She nodded and seemed to will herself upright. Without another word, she continued down the walkway under her own power.

"Curious," Simon said.

Amanda and I frowned at him, then realized he was watching the two Secret Service agents. Both were looking at Mrs. Harris's retreating figure, shaking their heads. Finally, the younger agent Coleman reluctantly detached and walked after her, while Hassall remained.

"Curious," Simon said again.

Simon, Amanda, and I remained on the porch while Congressman Harris and Slater ducked into a shadowed area near some bushes, to avoid the photographers and began to converse. We noticed them glance in our direction.

"You called it," I breathed to Simon. "Harris had to be the one who leaked the killing to the press."

A pensive nod. "But I never suspected he intended to capitalize on his nephew's death. That's what disgusts me the most. That this was so patently . . . ruthless."

Amanda's wrinkled brow mirrored mine. Simon wasn't given to hyperbole. She said, "Ruthless?"

"I'm convinced that's why Harris insisted that we not move Talbot's body. He wanted his wife to view it for the purpose of generating the anguished reaction we saw. So when she was photographed, she would be completely sympathetic."

"The fucking slimeball." She glowered in the direction of Harris and Slater.

"Two slimeballs," I corrected.

"Slater," Simon agreed, "orchestrated this. He's one of the most successful campaign managers in the country for the simple reason that he's mastered the art of dirty politics. In the past, he's been accused of slander and bribery, but nothing could ever be proved. Still, his underhanded tactics have made him something of a pariah among the political elite. Most ethical candidates wouldn't dream of hiring him for fear he'd create a scandal. I'm surprised that Harris is willing to take this chance."

I dimly recalled the criticism of Harris's choice of Slater. At the time it didn't get much press play because Harris had little chance of winning.

"Obviously," I said to Simon, "Congressman Harris is willing to do almost anything to win. So far, it's working. They've run a helluva campaign. What?"

Simon appeared deeply troubled. "It's probably nothing. But in Congress, Harris was known for two things: his supreme ego and his integrity. The latter quality is what set him apart. He often cast votes out of conviction rather than blindly following the orders of his leadership. It cost him significant political capital early in his career, even led to his removal from several key committees. Yet he never wavered in his practice. That took courage. Then there's the interview he gave last year, when he said he would never consider Slater as his campaign manager. Only a month later, he reversed himself and hired Slater."

Amanda and I shared a look. Simon was off on another tangent. She said, "And this relates to the murder because . . ."

"It's an inconsistency that bothers me. I'm curious why

someone who spent a lifetime adhering to certain standards of behavior would suddenly change. There must be a catalyst. Some reason."

"You bet there is," I chimed in. "The guy wants to be president so bad he can taste it."

"Perhaps," Simon said. "But character is an innate quality not easily altered. If power drove Harris, why spend a career alienating much of his own party? It certainly cost him the House Speaker's position." With a shrug, he added, "At any rate, this explains why Harris changed his mind about the press coverage."

Simon was suggesting that Harris hadn't originally intended to use Talbot's death for publicity, but had been convinced to do so by Slater. Was that a point in Harris's favor? Hardly. He'd still agreed to go along.

Truthfully, I didn't think Simon should be all that surprised that Harris had sold out his ethics. After all, this was what modern-day politics had become. Character and substance didn't matter. It was all deception and illusion, and the candidate with the most money and the best PR campaign invariably won. "Hell of a system," I muttered.

"What was that, Martin?" Simon asked.

"Looks like his highness wants to talk," Amanda said.

Harris was beckoning to us in a majestic manner. Egotistical slimeball or not, you don't blow off a potential president unless you're crazy.

"Martin—"

Simon stepped close and lowered his voice. "Do you really believe General Baldwin is innocent?"

"He's not capable of murder."

"But he was here."

"I'll talk to him again. He'll have an explanation."

He hesitated.

"Simon, if he is innocent, you will destroy him."

Silence. He was weighing the consequences of what I was asking. "Let me do the talking."

As Amanda and I trailed him down the steps, I felt a spark of hope.

He hadn't said no.

★ 23 ★

Harris was smiling as we approached him. It was a politician's smile—big and wide and insincere as hell.

He wanted something from us.

We stopped at the edge of the shadowed area, where he and Slater had taken refuge from the cameras. Hassall was planted several yards away, engaged in his mannequin routine.

Still smiling, Harris said, "Just wanted to say how much Teresa and I appreciate your cooperation. She needed to see Franklin. Prove to herself that he was really dead. She loved that kid."

"And you didn't?" Simon asked.

Christ— Amanda and I stared at him. We couldn't believe he'd dare to say this.

Harris had a puzzled look. He peered at Simon as if uncertain that he'd heard him right. I braced myself for the inevitable confrontation. No way would Harris stand for insolence from a—

Harris shrugged dismissively. "Hell," he said, "I guess it's no secret the kid and I had our problems over the years. But recently we've grown closer. Was our relationship perfect? No. But he was the closest thing I had to a son." His eyes narrowed. "And that's why I'm here, talking to you, Lieutenant. You heard Teresa. We want the bastard . . . the animal . . . who butchered our son. That's the only way we'll have peace. You understand me?"

Though his words came across as sincere, we knew he was going through the motions. His reaction to Talbot's corpse had already proven that he didn't give a damn about his nephew.

But for some reason, he wanted to make us think he did.

Simon said, "We're doing everything we can, Mr. Congressman."

"You know I was a DA? Prosecuted a lot of murder cases?"

Vague nods. We'd seen his TV ads, portraying his legal heroics.

"What about suspects?" Harris asked. "Anything yet?"

I held my breath, watching Simon.

He hesitated fractionally. "No, Mr. Congressman."

I exhaled. Amanda immediately fired me a worried glance. She was praying I was right about General Baldwin's innocence.

"No suspects?" Harris said. "What about Colonel Kelly? He's got motive. He hated Franklin ever since that incident when he accused him of . . ." He grimaced, unwilling to say the word. "Anyway, I told you he threatened Franklin on several occasions."

"We require proof of those threats. Until then, we—"

"You *have* proof. You have the message from last night. That's direct evidence of motive." His diction was clipped, exasperated.

Simon responded with a slow blink, as if surprised at something Harris had just said. He answered, "We've interviewed Colonel Kelly. He asserts he was drunk and only intended to frighten—"

"And you *believed* him? Come on, Lieutenant. Does the man have an alibi? Have you even *checked?*"

"We have, Mr. Congressman."

"And?"

"He doesn't appear to have one."

"Let me get this straight. Kelly had motive, opportunity, and no alibi and you *don't* consider him a suspect. What the hell kind of investigation are you running anyway?" He glanced at Slater who responded with a smirk.

Simon kept his cool. As a homicide cop who worked near the nation's capitol, he was used to working with self-important assholes. In a polite voice, he said, "We think there's another motive for the killing, Congressman Harris. We found some tapes that are suggestive . . ." He tapered off with a meaningful look.

Harris ignored the hint. "What kind of tapes?"

"We should discuss the matter in private, Mr. Congressman."

"Just fucking tell me, Lieutenant."

So Simon reluctantly did. Hassall reacted with surprise, but neither Harris nor Slater so much as raised an eyebrow. They'd both obviously known Talbot was gay and I wondered if this was why Harris had resented his nephew and never adopted him. Recalling Simon's comment about a homosexual relative being a detriment to a politician, I was pretty certain I knew the answer.

"Franklin was gay," Harris said, when Simon finished his description of the videos. "He taped his lovers. So what? Is that a crime?"

"If it was the motive behind the murder."

Harris snorted. "Be serious. Franklin was in the Air Force, remember? Why would he out anybody?"

Simon was silent.

"And didn't you tell me," Harris went on, "that Colonel Kelly believed Franklin was responsible for him not getting a star? You ask me, that's what probably set Kelly off. Pushed him over the edge."

Simon still said nothing.

"Lieutenant . . . Lieutenant . . ." Harris shook his head in a disdainful manner. "I know your reputation, but frankly I'm having some serious doubts here. Far be it from me to tell you how to do your job, but if I were you, I'd concentrate on Colonel Kelly. He hated my nephew and that's what we're talking about here. Hate." His eyes bored into Simon's.

"Colonel Kelly," Simon said quietly, "is still of interest, Mr. Congressman."

"He'd better be. Hassall, give the lieutenant my card. Santos, I expect you to brief me daily on your progress. When you decide to arrest Kelly, contact me immediately."

Harris stepped back, signaling he was finished. Looking toward the gate, he said, "Rolly, let's hold off on giving a press statement until the morning. I'm beat and we need to get Teresa home. I want her rested for her speech at Virginia Tech tomorrow. Any word on the network coverage?"

"The networks will show tape on the evening news. CNN will cover it live if General Murdock comes through with his endorsement."

"If? The bastard gave me his word."

"Murdock's catching grief from the military community. You haven't exactly been a big defense supporter over the years."

"Goddammit, I want his endorsement."

"I'll talk to him. He'll come around."

"He damned well better."

Harris and Slater walked by us down the walkway.

Amanda murmured to me, "Another connection to your alma mater."

It did seem curious that Virginia Tech kept popping up. Still, it wasn't unusual that the Harrises would go there. Notwithstanding the endorsement they were seeking, it was the largest university in the state, with an enrollment of more than twenty-five thousand. Toss in the parents of the student body and you were talking a lot of potential votes.

Agent Hassall came toward us, producing a card from a pocket. He passed it to Simon, accompanied by a "fuck you" look.

The man didn't learn.

Smiling pleasantly, Simon said to him, "I know Director McChesney."

Hassall stiffened at the name of the Secret Service chief.

"He's a personal friend," Simon said. "I wonder if he's aware of your rudeness or that you'd screwed up today?" He still had a pleasant smile.

A silence. Hassall squinted at Simon, trying to decided if he was telling the truth about his relationship to McChesney. A tongue flickered nervously across his lips; the answer was yes.

"There was no screwup," Hassall said. "It was a misunderstanding. That's all."

"What kind of misunderstanding?"

"It was a misunderstanding," Hassall said again. He hurried away.

Amanda said to Simon, "You really know McChesney?"

"We worked on several task forces before he became director."

"Oh, Lieutenant . . ." Harris had stopped at the end of the walkway and was looking at us. "It occurred to me that you might be reluctant to release information about my nephew's homosexuality. Not a problem. I believe it's crucial toward finding his killer. I *did* make it clear that I believe this is a hate crime?"

"Quite clear, Mr. Congressman."

"Good. Good. Just so there's no confusion." He continued across the lawn with Slater and a worried looking Agent Hassall.

"You thinking what I'm thinking, Marty?" Amanda said uneasily.

"Yeah. The military's in trouble if he pushes the hate crime angle."

She shook her head. "I actually considered voting for that asshole."

A surprising revelation because of Harris's liberal politics. Still, Amanda wasn't the first conservative to consider supporting him. Several prominent Republicans had raised eyebrows by endorsing Harris. This trend was apparently going to continue with the endorsement of General Murdock, whom Harris and Slater had been discussing. Murdock, who'd retired from the Army to become the commandant of cadets at Virginia Tech, was arguably the country's most popular military figure thanks to his spectacular orchestration of the second Iraq War. As to why a hawk like him would side with Harris, I couldn't even guess. Amanda's case, however, was a different story.

"Sure," she said, when I asked her. "I was really going to vote for Teresa Harris. You can't help but admire a woman like her."

Proving that for some, gender was more important than party affiliation.

"Congressman Harris," Simon called out suddenly. "A final question." He waved an arm over his head and ran across the grass toward him. And Simon never ran.

*

It didn't take Simon long to get an answer.

He spoke with the congressman for only a few seconds before Harris followed Slater into the helicopter. Hassall crawled in behind them and pulled the door closed.

Simon stepped away as the engine roared to life. He watched the helicopter lift off, then began retracing his steps.

"Okay, Marty," Amanda said, "any guesses why Harris wants this to be a hate crime perpetrated by Colonel Kelly? Because that's damn sure what he seems to want."

"Harris must believe he can use the hate crime angle to gain a political advantage."

"How? By indicting the Don't Ask, Don't Tell policy? Suggest it influenced Colonel Kelly to commit the murder?"

"That's the scenario the SECDEF was worried about."

The helicopter noisily chattered past us, heading east toward the Potomac River and the congressman's Maryland estate. As it disappear into the night, Amanda appraised me with skepticism. "I dunno, Marty. All that will do is put the military on the defensive and he's trying to *gain* their support."

I shrugged. "Even with Murdock's endorsement, Harris knows most of the military won't vote for him. Maybe he figures he's got nothing to lose by attacking Don't Ask, Don't Tell."

"I still don't see how that translates into a political advantage for Harris. It's not like the president is going to be tainted by this."

"He's the commander in chief. Chances are, he'll feel obligated to defend the military's position."

"But most of the public doesn't support gays serving

openly in the armed forces. Look what happened to Clinton. He got his ass handed to him over the issue."

I wasn't sure if her assessment held true any longer. Over the years, the American public had grown more tolerant and it was possible that—

"Uh-oh," Amanda said. "Bad news."

Simon was less than twenty yards away, striding rapidly, his lips pressed into a tight line. Obviously, Harris's response had displeased him. As he walked up, I asked him what the problem was.

"*Time*, Martin." He made an angry, stabbing motion in the direction of the departed helicopter. "I don't understand how Congressman Harris knew the time."

"Of?"

"Colonel Kelly's message. How could Harris have known when it was made?"

Amanda said, "I thought you told him—"

"I didn't. I only told him Kelly had left a threatening message. I never said anything about the time of the call. *So how did he know?*"

She was unsettled by the intensity of his gaze. "I . . .well, I suppose it could be because—"

She visibly started. I caught on a split second later and we both regarded Simon in shock.

"Simon, this is *crazy*," Amanda said. "You're suggesting that Congressman Harris would—"

"I'm not suggesting anything. I'm *telling* you that there are only two ways Congressman Harris could have known about the time of Colonel Kelly's message. The first is if Major Talbot had mentioned it to him or his wife. But the congressman informed me that he hadn't spoken with his nephew in several weeks and his wife hasn't mentioned any recent conversation. Now whether Harris was involved in

the murder, I don't know. What I *do* know is that someone
listened to Colonel Kelly's message and relayed its contents
to him. It's highly unlikely that this person would be one of
the maids, and since we know Talbot lived alone, that leaves
only—"

"The killer," Amanda said.

★ 24 ★

The night was cool and quiet. A light breeze felt good on my face. From the gate, we heard the scattered shouts from the reporters, calling out to us. In the distance, a dog began to howl. Amanda slowly shook her head, her expression dazed. She still had trouble grasping the impact of what Simon had just told us.

A man who would be president could be a killer.

She went still and stared off into space. It gradually dawned on me that she was trying to recall the conversation. To be absolutely certain.

"Simon's right," I said, breaking in on her thoughts. "Harris did mention that the message had been recorded last night." I'd remembered because of Simon's surprised reaction to this remark from Harris.

A nod of acceptance. Amanda briefly closed her eyes and when they opened, we heard her barely restrained rage. "His own nephew. The son of a bitch had his own nephew killed—"

"We don't know that," Simon said.

Amanda's head swung around to him. "Huh? Dammit, you just said—"

"The killer told Harris of the message. We still don't know Harris was involved in the murder."

"Get real. That proves Harris *knew* the killer. You think that might just be coincidence? Please."

"All I'm suggesting is to withhold judgment until—"

Amanda was too spun up and talked right over him. "What about the way Harris is pushing for this to be a hate crime? He practically *ordered* us to arrest Colonel Kelly. I wondered about that. We all did. Marty had this theory that Harris was going to use the issue to embarrass the military and the president, but now we know the truth. Harris wants Kelly arrested to cover for the real killer. It all fits. You know it does."

Her speech completed, she jammed her hands on her hips, defying him to respond.

"I agree with your assertions . . ."

"I'm thrilled."

"I agree Harris's actions are suspicious. I agree he appears guilty—"

"So what's the problem? Don't tell me you're still on the kick that he's got too damned much integrity to be a murderer."

"That can't be completely disregarded—"

"Like hell it can't."

"But what concerns me is what you mentioned earlier. The motive. What reason could Harris have for wanting Major Talbot dead?"

"They didn't get along. That resentment could have escalated to the point where Harris hated Talbot enough to kill him. Or possibly it was money. I mean Harris is shelling out over a million a year to support Talbot. I suppose Harris could have cut Talbot off, but that would have meant getting into a confrontation with Teresa." She saw I was about to chime in. "Let me finish, Marty."

As if I had a choice.

"It could also be," she went one, "that Harris was worried that Talbot might be outed and it would cost him votes. Sure, I know Harris said we could go public with Talbot's homosexuality, but that's conveniently after the fact. With Talbot dead; Harris knows the American public won't give a damn he was gay. This could be where the missing tape comes in. Let's say Harris knew it was going to be released and figured the only way out was to kill Talbot before . . ."

She trailed off, noting our dubious expressions. She sighed. "Bass ackwards, huh? If Harris was going to have anyone killed, it'd be the person who took the tape and not his own nephew."

Simon and I nodded. I said, "Harris has a sizeable lead in the election. I'm not even sure if he would have considered the tape all that damaging. If you noticed, he didn't seem all that interested in the other videos we found." I added, "I also don't buy the money motive. So what if he was shelling out a million bucks to Talbot each year? That's pocket change for a guy like him." My brow knitted at a sudden inconsistency.

"Yes, Martin?" Simon said.

It took me several seconds to follow the thread. "The torture still bugs me. Especially the penis jammed in Talbot's mouth. I can't believe Harris would order Talbot brutalized in such a fashion. Even if he wanted the killing to look like a hate crime, that act seemed unnecessarily sadistic. Harris could have told the killer to scrawl a note about Talbot being a fag. Something."

Amanda said, "The killer might have acted on his own."

"True, but . . ."

"Martin's intuition is correct," Simon said. "The killer didn't dismember Talbot's penis on impulse. Remember, Talbot was alive while this occurred. To me, this is crucial. I believe the killer was making a symbolic statement, to ensure Talbot understood *why* he was being killed."

"A cocksucker," Amanda said. "The killer was telling Talbot he was dying because he was a cocksucker."

"Ah, but that implies a hate crime. And if we rule that out and concentrate on the *placement* of the penis . . ."

He drifted off, looking at her. Waiting to see if she could connect the dots.

She did, saying, "Got it. The mouth. The killer put the penis in Talbot's mouth because he was going to talk, reveal something he shouldn't."

A nod of approval. A teacher pleased with a pupil.

Not that Amanda would see it that way.

She announced stubbornly, "It has to be Harris. He must have found out that Talbot was going to go public with something damning. Had him killed before he could."

"And the missing videotape?"

Her mouth hunted for an explanation. But the truth was, there was no plausible way to link the missing tape of one of Talbot's gay lovers to Harris.

"What if," she tossed out finally, "it was taken to confuse the real motive?"

"But the missing tape suggests blackmail and Harris *wants* this to be a hate crime."

Logic she couldn't deny. She responded with a frustrated grimace.

"The point is," Simon said, with a tolerant smile, "we must be careful not to jump to conclusions. Blackmail, a lover's quarrel, a hate crime—nothing can be ruled out. We have no choice but to follow every lead, beginning with the most likely. Do you understand, Martin? The *most* likely."

And he looked at me in a suggestive manner.

I had no argument. After all, Simon had gone out on a limb for me and deserved an explanation why General Baldwin was here this afternoon. I told him I'd like to question Major Coller first, since he might be able to confirm whether Talbot had a relationship with General Baldwin.

"We don't know when Coller will return home this evening," he said.

Translation: He didn't want to wait. I told him I'd go question Sam now.

"*We'll* question him," Amanda corrected.

Second translation: She didn't trust me.

As Simon, Amanda, and I entered the foyer, we saw the two med techs rolling the gurney with Talbot's body toward the hallway at the rear. By the staircase, Enrique was camped on the bottom step, simultaneously talking into a cell phone and scribbling in his notepad. Spotting us, he motioned emphatically with the pad, then continued to write.

"Mrs. Johnson," Amanda said.

A statement rather than a question. "Probably," I said.

Another cell phone rang and we automatically looked at the ones we were carrying. It was mine.

General Charlie Hinkle was on the other end and sounded upset. "You were supposed to fucking call me, Marty."

"Sorry, Charlie, it's been hectic and—Ow!" I felt an intense pain in my elbow. I wrenched free from Simon's grip. "*What are you—*"

Hang up, he mouthed.

I frowned, confused. Charlie said, "What the fuck is going on, Marty? Marty? You there? Dammit, quit screwing around—"

Simon snatched the phone from my hand. "General Hinkle, Lieutenant Santos. Martin will call you back in a minute." Amanda and I could hear Charlie sputtering as Simon canceled the call.

As he handed me back the phone, I said, "For chrissakes, Simon—"

"I didn't want you to do anything foolish."

I glared at him. "Define foolish."

He glanced around, saw no one was in earshot, then gave me a hard look. "No one," he said, "can know about our suspicions concerning Congressman Harris."

I was with him now, but thought he was overreacting. "Charlie can keep his mouth shut. I'll tell him to keep his mouth shut."

His eyes locked on mine. "And if he doesn't?"

"Simon's on to something, Marty," Amanda said. "General Hinkle will have to tell the SECDEF and the chairman of the Joint Chiefs. Once that happens, there's bound to be a leak. Someone on the staffs. Think about the fallout. The public and the media will assume it's all politically driven. That we're just trying to smear Harris."

I understood their concerns, but— "So we don't tell *anyone*? We keep our suspicions *completely* to ourselves?"

Solemn nods. Simon said, "We have no alternative. Once Harris becomes aware we're investigating him, he'll use the power of his position to stop us. And he will succeed."

"That's what worries me," I said. "Harris *is* too powerful. Without help, we haven't got a chance of getting him."

"You're admitting defeat, Martin. Don't."

"Like hell I am," I flung back. "I'm being a realist. To arrest Harris, we're going to need an airtight case. That means we need a boatload of evidence and then some. We can't collect it all on our own. We *can't*."

No response. He and Amanda looked at me, disappointment creeping into their eyes. My phone rang again. I made no move to answer it.

"It's your decision, Martin," Simon said quietly.

But it wasn't. Not really. It wasn't so much that I'd been outvoted two to one. Rather it was the growing realization that there was no good option. Whichever way we went, if Harris was guilty, he'd probably walk. The reality was that justice didn't apply to the rich and powerful. It just didn't.

"Screw it," I said and punched "talk."

Charlie chewed me out for almost thirty seconds before he got around to asking about the case. Under Simon and Amanda's attentive ears, I answered no to every question except: "Yes, Major Talbot was gay."

This generated more swearing from Charlie. While I waited for him to unscrew himself from the ceiling, I debated whether I should tell him that his worst fears might be realized. I decided to pass. If—and at this moment it was still an if—*if* Congressman Harris intended to portray Talbot's death as a hate crime, there wasn't much the DoD or the administration could do about it.

Why tell Charlie and give him an early coronary?

When I ended my conversation with him, Enrique had finished interviewing the maid Mrs. Johnson and was in the process of briefing Simon and Amanda on what he'd learned.

Referring to his notepad, he methodically went through the questions he'd asked her, paraphrasing her responses.

This was his style. Despite his cavalier attitude, he had a reputation for being smoothly thorough and deliberate.

Mrs. Johnson's negative answers outweighed the positives.

No, she had no idea who might have murdered Major Talbot, or why. No, she'd never heard him mention Colonel Kelly or General Baldwin. Yes, she did know Major Coller—he visited often. No, she never recalled him staying over. No, she hadn't known Major Talbot was gay. No, she didn't know anything about a video camera in the bedroom. Yes, it was a little over a week ago when Major Talbot installed the security cameras and purchased the guns. No, he never told her if there was something specific he was trying to protect himself against.

And so on.

I stood there, with my pen poised over my notepad, waiting to jot down something of interest. But all the information Enrique passed on was what we already knew or suspected.

Until he mentioned the priest.

"Mrs. Johnson," he said, "suggested we talk to Father Carlacci, Major Talbot's priest. He's the pastor of the Church of the Sacred Heart."

"On Randolph Street?" Simon said.

"Yeah. The two men were quite close. Father Carlacci dined here several times a month. He enjoyed good booze and after dinner, he and Talbot would retire to the study, where they'd spend half the night drinking and talking. Whatever they discussed, Mrs. Johnson doesn't know. They usually clammed up whenever she or Mrs. Chang were around. I said usually, because last Thursday Mrs. Johnson went to the study to refill their drinks. As she approached the door, she could hear them arguing. It was mostly Father Carlacci's voice she heard. She could tell he was angry and half in the bag. The door's pretty thick and Mrs. Johnson's hearing isn't all that good. Still, she managed to understand a few phrases. One because Carlacci repeated it."

He scanned his notes. " 'You'll have to tell them, Franklin. It can't continue. You'll have to tell them.' "

He glanced up.

"Who is them?" Simon said. "*What* can't continue?"

Enrique shook his head. "Mrs. Johnson didn't know. Right about then, she figured she'd better not intrude. As she left, she heard Major Talbot's response."

His eyes again went to his notepad. This time he looked up before he related what he'd written down down.

" 'They'll kill me, Father,' " he said. "She heard Major Talbot scream, 'They'll kill me, Father.' "

"Son of a bitch," a voice said.

It was mine.

Faulkner's arrival was Sister's second scene, and midday
a few plates on the stove were beginning to sizzle it.
He carried her over there, too. I rose to ask them
Faulkner couldn't come around and sit down near them
to the stove and.

With patience, Simon said, "Let me see if I continue.
Indicate those last bags, this felon didn't want
a blackmail then. Blackmail isn't false; it's terrible. As
far as you've got, there's clues there are.

She couldn't keep up her around. And it would only.

★ 25 ★

That was it. That was all Mrs. Johnson heard. Just three short sentences. Still, it was enough.

We could cross off hate crime and put blackmail into the possible but unlikely category. More importantly, we had a source who could provide us the motive and possibly the killer's identity. The question was whether Father Carlacci would tell us. Being a part-time Protestant, I had to ask.

"It depends," Simon replied, "on whether Father Carlacci considered Talbot's statements protected by the sanctity of the confessional."

"Talbot's dead," Amanda said.

"Doesn't matter." He paused, thinking. "I only glanced at the address list briefly, but— Yes. I'm certain his name was there. There were two phone numbers listed beside it. Martin, did you leave the folder in the bedroom?"

"Give me a sec." I stepped around him to go upstairs to retrieve it.

"That might not be necessary," Simon said.

I pulled up. Simon was frowning, searching his mental hard drive for the image of the page. I told him I needed to get the folder anyway, so I could confront Sam with Talbot's phone calls. When Simon didn't reply, I continued up the stairs.

The folder was on the coffee table where I'd left it. I made a quick check for Father Carlacci's name. It was there, along with the two phone numbers Simon had mentioned. The first was to the rectory where Carlacci resided, the second to his office. I searched for another name. Under Harris, five numbers were listed. Two were cellular, two were to their home, and one had no designation. Walking out, I plucked out the phone records and scanned the recent entries. The last call Talbot had made to the Harrises was two days ago, to one of the cell numbers—probably Mrs. Harris. It was a short call, under a minute.

Simon was right. From this, it appeared that Talbot couldn't have told either Harris about the threatening message from Colonel Kelly.

However, he could have told a couple other people.

Talbot made several calls after receiving Colonel Kelly's message; two last night and three today. One number I recognized. Talbot had called Sam's home number last night and spoke for almost five minutes. Sam must have known about Kelly's threat. He had to have known.

Shit.

Wedging the phone list in my jacket, I hustled down the stairs. By the time I rejoined everyone in the foyer, Simon was making a call. It's a good thing, having a photographic memory.

Simon phoned the rectory first, got a machine. He left an urgent message for Carlacci, then tried his office. Another machine. After clicking off, Simon placed a third call.

As with Major Coller, Simon wasn't taking any chances and ordered Arlington PD dispatch to send a patrol car to the church. Only this time, Simon wanted the officer to

ring the doorbell of the rectory and make every attempt to
awaken Father Carlacci, assuming he'd gone to bed.

"If he's there, have the father call me immediately. If not,
someone at the rectory should know where he is. Thank
you, Dee Dee."

Simon pocketed his phone, his expression troubled. I
read his concerns and asked him why the killer would know
about Carlacci. I added, "You think he could have been
Talbot's lover in the missing video?" This seemed pretty far-
fetched, but you never knew.

The Catholic in him appeared pained at his suggestion.
"This has to do with the torture, Martin. From the beginning I've wondered about it. Why was it so prolonged and
extensive?"

I hesitated, knowing this was too easy. "Obviously, Talbot
resisted talking."

"But why? What didn't he want to reveal?"

Blank looks from Enrique and Amanda. I felt similarly
puzzled. This was a question we'd already answered. Or
thought we had.

I said, "The killer had to torture Talbot to obtain the security room combination and possibly the location of the
videos—"

"Twenty-three," Simon said.

I looked at him.

"Major Talbot was stabbed twenty-three times. Two of
his fingers were crushed. Is it logical to believe he would
have withstood such agony to protect the security room
combination? Would you?"

"Well . . . probably not, but—"

I clammed up at Amanda's sudden expression of horror.
My eyes darted to Enrique. He'd gone pale.

At that instant, the realization hit me. "Oh, Christ . . ."

Simon nodded grimly.

An uneasy silence followed. None of us wanted to voice our acceptance of Simon's premise and what it meant. But deep down, we knew it was true. It had to be true.

Talbot's determination not to tell his killer what he wanted to know could only be described as heroic. His was in intense, unbearable pain. At some point, he realized he was going to die. Yet, cut after cut, he held out until his will was finally and inevitably broken.

No, it was ludicrous to believe Major Talbot suffered through such horror to keep from revealing the combination to the security room or even the location of the sex videos.

But if he was trying to protect friends . . .

Simon cleared his throat and we all focused on him. His expression was sad, almost mournful. "I pray I'm mistaken, but I don't think I am. Depending on the number of people Talbot took into his confidence . . ."

"We're talking about more bodies," Amanda finished.

Simon took the folder from my hand and flipped through the address list, looking at the names. So many names.

Including one who was a friend.

While we realized Talbot would only have shared his secret with those whom he trusted, we had no idea who those people were. And with well over a hundred names on his address list, we couldn't interview everyone in time. Certainly not before the killer acted.

We had a problem.

Simon closed the folder, looking at me. "We can't wait for Major Coller and Father Carlacci. We need General Baldwin to tell us what he knows. Time is of the essence. Hours can be crucial in preventing more bloodshed, including his own. Unless he cooperates, we can't guarantee his safety. Make sure he understands that."

"I will." His ominous tone scared me. I almost asked him to send a cop to watch Sam's place, but realized that would be a waste of time. The building already had security and with all the people coming and going, a police officer would have no idea who posed a threat.

"Of course," Simon said, eyeing me, "the crucial question is whether General Baldwin will cooperate?"

"I don't know." I didn't mention the call Talbot made to Sam last night. So what if Sam knew about Kelly's threat to Talbot?

"Even if he realizes what's at stake, Martin? That he himself could be in danger?"

"It would still be hard for him, Simon. If he confessed to being a confidante of Talbot's, he'd essentially be confirming they were lovers. He knows that admission would eventually become public. In a trial, it would have to become public. That's a humiliation he'd couldn't accept."

He said bluntly, "He'd rather die than admit his homosexuality?"

"I think so, yes."

"I'll get him to admit it," Amanda said.

She wasn't boasting so much as voicing a confidence based on fact. Amanda had a brutally confrontational interrogation style that regularly got results. While her odds of succeeding with Sam were somewhere between slim and none, one thing was certain; she wouldn't back off because he was a two-star.

Simon seemed to smile at her response. "Continue," he said to Enrique.

Referring to his notepad, he finally addressed the white sheets.

★ 26 ★

It was back in November, some six months earlier, when Major Talbot had changed to white bedding and sheets and had his bedroom and its furnishings painted blood red. No, Mrs. Johnson had no idea what possessed him to do this, or why. One morning, she arrived at work and found workmen renovating the room. Later that day, Major Talbot sent her out to shop for white bedding and sheets.

"Major Talbot," Enrique went on, "insisted the bedding and sheets had to be pure white and remain that way. If they became soiled in any way, they were immediately thrown out. Once, when Talbot was having coffee in bed, he spilled a drop on a pillow case. A single drop. Bleach would have taken the stain out. Still, the pillow case got tossed. He also had the maids throw out perfectly clean sheets several times. Ones without any stains that the maids could detect. Talk about compulsive, huh?"

Amanda's eyes crept toward Simon. She realized his purity theory might not be so crazy after all.

"And the color of the previous sheets Major Talbot used?" Simon said to Enrique.

"Beige and off-whites. He liked the lighter earth tones."

Simon nodded as if he knew this.

My cue. I said, "I take it the sheets in the videos *weren't* white?"

"They were actually a beige," he answered. "Quite light. One set even had a faint flower pattern. It was difficult to tell and I had to study the tapes to be certain."

I cut Amanda a look.

She dismissed it with a shrug. "I noticed the color disparity right off. Probably a girl thing."

"With your eyes closed?"

"Hysterical. Ha, ha. Remind me to laugh."

I almost said, you just did. But if I had, the room temperature probably would have dropped twenty degrees and we would have mixed it up again. One thing about Amanda, she could dish it out but couldn't take it. I asked Simon why we cared about the color of the sheets.

"Timing," he said. "Beige sheets tells us the videos were made prior to November. If Talbot hasn't had a lover since then, that further indicates he wasn't promiscuous."

"You're assuming he videotaped all his lovers?"

"If not, why bother to install the camera? Enrique, how many times were these unsoiled sheets thrown out? Four?"

He consulted his notepad. "Two."

"Oh?" Simon's slow blink followed.

By now, I'd had a pretty good idea of the point he'd been hoping to make. It was an offshoot of his purity theory. I said to him, "You were thinking that every time Talbot had sex in the bed, he tossed out the sheets."

"To him, they would be soiled both physically and spiritually. It's the only logical explanation. There is simply no other reason why . . ." He drifted off with an unfocused look.

I said sharply, "Simon."

Too late. He was gone. Trying to understand how he could be mistaken.

No one said anything. We'd been through this drill countless times and knew he wouldn't come back until he worked this through. The fun part was guessing when.

Amanda held up a single finger and I responded with two. Enrique didn't bet; Simon rarely took longer than two minutes.

Amanda won since we rounded down.

After less than thirty seconds, Simon began murmuring to himself, a sign his synapses were firing. "No, no. That wouldn't make sense because . . . yes, perhaps, but only if . . ." He fell silent for several more seconds. Abruptly, he said, "The sheets. Why? Why throw out them out? He wouldn't unless . . ."

His eyes suddenly widened. "Of course. *Of course*. That would explain—" He broke off with an angry grimace. "I've been a fool. I should have realized. But now I know. *I know.*"

"Know what?" Amanda immediately shot back.

But he'd spun away from her and began barking out instructions to Enrique. "Get Billy Cromartie. We need to determine how long the camera has been in the bedroom. We also need to make copies of the tapes. The maids should be able to tell us about the sheets. Particularly the one with the pattern. Go. Go."

Enrique pivoted and dashed across the foyer. By then, Simon was hurrying toward the staircase. He looked both tense and excited. Amanda called to him twice before he acknowledged her.

"The video tapes," he said. "Your suspicion was correct. They were meant to confuse the motive."

"And you know this because . . ."

That was all we were going to get because he was rushing up the stairs. Within seconds, he'd ducked into the hallway, leading to the bedrooms.

Amanda and I were alone in the foyer. She sighed. "He did say *tapes*, right?"

"Yes."

"So he's not talking about the *missing* tape? He's saying that the three we found were meant to confuse the motive?"

"Apparently."

She thought, then made face. "I got nothing."

"That makes two of us. C'mon. Let's see if we can sweet-talk Sam into telling us why Talbot was killed."

"Assuming he's not the killer," she said.

I let it go.

As we clicked our way across the tiled foyer, she said, "Uh, Marty, you do realize your watch is beeping."

Actually, I hadn't. I punched off the alarm and removed my phone to make a call. An important one.

★27★

When Nicole passed away, I promised myself I'd never let my daughter Emily go to bed without wishing her good night. In the five years since, I've kept my word. If I couldn't be with her in the evening, I always called. As a single parent, you have to remember the little things, so your child will always know how important they are in your life.

Amanda and I continued down the hallway toward the rear of the house. Forensic technicians were still visible in several of the rooms. Because of the sheer size of the home, they'd probably work through the night and the way this case was going, we would also.

"Emily?" Amanda said.

A conclusion she'd reached because I'd punched the speed dial. She asked to talk to Emily when I was finished. "A little girl talk about her dance."

I figured as much. During the past three years, Amanda had become a big sister to Emily. It's a relationship I've continued to encourage, despite the difficulties between Amanda and me. Emily needed a female role model and I learned long ago that even if I started shaving my legs or listening to adolescent boy bands, I'd never come close to fulfilling that bill. Ask any dad whose gone shopping with his daughter to buy her first bra and he'll know where I'm coming from.

My housekeeper Mrs. Anuncio answered on the fourth ring, which was two past her norm. She's originally from Colombia and has been looking after Emily and me since Nicole died. I said, "Hi, Mrs. A—"

"You wait." She put down the phone and went away.

I sighed. Almost seventy, Mrs. A was set in her ways and ran the household like it was her personal fiefdom. While she doted on Emily, she tolerated me as a necessary evil. It wasn't anything personal. My crime was being a male, a gender she's despised ever since her husband ran out on her.

Amanda and I walked quickly. We cruised through the churchlike great room, pushed through the glass door onto the patio, then made our way across the pool deck. I heard a faint scraping sound at the other end of the line. "Em?"

It was Mrs. A. I told her I wanted to speak to Emily.

"She sleep."

"Already?" The dance ended at ten-thirty and I'd set my watch alarm for eleven fifteen, assuming Emily would be too jazzed to go right to bed. "All right, tell her I called—"

We were approaching the rear gate. I came to a sudden halt and pressed the phone to my ear. Amanda blew past a couple steps, then looked back with a frown. I held up a finger to her, listening intently. There it was again. In the background, a muffled female voice called out to Mrs. Anuncio, as if through a door.

I said to Mrs. A, "I thought you said Emily was asleep."

"She wake now," she said simply.

"Is that a fact?"

"*Como?*"

"Never mind. Put her on the line, Mrs. A." I rolled my

eyes, garnering a smile from Amanda. She knew how exasperating Mrs. Anuncio could be.

As I waited, I realized I could hear breathing. Mrs. A was still on the phone.

What's with her? "Mrs. A, will you please go get—"

"I no get her."

"What?" I was taken aback. "Why not?"

"She shower. Talk tomorrow."

I was confused. It almost seemed as if she was trying to prevent me from talking with Emily. "How can she be in the shower if she just woke up?"

"She shower," she repeated stubbornly.

That did it. My irritation meter was pegged on high, but I tried to remain calm. "Mrs. Anuncio, listen to me. I don't care if Emily is in the shower. I want you to take the phone to her—"

I heard Emily call out again. Her voice was louder, more distinct, as if she'd opened the door. I immediately recognized the telltale slurring of her words. For a moment, I tried to deny the implication. My daughter would never—

Emily called out a third time. This time there was no doubt.

I gripped the phone so hard I thought I might break it. "My God, she's *drunk*. Emily is drunk."

Amanda looked stunned. In an instant, she was by my side, squeezing her ear next to the phone.

"No drink," Mrs. Anuncio insisted. "Sick."

"*Goddammit*," I exploded. "*Don't lie to me.* I want to know how Emily got drunk and why you are lying—"

My mouth froze in the open position. There wasn't any point in saying anything more because Mrs. A had hung up on me.

★

I lowered the phone and sagged against the fence. My mind felt numb as I tried think this through, comprehend why it had happened. From somewhere I dimly heard Amanda's reassuring voice. Moments later, she appeared before my eyes, her face filled with concern.

"It's okay," she said. "It happens. Kids experiment. It's called growing up."

"Not Emily."

"Meaning what? She's not going to grow up."

"Of course not, but—" I gazed off into the night to reign in my emotions. Without looking at Amanda, I said, "It's just that I've tried so hard to make sure she was raised right. Knew what's important. And now, it seems as if . . . as if—"

"It was all a waste of time? Is that it? You believe you failed her somehow?"

I swallowed, felt myself nod.

"You think this wouldn't have happened if Nicole had been alive?"

"It . . . wouldn't. I've been working long hours. Nights. I haven't been there for Emily—"

"Cut it out."

I gave her a look of annoyance.

She said, "You're pathetic when you get like this. Stop it."

"Now hold on—"

"I told you about your martyr complex. This compulsion for accepting the blame for other people's actions. It's pathetic. It really is."

"*She's my daughter and she's drunk.*"

"So what? You didn't serve her booze or tell her it was okay to get pickled. She made that decision *on her own.*"

"That's not the point."

"It's *precisely* the point. She's not some computer you can program. She's a teenage girl. She's going to make errors in judgment. When she does, you have to realize it's not your fault. It's *hers*."

My anger faded as I realized what she was trying to do. Still, I couldn't accept her rationale and told her why.

"You don't have kids," I said. "You don't understand what it's like to raise a child. Emily's my responsibility. Mine. Any decisions she makes, any values she has are a reflection of me. What I've instilled."

She listened calmly as I spoke, giving the impression that she empathized with my position.

Not quite.

"Fine," she said mockingly. "You're right, Marty. You're absolutely right. I don't have kids. I can't possibly know what I'm talking about. I haven't a clue what it's like to be a teenage girl and you do—"

Not again. "Amanda, all I'm saying—"

"I *heard* you, Marty. And I'm holding you to what you said. You want to blame yourself for Emily getting drunk, be my guest. God forbid she ever tries pot or has sex—don't look at me like that. She's a *teenager*. These things happen. When they do, you can really screw yourself in a circle. Hell, you'll probably spend a year in therapy, trying to figure out where you went wrong. It's a shame. It really is. Someday you'll wake up and realize life is a lot more enjoyable when you're not laying guilt trips on yourself."

I didn't reply. There wasn't any need. We both knew the guilt she was referring to had nothing to do with Emily. Rather, it was the rationale she'd used to justify her martyr comment.

She'd once told me that she believed the main reason I've held onto my wife Nicole's memory so long was because I felt guilt over her death. That I considered myself somehow responsible.

The truth was, I did feel guilty for one simple reason that made perfect sense to me. I was alive and Nicole wasn't.

"Who are you calling now?" Amanda asked.

Sara Winters was my neighbor who had driven Emily home from the dance. She'd intended to call me in the morning, to tell me about what happened with Emily. "The news mentioned you're working on the murder of Congressman Talbot's nephew and I didn't want to upset you."

"Tell me now."

At this, Amanda again pressed close to listen to Sara's account.

It wasn't as bad as we thought.

When Sara arrived at the dance, she couldn't locate Emily. With the help of her daughter, Sara learned Emily had gone with a group of friends to Larry Nelson's place. Larry was a farmer and had a couple of high school sons who were pretty wild.

"Larry and Marge were out of town," Sara said, "so the boys decided to have a party in the barn. Must have been fifty, sixty kids there. Most were drunk or close to it. I called Deputy Haney and he shut the party down. He said he'd talk to you tomorrow. If it helps, there was a big bowl of fruit punch that some of the girls were told contained no booze. But it did. Quite a bit, according to Haney. So, does it, Marty? Help, I mean?"

"It helps, Sara," I said.

"You ask me, that's probably what happened with the younger girls. They're all good kids like Emily. They'd never had alcohol before. They didn't know what they were drinking."

"I appreciate all your help, Sara."

"Anytime. I'm just sick about this, but you know how it is with kids. Lord love 'em. Anything else you want to know?"

I asked her how bad off Emily was.

"I had to stop the car so she could throw up. She felt better afterwards. She'll be fine by morning, other than a hangover."

"Thanks again, Sara."

"Night, Marty. Try not to worry, huh?"

"I won't," I lied.

As I put my phone away, Amanda stepped back, looking as relieved as I felt. Her response was understandable. In some respects, she was closer to Emily than I was. She certainly had a better rapport. She said, "Guess we should have known better. Checked the facts before overreacting."

We, not you. I smiled my appreciation to this gesture. "She still shouldn't have gone to the party."

"Chill, Dad. She's paying for it. It'll be a long time before she touches booze again. You got off easy."

When I thought about it, I realized I had.

I pushed away from the fence and reached out to unlock the gate. Amanda had the same idea and our hands met on the latch. This time neither one of us jerked away.

Her fingers lingered on mine longer than necessary before she withdrew it. She said softly, "You're a good father. You have no reason to ever feel guilty about the way you're raising Emily."

"I know, but sometimes it's difficult to—"

"Or about anything else."

In her gaze, I sensed rather than saw the message it contained. I nodded I understood and she smiled. I waited for her to turn away, but her big eyes remained focused on mine. Standing so close to her in the semidarkness, it occurred to me that this might be my last opportunity. I had to ask her now.

Gathering my nerve, I drew in a breath—

She turned away. "You hear something?"

Someone was calling to us.

Enrique jogged across the pool decking, shouting for us to stop. Behind him, we could see Simon striding briskly, talking on a cell phone. Under an arm, he'd jammed the folder I'd given him and in his free hand, he carried—

"A *pillow?*" I said.

"Must be evidence," Amanda said.

Approaching us, Enrique slowed to a walk, speaking rapidly. "Change of plans. Officer Hannity called. Simon's talking to him now. If it pans out, you'll only need to question General Baldwin to verify. The problem is getting there without tipping off the press. They know Simon's limo and are sure to follow. Simon's got an idea that should work. I'll drive the limo and—"

So much for being deliberate. Enrique's words were bouncing around too fast for me to understand. I told him to take a breath and he sucked one in, loud enough for us to hear.

I said, "I assume Hannity was one of the cops conducting surveillance—"

"Right. Major Coller. He just came home." He grinned. "Officer Hannity says our boy is toasted. Took him forever to get his key in the door. But, hey, if the man was sober enough to drive, he can talk."

I found myself getting caught up in his excitement and forced myself to calm down. Even if Coller knew who orchestrated the killing, that was still a long way from proving murder.

"And Simon's idea?" Amanda said.

Enrique explained in under a minute. By then, Simon had joined us. "We'll be there in ten minutes, Hannity," he said into his phone.

As he ended the call, he said to Amanda and me. "Hannity will advise Coller we're on our way. You understand what to do?"

We nodded.

Eyeing the pillow, she said, "You sure you'll be comfy enough?"

"I think so. The ride shouldn't take long and—" Simon stopped; he realized she was teasing him. His face frosted over and he stiffly turned away, walking through the gate toward the cars.

"Not smart, Amanda," I said. "You know how sensitive he is."

She grinned. "Oh, come off it, Marty. He's taking a pillow. Who does that?"

Only Simon.

Amanda pulled her Saab up to the northwest edge of the house, just far enough to provide us with a view of the front gate. I sat beside her in the passenger seat, and as she braked to a stop, we both hunched forward, watching the limo continue down the drive ahead of us. Approaching the gate, it slowed, tucking in behind a phalanx of uniformed officers who began clearing a path through the crowd of media.

"The fish are biting," Amanda said.

Through the fence, we could see a number of press types bolting for their vehicles. As the limo turned onto the road, cars and vans began pulling in behind it. Several almost collided. Horns blared.

I checked the dashboard clock: 11:23.

Precisely three minutes later, I said, "Okay."

Amanda tapped the gas and we rolled down the driveway. Ahead, the gate which had closed, was beginning to open. The cops were again positioned in a wedge, ready for battle.

"What do you think?" Amanda said. "Got rid of about a third?"

A reference to the press. "Maybe a little less."

"Show time," she said, seconds later.

We crept through the gate and the flashes began to pop. Because of the cops, no suicidal cameramen threw themselves at the car. Once we cleared the crowd, I looked back. No one bothered to tail us. A given. Simon was the lead investigator and we were his helper bees. We didn't count.

As the car picked up speed, I settled back for the short ride and wondered what Major Coller could tell us.

★ 28 ★

The drive to Major Coller's should have taken around eight minutes. Amanda kept the pedal to the metal and turned into the townhouse complex in a shade under six. To call it a complex was an exaggeration. Actually, it was an L-shaped pattern of no more than two dozen town homes located on a quiet street, across from a wooded park.

Coller's residence was easy to find. All we had to do was look for the police cruiser and glance to the right. Number sixteen was the fourth residence from the end, the one with an American flag hanging out front.

Amanda swung in beside the cop who was leaning against his car, waiting for us. He pushed upright as we emerged. He was a baby-faced black man with forearms the size of my thighs. His nametag confirmed he was Hannity.

Amanda and I flashed him our flip-top IDs. I said, "I understand you spoke to Major Coller . . ."

"Right. Passed the message about you coming." Officer Hannity squinted as if puzzled by something.

I said, "How drunk is he?"

"Drunk enough. He's damn lucky he managed to drive here in one piece. Look, I thought Lieutenant Santos was coming."

"He's here," Amanda said.

"Oh?" Hannity's eyes shifted to the back seat of the Saab. It was obviously empty. He returned to us, appearing even more confused.

Just then, we heard a tapping sound. It was followed by a muffled and angry voice. As we focused on the trunk, a flicker of comprehension crept across Hannity's broad face. "Ah, hell. You're not telling me—"

"It's a long story," I said.

The tapping and shouting continued. We stood there, listening to it.

"He's getting pissed," Amanda said. "Guess we better let him out." She sounded disappointed.

"And me without my camera," Hannity said, grinning. "Shit, I come back with a picture of the lieutenant crawling out of a trunk, I'd be a hero. I wouldn't work nights for a month."

I looked at Amanda. She always brought a camera on an investigation.

She hesitated, tempted. But she ultimately shook her head. A sensible decision. Hell hath no fury like a Simon scorned.

As we stepped around to the trunk, Amanda thumbed the release on her key chain. The lid popped open and Simon sat up, looking like a furious, albeit immaculately dressed, jack-in-the-box. For an instant, I thought he might be angry enough to swear.

"*This*," he seethed, "was not amusing."

I said, "It was your idea."

He glowered and thrust up the pillow. This generated another grin from Hannity. Bad move. Simon cut him a look and the grin vanished.

After Amanda and I helped Simon out, I tossed the pillow in the trunk and shut the lid. We watched as Simon went through his primping routine. Appearance, of course, was everything.

Pocketing his comb, he held Hannity in a menacing stare. "Not a word. You understand. Not a word."

Hannity didn't quite snap to attention, but he came close. "No sir," he barked.

Simon pivoted and headed across the parking area toward Coller's residence. As Amanda and I swung in behind him, we heard Hannity say, "Uh, Lieutenant—"

Three heads turned.

Hannity nervously appraised Simon. Gun-shy.

"Go on," Simon said impatiently.

Hannity began, "It's . . . it's about what you said. If I saw anything suspicious . . ."

"Yes, yes . . ."

"It's probably nothing, but . . . when I was walking over to talk to Major Coller, I saw this BMW. A black M5. It slowed like it was going to turn in, then sped up and continued on by."

Simon said, "And you think it was because he saw you?"

"Not only that, sir. You see, one of the reasons I noticed it was because I'd seen a black M5 parked over there, when I first arrived." He pointed to spaces at the far end of the asphalt, perhaps thirty yards away. "When I showed up, it sat there for maybe a minute, then pulled out."

"Did you have a description of the driver?"

"Windows were tinted dark. I could tell there was one person in the car. I think it was a man."

"Think?"

"It had to be a man. See that light—" He pointed to a lamp pole, behind where he'd indicated the car had parked. "I saw the guy's outline. After I parked, I noticed him sitting there, looking at me. Kinda made me wonder, so I kept my eye on him. I was thinking about checking him out, when he drove off. Anyway, he was a pretty big guy. That much I could tell."

"A license number?"

"I tried to get it, the second time. The problem was I had to run out to the street to see it. By then, the car was almost a block away. It had temp tags, though. Like from a dealer."

Simon asked if that's how he'd concluded it was the same car he'd seen earlier, because of the temp tags.

"Actually, Lieutenant," Hannity said, sounding a little embarrassed, "I never paid attention to the tags the first time. But can't be too many people afford an M5 who live here. Those go for seventy, eighty grand, easy."

Simon gazed out across the rows of moderately priced vehicles and nodded as if he agreed. He didn't; he was pondering the same thing Amanda and I were.

What if the driver *didn't* live here?

"How long ago did you speak to Major Coller, exactly?" Simon asked suddenly.

Hannity fingered the radio mike clipped to his lapel. "Maybe two minutes after we spoke. Not more." He checked his watch. "Call it eleven twenty-five."

"It's eleven forty-one," Amanda said, her eyes rising from her wrist.

Sixteen minutes.

And Coller's townhome had a back door.

I took out my pistol, eyeing Simon. "Better safe than sorry."

He issued instructions. Because Simon had gone to Kennedy Center, he didn't have his weapon so Hannity passed him the shotgun from the patrol car. He and I continued to Coller's front door, while Amanda and Hannity ran around to the rear.

"I'll cover you," he said, chambering a round.

I nodded and rang the bell.

Footsteps.

When I was sure, I stepped away from the door. "Someone's coming."

Simon was partially turned, scanning the parking area. I kept my gun trained on the door.

The sound of a lock clicking open. The door opened a crack and a handsome blond man tentatively peered out, swaying slightly. It was him, the man from the video. His eyes popped wide at the sight of my pistol. "Jesus."

By then I was lowering the barrel and reaching into my jacket. "It's okay, Major Coller. Sorry for the scare. I'm Agent Collins of the OSI. This is Lieutenant Santos."

He relaxed. "Right. You got some questions for me. Man, you guys don't screw around." For someone who was pickled, his voice was surprisingly steady.

After an attempt to focus on my credentials, he gave up with a shrug. "Looks good to me. What's this about, fellas?"

He opened the door and stood there smiling. I started to ask him if we could come inside when I felt a stinging sensation on my ear. It wasn't particularly painful. It felt like a bee sting or the prick from a pin, but I knew it wasn't either.

Because an instant later, Major Coller's throat exploded in a sea of red.

Time slowed and mist touched my face.

I saw Coller's startled expression as he pitched violently back. I saw him collapse to the floor and clutch for his throat. I saw the blood spurt between his fingers as he frantically tried to stop the bleeding. I heard his wheezing gurgles as he struggled to breathe. I saw and heard it all.

Right up until I felt Simon shove me in the back, screaming at me to get inside.

★29★

I sprawled through the doorway, stumbled over Coller and fell onto the hallway floor. From behind, I heard the sound of splintering wood. I rolled over against a staircase railing, just as Simon dove in beside me. His shotgun banged off my head and I swore. An instant later, something thumped into the carpet, inches from Coller, who was rolling around, clutching his throat. Another thump. Coller's shoe jerked and blood spurted from it. He tried to scream and gurgled instead. Simon yelled at me to pull him back, out the way. I hollered back that I was fucking trying.

I'd jammed my pistol in my holster and was reaching for Coller. He squirmed and thrashed wildly. I finally managed to grip him under the armpits. His shirt and chest were soaked with blood. I pulled as hard as I could and we began sliding back. Another bullet struck the carpet where he'd been lying. Simon joined in by pulling on my arms and we dragged Coller into a small living room, bullets thumping behind us.

We lay there panting, ears straining. But it was silent. There were no more thumps.

From the rear of the house, someone began banging on a door. Simon and I sprang to our feet, raised our weapons—

"Simon, Marty!" Amanda called out. "What's going on in there? What's wrong?"

That's when I realized we'd never heard the shots.

"Stay with him," Simon said. "Try and question him."

I looked at Coller. He'd stopped thrashing and his gurgles were weakening, becoming almost inaudible. I said to Simon, "He's hit in the carotid artery. There's no way he can—"

Simon crawled into the hallway. He turned right, heading toward the front door. I shook my head, thinking he was crazy to risk it. Seconds later, I heard the door slam shut confirming he'd made it. From the back of the house came more insistent pounding. Amanda: "Dammit, Marty, what the hell is going on?"

"Shooter. Sniper with a silenced rifle. He got Coller—"

"Jesus!"

"Hannity, radio for an ambulance and back up!" I stared down at Coller. His eyes were closed and frothy red bubbles oozed through his fingers. "Can you hear me, Major?"

Nothing.

More pounding. Amanda: "Marty, open the fucking door."

"Go around to the front. See if you can locate the shooter."

The pounding stopped.

To Coller, I said gently, "I know you can't talk so don't even try. Just listen. Someone killed Major Talbot tonight and has also shot you. Do you know who might want you both dead?"

His eyes fluttered open. I saw the fear in them. He seemed to nod, but it could have been my imagination.

"Is it Congressman Harris?"

He stared at me.

"General Baldwin?"

Again, nothing. He was still staring. After a few seconds, I realized he was never going to respond to me or anyone else again.

He'd just died.

I shook my head pityingly. In the ensuing stillness, I became aware of a dull pain in my ear lobe. My hands were matted with Coller's blood, so I gingerly touched the tip with my wrist. Torn flesh. It dawned on me how close I'd come and I began to tremble. It was all I could do to force myself into the hallway and search for Simon.

"Up here, Martin!"

Even though the front door was closed, I wasn't taking any chances. I hugged the right wall and at the last moment, dove onto the stairs. I scurried up half a flight and entered a dining room. Simon was on his knees, peeking through shades, talking into his cell phone. He was telling someone—dispatch—that the shooter must be in the park.

He glanced back with a questioning look. I interpreted it and shook my head. "Coller," I added, "seemed to know who might be behind the murders, but died before he could identify him."

Simon's face darkened with a smoldering anger. As he relayed the news of Coller's death, I skirted around the dining table and cautiously peered out the edge of the window.

The park was located directly across the street. It was quiet and dark. My eyes scanned the silhouettes of trees; nothing moved. I shifted to the parking area, which was visible about a hundred yards to the right. No cars, but it didn't mean much. The park occupied a city block and there were several access points.

How long since the last shot? Three or four minutes. Plenty of time for the killer to be long gone.

In the distance, I heard sirens. Easing from the window, I contemplated the pistol I was holding. As with my hands, it was sticky with blood. I glanced at my shirt and jacket. More blood. I checked out Simon. He was completely un-blemished, since he'd never actually touched Coller.

That wasn't by accident.

My ear began to throb and I told him I was going to find a bathroom and clean up. He nodded absently and kept talking into the phone. I also had a call to make. As I swung around to leave, I unclipped my cellular, then paused at a question Simon asked the dispatcher.

He'd inquired about the officer who had been sent to the rectory—whether he'd turned up anything on Father Carlacci. There was a brief delay as the dispatcher contacted the officer and received his answer.

From Simon's disapproving hiss, it wasn't the response he was looking for.

"Send three more units to secure the church perimeter," he ordered. "I'll be leaving here soon. Has anyone advised Sergeant Tasker—transfer me. Henry? Simon. You heard? Fine. We need to locate Father Carlacci. Contact the arch-diocese— The church secretary should know where he is. If that's the case, we'll need keys to the rectory. No, don't mention our suspicions. I don't want to alarm anyone un-necessarily."

Simon punched off and slumped wearily against the wall. "The rectory is locked and no one answers the door."

"It's Friday night. Father Carlacci didn't sound like a wallflower. He could have gone out for a drink."

"And the other two priests who reside there?"

I tried desperately to come up with a plausible response. It was denial. I didn't want the killer to win again. Not tonight.

Not ever.

I knew then what I had to do. I suppose I'd known it all along.

I checked my watch. Almost midnight. Sam's party would be wrapping up.

As I voiced my intention to Simon, he began shaking me off. "Amanda goes. You're too close to General Baldwin."

"It's better if I see him alone. I can make him talk to me if I'm alone."

"He didn't tell you anything before."

"This time he will. I'll make him tell me."

He continued to argue with me—until I explained how I could force Baldwin to talk to me.

He regarded me with surprise. "You'd be willing to go that far?"

"We got two bodies and no telling how many more could turn up. Yeah, I'd go that far."

He grudgingly nodded for the simple reason that he really didn't have a choice. Sam was Air Force and I was the chief military investigator. I could question him any damn time I wanted.

He glanced at the cell phone in my hand. "General Hinkle?"

"I need to report Coller's shooting."

"Perhaps I should do it."

The control freak in Simon talking. He was worried I might let something slip about our suspicions concerning Congressman Harris. I told him, fine. He could make the call. I didn't care.

Simon added, "I'll have Enrique swing by General Baldwin's and drop off Major Talbot's address list."

We'd discussed this. Our hope was that Sam could identify likely candidates with whom Talbot might have shared his secret. By likely, we were talking about fellow gays and more specifically, potential lovers.

The sirens were almost on top of us. We heard a squeal of brakes and the slamming of car doors. Anxious voices shouted out Simon's name. He hollered back that he was okay and would meet them around the back.

"Give me five minutes," I said to him. "And ask Enrique to bring me a clean shirt."

His expression became concerned. "Have the EMTs treat your injury first."

"I will." I smiled faintly. "Thanks for the shove, huh. If you hadn't, I'd probably be dead."

"Not necessarily."

I stared at him as if I hadn't heard him correctly.

"The shots, Martin. If you'll recall, the shooter only fired one that was close to us—"

"Close? *He hit me.*"

He shrugged. "He had no choice. You were in the line of fire. We both were. But there were no more shots until we were clear of the door. And those were well away from us."

"Sure. We weren't the target. He was trying to kill Coller."

"Precisely. If he wanted to insure Coller was dead, why keep aiming low, toward his legs. Why not go for his chest or head? To me, there is only one explanation, he was trying to keep from hitting us."

I tried to dispel his argument, but couldn't. From what I could recall, it certainly did appear as if the killer had aimed low.

"A cop," I said. "I guess he didn't want to kill a cop."

"A curious standard for a ruthless killer, don't you think?"

It was. But the shooter could have a connection to cops. Maybe he'd even been one.

My ear was pulsing again and I wanted to leave.

"Ah, Martin, there's something we need . . . we *must* discuss."

I frowned at his insistent tone. "Oh? What?"

He sat there, looking up at me. Twice he seemed on the verge of speaking, but never did. With a deep sigh, his eyes dropped to the floor and he shook his head regretfully.

A suspicion began to form. "Is this about Amanda?"

No response. He continued to fixate on the floor. I didn't say anything. I just waited for him to gather up the nerve.

Finally his eyes crawled up to mine. "Please understand, I never believed you would act upon your feelings. That's why when Amanda asked my opinion, I told her she should move on. Frankly, I believed it was in her best interest emotionally. She couldn't spend the rest of her life waiting for you to decide. It wasn't fair to her or you." He paused, looking at me. "Martin, this isn't easy—"

"Tell me."

His mouth opened as if to do so. But he still couldn't bring himself to admit what we both now knew. Again his eyes retreated to the safety of the floor.

I suppose I should have left then. But I wanted him to tell me to my face how he'd screwed me over. I said, "There really isn't a Bob, is there?"

He glanced up with mild surprise. "No, no. He does exist. Amanda is very much in love with him and he with her."

"I see." I swallowed hard. "Go on."

"You should hear the rest from Amanda. She should be the one to tell you."

"I want you to tell me."

Another pause. Longer than the first. I thought he'd chickened out and wasn't going to admit that he was really—

"The truth is," he said, speaking up suddenly, "I've developed a great affection for Amanda. I believed she had a right to happiness. I've asked her to tell you of her engagement for weeks, but she wanted me to do it because it was ultimately my responsibility. Their getting together. If you should be angry with anyone, be angry with me."

He abruptly rose and stood before me.

I don't know what he expected me to do. Maybe take a swing at him or cuss him out. Any other time, I might have reacted that way.

But the man had just saved my life.

"Are you really Bob?" I heard myself ask him.

Another surprised reaction. "You're actually serious?"

"You better believe it."

He began to laugh. "Bob, *me*?"

"Simon this isn't funny—"

"But it is. The irony is exceptionally funny. You of all people should know I'm not Bob."

"What the hell is that supposed to mean?"

"Ask Amanda. You'll have to ask Amanda or perhaps Emily."

"*My daughter?* What does Emily have to do with this?"

He shook his head and continued to laugh.

I walked out.

★ 30 ★

In a guest bathroom on the second floor, I began to clean myself off. I was a mess. In addition to the blood on my clothes, the bottom tip of my ear lobe was missing and more of Coller's blood dotted my face.

I sighed. When it rains, it floods.

In my head, I still heard Simon's laughter. No way he'd faked that reaction to throw me off. Curiously, the fact that he wasn't the mysterious Bob made me feel even worse. If Amanda fell for Simon, I could understand it. The guy was brilliant and a zillionaire.

But Bob also apparently had bucks. And maybe he was brilliant too.

You of all people should know I'm not Bob.

That remark ate at me. Did Simon believe I *knew* Bob? Obviously, he must. And what about his comment concerning Emily? Had Amanda told Emily about Bob? Again the answer seemed obvious.

So I was the only one left out of the loop.

I searched my memory for everyone I knew named Bob. There were six. Two were married and one was an uncle on my mother's side. None were rich.

Fuck.

I'd almost finished washing up, when I heard a knock on the door. "EMT," a male voice said.

I opened the door, still stripped to the waist. A burly medical technician stood there, carrying a doctor's bag. A woman tentatively peered out from behind him.

Amanda.

"Go away," I said.

The man blinked. "Whatever you say, buddy. I was told to treat your ear."

Amanda said, "Marty, I know you're upset, but we need to talk. Please."

I said to the technician, "I was talking to the woman."

His head swiveled between Amanda and me. "Look," he said, reading the situation, "maybe I should come back when you two—"

"No," I said.

"Yes," Amanda said.

More head swiveling. He made his decision and started to leave. I said, "Get back here."

He froze.

I said to Amanda, "I've got nothing to say to you. You've had your fun."

"If you'll let me explain. It's not what you think—"

"Simon says you're in love with Bob."

She hesitated.

I said, "Well?"

"Yes, I am, but I want you to know—"

"You thought it was funny as hell to play me along. Make me think I had a chance when I didn't. Don't deny it. You know damn well that's what you were doing."

"Look, I can explain about that—"

"Not to me. Tell someone who cares." To the med tech, I said, "Get in here."

As he reluctantly stepped inside, I started to close the door. I paused when I saw Amanda's eyes mist. "Marty, you could have been killed. If that had happened, I'd have never forgiven myself. We have to stop these juvenile games and—"

I shut the door on her . . . hard.

"Man," the tech said. "You always this big a jerk or you just having a good day?"

"Just bandage the ear, huh?"

As he attended to me, I didn't expect to feel much pain, but I did.

"Asshole," he said, when he left.

I emerged from the bathroom carrying my white dress shirt. I was looking very *Miami Vice*, wearing my jacket buttoned up over my bare chest. I went down to the first floor, continued past the living room where Coller was lying dead, and entered a tiny kitchen. Simon and Amanda were there, talking with a couple of uniformed officers. Simon was telling them to put out an APB for the black BMW with dealer tags. Noticing me, he pointed to the back door and said my ride was waiting. I nodded to him, but my attention was on Amanda who was looking at me as if I was something stuck to the bottom of her shoe.

Where did she get off being upset with me? I was the wronged party, not her.

Stepping past her, I shot her a withering glare.

Kiss my ass, she mouthed.

I puckered up.

"Stop it," Simon ordered. "Both of you." I glanced back. The two cops had wiseass grins. So much for being subtle.

I continued out the door. The cop was waiting on the dime-sized lawn. He escorted me down a concrete pathway toward the far end of the complex, where his cruiser was parked. Several residents called out to us, asking what was going on. We told them to go back inside, lock their doors, and someone would be around shortly to explain the situation to them. The "shortly" part was, of course, a lie.

As we drove away, I glanced toward the park and saw it fronted by an armada of flashing police vehicles, officers shielded behind them, their weapons pointed. That's how they would remain until SWAT arrived and cleared the park for the killer.

I made two calls, listening with my good ear. The first was to Enrique who informed me he was going through his wardrobe, picking out a shirt for me. And yes, he'd dumped the press who were tailing him.

"I drove straight to my apartment. You should have seen their faces when I told them Simon wasn't in the limo. I even let them take a look inside. Man, were they pissed. Especially Chrissy Sweeney over at Channel Five. Jeez, that lady can swear. So what color shirt you want?"

"What are my choices?"

When he told me, I said, "The blue."

"It's actually more of a purple."

"Fine. The red."

"It's actually more of a pink."

We went through three more colors. Everything was actually something else. I think he was saying this to yank my chain.

"Just bring me a fucking shirt," I said.

I clicked off. The cop was grinning. I pointedly ignored him and called Sam. When he answered instead of the waiter, I knew the dinner party was over. That was a good thing. His response to my request was not.

"Marty, I'm tired," he said. "I'm not answering any more

questions. To you or anybody. I told you I don't know anything."

I anticipated this response and was ready. I hit him with my first kicker, saying, "Someone blew away Major Coller tonight—"

"Aw, Christ—"

Then the second: "And I believe you could be next."

The phone hissed.

I expected some kind of shocked reaction and a demand from Sam why I would conclude he might be in danger, but the silence continued.

Which meant he already knew.

"Sam . . ."

"Don't do this, Marty. Don't fucking come here. Leave me out of it."

"You lied to me from the start. I know you and Talbot had a relationship."

"You're reaching. You can't prove a damned—"

"I've got Major Talbot's phone records. I'll also bet if we show your picture to the maids, they'll remember you. Or maybe I should show a picture of Talbot to the guard in your building. How many times did he come by, Sam?" This wasn't a guess; they had to liaise somewhere.

"Why are you doing this, Marty? So I was friendly with Talbot? So what? I'm telling . . . I'm *asking* you to leave me out of this. Please."

"Say it. You were lovers. Say it."

"We weren't."

"Say it, Sam."

"We weren't. *We weren't.*"

I heard the panic in his voice then. This was unexpected. Sam had spent a lifetime developing a hard-nosed military persona and I didn't think he would began to crack so soon.

But he was.

I didn't want to finish this over the phone. I didn't want to push him completely over the edge when there was no one to catch him. I didn't.

But he'd given me an opening. One I had to take.

What to do about the cop. Since the mention of Talbot's name, he'd been following my conversation with interest. I covered the mouthpiece and growled, "You repeat any of this, I'll deny it."

His face went blank. "Repeat what?" he said coolly.

This guy was going to make chief. Gathering myself with a deep breath, I bluntly asked Sam who killed Major Talbot.

"How the fuck should I know?"

"Because I think he told you . . ." I paused for effect. "And I know you were at his place shortly before the murder."

"You're fucking crazy."

"You were *seen*, Sam. Two witnesses saw you outside his gate."

"They're mistaken. I was nowhere near—"

I went for it then. Played my last kicker. "I'll do it if I have to, Sam."

"Do what?"

"Turn you in."

A long pause. I heard him slowly exhale. "I don't believe you."

"Try me."

"It'll be your word against mine."

"Don't forget Randy's police report, where he swore he saw you in that gay bar. And once we keep digging, I'm sure we'll uncover other instances where you visited—"

"You fucking son of a bitch."

"The truth. All I want is the truth."

"Why?" he exploded. "What the hell would you do with it?"

Bingo.

I said softly, "Son of a bitch. You *do* know who killed Talbot."

Silence.

"Sam," I said, "I'm sorry you're gay. I'm sorry your secret may get out and your career may be over. I'm sorry your family may find out and I'm sorry you're mixed up in a murder. But we've got two dead people and you have information that will help us find the killer."

Still nothing from Sam. I didn't press him any more. I'd played the guilt card and it was up to his conscience to do the rest.

When he finally responded, his voice was resigned, accepting. "You're right about . . . all of it. I know who . . . who must have killed Franklin. But even if I told you, you'd never be able to arrest them. They're too powerful. I tried to tell that to Franklin. I told him what he was doing was dangerous. I said to let it go. Just let it go. But he couldn't. He was like that. Always tried to do what's right. That's what I admired most about him. His integrity. Part of it . . . most of it was his faith. He always had that as a barometer, to judge himself. I'm religious, but nothing like him. If I was, this wouldn't be so damned hard. There's a certain freedom in believing in something bigger than you. But for people like us . . . Franklin and me . . . there was a problem. It was always there, hanging over us . . . reminding us that we were different . . . unworthy. That scared Franklin . . . terrified him. He tried so hard to make himself worthy, deserving. But in the end, he knew . . . he had to know . . ." He trailed off without completing the thought.

I was squirming with anticipation. I said, "You're telling

me Congressman Harris had him killed, right? Shit, of course you are." The cop's head snapped around. I gave him a hard look and he turned away. I said to Sam, "Who else? Who else was involved?"

Sam resumed speaking as if he hadn't heard me. His tone contained an affectionate, reflective quality. "I was the senior officer. I should be the one who guided him, but it was the other way around. He taught me about courage and grace and . . . well, the specifics don't matter. What does matter is that I'm not afraid to come forward. Not any longer. Not when I think about how they killed Franklin. Like some animal. Fuck those assholes. *Fuck them.*"

The phone hissed. I said, "I need the names, Sam."

He sighed. "I'm so damned tired and I need a drink. When you get here, I'll tell you everything. I'll even show you the tape they sent. They counted on it to keep me quiet."

I realized what tape he must be referring to. Now it was clear why his decision to cooperate had been so excruciating. "The names. Just give me the names."

"Marty, please . . ."

He was teetering emotionally. If I pushed him now, I could lose him.

I backed off.

"All right, Sam." I expected him to hang up.

But he still wanted to talk. He asked me if I had known that Franklin was a fellow alum from Virginia Tech. I told him I had.

"I suppose that's the main reason we hit it off. We had so much in common. The corps, the Air Force, the pressure of being different. He was the one person who understood what I went through because he'd experienced the same thing. I never had that before. Someone to confide in. Christ, I'm going to miss him."

His voice trembled with emotion. I didn't say anything. Sam was looking for a response; he just wanted someone to listen.

"You know he also liked to ski. It's true. At school, he used to go to Clayter Lake every chance he had. Camp out just like we did. How's that grab you? Two gay guys from the corps who liked to ski and we end up getting together. What are the odds?"

A direct question. "Pretty small."

"We should do that soon, Marty. You and me. Go there and spend a weekend. Franklin would like it if we did. He and I talked about going all the time."

"That'd be nice, Sam."

"How about when this is over? It'd be like old times. We could forget about all this. Forget about everything."

"Anytime you say."

When Sam quietly clicked off, I could almost see his smile. For the briefest moment, I too felt excitement at the prospect of rekindling our friendship. Then reality set in and I realized we were fooling ourselves. I was about to create a chasm between us that could never be bridged. From now on, whenever he saw me, he would be reminded that I was the person who had destroyed his life and career. Could he ever forgive me? I doubted it.

That's why we'd never go skiing together.

★31★

After we turned into Sam's apartment building, I made the cop cruise the lot to check out the cars. We didn't spot anyone watching nor did we see a black BMW M5. By the time we circled back, Enrique was parking the limo against the concrete island across from the entrance. The cop pulled in beside him and as I got out, I almost choked at the shirt Enrique was holding.

Charitably, the color could be described as green. More accurately, it was luminescent aquamarine.

The cop was laughing as he drove off.

I glared at Enrique as I took the shirt. "You're enjoying this, aren't you?"

"Hey, don't blame me. Right after I talked to you, Amanda called. She suggested the shirt. She also has a message she wanted me to pass on. How's the ear? I meant to ask before. Jesus, that was close, huh?"

"For me. Coller wasn't so lucky."

"I heard. I wish I would have been there. Maybe I could have done something to stop the guy." This wasn't bravado. As a former SEAL, he had a supreme confidence in his abilities.

"You couldn't," I said. "The shooter was too good. He couldn't have had more than a six-inch opening to hit Coller. Yet, he got him on the first shot from at least three hundred yards."

"So we're talking a professional trigger man." He paused thoughtfully. "Or someone like me. With military training."

I nodded. Along with a possible cop connection, the latter was something I'd been tossing around.

Following up on the obvious, Enrique asked if either General Baldwin or Colonel Kelly had sniper or marksmanship training.

"Possibly Kelly. He was Army Ranger. Sam . . . General Baldwin's out. He's an Air Force pilot and never trained as—" A memory floated back, one that had nothing to do with Sam's gun collection. "Correction. Sam does have marksmanship training. All the Baldwin boys were trained to shoot expert, in case they joined the Army."

Interest flashed in Enrique's eyes. He knew Sam had been spotted outside of Major Talbot's home prior to the murder. Now if he could also be placed in the vicinity of Coller's at the time of—

"Forget it," I said. "Sam didn't shoot Coller. Why would he?"

He shrugged. "Just covering all the options. It's what, ten, twelve minutes from here to Coller's. Baldwin could have taken him out and beat us here easy."

I was about to tell him that wasn't possible because of my call to Sam. Then I remembered I'd phoned him a good twenty minutes after the shooting. Mentioning Sam's dinner guests as his alibi was also out; I didn't know what time they left.

I settled on option number three.

"Sam knows who the killer is and has agreed to tell me."

End of discussion. Enrique looked dumbfounded. "No *shit*."

"No shit."

"So we'll soon know—"

"Everything."

I stepped over to the back of the limo to change. As I opened a door, I reminded him of Amanda's message.

"Oh, right." He dug out his notepad and began flipping pages.

"Must be some message," I said dryly.

"She told me to write it down, so there wouldn't be any misunderstanding." Tilting the pad toward the limo's interior light, he read, "Tell Marty he's petty, childish, and vindictive. Tell him my actions were completely justified and that he is wrong about everything."

He glanced up, making no attempt to hide his amusement. "She also mentioned that you should rent the video *Sleepless in Seattle*."

I just looked at him.

He shrugged. "Hey, I'm only the messenger. That's the Tom Hanks movie, right? About a guy who was widowed and ends up falling for Meg Ryan."

I was nodding. I remembered the story because it had come on HBO only last month. Obviously Amanda was making some comparison between me and—

And then I realized what it was. Amanda was telling me to be more like Tom Hanks's character. Accept Nicole's death and move on emotionally.

Cute. Like I said, Amanda always had to get in the last word.

"I understand you and Amanda had a little disagreement about her engagement to Bob," Enrique said.

"She told you that?" This surprised me. I didn't think she knew Enrique that well.

"Simon mentioned it." He said this with an odd smile.

I read it, saying, "I take it you know Bob."

"We've met." Still smiling.

"Cut the shit. Who is he?"

"Simon said not to tell you."

"Oh, for—"

"He met Amanda through Simon. That's all I can say."

"At least tell me if I know the guy."

His only response was that silly smile. I sighed, realizing that was the only answer I was likely to get. But as I stripped off my jacket and laid it on the back seat, his head dipped once.

I knew Bob.

I finished buttoning up the green shirt. I was wearing it untucked not as any kind of fashion statement, but because I wanted to hide the gun holstered to my waist. I'd opted not to don my jacket because it gave me the willies, walking around in clothing stained with a dead man's blood.

I began emptying my jacket pockets. As I removed my credentials and the faxes of Talbot's phone calls, I asked Enrique if he had the folder with the names and addresses of Talbot's acquaintances.

"Simon stuck it in one of the storage compartments." He ducked inside the limo, fumbled around in the area near the swing-out desk, then reappeared with the folder. I handed him the phone list to file inside it.

As he did, he frowned at something in the folder. Glancing down, I glimpsed the picture of General Baldwin.

He shut the folder and handed it to me. "Mind waiting until I talk to Simon?"

230   PATRICK A. DAVIS

"Why?"

"We have a problem. It'll just take a minute."

"What kind of problem?"

He hurried away and took out his cell phone. He kept walking until he was well out of earshot. As if that wasn't enough, he spoke to Simon in low tones. Watching him, I realized there could only be one explanation for his reaction; he'd recognized Sam. But why all the secrecy and what was this comment about a problem?

Enrique's conversation with Simon crept into the third minute. He seemed to be arguing with him. To hell with it. I had to question Sam.

Enrique stood between me and the entrance and as I walked toward it, he shook me off and drifted back. I ignored him and kept going. When he backed into the steps, he angrily cupped the phone and ordered me to stay the fuck back.

So I pulled up, not because of what he said, but the way he said it. Enrique rarely displayed anger. He consider it uncool and unprofessional. Yet just now, he'd almost bit my head off to prevent me from hearing what he said.

Once his conversation ended, I hurried forward to find out why.

"Simon said I should tell you," Enrique said.

He spoke with the enthusiasm of a man with a gun pressed against his head. I said, "And you don't want to because . . ."

"It's nothing personal, Marty. A lot of lives will be ruined if the word gets out."

"What word?"

He hesitated.

"I'll promise not to kiss and tell. Scouts honor."

His eyes dissected me. "I'm fucking serious about this. You can't tell Amanda or anyone in the OSI. *No one*."

"Fine. Anything."

He drew in a breath, let it out. Still undecided.

I prompted, "You recognized Sam, right?"

A slow, painful nod. "It . . . it was almost a year ago, in a gay club."

Big surprise. "And the significance is . . ."

"Remember when I said Major Talbot looked familiar? That I might have seen him . . ."

"Right."

"I've been knocking myself out, trying to remember. When I saw General Baldwin's picture, it hit me. It was in that club. They were both there that night. Talbot and your friend Baldwin. I briefly spoke with Baldwin. I only saw Talbot when he walked up to Baldwin and they went off to dance. You could tell they were a couple."

This revelation didn't come anywhere close to explaining his reluctance to confide in me. I said, "You mentioned lives could be destroyed . . ."

"If the word ever got out about the club. That it even exists."

I still didn't get it. I said, "There are a lot of gay clubs around—"

"Not like this one, Marty. It's exclusive as hell and very private. It's more like a resort. It caters to wealthy and powerful gays and lesbians. Gives them a place where they can go without fear of being outed." He saw my eyebrows creep up. "You're catching on. My guess is the club is where Talbot met Benny Rider and Ross Pelman. A lot of celebrities are members. Politicians too. Occasionally guests like me get invited, but only after we've been vouched for by a member and only after we sign documents promising never to reveal anything about the club. Even then, we're restricted to certain sections."

"Where's this club located?"

"In the country. About thirty miles northwest of Manassas. The place isn't all that large, but it sits on a lot of acreage and is surrounded by trees. You could drive right by it and never know it was there."

"Who owns it?"

"No clue. A guy in a white dinner jacket seemed to be in charge. I think someone mentioned he was the manager."

"The name of the club?"

"Doesn't have one. People refer to it in whatever ways works for them. The club, the farm, the ranch. Not having a name is part of the security angle. It's hard to talk about a place that doesn't have a name. And that's what the members are paying for. Absolute security. Some couples come there and don't want to mingle, so they don't. They're escorted in through a separate entrance and stay in isolated bungalows, guaranteeing their anonymity. Everyone coming in is searched for cameras and recorders. It's also fenced to keep visitors out. So far, all the security has worked like a charm. Place has existed for years and no one in the straight world knows about it. Hell, most gays don't either. But this investigation could change all that. If you and Simon aren't careful, a lot of people could get hurt. It's not right."

He shook his head, staring at the folder in my hand. I'd already figured out the connection he was making and held it up, saying, "The problem you mentioned earlier. If Talbot met two of his lovers at the club, he might have met others whose names are listed in here. One of them might be the killer."

He nodded gloomily.

I smiled. "Relax. I don't think we'll have to investigate the members of the club. Sam as much as told me that Congressman Harris was behind the murders."

Enrique's reaction puzzled me. Instead of relief, his brow furrowed in confusion. "That doesn't jive with what Simon told me."

"Which was . . ."

"He got excited when I described the club. He said it could hold the answer to the killings."

Now it was my turn to be confused. I asked him if Simon explained why he'd concluded this. Of course, he hadn't.

"Wait here," I said. "Sam will tell me if a club member is involved."

The same entry drill into the apartment building as before.

Peering through the glass door, I spoke my name into the intercom. At the buzz, I pushed through into the lobby. Since midnight had come and gone, a shift change had occurred and a different guard sat behind the security desk. He was an elderly gentleman with a pleasant face. At the moment, that face was trained on me as I approached.

"General Baldwin left this for you, Mr. Collins." He held up a white envelope.

I took it from him, sickened.

"Do what you have to do."

And below: "I'm sorry."

Those were the only words scrawled on the page inside. It wasn't even signed.

The guard said that Sam had left not more than ten minutes ago. That told me two things: He'd rushed out the moment he'd hung up and never had any intention of meeting with me.

I'm not afraid any more.

But of course Sam was still afraid. In the end, when he had to decide, his fear won out.

I tried to feel anger for him, but couldn't pull it off. In my heart, I realized Sam wasn't acting to preserve his own self interests. Not entirely. Since birth, he'd been conditioned to protect the piece of plastic he wore on his uniform, the one above his left breast pocket that said Baldwin.

And there was also that videotape.

A charge of homosexuality was one thing. Depending on the proof I could dig up, Sam could still deny it, possibly accuse me of having a vendetta against him. At the least, he could create doubt in people's minds.

But not if the tape became public.

Before I left, I asked the guard if he knew which vehicle Sam had driven off in.

"He has a green Caddy."

There were several in the parking lot. "Did you see him drive off in it?"

"No. But it's the only vehicle he has."

As I walked away, I considered calling Simon to put out an APB, but realized that was a waste of time. Regardless of what I did, Sam wasn't going to cooperate until I gave him a reason.

Like finding that original of the tape he was being blackmailed with.

I shook my head. If the tape was in Congressman Harris's possession, it might as well be on the moon.

Exiting the building, I called Simon to relay the bad

news. When he answered, his voice sounded strained and for a instant I thought I had the wrong number.

"We've entered the rectory, Martin. We've found two, so far."

"Two?"

Then I realized he meant bodies.

★32★

Four. We now had at least four victims.

Enrique drove like a madman, wheeling the limo in and out of traffic and riding the horn. Normally the drive to the Church of the Sacred Heart on the north side of Arlington should have taken close to twenty minutes. We made it in fifteen and change.

Unlike the scene outside Talbot's residence, there was no media circus present. That would change once word of the killings got out. A female cop manned the driveway and as we turned in, she made a circling motion, indicating we should go around back.

We followed the asphalt around the stone church, wound past a gym, and arrived at a rambling two-story Victorian house with a large front yard. Four blue and white cruisers were jammed in the circular driveway, their lights flashing. Several civilian vehicles sat in a small parking area about thirty yards to the right. One was Amanda's Saab. Enrique squealed to a stop behind the cruisers and we hurried up a long brick walkway toward the front door.

Two uniformed officers were stringing yellow crime scene tape around the perimeter of a the yard. Under a light post beside the walkway, a third cop—a sergeant—was interviewing a frightened looking Hispanic man in coveralls. Addressing the sergeant by name, Enrique asked him how many victims were found.

"A woman and couple priests."

We were up to five.

"One of them Father Carlacci, Eddie?"

"Haven't heard." Eddie kept looking my way, as did the Hispanic man. Like the majority of the human race, they'd never seen a glow-in-the-dark shirt before. I felt compelled to explain my presence by informing Eddie that I was an agent with the OSI.

"Uh-huh." Eddie's skeptical gaze shifted to Enrique as he gestured to the Hispanic man. "How about giving me a hand, Enrique? This guy's a church janitor and doesn't speak much English. He's from Colombia."

Enrique rattled Spanish to the janitor. The man's head bobbed and he said *si* a couple times.

"Give me a minute, Eddie," Enrique said.

We reached the front stoop and donned latex gloves. The door was partially opened and we heard faint voices. Enrique went in first and I followed. "Careful," he said.

It was the woman.

Her body lay sprawled in the middle of the alcove, maybe five paces from the door, legs angled toward us. She was a matronly woman in her early sixties, with a pile of brown hair. In her youth, she'd been pretty, but she didn't look pretty now. She'd been shot once in the base of her scalp, the bullet angling up and exiting her forehead. She stared out with sightless eyes, her head resting in a pool of tacky blood. The wire glasses she'd been wearing were lying a couple feet away, the frame bent, the lenses cracked.

Enrique knelt, touching her upper arm with the back of his wrist. "Cool. Blood's dry. Dead for hours."

A shell casing lay against the wall, just inside the door. I bent down to inspect it.

"Looks like a forty-five," Enrique said.

"It is."

The casing told us the weapon was an automatic. The fact that the killer hadn't picked it up indicated he hadn't considered it incriminating, probably because he intended to ditch the gun.

Rising, I verbalized what had transpired. "She answered the door. As the guy followed her inside, he shot her."

"One cold bastard," he grunted.

The operative word was cold. This proved Simon's earlier assessment was wrong. A guy this ruthless wouldn't give a damn about killing a cop.

We carefully stepped around the body. The house was a cavernous, rustic structure that had been built near the turn of the century. The walls were covered with my grandmother's flowery wall paper and there was a slightly musty smell. A worn oak staircase rose before us to a railed landing with a missing spindle. To the our left was a dining room; to the right, a living or family room. The voices were coming from the second floor and we could hear a woman sobbing.

"Hello, Millie," Enrique said. An attractive female cop with curly brown hair had materialized in the entryway of the living room.

Millie managed a wan smile. "Thought that was your voice, Enrique. Second victim's in here. Father Garrigos. Lieutenant Santos figures he heard the shot that killed Mrs. Talley."

As we moved toward her, Enrique asked if Mrs. Talley was the housekeeper.

"A volunteer," Millie said, easing into the room to let us in. "According to the church secretary, Mrs. Blake—that's who's crying—Mrs. Talley came over once a week to look after the priests. Helluva thing, huh?" She gestured with a thumb. "On the rug."

We entered a cozy space dominated by a flared-back couch and two user-friendly recliners, all arrayed around an ornate coffee table. Across from the couch was a cabinet with a television and that's where Enrique and I were looking now.

Specifically at the throw rug in front of it, where the body of a wavy-haired man in his thirties lay sprawled on his back. He was dressed casually in Docker slacks and a pullover shirt, sans a priest's collar. Like Mrs. Talley, he'd been shot in the head. Unlike her, he had also been shot in the chest.

"Chest first," Enrique said. "Then the head to finish him off."

The powder burns on Father Garrigos's forehead verified the sequence. Recalling the silenced rifle used in Coller's murder, I asked Millie why Simon was so certain Father Garrigos had heard the shot that killed Mrs. Talley.

"His drink." She indicated a glass lying on the floor beside the farthermost recliner. "It's like he got out of his chair in a rush and dropped it."

I nodded, noting an open Bible on an end table beside the recliner. Enrique's head began shifting between Garrigos's body and the recliner. He was thinking that the priest had only managed to make it a few feet before being shot. I glanced around for shell casings and spotted one back by the entryway. A second winked up from beneath the lip of the television cabinet.

The killer had moved fast.

Too fast?

He wouldn't have had time to plan this killing. Once he'd obtained Carlacci's name from Talbot, he'd have been desperate to silence the priest before Talbot's murder became public. Since two other priests resided here and there was only one more victim, it came down to whether our boy had called first to ensure Carlacci would be present. If not and we got lucky—

I shook my head at Millie's response. So much for luck.

We left to view Father Carlacci's body.

Mrs. Blake was crying softly as we made our way up the stairs. We crossed the landing into a darkened hallway, rooms running down either side. A cop stood at the far end, watching us with more than passing interest. By now I'd had my flip top OSI credentials hanging from my shirt pocket, to prove I was a military investigator not a *Miami Vice* throwback. As we continued toward the cop, we peeked into a room where the crying was coming from.

A petite woman with black hair sat on a brass bed, hands over her face. Amanda hovered over her, speaking in comforting tones. Noticing us, Amanda shook her head and kept on talking.

Enrique and I went down the hall.

As we walked up to the cop, he nodded to a doorway. From within we heard Simon's voice.

We entered a bedroom that was much larger than the first. It was austerely furnished; a bed, a night stand, two dressers, and little else. Father Carlacci apparently took his vow of poverty seriously. Faded flannel pajamas and a threadbare robe were laid out at the foot of the bed. As he conversed on the phone, Simon sadly contemplated the clothing, his free hand working his rosary.

". . . if Father Carlacci mentioned something to you?" Simon was saying. "Some reason for the murders? We know Major Talbot confided in him regularly and we're convinced—" He noticed us. "Excuse me, Father."

Covering the phone, his face smoothed into a mask. He announced, "They killed priests."

As if that was the ultimate sin. To Simon, it probably was.

His eyes seemed to look right through me. "You understand this alters everything now."

I frowned. "Alters it how? What are you going to do?"

His gaze chilled, matching the temperature in his voice. "Whatever is necessary, Martin."

Ominous words. I glanced at Enrique. Unlike me, he didn't seem the least bit troubled by them.

Simon viewed the world through his own ethical prism. If he considered a goal just, then any method he employed to achieve that goal was equally just. On occasion, he'd been known to play fast and loose with the Fourth Amendment. While I've never seen him do anything blatantly illegal—he might bully an uncooperative suspect or bribe a parking attendant to search a suspect's car—I've heard the rumors. The most notable instance occurred during the arrest of the child killer whom Enrique had almost beaten to death. The case against the killer had been questionable until Simon miraculously discovered key evidence in the suspect's previously searched apartment. Immediately the rumors started flying that Simon had planted the evidence. While nothing was ever proved, the rumors persisted to the point where I asked Simon if it was true. Had he planted evidence?

I didn't really expect him to tell me. Despite our friendship, he'd be crazy to admit to anything.

But he did . . . sort of.

"I did what was necessary," he said.

Almost identical to the words he'd used just now.

"Simon," I said. "I wouldn't do anything rash. We have to play this one by the book. We'll never make a case stick if we—something funny?"

He was watching me with tolerant smile.

"You misunderstood, Martin. By "necessary," I was referring to my determination to leave no stone unturned in resolving this case." He actually said it with a straight face.

"You're telling me you weren't determined before?" I mirrored his straight face, but tossed in a cynical tone.

"Not to this extent. Now it's personal."

An oblique reference to the connection he felt for the dead priests, a fraternity he'd almost joined.

We could have danced around this subject for another round, but nothing I could say was going to change Simon's mind. He was a man on a mission and would pursue the killer with the passion of a zealot, legal niceties and police protocol be damned.

I shook my head at him. "Do me a favor and keep me out of it."

He looked hurt. "Martin, you of all people should know my standards of conduct."

Precisely.

"Father Carlacci in there?" Enrique asked.

He was focused on a doorway in the opposite corner. Through it, we glimpsed white tile and the edge of a sink. On the floor, we could also make out the glint of shell casings.

Simon nodded. "He was shot three times.

As Enrique and I walked over to the bathroom, he resumed his conversation on the phone.

★ 33 ★

The nude body of Farther Carlacci lay slumped in the bottom of a tub, knees bent, his torso tilted in our direction, his head hanging limply off to the side. He was a small, wiry man who looked about seventy. Midway up the tile backsplash, we noticed two starred bullet holes, confirming he'd been standing when he'd been shot. Edging closer, Enrique and I saw that both rounds had struck Carlacci in the side of his chest. As with the other priest, a final shot had been fired from close range into his head.

"Still a few water droplets," Enrique said. "The killer must have left the shower on."

This explained the lack of blood in the tub. Refocusing on Carlacci's chest wounds, I noted they were within an inch of each other. "Our boy is good with handguns too."

"Three," Enrique murmured.

He was standing beside me and reacted to my frown.

He shrugged. "When I called Simon from General Baldwin's apartment, I mentioned that Colonel Kelly and General Baldwin might have had marksmanship training. He said that made three."

"He tell you who the third person was?"

"Uh-uh. He did say they weren't a suspect." He contemplated Carlacci. "Kinda risky, don't you think? The way the killings were carried out."

This was something I'd noticed also. "Yeah. The killer was lucky Carlacci was in the shower. If not, he'd have heard the shots. Maybe gotten to a phone."

"A pro wouldn't take that chance. He'd have rounded everyone up first before killing them."

"The killer could be an amateur. One who can shoot."

"That's what I don't get," Enrique said. "If Harris is behind the murders, you'd think he'd hire a pro. Someone who knew what he was doing and could be trusted to keep his mouth shut."

"Harris is a politician, not a mob boss. It's not like you look up hit a man in the Yellow Pages."

"I guess . . ."

He still appeared unconvinced.

I'd seen enough and was about to go when I noticed Enrique toss me a couple of quick looks. After the third one, I asked him what was on his mind.

"No offense Marty, but Simon's right. Your way won't work. You'll never get a guy like Harris, playing by the rules."

In the past, I'd had similar conversations with Simon and Amanda. Was I the only one who believed the oath we took as cops actually meant something? "So you believe the ends justify the means?"

"Sure. Sometimes."

"Enrique," I said patiently, "we're cops. We're supposed to follow the law. We represent the law."

"Even if it means a killer walks."

I met his measured gaze with one of my own. "Even then."

"The bastard killed five people, Marty. *Five.*" For emphasis, he looked at Carlacci's body, then refocused on me.

"Doesn't matter."

I waited for the inevitable look of disgust. When it came, it was accompanied by a slow head shake. Watching him, I began to wonder if maybe it hadn't been an accident when he almost killed that child murderer.

He said, "So the way you see it, the law should always be followed, even if the guilty go free. There are no exceptions."

Trying to get me to back down from an absolute. "None."

"I see." He studied me. "You wouldn't bend the rules to prevent a multiple murderer from becoming president?"

I hesitated.

"Yeah. Thought that might make you reconsider." He winked. "Welcome to the club."

I wouldn't go that far.

Simon was still on the phone as we left the bathroom. While Enrique left to play the Spanish version of twenty questions with the janitor, I eavesdropped on Simon's conversation, then verified my suspicions by asking the cop in the hallway if Simon was talking to the third priest who resided here.

"Yeah. Father Coughlin. He's on a Catholic retreat near Richmond. He's damned lucky to be alive. He left right after dinner. If he'd hung around for another thirty minutes—"

"Hold on. You *know* the time of death?"

"The lieutenant figures it's around eight P.M., give or take. He talked to that lady down the hall . . ."

"Mrs. Blake."

"She said that the priests ate at seven. And the dead woman . . ."

"Mrs. Talley."

"Always went home after she finished washing the dishes. Usually that was around eight-thirty or so. Since there are still dirty dishes in the kitchen, the lieutenant figured the killings had to occur before . . ."

He kept on talking, but I was no longer listening to him. Not since Simon had said a word that caught my interest.

Blackmail.

I reentered the bedroom to find Simon pacing, his expression grim. "That's *all* Father Carlacci shared with you, Father? He only said that Major Talbot was being blackmailed? He never explained why— *Think*, Father. Did he ever mention a videotape or Major Talbot's homosexuality? I see. So much of what Carlacci learned *was* in the confessional. Yes, yes, I understand the information is sacrosanct. Again, I'm sorry for your loss. I should be here when you arrive. If you can think of anything else . . . thank you, Father. Drive safely."

Simon's pacing ended when he punched off the call. His eyes dropped to his rosary beads and he deflated a little.

Disappointed.

I said, "The missing tape. That has to be it. That's what Major Talbot was being blackmailed with. And Sam must be his lover on it, which is why they're targeting him. Hell, it all fits."

Simon nodded absently. Pocketing his phone and rosary, he closed his eyes and mouthed a silent prayer. Further evidence of the turmoil he felt over the death of priests.

At the sudden squelch from a radio, his eyes snapped open. We heard Enrique's tinny voice asking Simon to come downstairs. The cop in the hall reached for his lapel mike, watching Simon expectantly.

I said, "Enrique's questioning a church janitor. The guy might have seen something."

Simon immediately turned for the door. To the cop, he said, "Tell him I'm on my way. And remember, no additional radio calls until I tell you."

The cop nodded and made the call.

As Simon swung out into the hall, I tucked in beside him. I said, "Assuming Talbot was being blackmailed to keep quiet about something he knew—"

"He was."

"And Congressman Harris is behind the killings—"

"We have no proof of that."

"Give it a rest, Simon. Sam told me—"

"That," he said, "is precisely what bothers me. *Your* conversation with General Baldwin."

I waited for him to elaborate. He didn't. We strode past the bedroom with Amanda and Mrs. Blake. Except they weren't there. As we started down the stairs, I asked him to explain what disturbed him about my conversation with Sam.

He hesitated. "You might not like it."

"Try me."

"I don't think we can trust General Baldwin."

"Oh, for—"

"Why the delay, Martin? Why didn't he simply tell you Harris was responsible for Talbot's murder?"

"I told you. He was scared because of the videotape. He couldn't bring himself to—"

"According to you, he'd already *implied* it was Harris. If that was Baldwin's purpose, to identify Harris as the person behind the killings, why not remove any doubt and accuse him by name? What did he have to gain by waiting?"

My mouth opened, then fell shut. I had to admit he was on to something, since Sam had no intention of meeting with me.

"No, no," Simon said. "General Baldwin knew exactly what he was doing. He was being intentionally vague so he could later deny that he'd ever accused Congressman Harris."

It took me a second. "To keep Harris from finding out he was the one who talked?"

We reached the ground floor and continued toward the front door, which stood open. "Actually," Simon said, "I was considering a more worrisome possibility." And the look he gave me told me this was the part I wasn't going to like.

"Let's hear it."

Approaching Mrs. Talley's body, Simon came to a stop, his eyes locked on mine. "Ask yourself how the killer learned that Talbot was going public with information he knew. Would Talbot have told him? Highly unlikely. That leaves two remaining possibilities. One, someone close to Talbot betrayed him. Two, there never was any betrayal because it was the person close to Talbot who killed him." He gave me that look again, indicating this was the option he favored.

"Simon, how many times are we going to go through this? Sam didn't murder—"

"*Enough*. For your sake, I've tried to be patient, give him the benefit of the doubt. But the evidence indicates—"

"I don't care. I'm telling you that Sam would never—"

We stood there bickering, neither one willing to listen to the other. Simon emphatically jabbed a finger into his palm, ticking off the facts against Sam. "He was *seen* at Talbot's. He *is* a trained marksman. He *attempted* to shed suspicion on Congressman Harris. He had *motive* and *opportunity*—"

"Just a damn minute," I fired back. "Sam might have an alibi for Coller's killing."

"*Might?*"

I told him I couldn't check because the guard on duty had gone home. "I'll find out first thing in the morning. The guard can tell us whether Sam left his apartment tonight."

"And if he did leave . . ."

He left the statement hanging. Trying to nudge me into a conditional admission of Sam's guilt. It wasn't going to work because, for once, I actually knew something he didn't.

I let him in on the secret now.

Simon slow-blinked me. This was a curve he hadn't seen coming. "You're sure?" he demanded. "You are absolutely certain?"

I went back to my conversation with Sam, recalling his words and affectionate tone. I analyzed my impressions and tried to be objective in my conclusion.

"I'm sure," I said. "Sam loved Major Talbot."

I could see Simon struggling with himself, undecided as whether to—

"Trust me," I said quietly. "I'm right about this."

Simon measured my sincerity, a flicker of acceptance crossing his face. He realized I wouldn't lie to him. Not about this. He sighed, "Martin, how do you explain the fact that in all likelihood, Major Talbot only told two people of Colonel Kelly's threatening message?"

He was referring to the phone calls Talbot had made after receiving the threat. I said, "You traced the numbers—"

"Yes. He made three calls today; one to a dry cleaner, one to his office, and one to General Baldwin's cell phone." His eyes narrowed. "Last night, he also phoned General Baldwin at his home, then immediately afterward called Major Coller. Rather suggestive, don't you think?"

It was more than suggestive. The back-to-back calls all

but confirmed that Talbot had phoned to relay something important.

Like Colonel Kelly's threat on his life.

"Since Coller's dead," I said slowly, "you think Sam had to be the one who contacted Congressman Harris and told him about Kelly's threat."

"It's more than that, Martin. It's *why* he would have done so."

I read the inference. He was saying that the reason Sam had passed on the threat was so that Harris would have a convenient patsy to hang Talbot's murder on. If true, this was damning. It indicated that not only had Sam betrayed Talbot, but he also knew the consequences of his betrayal.

Talbot's murder.

Simon continued to stare at me, waiting for my response. I thought hard, trying to come up with another scenario. Something that was even remotely plausible.

There was one. It wasn't a complete stretch because of what Major Tenpas had told me.

"Coller," I said. "Major Coller must be the one who contacted Congressman—hear me out." He was about to interject and I spoke rapidly to prevent him from doing so. "It's not as crazy as it sounds. Coller was supposed to be very ambitious. He was quitting the Air Force to work for the Harris campaign. Maybe that's how he got the job. Because he was willing to sell out Talbot."

Another time-delayed blink. A second curve I'd thrown by him. I was on a roll.

"And Harris," he said, "had Coller killed because he could implicate him."

A statement more than a question. "Sure. Coller knew too much."

Just then, we heard a shout and looked out the front door.

We spotted Enrique standing between the janitor and the sergeant named Eddie, who was taking out a cell phone.

"Simon," Enrique called out. "Eddie says you think the killings happened around eight?"

"Yes."

"You're sure?"

"Yes."

Enrique grinned. "Then we got a break. Hector saw them. He saw the killers."

Plural.

As Simon and I headed toward the door, he said stiffly to me. "Perhaps, Martin."

Not exactly an endorsement of my suspicions about Major Coller, but I'll take it.

★34★

Simon and I made our way down the walkway toward the lamp post, where Enrique and the janitor waited. Eddie had drifted away from them, talking loudly on his cellular. He said, "That's right, Jeff. We're staying off the radio until the scene gets processed. After the Talbot killing, the last thing the lieutenant wants is more goddamn press—"

Looking past Eddie, I saw Amanda assist Mrs. Blake into the front seat of a police car. After closing the door, she leaned through the window and gave Mrs. Blake a hug. As she did, two cops contemplated her backside with leering smiles. Amanda suddenly turned and caught them looking. The old Amanda would have chewed them out, or at least emasculated them with a blistering comment. This Amanda just coolly walked away, looking beautiful and remote. The cops grinned, elbowing each other.

At that moment, I realized her transformation was complete; Amanda had really changed.

"Does Amanda really love this guy Bob?" I asked.

"Yes," Simon said.

"So it's too late for me?"

"Does it matter?"

"Very much."

"I see." He paused. "Do you love her?"

I watched Amanda join Enrique. Up to now, I hadn't been willing to admit even to myself that I —

"Yes," I said softly, "I love her."

His pace slowed. "You're certain of your feelings?"

I nodded.

He was quiet for a moment. With feeling, he said, "I care for you both, Martin. But you hurt her before and I won't allow you do so again."

"I won't," I said. "But I have to know if it's too late."

"That's up to Amanda."

"At least tell me if I have a chance."

Simon's expression softened. "You always have a chance."

So it wasn't over. While I realized the odds could be a hundred to one against me, I didn't care.

I had a chance.

Enrique watched our approach, engaged in an anxious two-step. The instant we reached him, he practically leapt at us to describe what the janitor saw.

Enrique spoke in his newscaster precise style, consulting his notepad.

The janitor's name was Hector Cruz. He'd been hauling trash to the Dumpster, when he spotted the car driving up to the rectory. It was between seven forty-five and seven-fifty P.M. Hector knew this because he'd been listening to a radio station over his Walkman and the quarter-hour commercial break had just ended.

Hector saw two men get out of the car. He couldn't see them well because it was dark and they were too far away. Both seemed average in build, one taller than the other. He recalled they were dressed similarly in lightweight jackets and baseball caps. The jackets and caps looked black. He believed they wore jeans.

No, he never saw them enter the rectory. By then, he'd gone back inside the church.

"That's all?" Simon said, when Enrique finished. "Two nondescript males in black jackets and baseball caps."

Enrique pointed to the Dumpster, which was situated between the gym and the church. "What do you expect, Simon? We're talking a distance of what, eighty, maybe a hundred yards. And the Dumpster can't be twenty feet from the side door of the church. Mr. Cruz only saw the killers for a few seconds, when he walked back to the church."

"A Walkman, huh?" Amanda said.

Enrique nodded. "That's why he never heard the shots."

"Been tough to hear them anyway," I said, "once he was in the church."

"What about the car?" Amanda asked.

"A silver sedan. Four door."

Not the black BMW we expected. She said, "No make or model?"

"No." He added, "He did say it looked expensive."

"He must remember *something* about the killers' appearance," Simon said. "Gained at least an impression of their ethnicity or age or hair—"

"They had on jackets and caps, Simon."

"Even so—"

"The height difference," Enrique said. "He did say it was significant. It would have to be for him to notice."

Simon squinted, suggesting this meant something. He became still, his brow deeply knitted. I hoped this wasn't going to take long.

It didn't.

"How different?" Simon asked Enrique. "Six inches. A foot?"

Enrique shrugged. "He said quite a bit."

"Was the smaller man unusually short or—"

"His impression was the other person was tall. But he made a point of saying he couldn't be certain because—"

Simon impatiently stepped around him to talk to Hector. Enrique glanced quizzically at me. I shook my head; I couldn't venture a guess at Simon's sudden interest. Amanda gave it a shot, pointing out that an unusually tall killer would be easier to identify.

A given if you had a suspect pool. But none of the players whom we'd come across could be described as unusually tall except for—

"General Baldwin?" Amanda said, as if reading my mind. "He's tall, right?"

"Six-five." I added, "I saw him at his dinner party at nine."

"That gives him an hour. He could have left the party and returned." This was Enrique.

"With the secretary of the Air Force and a congressman as dinner guests?"

That quieted them. Neither could fathom Sam slipping out on high-powered guests to slaughter three people, then return for dessert.

Hector looked understandably nervous as Simon addressed him. Simon tried to disarm his concerns with a beaming smile. He reinforced it with soothing Spanish and Hector visibly relaxed.

In response to a question, Hector pointed to the driveway, where one of the cop cars was parked.

"The killers parked there," Enrique said.

More conversation in Spanish. Simon gestured to a section of the walkway close to the house. Hector seemed puzzled. He shook his head.

Enrique said, "He's asking him who walked up to the house first. The passenger or the driver? Hector thinks it was the passenger, but can't be sure."

"Do we care?" Amanda asked.

"Simon," Enrique explained, "thinks the one in charge would go first."

"Do we care?" Amanda repeated.

Simon held his hand adjacent to his head, palm parallel to the ground. His question about the height.

Hector thought for a moment, then moved next to Simon. He was at least five inches shorter than Simon's six-two. He squinted at Simon's head, then placed his hand several inches above it.

"More than a head taller," I said.

Simon asked another question and Hector responded.

"He thinks the driver was the tall one," Enrique said. "Again he isn't sure."

Simon began walking toward the driveway, motioning Hector to follow. After several paces, he lowered his voice and asked another question.

"What's *this*?" Amanda said. "Is he—hell, he is. He's trying to keep us from hearing him."

The cops were standing around with blank expressions. None appeared to follow the conversation.

"Not us," I said to Amanda. "We don't speak Spanish." I looked at Enrique.

Instead of appearing irritated, he had a stunned expression.

"You heard what Simon asked?" I said, jumping on the obvious.

A hesitant nod. "A couple words. Simon wants to know if—"

Simon spun toward him. "No," he ordered harshly. "Not a word."

Enrique flinched, shocked at his tone. His mouth obediently closed.

Amanda glared at Simon. "What the hell is this? We're on the same team, remember?"

The cops watched this confrontation with spreading smiles. It wasn't often they saw someone get into Simon's face.

"It's nothing," Simon said to Amanda. "It's an impossibility. It can't be done."

"What can't be done?"

His attention was back on Hector. The two men ducked under the yellow tape and drifted toward the driveway, speaking in hushed tones.

"It *is* impossible," Enrique murmured. "But why would Simon ask? Why in the world would he even consider the possibility that . . ."

Amanda and I watched him. He was slowly shaking his head, looking completely confused. Brushing past us, he headed down the walkway, still talking to himself. Amanda and I frowned, staring after him.

"You catch what he just said, Marty?"

"Something about a person being in two places at once."

★35★

Enrique went over to the limo and climbed in the back. He left the door open and we could see him sitting there, staring into space. While Amanda and I had no idea what question Simon had posed, Enrique's reaction did confirm one thing.

Simon was thinking out of the box again.

"He's finished," Amanda said.

A reference to Simon who'd removed his wallet and was handing Hector several bills. From Hector's response, we knew they were big. He smiled broadly and thanked Simon profusely. As Hector walked toward the church, Simon negotiated the crime scene tape and made his way over to Amanda and me.

His determined expression made it clear it was no use pressing him for answers, so when Amanda gave me a questioning look, I shook her off.

So much for accepting my input.

Once Simon got within earshot, she demanded, "When will you tell us?"

He shrugged. "There's nothing to tell. It can't happen."

"Then why are you worried?"

"I'm not." His denial contained a weary quality; he didn't expect us to believe him.

"*It?*" Amanda pressed, fulfilling his expectation. "What's it? What can't happen?"

Ignoring her, Simon addressed Eddie, who'd worked the phone earlier. "What's the estimate for the ME and forensics?"

"Thirty minutes for forensics, Lieutenant. At least an hour for an ME, Doc Page."

Simon nodded and started back down the walkway, away from the house.

"Where are you going now?" I asked.

"Church," he said, without looking back. "I need to think."

"I'll go with you."

"No. I need to be alone. I need to understand."

"How two people can be in the same place at once?"

I had to hand it to Simon. He never reacted in any way. He just calmly scooted under the tape and kept walking as if he hadn't heard me.

But the farther he moved away from us, we saw his head bend and his shoulders droop. No doubt about it; Simon was deeply troubled.

Amanda said, "You realize what this means, what it has to mean."

"He believes it's Congressman Harris."

"How? It has to be more than Hector's description of the killers. There wasn't much there."

"Obviously there was enough."

For the next several minutes, we tried to come up with likely candidates who might fit Hector's vague description of the killers. The problem was that we had to rule out everyone in Harris's entourage. During the killings of Talbot and

the priests, they were either in Pennsylvania or on an air-
plane. With regard to Coller's murder, they wouldn't have
had time to drive to Arlington from the congressman's
Maryland home, after being dropped off by the helicopter.

"The Harris estate is near Fort Washington, right?"
Amanda said.

"Yeah. Take at least forty-five minutes to drive to Coller's."

She watched Simon disappear into the church. "It's impossible. You can't be two places at once. Too bad. I was
hoping to nail that dirtbag campaign manager Slater. He's
what? Five-eight or-nine? He could have been the shorter
perp."

"Guys like him don't soil their hands on something as
dirty as murder."

"A girl can always hope." She said it without a smile.

I said, "Colonel Kelly and General Baldwin are also
out. Kelly's too stocky to be either killer and we know
Simon wouldn't have any qualms about arresting either of
them."

She faced me. "So we're back to square one. It's people
we haven't met. Either pros or some other staff members."

I told her I was leaning toward the latter because of the
risky manner with which the priests' murders had been carried out. I added, "Assuming they were staff members or acquaintances of Harris, I'm wondering how Simon recognized them. Chances are he wouldn't have met them
either."

"Simon's connected politically, right? Goes to fund-
raising dinners and cocktail parties. He might have run
across them somewhere."

"What about Enrique? He seemed to know them too."

"He's Simon's shadow. He could have been present
when Simon met them."

Perhaps but—

I shook my head. "Simon still must have a *reason* for suspecting them. Something beyond their appearance. Something that told him these people might be capable of murdering—"

And then it came to me. I felt a step slow. I should have made this connection sooner. "Shit, *shit.*"

"What?"

I relayed what Enrique told me. That Simon mentioned a third person in addition to Colonel Kelly and Sam who possessed marksmanship skills. "Simon didn't consider them a suspect, probably because he believed the person had an alibi."

She digested this with a slow intake of breath. "So that's why Simon thinks it's Harris, because this person is connected to him. Someone who could shoot . . ."

"Yes."

"But Simon can't get around the alibi. Until he does, he won't tell us anything. He's afraid of being wrong."

"You know Simon."

"Yeah." She scowled. "Mr. Insecurity. He say anything else I should know?"

I gave her a rundown of my conversation with Simon, including his suspicions of Sam, my conclusion that Sam loved Talbot, and Simon's grudging acknowledgment that Major Coller might be the person who betrayed Talbot. Because of my promise to Enrique, I withheld Simon's comment that the gay club might hold the answer to the killings.

"Coller sold out Talbot, huh?" Amanda said. "*That's* a twist." Her tone suggested she was having trouble with this.

"It was either him or Sam, and I know it wasn't Sam."

"Any chance that General Baldwin only *pretended* to

be affectionate toward Talbot, in order to throw off your suspicions?"

I hesitated. "Of course there's a chance—"

"But you don't believe it."

I didn't reply. She knew damn well I didn't. She still appeared skeptical, but before she could pursue the topic, I asked her if Simon had mentioned anything I should know.

"A couple items. Doc Cantrell called him with the time of death. Since we don't know when Talbot had lunch, all she could tell us was that it was five hours after he ate, give or take thirty minutes."

Assuming Talbot ate around noon, that still put his murder around five in the afternoon. "And the second item?"

She gave me a knowing look. "The black BMW. We think it belonged to Major Talbot. Teriko found the purchase agreement in Talbot's files. He bought a black M5 last week."

I stared at her.

"Go figure. The killers must have taken it, but why? Did they get some kind of perverse jollies using Talbot's own car when they took out Coller? If so, why didn't they use that car when they came after the priests?"

"They probably realized the car was spotted by Officer Hannity."

"Maybe." Her brow crinkled. "Another thing I don't get is why there was only one person in the car when Hannity spotted it? It wouldn't make sense for the second guy to be hiding in the park. How would he know he'd need to take out Coller with a sniper shot?"

This break in the killers' MO did seem odd. We now realized they must have teamed up to kill Talbot—one of them must have driven off in his BMW—and they also both attacked the priests. Yet, when going after Coller, they didn't pair up. Was this a matter worth concerning ourselves over? It might be.

If the second killer had targeted another victim whose body we still had to discover.

I rubbed my face hard at the possibility.

"You think Simon will talk to us when he comes out?" Amanda was again looking at the church.

"Not unless he can get around the alibis."

She gave me a sideways glance. "So you could be wrong about Slater dirtying his hands? Or maybe Harris was the third marksman? If we want to get really crazy, we could even throw Coller's name into the ring—"

She stopped when something occurred to her. "Jesus," she said.

"What?"

She focused on me, her voice excited. "That's the answer. That's why there was only one killer in the car. You don't see it, Marty? What if Coller *was* the smaller killer? He fits the description. Slender, average height. He also must have been in on the Talbot killing. We knew Talbot wouldn't let strangers into his house. Once Coller did his part, he became a loose end to be disposed of. Hell, it makes sense. You know it does."

I had to nod my agreement. She stood there, grinning as if this was a breakthrough in the case. It wasn't. Even if her theory proved true, it still shed no light on the second killer's identity or who was behind the murders.

When I mentioned this, her grin faded and she turned to gaze toward the church.

"Screw it," she said wearily.

★36★

There was no reason for us to remain. The Arlington PD had responsibility for processing the crime scenes and we'd only be in the way. In the morning, Amanda and I would attempt to crack the case by interviewing Sam. This time I was confident he'd cooperate.

In hindsight, my threat to formally charge him with homosexuality had been a mistake. It came down to credibility . . . mine. Sam hadn't believed I'd go through with it. His attitude would change once I informed him that I still intended to expose his homosexuality, only not to the Air Force.

I was going to tell his father.

Would he fear being shamed in the eyes of his family as much as public humiliation? My hunch is that he'd fear it even more.

Still, I clung to the hope that I wouldn't have to follow through on this threat. It depended on Sam. Twenty-five years ago, he'd been a good man and I hoped he still was.

As we walked toward the spillover parking area where Amanda had parked, I thumbed Sam's number into my cellular. When his answering machine came on, I said, "They killed three more people, Sam. Two priests and a woman. How many more have to die?"

Short and sweet and laden with guilt.

As I clicked off, Amanda said, "I almost feel sorry for him."

I tried to hide my surprise and failed.

She sighed. "Guess I'm mellowing with age, but I've been wondering what I'd do if I were him. Talk about getting caught between a rock and a hard place. You think about that? What you'd do if you were in his shoes?"

"All the time."

"And?"

"I'd like to believe I'd come forward . . ."

"But you don't know."

"I don't think anyone can know. You can't, unless you're a Baldwin."

She nodded; she understood what I was trying to say.

"That's why I feel sorry for him," she said.

We strolled past the limo. Enrique was slumped against the rear seat, eyes closed. I called out we were leaving. He cracked open his eyes, nodded, closed them again. Amanda asked me where General Baldwin might have gone tonight, after he ditched me.

I shrugged. "He might have driven around for a while, then returned to his apartment. Or maybe he got a hotel room or is staying with family."

"Parents?"

"Unlikely. That's a four-hour drive. They live in Blacksburg."

"Virginia Tech again. Curious how everything seems to connect to there. You, Talbot, General Baldwin, his folks, the Harrises speaking there tomorrow."

I passed on a response. We realized it was only coincidence.

We arrived at her car. As I swung around to the passenger side, I saw her smile at me over the roof. "It is hideous. I almost feel guilty."

A reference to my shirt. "Almost?"

Her smile faded. "You don't want to get into this, Marty. Believe me."

She didn't have to tell me twice.

Climbing into the Saab, I glanced at the clock on the dash. It was after two and I felt physically and emotionally exhausted, with an emphasis on the latter. And I still had one last ride to take on my emotional roller coaster.

Settling into my seat, I looked at Amanda and wondered when to buy the ticket.

She started the car. "You get my message?" Her tone was curiously up-beat and I wasn't sure why.

"Yes," I said cautiously.

"Well?"

"I don't recall the specifics, but essentially I'm an asshole."

"Not *that*. What about *Sleepless in Seattle?*" She was staring at me now.

"I understand the anology."

"Really?" She seemed surprised.

She backed up the car and turned onto the asphalt road. "Good," she said. "That makes everything easier. If you know how all this came about, you also understand our intentions. Why Emily did what she did and why Simon and I agreed to—"

I was tired; that one almost got by me. "Hold it. What does Emily have to do with— "

My cell phone rang. I'd been spring-loaded for a call and snared it free from my belt, focusing on the caller ID.

Only it wasn't Sam; it was General Hinkle, calling from home.

In a disappointed voice, Amanda said, "If you have to ask about Emily, you don't understand. You can't. I was hoping I wouldn't have to—"

She broke off, so I could speak into the phone.

I said into it, "It's your dime, Charlie—"

General Charlie Hinkle exploded in a verbal barrage, loud enough to hurt my ears. His words spilled out so fast, I barely understood him. Something about a conference call he'd completed with Chief Novak of the Arlington PD and the secretary of defense—

I swore and ordered Amanda to stop the car.

"Huh?"

"*Stop the car.* We have to arrest Colonel Kelly."

After Amanda drove back to the parking area, she killed the engine, watching me. In my ear, Charlie was still talking, his voice having receded below the pain threshold. My mind raced as I tried to take everything in. From his conversation with Chief Novak, Charlie knew about the murders at the rectory, but they had little bearing on the decision to arrest Colonel Kelly. He said, "Call me ASAP the moment Kelly's in custody. The SECDEF has a press release waiting. The military wants to appear as if we're cooperating completely."

Amanda edged closer to me, trying to listen. As I held out the phone between us, I said, "He didn't do it, Charlie. Colonel Kelly didn't kill anyone."

"Prove it later. After he's in custody."

"We have descriptions of the men who killed the priests. It couldn't have been Kelly."

"So he had help. Or maybe those killings aren't related to Talbot's."

I made a derisive, sucking sound.

"Look," he said irritably, "this isn't a fucking debate, Marty. Congressman Harris has us by the gonads and is squeezing hard. He called the SECDEF and as much as promised he'd publicly accuse the military of a coverup if he didn't get results and fast. By results, he made it clear he wanted Kelly arrested. When I spoke with Santos after the Coller killing, he told me he didn't think Kelly was involved, so that's what I passed on to the SECDEF. Now I look like a fucking jackass—"

"Kelly is being framed. Only the killer could have provided the—"

"God dammit, you listening? We're talking five murders and everyone in the world knows who the prime suspect is now. We don't make the arrest and every talking head in the country will be screaming coverup. Hell, *I'd* be screaming coverup. Maybe you're right. Maybe Kelly's not guilty. Right now no one gives a damn. No one can *afford* to give a damn. They're looking for political cover and Colonel Kelly is it."

He was breathing hard.

I said, "I'm not sure I can do this. Arrest an innocent man."

"You're *assisting* in the arrest. The Arlington PD has the lead."

"I can't do it, Charlie."

Amanda nodded approvingly.

"I see." Charlie's voice was like ice. "You don't want to participate, that's your call. But you'll be disobeying a direct order, which means you'll be through with the OSI. You understand what I'm telling you, Marty? Finished. I mean it."

I was silent.

"Marty?"

"I understand."

"What's it going to be?"

The phone hissed. Amanda gave a resigned sigh and whispered, "Better say yes."

I said nothing.

She watched me in growing alarm. Her hand snaked over the mouthpiece. "You're not actually thinking of quitting?"

"Maybe."

"Marty, this is crazy It's not worth destroying your career over."

"It is to me."

"You'll regret quitting. You know you will. Say yes."

Charlie said, "Marty, I'm waiting."

Amanda was still talking, trying to convince me to say yes. Her tone contained an insistent quality that hinted at desperation. *She really wants me to stay. This from the woman who didn't want to have anything to do with me only hours earlier.*

If I said this didn't influence my decision, I'd be lying. Still, there was another consideration that was equally compelling.

How could I prove Kelly's innocence if I quit?

I nudged Amanda's hand from the phone. She resisted me until I told her I was going to say yes. Her face flooded with relief. She saw me watching her and dropped her eyes, as if embarrassed by her reaction.

"You win," I said to Charlie. "I'll arrest Kelly."

"Fine," Charlie said, his tone relaxing. "Now listen up. Here's the way it will work. The SECDEF wants credit spread out equally between the military and the Arlington PD. Chief Novak agreed and . . ."

As Charlie explained how the arrest would go down, I began regretting my decision. Even Amanda had to sit back from the phone, too disgusted to listen.

"Remember," Charlie said, "I want a call the moment he's in custody."

I said mechanically, "Yes, sir, General Hinkle."

"You trying to be a wiseass?"

"No, sir, General Hinkle, sir."

"Screw you, Marty."

"Anything you say, General—"

He hung up with a bang.

I smiled at Amanda. "Thanks for the advice."

"Sure." She returned an awkward smile of her own, then reached for the door. She still seemed embarrassed and it was apparent why. In an unguarded moment, she'd let her defenses down, made it known she still cared for me. The question I had was, at what level? Had she merely reacted out of concern for a friend or was it something more?

Don't read too much into this, Marty.

I'm only human.

She opened the door, then frowned. "Who are you calling?"

"Simon. Make sure he knows."

"He knows."

She pointed in the direction of the church. We could see a figure striding rapidly along the asphalt road toward the rectory. It angled toward the limo, waving both arms.

"Enrique!" Simon shouted. "Turn on the TV to CNN!"

★ 37 ★

No hot tub.

But Simon's limo had practically everything else a millionaire homicide cop could want.

In addition to the previously mentioned swing-out desk with the built-in laptop computer and the satellite phone, fax, and Internet system, there was a stocked bar, a fridge packed with goodies, a sound system that could power a rock concert, and a plasma screen TV mounted to the roof in a fashion similar to those on aircraft.

Simon, Enrique, Amanda, and I were seated along the rearmost seats, watching the screen. We were joined by several cops, who were kneeling on the ground, peering through the open rear doors. A commercial was playing. A man dove on a satin-sheeted bed and slid right out a second floor window, landing in bushes. It was funny, but no one laughed.

I said, "Try Fox or CNBC."

Enrique raised the remote.

Simon said, "It's only playing on CNN."

The remote dropped.

The commercial ended and another came on. Simon's cell rang and he listened, grimaced in displeasure, then advised someone he'd be at the Days Inn in thirty minutes.

Disconnecting, he said to Amanda and me, "The warrants will be waiting for us."

He was referring to the ones we needed to arrest Kelly and search his room and vehicle. The speed with which they'd been processed indicated the Arlington PD wasn't wasting any time.

Simon grimaced again and started telling us about a tip that had been called in. Before he could reveal specifics, Enrique grunted, "About time."

On the TV, we saw a rolling banner that said breaking news.

Charlotte Steiner, the CNN late night anchor, appeared at her desk, her pretty face appropriately subdued. She provided a recap of Major Talbot's murder and reminded the audience that a year earlier, he had been accused of homosexuality.

"The man who accused him," Charlotte went on, "is Air Force Colonel Brian Kelly. While the police haven't named Colonel Kelly as a suspect, CNN received an exclusive videotape that places him at Major Talbot's home on the afternoon of the murder. In the video you are about to see, please note the time and date in the lower right corner . . ."

As Charlotte droned on, an image appeared over her left shoulder. We saw a shot of the Talbot's driveway and front gate. A wide-angle view, taken from above.

"One of the missing surveillance tapes," Amanda concluded.

"Anyone make out the time?" I asked, squinting. The screen was only eight inches high and a foot wide; the video less than a quarter of that.

"Four-forty-two," Simon said.

I said, "Sam was there about twenty minutes before, right?"

"It doesn't necessarily clear General Baldwin, Martin. He might be in the house."

"If he was, he'd never let them kill Talbot."

Simon smiled; he had only been yanking my chain—I think.

"A car," Enrique said. "An SUV."

The surveillance image filled the screen and Charlotte continued to talk in a voice-over: "Colonel Kelly will soon emerge. CNN independently confirmed his identity, though some viewers might recognize him from the extensive coverage of the homosexuality charge he brought against . . ."

I tuned her out, watching the SUV roll to a stop in the driveway. It was a tan or gold Ford Explorer, that matched the description of the vehicle that Kelly said he owned. The driver's door opened and a stocky man in civilian clothes emerged. Even though the angle was taken from above, there was no doubt it was Colonel Kelly.

He strode in a determined fashion toward the call box, pressed the button, and spoke into it. The camera followed, keeping him centered in the screen.

Kelly waited and spoke again. We had a view of his face from an oblique profile. He frowned, as if puzzled. He pressed the button again and we could see him talking. He shook his head and seemed increasingly agitated. He abruptly turned away and we caught a frontal shot of his face.

"Uh-oh," Enrique said. "The man is pissed."

An understatement. Kelly's face had been coldly furious. He stalked toward his Explorer, the camera following.

"It's almost as if he expected Talbot to let him in," Amanda said.

Kelly opened the driver's door and leaned across the seat.

When he stepped back, he appeared to be holding something in his right hand.

"Anyone see what it is?"

"Not yet."

Kelly walked back toward the gate. We glimpsed the object then, sunlight glinting off the shiny—

"There," Charlotte announced over the TV. "You can see it now. It's a knife."

Kelly stopped several feet from the gate and waved the knife into the camera. It was enormous. The blade had to be eight inches long and three inches wide. It resembled a Bowie knife, except with a slight curve.

A cop grunted, "This guy must think he's Crocodile Dundee."

Enrique said, "It's too big to be the one used on Talbot. That blade couldn't be more than an inch wide."

Colonel Kelly continued to wave the knife at the camera. As he did, his mouth spread into a crazed half smile.

"He's saying something," Amanda said.

I immediately deciphered the words he was forming. It wasn't hard; they were easily recognizable.

Fuck you, fag.

Message delivered, Kelly again smiled menacingly.

"Hey," another cop said, "he's not moving, is he?"

Kelly's image had indeed frozen. For several seconds, he continued to stare out at us, the knife extended, the crazed smile fixed to his lips.

"Jesus," Amanda said, "they're really playing this thing up. No wonder everyone's screaming for his arrest."

Out of the corner of my eye, I noticed Simon shake his head. He didn't want to arrest Kelly any more than I did, but realized that decision was out of our hands.

The bastard Harris had outsmarted us.

The monitor changed to reveal Charlotte Steiner at her anchor desk. In a conspiratorial voice, she said, "That's the extent of the video we received. CNN has learned from an unnamed source that the authorities will soon be acting upon—"

"Turn it off," Simon said.

For several moments no one spoke. We were all wondering the same thing, a possibility we were forced to consider.

Could we be mistaken? Could Colonel Kelly have murdered Major Talbot?

But that notion was ludicrous. Kelly wouldn't have taken the surveillance tapes only to incriminate himself by releasing one to CNN.

Amanda said, "Ten bucks says Colonel Kelly never entered the grounds. If he had, the killers would have released video of him going inside."

Tacit nods all around.

Expanding on this theme, she continued, "They must have called Kelly. Used some ruse to get him there."

I pointed out that since no call to Kelly had been made from the house, the killers must have contacted him before they'd arrived. I said, "We can check Kelly's phone records, but chances are—"

"A pay phone," Simon said. "They would have used a pay phone."

Another given. These people were too smart not to have covered their tracks.

"The knife," Amanda said. "They couldn't have known Kelly would have a knife. Pull it."

Simon shook his head. "They only wanted him there, so he'd be recorded on tape. The rest was all Kelly's doing."

Another long silence fell upon us. It was as if we were

stalling, unwilling to take the next step. Simon checked his watch and signaled Enrique with a look.

It was time.

As Enrique crawled out to get behind the wheel, I waited for Amanda to slide out the opposite door. We'd follow in her Saab.

With a gloomy sigh, I said to Simon, "You've got to hand it to them. They covered all the bases. Even if we can't tie Kelly to the other murders, they made sure we can connect him to Talbot's."

"They have tied him to the other murders, Martin."

I frowned at the remark. From behind, Amanda said, "They can? How?"

"The phone tip," Simon said.

He looked angry as he explained.

It was over.

After Simon related the details of the tip, that was the one thought that gripped me. The case was over and we'd lost. The only thing that could help Kelly now was an alibi. If someone would swear they had seen him at the time of the priests' murders.

But I remembered what the bartender Joseph had told me: *The guy shows up almost every night at nine and never stays more 'n an hour. Like clockwork.*"

Maybe the killers knew that somehow. Knew his routine. If Coller was involved, he would have known Kelly lived alone and realized there was a better than even chance that the colonel wouldn't have an alibi for 8 P.M., when the priests were killed.

Or maybe the killers realized it didn't matter. Alibi or not, it would be almost impossible for Kelly to explain away evidence this damning. Even if he couldn't have physically committed the murders, he would be judged responsible.

I was overwhelmed with a numbing frustration. I felt as if I was running a race where someone kept moving back the finish line. I wanted to call General Charlie Hinkle and tell him he could take my job and shove it. I wasn't going to be a part of this.

Exiting the limo, that was the decision I'd made. I even got as far as to reach for my cell phone.

"Martin . . ."

Amanda and I turned around. Simon had rolled a window down and was staring at us . . . or rather me.

"Don't be discouraged," he said. "They haven't won yet."

"The hell they haven't," I flung back. "Harris is going to be the president. He'll have the biggest bully pulpit in the world. With him twisting arms, Colonel Kelly doesn't have a chance. The poor bastard will be lucky if he doesn't get the death penalty."

Simon was silent, looking at me.

Smiling.

Slowly it dawned on me what he was really saying and I felt a stirring of hope. I had to be certain and was going to ask him straight out. This time I was going to demand an answer.

Before I could question him, the limo's engine roared to life and Simon began whirring up the window. As he did, he continued to look at me with that same curious smile.

"Well, I'll be . . ." Amanda said. "He knows, doesn't he?"

"He knows something."

★38★

What did Simon know and how did he know it?

Those were the two questions I felt compelled to answer during the ride to the Days Inn. To gain insight into what Simon was thinking, I compiled a list of additional questions in my notepad, based on comments he'd made that I hadn't understood.

With Amanda's input, it took me five minutes to complete the list, which included remarks and possible explanations.

1. Why was Simon interested in the color of Talbot's sheets?
   - Timing?
   - If so, did it really matter how long Talbot had been using white sheets?
2. Why did Simon want Billy to tell him how long the video camera had been installed in Talbot's bedroom?
   - Again timing?
   - If so, why was it important to know how long Talbot had been videotaping his lovers?
3. Why did Simon say the videotapes were meant to confuse the motive?

- He said tapes, not tape.
- Was he referring only to the tapes that were left behind and not the one taken to blackmail Talbot and Sam?
- Makes no sense. The missing tape was the one that suggested the blackmail angle.
- If true, why didn't Simon say so?
4. Why did Simon tell Enrique the gay club was crucial to the case?
   - Did he believe a gay member was the murderer?
   - Possibly. Two of Talbot's lovers were celebrities.
5. Who was the third marksman?
   - Congressman Harris?
   - Roland Slater?
   - A member of Harris's staff?
   - A club member? (A celebrity?)

Except for question number four, Amanda and I discussed each entry. We knew there had to be a pattern, but we couldn't see it.

It was frustrating.

We felt foolish.

We wanted to give up.

But instead of doing so, she hunched over the wheel, her brow knitted in thought. Following her lead, I fixated on the page, forcing my tired mind to wander over each line.

Nothing on the first pass. Or the second. But during the third I finally saw it.

A connection.

· I began to tremble. My eyes shifted between the words "timing" and "sheets."

They darted to the second entry: "Why did Simon want

Billy to tell him how long the video camera had been installed in Talbot's bedroom?"

I looked at the fourth question. The one about the club.
I focused on a single word.

"Celebrities."

Then back to the third question: "Why did Simon say
the videos were meant to confuse the motive?"

And he said "tapes."

All of them.

That's when I knew. I murmured, "Oh, God—"

Amanda's head swung around. "You got something?"

My mouth felt like sand. "Yes. I think . . . yes."

"Well?"

I glanced over to tell her. More than anything, I wanted
to tell her. Share this revelation.

But I'd made a promise.

"I can't say."

"*What?*"

"I can't say," I repeated.

She stared at me in disbelief. That reaction instantly
gave way to anger. "What the hell is this, Marty? You
pulling a goddamn Simon on me?"

"No. I just can't—"

"*Son of a bitch.* I can't believe you. I really can't. We're
supposed to be cooperating together—"

She was completely incensed, looking at me more than
the road. I said, "Amanda, take it easy—"

"*Screw you.* I don't know what the hell you're trying to
pull—"

"Watch out!"

Her head snapped around to the front. Simon's limo had
stopped at a light and we were about to plow into the back.
She jammed on the breaks and we were thrown against our

shoulder harnesses. We squealed to a stop, a foot from impact.

The car was quiet. No one said anything.

The light changed and she stepped on the gas.

"You're a fucking asshole, you know that?"

We rode the rest of the way in silence.

Press Wars II.

That's what we were confronted with when we drove into the Days Inn parking lot.

The east end was packed with press vans and satellite trucks, the occupants held at bay by two cops. One was Officer Hannity, the guy who'd been with us at Coller's place.

An armada of police vehicles were parked by the hotel entrance, a knot of officers visible on the steps. Two men in civilian clothes—probably hotel employees—were setting up a wooden podium on the sidewalk out front.

They're looking for political cover and Kelly is it.

Here's how the arrest is going down . . .

I shook my head. Arresting Kelly was one thing. That I could stomach. But to make a public spectacle of it, parade him in front of the—

I stared at the TV cameras and glanced at my shirt. While I'd lost the war over this thing, I was at least going to win a minor battle. When Charlie and the SECDEF saw me on TV, they would be a couple of very pissed-off campers. They would consider my attire unprofessional and embarrassing to the good name of the military. In the scheme of things, it wasn't much of a victory.

But it made me feel a little better.

Amanda followed the limo to the west side of the building, where two more police cruisers sat, noses angled toward a tan Explorer. A couple patrolmen and a plainclothes detective waited between the vehicles, eyeing us expectantly.

The limo's brake lights came on and we stopped behind it. By the time Amanda and I got out, Simon and Enrique were strolling over to the detective, a pint-sized guy with a goatee. The guy held up something to show them. We couldn't tell what it was because Enrique blocked our view. Two steps later, he angled to one side of the detective and we got a good look at the item.

A large knife in a leather sheath.

Amanda slammed the door of the Saab, to remove any doubt that she was still thoroughly ticked off. I trailed her at a safe distance.

"It was in the glove compartment, Lieutenant," the detective said to Simon, as I sauntered up. "It's clean. No blood." He offered the knife to Simon who declined with a head shake.

"You find the gun, Hal?" Simon asked him.

"Yeah," the detective grunted. "Under the couch where the caller said it would be. It's a forty-five, recently fired. Show the man, Paul."

One patrolman stepped over to a cruiser, reached into a cardboard box sitting on the passenger seat, and produced a large automatic.

He brought the gun over to Simon, who slid on latex gloves. Hal trained a penlight on the weapon, so Simon could inspect it.

After sniffing the barrel, Simon popped out the clip and thumbed out the remaining rounds. "At least six are missing."

Which matched the number of shots fired at the rectory.

After reinserting the clip, Simon returned the pistol and

rounds to the cop. "Have you finished searching Kelly's room, Hal?"

"Just about."

"Did Kelly resist?"

"He was asleep. Had no clue about the CNN video or what we were doing there. Practically keeled over, when we found the gun. Swore he didn't know anything about it."

"Did he have an explanation for how it got under the couch?"

"You better believe it. Said it had to be the guy who showed up in his room a little after ten tonight. Here's a grabber, Lieutenant: He said it was that Air Force major who was killed by the sniper—"

"Major Coller," Simon said.

"Colonel Kelly went off on Coller big-time. He said he was the bastard who suckered him into going over to Talbot's place this afternoon."

Amanda cut me an I-told-you-so look. One punctuated by a withering glare.

I sighed.

Simon eyed Hal, "So Kelly *had* expected to meet with Talbot at his home?"

Hal nodded. "Some crap about a promotion. According to Kelly, Talbot was going to put in a good word for him with his uncle, the congressman. Convince him to help Kelly get promoted to general. Kelly said he thought it was all bullshit, but figured he had nothing to lose by showing up."

"Who answered when he called on the intercom?"

"Nobody. That's what pissed Kelly off. He figured Talbot was fucking with him, so he decided to fuck with him back. That's why he pulled the knife."

"He always carry the knife in the car?"

"For the last couple weeks. Since we had those car-jackings in Old Town."

"No rifle has turned up?"

Hal shook his head. "I checked out the obvious places in the room, Lieutenant. I got a guy crawling through the Dumpsters. We get through here, I'll have my men sweep the area, see if we can find a likely place where Kelly might have dumped it."

Amanda was frowning at this part of conversation, as was I. I tossed out, "Was the rifle also mentioned in the tip?" If it was, Simon never told us.

"No," Simon said. "We're only trying to preclude the possibility that someone might try and link the rifle to Colonel Kelly. Frankly, I'm curious why they didn't do so; it would have sealed the case against Kelly."

A valid concern.

Simon asked Hal if Kelly had an alibi for 8 P.M. tonight.

"Uh-uh." The detective gestured across the street, toward Quigley's bar. "He was over at that bar from nine to ten. Other than that, he was in his room."

"No visitors?"

"Only Coller." He hesitated, as if to add something.

"Yes?"

Hal shrugged. "Probably nothing. Colonel Kelly had just returned from the bar, when Coller knocked on the door. Kelly thinks he was waiting for him.

Simon digested this with a nod. "You have the arrest warrant?"

Hal patted his jacket.

"Let's go," Simon said.

★39★

We entered through a side door, to avoid the reporters. Taking the elevator to the fourth floor, we emerged into a quiet corridor. Midway down, we saw an open door, a cop the size of a house standing outside. As we approached the room, two female forensic technicians materialized, carrying evidence boxes and bags of clothing—items they would check for blood or fibers, anything that could connect Kelly to Talbot's killing.

When Simon asked, they shook their heads no. They'd found no other weapons.

We filed inside the room to find Colonel Kelly seated on an unmade bed. He was dressed in a short-sleeved shirt and slacks. A tough looking female detective and another uniform hovered over him. In contrast to his arrogant demeanor at Quigley's, Kelly appeared docile, almost frightened.

The colonel knew he was in trouble.

He watched us enter with blinking eyes. Seeing me, he sprang to his feet, his voice containing more than a trace of panic.

"Collins," he said. "I didn't do it. I didn't kill Talbot.

What you saw on the video. I didn't mean anything by it. I was only trying to scare him—"

"Don't say another thing," I said. "Not one word until you get a lawyer."

Hal and the female detective glared at me, but Simon nodded his approval.

"*I didn't do it.*" Kelly's voice rose shrilly. "Someone had Coller set me up. That person must have killed him. Why can't you guys see it? I'm being set up. *Someone is setting me up.*" His eyes darted around, searching for a face who believed him. Everyone gazed back with practiced, detached expressions.

Including me.

Simon came forward with the warrant and formally placed Kelly under arrest. As Kelly was being cuffed by the female detective, he continued to protest his innocence.

"I told you," he said to me. "I told you I was the easy choice."

His eyes locked on mine accusingly, implying that this was somehow my fault.

I wasn't going to respond, but couldn't help myself.

"Yes," I said. "You told me."

He continued to stare at me, as if he expected something more. But there was nothing else I could tell him. No reassurance I could provide.

However, there was something I could do.

"Simon, can I talk to you for a minute?"

As we moved to the area by the wash basin, I whispered my request to him.

He studied me for a long beat. "Your superiors will be angry. They wanted the arrest telecast."

"Screw them. Kelly doesn't deserve to be humiliated."

A tiny smile.

As he stepped away, I saw Kelly's eyes focused on me. I told myself to ignore him, but his eyes remained on me.

I turned my back on him and walked out.

It wasn't my fault.

If anything, Kelly bore much of the responsibility for his predicament. He was the one who left the threatening message, waved the knife into the camera. He's the one who made himself the perfect patsy.

It wasn't my fault.

But as I took the elevator to the ground floor, I kept going back to what Amanda said to me, after we'd learned that my daughter Emily had gotten drunk.

Someday you'll wake up and realize life is a lot more enjoyable when you're not laying guilt trips on yourself.

It better happen soon because I wasn't having much fun now.

I was leaning against a wall by the elevators, staring blankly at the lobby entrance. Through the glass doors, I watched the cops position themselves into a human wall before the podium. One spoke on his radio. He said something to the others and everyone looked in the direction of the reporters. Moments later, the first surge of media appeared, running.

The elevator dinged and I pushed upright.

Hal and the female detective emerged first, leading a sullen Colonel Kelly. Instead of continuing into the lobby and the waiting dog-and-pony show, the trio hung a left into a hallway that funneled to the side exit. Kelly would be slipped into an unmarked car and quietly driven away.

Enrique and Amanda appeared next. He acknowledged

me with a grim smile, but Amanda blew by without a glance. Simon brought up the rear and eased on over. "Ready, Martin?"

I looked at him as if he were crazy.

His expression turned sympathetic. "If it helps, Colonel Kelly won't be in custody long."

The confirmation I'd been seeking. I went with it and said casually, "How much do you know?"

He shrugged. "It's still not clear who was responsible for the murders."

"It isn't?"

He continued as if he hadn't heard me. "But I know where to find the answer."

"The gay club?"

He tried not to show surprise and almost made it.

I explained, "Enrique told me you believed the club might be crucial to the case. I didn't understand why until I put that together with Talbot's videotapes."

An approving flicker in his eyes. "So you realize the blackmail went beyond Major Talbot and General Baldwin?"

I nodded. "You got a line on who owns the club?"

"Not yet. I asked Enrique to call his friend, the one who is a club member, to see if he could provide the owner's name."

"The friend wouldn't, huh?"

"Enrique is reluctant to call him. His friend has a high government position and he doesn't want to involve him."

"Hey," a voice called out, "you guys going to do this or what?"

We looked toward the lobby entrance. Amanda stood beside Enrique, her arms folded, one foot tapping.

As we started toward her, Simon observed, "She's seems irritable."

"She's upset because I wouldn't tell her about the club."

I gave him a sideways glance. "We can't keep this from her."

"I'll talk to Enrique."

We passed a timid looking woman at the reception desk. I threw her a smile. She stared back mutely, making no attempt to return it. I didn't take it personally; it was probably the shirt.

I said to Simon, "You mentioned you don't know who is responsible for the murders . . ."

"No."

"But you believe Harris is involved?"

No response. Even now, he was still reluctant to commit himself. We were almost to the glass doors. I said, "C'mon, Simon. We both know he has to be—"

"An unwilling participant, Martin."

Another suspicion verified. Congressman Harris, it appeared, was also being blackmailed.

We stepped onto the rubber pad and the automatic doors slid open. Instantly, we were greeted by a barrage of questions and the flash of cameras.

"What other evidence do you have besides the surveillance video, Lieutenant?"

"Did Colonel Kelly commit all the murders?"

"Was it a hate crime?"

Simon asked me, "How do I look?"

I gave him a once-over. "Fine. Perfect."

Apparently my assessment wasn't good enough, considering he was about to go on national TV. Simon began smoothing imaginary creases from his jacket. My phone rang and I knew it could only be one of two people. One I wanted to talk to; the second I didn't. After checking the caller ID, I offered the phone to Amanda.

"Tell Charlie that Kelly is in custody."

"So General Hinkle can read me the riot act because we didn't arrest Kelly on camera. No thanks."

"I haven't got time to talk to him now."

"So don't." She shrugged.

The phone kept ringing. Amanda ignored it and me. Simon said to her, "You can blame me for Kelly's arrest."

She just looked at him.

I said to her, "If I don't answer, he'll call you."

That finally convinced her. She made a face and took the phone. I gave her a smile. "Wish me luck?"

"Break both legs," she said, moving away. She sounded as if she meant it.

"I'll take the lead," Simon said to me. "Remember, we need to present a united front. It's important that you support my conclusions."

I frowned. "Why wouldn't I?"

He passed through the doors and continued down the steps toward the podium. I followed him, curious why he felt the need to tell me this.

Three minutes later, I had my answer.

★40★

That son of a bitch.

I could believe what I was hearing. Simon had no desire to convict Colonel Kelly in the public's eyes. I knew he didn't.

Yet, rather than simply tell the press what they already knew, that Colonel Kelly had been arrested for the murders of five people, Simon methodically laid out the case against him.

He told them about the threatening phone call and Kelly's anger about being passed over.

He told them Kelly didn't have an alibi for any of the killings.

He told them about the pistol found in Kelly's room.

He told them Kelly was a former Army Ranger and a marksman.

He told them everything. He spoke for over twenty minutes. Afterward, he answered questions for another ten.

By the time he'd finished, I was steaming. When he drifted back from the podium, I growled under my breath, "What the fuck are you doing?"

Simon continued to smile into the cameras. To me, he whispered, "Tell them you agree."

"Like hell."

"Martin—"

"No."

"They must believe we're no threat."

"Huh?"

"*Do it.*"

He stared straight ahead, the plastic smile stuck to his face. Beneath it, I saw his teeth were clenched.

I muttered, "I hope you know what you're doing."

Moving up to the podium, I gazed out into the sea of lenses. As I introduced myself, I noticed several reporters sprout big grins. They were reacting to my seventies disco look and the bandage on my ear didn't help. One guy asked loudly if I was working undercover. A second wanted to know if I cut myself shaving. They both got laughs and I could picture Charlie turning about five shades of red as he watched this.

To keep him from throwing something at his television, I began my spiel by mentioning the cover-your-ass items he'd wanted me to emphasize. I reminded everyone that this was a joint military and civilian operation, with credit for the arrest to be shared between the two agencies. I explained that Kelly's arrest would never have been possible without the full cooperation of the military in general and the Air Force in particular. Next, I made the equivalent of a public service announcement, saying the military has a standing policy to vigorously pursue any alleged hate crime, whether it be based on gender, race, or sexual orientation. In light of the military's Don't Ask, Don't Tell policy, the last item could be construed as hypocritical, which was why I blew past it without bothering to elaborate.

This was not the time to get into a debate over gays serving in the military.

Since Simon had covered the particulars of Colonel

Kelly's arrest, I wrapped up my remarks by stating that I, as the military's lead investigator, fully supported the conclusions of my counterpart from the Arlington PD, Lieutenant Santos. My entire account took less than five minutes, which was two longer than I'd intended. When I finished, the questions began. I smiled politely and shook my head. "Sorry, I'm not taking questions."

"Agent Collins," a nasal-voiced woman sang out. "Do you believe the military's antigay policy bears any responsibility—"

I couldn't get away from the podium fast enough. Simon and I hustled up the stairs into the hotel, the questions following us.

The lobby doors closed behind us. It was quiet.

Enrique and Amanda were waiting where we'd left them. She handed me my phone. "General Hinkle called again. He's hot. He wants you to call him ASAP." She sounded absolutely thrilled at the prospect of me getting my ass chewed.

I promptly stuck the phone on my belt.

"Hey," she said. "Did you hear me? You're supposed to call him."

Ignoring her, I gripped Simon hard by the elbow to show him I meant business and guided him to the far end of the lobby. Lowering my voice, I said, "Start talking."

He sighed. "I made a mistake. Harris might know about our interest in the club—"

He clammed up at the sound of clicking heels. I turned, saw Amanda coming over, her eyes stubbornly defiant.

"What club?" she asked Simon.

He didn't reply.

Her face darkened. Her eyes went to me, then back to him. "I asked you a question."

He still said nothing.

She began a slow burn and Simon and I braced ourselves for ignition. But rather than torching off, Amanda
twirled and walked quickly toward the hallway leading to
side exit.

Aw, hell—

I said, "Where are you going?"

She picked up the pace. She was almost to the hallway.

"Amanda, you don't understand—"

She spun to me, her face flushed more with hurt than
anger. "I understand that I'm *tired*. I'm tired of the bullshit.
I'm tired of dealing with this boys' club you got going. As far
as I'm concerned, you two can go to hell."

The woman at the reception desk stared at her in shock.
When she glanced my way, I jerked my head. She took the
hint and disappeared into the back.

No one spoke. Amanda shook her head disgustedly at us
and turned away.

I grunted, "Simon."

He said, "Wait, Amanda."

As she swung back around, he said, "Enrique?"

All eyes went to Enrique. He gazed back with a pained
expression. What he feared was about to happen.

While I felt sympathy for his inner turmoil, I thought his
expectations were unrealistic. Did he really believe the
club's existence could remain a secret?

"It's okay," Simon said to him. "We can trust her."

Enrique glanced at Amanda. "It's not you. It has nothing
to do with you."

"What the hell is it then?" she shot back.

"It's okay, Enrique," Simon said again. "If we're discreet,
no one else besides Amanda will know."

Enrique sounded tired. "Save it, Simon. Five people are dead. We both know you can't guarantee—"

"I promise I will try."

Enrique gazed at Simon, weighing his sincerity. "You called the state police about a search warrant." His tone made it sound like a crime.

"So rather than compromise the club's members, you would prefer the killers go free?"

Enrique stiffened at the insinuation. "Of course not. It's just that I think a warrant should be a last resort. Something used only if—what?" He was puzzled by Simon's sudden smile.

"We have no disagreement, Enrique."

"No?"

"A warrant *is* my last option. I'm hoping to enter the club without one."

Instead of appearing pleased at this concession, Enrique's handsome face knotted in a grimace. "That's just it, Simon. I've been knocking myself out, trying to figure out a way inside. The security is damned tight. Even if we got cooperation from a member, I don't see—"

Simon said, "There might be a way."

"How?"

Simon went over and put an arm around Enrique's shoulder. The two conversed in Spanish. Amanda scowled at this.

More secrets.

Enrique appeared startled by something Simon said. He stared at Simon as if he didn't believe him. Simon nodded and Enrique actually smiled.

After another exchange of Spanish, Enrique hurried out the double doors. Most of the media were still hanging around. A number of the correspondents had dispersed and were talking into cameras, filing their reports.

"Amanda. Martin."

Simon was motioning us over. As Amanda and I strolled up to him, she said, "You will tell me everything." More command than question.

"What I can."

She bristled at the condition. "Not good enough. I want to know—"

Simon shut her up by talking about the club. Her eyes widened in amazement, once she grasped its connection to the case.

"You're sure about this?" she said. "There's no possibility you could be mistaken?"

"None," Simon said. "The videotapes and camera were planted. Major Talbot never videotaped his lovers."

A phone suddenly rang shrilly at the front desk. Amanda didn't react. We could almost see the gears spinning in her head as she tried to think through the implication of what Simon had revealed. Precisely what it meant.

Simon and I didn't say anything. Amanda didn't like to be spoon-fed, so we watched her and waited.

I looked outside, searching for Enrique. He was talking to an elderly gentleman with a distinctive mane of thick white hair. I recognized the man, having seen him on a number of cable news shows. He was a prominent investigative reporter for *The Washington Times*. I found it more than a little curious that Simon had sent Enrique out to talk to him.

Then again, perhaps it wasn't so curious after all.

Would Simon go this far? In a heart beat. But Enrique was a different story. I couldn't see him signing on to what Simon intended.

Yet, for some reason, he appeared to be doing just that.

The reporter handed Enrique a business card and they shook hands warmly. Seeing this, I realized the reporter had to be one of Simon's regular contacts, someone who quietly did him favors for a price.

This favor was going to cost Simon big time.

Leaving the reporter, Enrique glanced around, as if hunting for someone. He threw up a hand and appeared to call out. I frowned, noticing the person who'd responded wasn't another press type, but a cop.

As Enrique walked over to Officer Hannity, I shifted my attention inside to hear Simon's response to a question Amanda had just posed.

She said, "It can't only be because of Talbot's white sheets, right?"

"It wasn't," Simon said.

He proceeded to explain how he'd concluded the video-tapes and camera had been planted.

★ 41 ★

"It bothered me," Simon said, "that the videos showed Talbot sleeping with lovers on colored sheets, when we knew he'd been using white bedding for the past six months. I entertained the notion that Major Talbot had abstained from sex during that period, at least in his home. But if that was true, then why throw out his bedding on two occasions?"

"Sex," Amanda said, voicing the response he wanted. "He had sex."

Simon nodded. "I asked myself why *hadn't* Talbot video-taped those trysts? He'd taped others; why not these two? Was he in the habit of asking his partners for their permission? Unlikely. The camera was hidden; it's *purpose* was to secretly tape— Yes, Amanda?"

She was squinting at him. "Couldn't those acts have been taped and the videos taken by the killers?"

"I considered that. Still, it troubled me that the remaining videos only revealed colored sheets. It could have been a coincidence, but I also realized it was possible that the videos weren't recorded in Talbot's bedroom. He was deeply religious. He'd painted his room the color of Hell to remind himself of the consequence of sin. It seemed incompatible that someone like him, someone so devout that he disposed of his sheets in order to symbolically cleanse himself of his sin, would be in a habit of recording those same sinful acts. I decided he wouldn't.

"But how to prove it? The tapes didn't show when they'd been recorded, a fact I found rather convenient. When I asked Billy whether there was any chance of retrieving that information—"

Amanda said, "You believe those tapes *did* contain a date and time?"

"The originals probably did, since they were recorded for the purpose of blackmail. According to Billy, it's a relatively simple matter to digitally edit out the time and date."

"Can't that information be retrieved?"

"Not from a copy. And I'm sure that's what we found, copies made from the original, once the date and time were removed." He shrugged. "So that left us with only the video camera. I had to know if it had been installed after Talbot had begun using the white sheets. I didn't have much hope that Billy could give me an answer. How can one know how long a camera has been in place?"

He smiled at Amanda. "This is where we were fortunate. It took Billy less than twenty minutes to come up with a time period. Ironically, it was Major Talbot's own surveillance company which provided the answer. They recognized the model number as a video camera which had come on the market only recently. Since March, some four months *after* Talbot began using white sheets. The camera is a wireless model known for its ease of installation. I'm sure that's why it was chosen by the killers. Because they could install it quickly."

Simon's eyes hardened. "And *that* was their mistake. If

they hadn't chosen that camera, that specific model, we never would have known the tapes were planted. But they did choose the camera and now we know. We were fortunate."

He fell silent, looking at Amanda, anticipating more questions.

I knew of at least two she must have on her plate, both biggies. She alluded to one of them, saying, "You mentioned the tapes and camera were planted to confuse the motive— "

"They were."

"But the purpose of the tapes was to implicate one of Talbot's gay lovers and *not* Colonel Kelly. Yet, he's the one they're framing. It makes no sense."

"Ah, but it does," Simon said. "Talbot's murder was a well orchestrated operation. It must have been planned over an extended period of time. Several days or perhaps even weeks— You see it now, Martin?"

I was nodding. "I'm beginning to. You're saying they had a plan in place *before* Coller told them about Kelly's threatening call . . ."

"Well before."

"A plan which included framing one of Talbot's lovers for the murder. That's where the videos came in. They had to give the police somewhere to look . . ." Amanda's eyebrows shot up; she'd caught on. I continued, "What I still don't understand is why they didn't shelve this part of the plan, once they decided to target Colonel Kelly."

Simon shrugged. "Insurance. There was no guarantee Kelly would arrive at the appointed time at Talbot's home. Even if he did, they couldn't know whether Kelly would allow Coller into his room, to plant the gun. So they had a backup in place, should it be needed."

"The missing tape," Amanda said. "Or rather, the one

they made us *believe* was missing. That's their backup. They intend to release that tape if Kelly doesn't work out."

"Yes," Simon said.

And we all knew who starred with Talbot in that tape.

Simon and Amanda looked to me, a mixture of understanding and empathy creeping into their eyes. Like me, they realized this must be the primary reason Sam hadn't come forward.

A rock and a hard place.

Hell, we hadn't known the half of it.

I recalled my conversations with Sam and all the guilt I dumped on him. *Nice going, Marty.*

"Do you know where General Baldwin might be?" Simon asked me.

"No." I shrugged. "He might have returned to his apartment."

"He hasn't. I contacted the security guard. I also left messages on General Baldwin's voice mail."

It didn't surprise me that Simon had bypassed me to contact Sam. Even with what we knew, we had to have Sam's help in breaking the case.

I said, "I'll track him down in the morning. I'll contact his family and his exec. A two-star can't hide. Someone will know where he is."

Simon didn't look happy about the delay, but what did he expect from me? It was almost 4 A.M. on a Saturday morning.

Amanda gave a suggestive cough to get our attention. Once she had it, her eyes fixated on Simon, her expression a mask. It was her game face. She was about to ask Simon the second key question and anticipated a nonanswer.

"All right," she said to him, "now tell us who you believe committed the priests' murders."

Simon hesitated. "I don't know."

Her beautiful jaw tightened, but when she spoke, her voice remained calm. "You sure as hell suspect someone."

"I don't know," he repeated.

This time there was no slow burn. Once again, Simon was withholding information. In light of what she had just gone through, it was too much. She exploded angrily, "God damn you, Simon. I'm tired of—"

The words died in her throat.

Her anger was replaced by a perplexed look. She was confused by what she was seeing. She stared at Simon, to be sure it was there.

The expression of deep sadness.

He said quietly, "I want to be wrong, Amanda. I want so much to be wrong. Can you understand that?"

Amanda didn't seem to know quite how to respond. She nodded as if she understood, but she didn't.

Moving away from him, she glanced at me as if to say, *What the hell?*

I shook my head. "Simon?"

When he turned to me, I asked him a question I knew he would answer, because he had already partially done so.

I wanted to know about the the mistake he'd made.

Simon had phoned a friend from the state police, a lieutenant who supervised the night shift, to inquire about the possibility of obtaining a warrant for the club.

"What I wanted," Simon said, "was for him to make a few discrete inquiries, see if there would be any difficulty with obtaining a warrant, should it come to that."

Amanda said, "Political difficulties?"

"Yes. With Congressman Harris's involvement, I assumed there would be problems. My concerns proved valid; my friend didn't even have to check. He was familiar with the club because of an incident last year. Two teenage boys had stumbled onto the resort and were roughly treated by the security guards. One of the parents filed a complaint, which was immediately shelved. The state police were ordered by someone in the governors' office to drop the matter."

This didn't come as any surprise. Harris's political influence was well documented.

Amanda said, "Did your friend know the purpose of the club?"

"The police were told it's an exclusive spa, which caters to celebrities who covet their privacy."

This wasn't far from the truth. I said to Simon, "I still don't understand why the call was a mistake."

"By itself, it wasn't. It was more the timing and sloppiness on my part. I'd been speaking to my state police contact when Chief Novak called about the CNN video. In my haste to talk to the chief, I switched over before I could caution my friend not to mention my interest in the club."

I said, "And he did?"

"To several detectives. One who spent several years on the governor's security detail. This woman became concerned over my interest. She repeatedly asked my friend why I would want to search the club."

"Oh, hell," Amanda said. "We're screwed."

I asked Simon, "Has this detective passed on your interest—no?"

He shook his head. "Once she began asking questions, my friend realized he'd made an error. He ordered her not to contact anyone in the governor's office. She agreed, but only because he was pressuring her. Once she gets off shift, he's convinced she'll contact someone in the governor's office."

Now I understood his Kelly-bashing press conference.

"That's why you went after Colonel Kelly. You're hedging. Should the detective contact someone in the governor's office, you're hoping that person might not relay the information, if they believe you're convinced of Kelly's guilt."

He nodded.

Amanda asked, "When does the detective get off shift?"

"Seven A.M."

She checked her watch. "Less than three hours from now."

"Yes."

Simon's gaze shifted between her and me. He didn't bother to voice what he was thinking because he didn't have to.

Amanda turned to me with tired eyes. We'd been up close to twenty hours and were running on fumes. Could we keep going?

It wasn't really a question; we had no other option. We couldn't take a chance on evidence being destroyed.

Amanda said to Simon, "The detective might have already made the call. It could already be too late."

"Does it matter?"

She shook her head.

"The sooner we get going, the better," I said.

"Not so fast, Marty," Amanda said. "First, I want to know how we're going to get inside without a warrant?"

She folded her arms and looked right at Simon in a particularly determined way.

Simon detailed his plan. The big pieces I'd guessed. When he fell silent, I saw Amanda nod her approval, indicating she believed it might work. I was also cautiously optimistic.

It depended on the club manager, whether he could be intimidated.

"We'd better leave separately," Simon said to us, "to preclude anyone following."

The press didn't miss much. They'd seen Amanda and me arrive in her car and would wonder why we were leaving it behind, to go off with Simon in his limo at four in the morning.

Since the Pentagon was nearby, Amanda told Simon we'd wait for him in south parking, near the Corridor Two bridge. As we started to leave, Enrique reentered the lobby and handed Simon a business card. He was smiling cheerfully. "Eric Olson says it's a go."

The reporter.

Simon pocketed the card. "Officer Hannity?"

"He said the driver of the M5 definitely wasn't short. Far from it."

"Hannity is certain?"

"Yeah. The driver sat up pretty high in the seat. Hannity remembered because the guy had to hunch over to watch him through the windshield."

Our tall friend.

"So," Enrique said to Simon, "we going to do this now?" He was smiling again, his tone eager.

Nodding to Amanda and me, he said, "We'll wait a few minutes, then meet them at— "

As he explained the plan, Amanda and I resumed our trek toward the hallway at the rear of the lobby. Before we turned the corner, she said, "He looks pretty happy, doesn't he?"

She was looking at Enrique, who couldn't seem to stop smiling as he conversed with Simon.

We continued toward the side exit. Amanda appeared troubled. She asked, "You think he believes Simon is only bluffing?"

"Probably."

"To get into the club, Simon might have to act on his bluff. Actually go through with it."

"And he will."

"Enrique has to know that, right?"

"I'm sure he's considered it."

"Then I don't get it. Why the hell is he so happy? His worse nightmare could come true."

We came to the door and I faced Amanda. "Whatever the reason, I wouldn't worry about it. Only Enrique knows where the club is located. To ensure his cooperation, Simon probably told him a lot of things. The thing to remember is that Simon wants these killers even more than we do." I pushed open the door for her. "After you."

She still looked uneasy as she went past me into the night.

There weren't many benefits for working early on a Saturday morning, but the lack of traffic was one. As we drove to the Pentagon, we were practically the only car on the road, the drunks and party animals long gone.

Six minutes after departing the Days Inn, Amanda curved onto the perimeter road that looped the Pentagon's cavernous south parking. I was in the middle of a yawn when Amanda suddenly jammed on the brakes. Looking over, I saw her squint at something in the distance, to my right.

"It's probably not it, Marty. It's probably just a coincidence."

The apprehension in her voice countered her words. I immediately shifted around in the seat to match her gaze. Under the bright lights, I spotted several vehicles scattered across the near empty asphalt. The nearest was a van. A row past it, I saw a red sedan and —

I went tense, staring. My first reaction was that it had to be a coincidence. It couldn't be anything else.

That's what I told myself right up until the moment Amanda turned toward the vehicle and flashed her high beams.

"You see the plate?" Amanda asked.

"I see it," I said.

We were looking at a temporary dealer's tag affixed to the bumper of a shiny black BMW M5.

★42★

Amanda pulled up behind the BMW and killed the engine. "This has to be part of the plan to further incriminate Kelly, right? Or possibly General Baldwin, since he was their second option."

"Yeah . . ." Nothing else made sense.

She gave me a long look and I had a pretty good idea what was coming. With an apologetic cough, she said, "Uh, Marty, I have to ask one more time. About General Baldwin's alibi—"

"He wouldn't have left his dinner party to kill the priests. You know he wouldn't."

She nodded. Still, I knew she would continue to harbor suspicion of Sam until she could explain away the one constant in the case that kept pointing to him.

One of the killers was tall.

She gestured to the glove compartment. "Hand me the flashlight, huh?"

We stepped over to the BMW, donning latex gloves. She tried the driver door while I tugged on the passenger side handle. Same result. Locked.

She splayed the flashlight beam over the interior. It appeared showroom clean, not so much as a scrap of paper or a speck of lint visible. When she backed away, we saw car lights winding along the loop. I watched until I was sure and waved my arms.

When the limo came to a stop, we expected Simon to get out and inspect the BMW. Instead of doing so, he stuck his head out of a window, gazed at the car for no more than a few seconds, then said to Amanda and me, "The doors are locked?"

We nodded.

"Have you called it in?"

"No," she said.

His jacket began ringing. Reaching for his cell phone, he said, "We'll report it later. Get in. We have a long drive."

As she and I walked around to the opposite door, neither of us showed the least bit of concern over Simon's lack of interest in the car. Like us, he believed it had been placed here as part of the frame-up.

I opened the door for Amanda. As she started to crawl inside, Simon said, "Could you give me a few moments?"

I bent down, saw him smiling apologetically. "It's a personal call."

"Sure," Amanda said. "Not a problem." She stepped back and I shut the door.

To me, she said, "A personal call at four-thirty in the morning?"

"It could be a family crisis. Or maybe it's someone out of the country."

"You believe that?"

I hesitated and shook my head.

For the next several minutes, we waited outside the limo, wondering what it was that Simon hadn't wanted us to hear.

★

Simon was hungry.

That's what he told us after he rapped on the window, signaling he was done with his call.

Entering the limo, Amanda said to him, "You want to stop *now*?"

"It could be some time until we get another chance."

"I thought you were in a hurry to get to the club."

"Another few minutes won't matter."

Actually, it turned out to be almost forty minutes. We pulled into a Denny's a few blocks away. Amanda and I ordered two breakfast specials and ate quickly. Simon and Enrique lingered over their meal, had a second cup of coffee. Suddenly, they didn't seem in a rush to get to the club. When I asked Simon what was behind this sudden attitude change, he repeated he'd been hungry. He smiled as he replied, his tone sincere. He wanted Amanda and me to believe him.

Not a chance.

The drive to the club took a little over an hour. As beat as we all were, no one risked a nap because we knew we'd feel worse when we awoke. Following Highway 66, we cruised past Manassas, then turned north onto State Road 15. During the ride, I called General Hinkle and his disjointed voice indicated I'd woken him up. That's probably the reason he really didn't jump down my throat. He told me that the next time I went before the press, I'd better be wearing a fucking suit. I said I would.

"You heading home now?" he asked.

"Yeah." It was easier than getting into another argument with Charlie about why I should continued to pursue the case.

"Okay. Good work. The SECDEF and the president are happy this thing's finished. Call me tomorrow, but not too early."

"Don't worry."

Somewhere past Antioch, Enrique made a left onto a two-lane blacktop. After winding through several miles of forested countryside, he made another left onto another blacktop road. By now, the sky was beginning to lighten and we could make out signs affixed to trees.

In big red letters, several said, PRIVATE DRIVE, KEEP OUT. Others: TRESPASSERS WILL BE PROSECUTED.

We continued down the road for another half-mile. Rounding a bend, Enrique said, "The gate's just ahead."

Moments later, we spotted it no more than fifty yards ahead. A seven-foot-high chain link gate, a brick guard shack beside it. The fence continued into the woods and was topped by barbed wire. Every few feet along it, we saw more red signs proclaiming this was private property.

As we rolled up to the gate, a muscular young man in a guard's uniform stepped from the shack, signaling us to stop.

Lowering his window, Simon called out to him. The guard came over to his door and studied him for several seconds, trying to place him.

When he drew a blank, he said, "This is private property, Mister. You'll have to leave."

Simon showed him his badge. "I'm a homicide lieutenant. I'd like to speak to the person in charge."

The guard's face registered surprise. "Mr. Crenshaw is asleep."

"Is he the manager or the owner?"

"Mr. Crenshaw is asleep," the guard repeated, his tone hardening. "Do you have a warrant?"

"I'm afraid not."

"Then you'll have to leave, Lieutenant. I'm sorry."

Simon smiled affably. "Contact Mr. Crenshaw. I know he'll want to talk to me."

"Lieutenant," the guard said, puffing up his muscles to make sure Simon noticed. "This is private property and you are trespass— What's this for?"

The guard squinted at a business card that Simon was holding out to him.

"Mr. Olson," Simon said, "is a reporter for *The Washington Times*. If Mr. Crenshaw doesn't talk to me, Mr. Olson will release a story about this institution."

The guard stared at the card, his belligerence replaced by uncertainty. He glanced at Simon, but still seemed reluctantly to do as he asked.

"Included in the story," Simon went on, "will be an exposé on the blackmail this establishment was engaged in. Specifically, how club members were—"

That did it. The guard snatched the card from him and hurried toward the guardhouse. He stepped inside and made a phone call. More than once, he anxiously glanced our way.

Encouraging. He wouldn't be reacting this way if he'd been tipped off we were coming.

Amanda said, "Big Brother is watching."

She was peering up at a surveillance camera mounted over the guard shack. It was pointed directly at us. I resisted the urge to stick my hand out the window and wave.

The guard hung up the phone and walked back over to Simon. In contrast to his earlier confrontational manner, his tone was exceedingly polite. He even flashed a smile.

"Mr. Crenshaw will be here in few minutes, Lieutenant."

"Thank you."

When the guard stepped away, Simon unlatched a seat

back, revealing a storage compartment. From within it, he removed one of the tapes we'd recovered from Talbot's bedroom, inserted it into the VCR player mounted above his head, then settled back in his seat to wait.

Three minutes later, we saw the car drive up.

★ 43 ★

It was a pale blue Mercedes coupe that easily cost what I made in a year. The car stopped on the other side of the gate and a slender, silver-haired man with a lengthy ponytail got out, smoking a cigarette. He wore silk pajamas and a satin robe with Chinese lettering.

The gate was already motoring open and the man slipped through it, pausing to converse with the guard, who passed him Eric Olson's card.

The man scowled at the card, fired the cigarette to the ground, and walked purposefully toward the limo.

We were climbing out.

"I'm David Crenshaw, the manager," the man said, stopping before Simon. "You Lieutenant Santos?" He spoke with a British accent that didn't sound quite legit.

Simon nodded and started to introduce Amanda and me.

Crenshaw interrupted him before he could finish. He demanded, "What's all this about, making some threat to expose us with a story in the *Times?*"

"It's no threat, Mr. Crenshaw," Simon answered smoothly. "It's what will happen if you don't allow us inside. Call Mr. Olson. His home number is on the card."

Crenshaw's eyes went to the card and back to Simon. "And the blackmail comment?"

Simon gave him a hard look. "I think you know."

Crenshaw bristled. "I don't know what the hell you're talking about. What I *do* know is that you are out of line, Lieutenant. Your strong-arm tactics aren't going to work. Not with me. You're making a baseless, unsubstantiated allegation. If you print one word of it, I'm going to slap you and the *Times* with so many lawsuits it will make your head spin. I'm also going to have your badge for this. Don't think I can't. Now get out of here before—"

Simon cut him off. "Shall I show you, Mr. Crenshaw?"

"I'm not interested in anything you have to say." Ponytail flying, he turned in a dramatic fashion and strode toward the gate. "Pete," he ordered the guard, "call Bruce and Vance. Have them escort the lieutenant and his party off the property."

"Mr. Crenshaw," Simon said. "You'd better take a look."

Crenshaw kept on walking.

"You'd better look," Simon called out again. "Unless you want to spend the rest of your life in prison."

Crenshaw made it two more steps before he stopped. He slowly faced Simon and said icily. "Is that another threat?"

"It's the truth. You could be charged as an accessory to as many as five murders."

Crenshaw worked hard to keep his face blank, but you could see that Simon's accusation had gotten to him. A tense line appeared around his jaw and he began nervously shifting his weight from one foot to the other. "I don't know anything about murder."

"Or blackmail?"

"I have nothing to say. Your charges are preposterous.

Absolutely groundless." The sudden twitching of his left eyelid suggested otherwise.

"We'll see. Please get in the car, Mr. Crenshaw."

He stiffened. "Why?"

"In the car. It won't take long."

"Are you going to arrest me?"

"If necessary." This was a bluff. While Simon had the ability to make arrests outside his jurisdiction — it was an authority he'd been granted because of several task forces he'd worked on — he had no evidence to do so.

Still, Simon's threat had the desired effect. It appeared Crenshaw *was* someone who could be intimidated. Whatever resistance remained in him fell away and what could only be described as panic swam across his face. His eyes darted to his car and for a moment, I thought he might drive away.

"Don't be a fool," Simon said, moving forward to prevent his escape. "You will only make things more difficult for yourself. I know what crimes have been committed and I know who is responsible. I know everything, Mr. Crenshaw. *I know.*"

Another bluff?

Crenshaw clearly didn't believe so. He deflated under the intensity of Simon's gaze. The guard started to walk toward his boss. Amanda placed her hand on her gun and eyed him coldly. The guard froze, then wisely retreated.

There was a long silence. In the distance, we could hear birds chirping. Crenshaw appraised Simon bleakly. "It seems I have no alternative."

"Cooperation."

"I'm only an employee. I wasn't aware of anything illegal."

Simon nodded sympathetically. "I understand. If you'll come with me . . ."

As Simon escorted Crenshaw to the limo, Amanda and I hurried around to the other door. Once we had a quorum, I pointed the remote. When the video came on, Crenshaw put his head in his hands.

"I'm only an employee," he said again.

The video continued to run. Major Coller and Talbot were locked in a passionate kiss. Coller broke away with a seductive smile. Talbot excitedly pulled Coller to him and—

"Turn it off," Crenshaw said.

I clicked the remote and the image disappeared.

Crenshaw was staring dejectedly at the floor, one hand fingering his ponytail. The fingering stopped and he looked up with dull eyes.

"You know both men were murdered yesterday," Simon said quietly.

A blink of surprise. "I knew about Talbot . . . from the news. I didn't know about the second man."

"His name is Coller. You're not familiar with him?"

"He wasn't a member. I vaguely recall he came here once or twice with Talbot. The last time about five, six months ago." His eye twitched. He rubbed it, focusing on Simon. "I'm not sure what you're after, Lieutenant. I had nothing to do with their deaths."

"Do you know who did?"

"I told you I don't know anything."

"Don't lie to me."

Crenshaw's eyelid twitched faster. He ignored it. "I'm not lying. I don't know anything about their deaths. For God's sake, I'm no killer." His gaze shifted to Amanda and me, as if trying to convince us.

I asked how long he had worked at the club.

"Six years. Since it was built. I was hired to—"

"You've been the manager that entire time?"

"Yes."

"You must have been aware that guests were being video-taped and blackmailed?"

He hesitated.

"Mr. Crenshaw," I said. "You're the guy in charge. You had to know."

"I . . . I . . ." Crenshaw gave up on a denial, realizing it would be pointless.

"Who is the owner?" This question came from Amanda. She was impatient and wanted to know.

Crenshaw licked his lips, looking frightened. "If I tell you, he'll kill me. You don't know him. I tried to leave him once. Quit. He said he'd kill me if I did. He meant it." His voice cracked and I noticed he'd lost his English accent.

"We'll find his name eventually," Amanda said.

"Not from me."

"We'll protect you," Simon said.

"You *can't*. He's too powerful. He has contacts every-where. Important contacts. People who will do what he asks, no questions."

"People he's been blackmailing?"

"Mostly. They can't afford to be . . . compromised."

"When the story breaks," Simon said, "his influence won't matter. The word will be out and he will be finished."

Enrique showed no reaction to this statement. Obviously, Simon had told him something to alleviate his concerns that this could all become public.

"The name," Amanda said to Crenshaw. "Give us the owner's name."

Crenshaw's mouth worked soundlessly. He still couldn't bring himself tell us.

"You said you wanted to leave," Amanda pressed. "This is your chance. Give us his name."

"What about prison? I couldn't handle prison."

Simon said, "If you had nothing to do with the murders—"

"I didn't. I swear to you."

"Then you won't serve any time. I give you my word."

My eyebrows inched up at this remark. So did Amanda's. Last we checked, blackmail was still a crime and Simon wasn't a judge or DA.

Crenshaw said, "I also want my cooperation kept confidential. I won't testify against him or sign affidavits."

A condition Simon couldn't possibly agree to. But he did without hesitation, nodding his acceptance.

"Okay," Crenshaw said.

Lowering his voice as if afraid someone would overhear, he revealed the owner's name. None of us displayed surprise upon hearing it. While he hadn't been one of our prime suspects, he'd been on the list. Beside, Amanda had the guy pegged.

Slater was a scumbag campaign manager.

★44★

"It's absolutely beautiful," Amanda said.

We were following Crenshaw's Mercedes. A quarter mile from the gate, the thick forest transformed into a pastoral setting reminiscent of a Greek postcard. Before us were colorful gardens and picturesque water fountains. Past them towered a Mediterranean villa that easily approximated the size of a small hotel. Paths led off in various directions, several ending at iron gates, vine-covered bungalows visible behind them. Over to the left I saw tennis courts and beyond them, a building that looked like a stable.

To carve this Garden of Eden out of the forest must have cost millions and I asked no one in particular how Slater had footed the bill.

"He was a blackmailer," Amanda responded, as if that said it all.

"*Before* he built this place?"

She saw my logic and didn't reply.

"Slater could have funded the construction on his own," Simon said. "He's wealthy in his own right. He was a television producer, prior to becoming a political consultant."

Explained his expertise with videos.

The Mercedes stopped in front of the villa and we

parked beside it. Climbing out, I took a look around. I didn't see anyone, but I didn't expect to. It was 6:30 A.M. After a hard night of partying or whatever, the guests would still be asleep, probably for several more hours.

Simon asked Crenshaw, "Were all your rooms set up with video cameras?"

"Only the bungalows. Those we assigned to the more . . . exclusive guests."

I said, "Those who were worth the trouble of black-mailing?"

A wan smile.

"Where are the videotapes?" Simon asked.

"In my office."

Crenshaw led us up the stone steps into the hotel.

The interior of the villa was as dramatic as the grounds. Ornate chandeliers dangled from vaulted ceilings that had to be twenty feet high. The floor was polished Italian marble, the walls a soft coral stucco, accented by rich mahogany trim. Gilt framed paintings and brightly colored frescos adorned the lobby area, enhancing a feeling of wealth and elegance, which, of course, was the intention.

Roland Slater wanted to attract people who could afford to pay.

Stopping by the reception desk, Crenshaw spoke briefly to a young woman. He must've told her we were cops, because she looked startled.

"This way," Crenshaw said, walking past us.

He led us down a long corridor, past a glassed-in bar and lounge, complete with a dance floor and a metallic disco bulb. At the end of the hall, he made a left into a narrower passageway and pushed through a door marked "Administration."

We entered a cramped anteroom with a secretary's desk and a modest sitting area. Crenshaw continued to another door affixed with a gold nameplate inscribed with his name.

We followed him into a roomy office dominated by a large desk, several leather armchairs, and a cherry television cabinet. Stepping around the desk, Crenshaw knelt at a chest-high steel safe tucked in the corner and dialed the combination. At a click, he opened the door and reached inside.

"Step away," Simon said.

Crenshaw moved back.

Squatting down, Simon removed videotapes and passed them to Amanda and me. Before we placed the tapes on the desk, we read the labels. A majority of the names were repeats, indicating they'd visited more than once. Several were celebrities and high-ranking government officials. Five were prominent members of Congress, the most notable being Senator Tobias Hansen, the conservative senator who'd bucked his party by endorsing Congressman Harris for the presidency.

Seeing Hansen's name suggested that Slater hadn't blackmailed individuals solely for monetary gain. This suspicion was validated when we saw another tape with the name of the retired general and recent Gulf War hero, who was now the commandant of cadets at Virginia Tech.

"Now we know why General Murdock is supporting Harris," Amanda said.

I still couldn't believe it. I thrust the tape out to Crenshaw. "General Murdock is gay?"

"His daughter."

He said it with a little smile, as if he found the irony that a general would have a lesbian daughter somehow funny.

I saw red. He was a scum-sucking blackmailer who destroyed reputations and lives. It was all I could do not to jerk him by his ponytail and slap the smile from his—

"This the last one, Martin," Simon said.

He was holding out a tape to me. As I took it from him, I read the name on the side.

Harris.

Another piece of the puzzle—the key piece—slipped into place. We now understood why Congressman Harris, a man with a reputation for integrity, had become involved with a disreputable political guru like Slater.

I shook my head as I set the tape on the desk. Simon had called Harris an unwilling participant. But blackmail or not, he *had* participated and five people were dead.

So much for his integrity.

"How many?" Simon asked, contemplating the tapes on the desk.

"Forty-eight," Amanda answered. "But there are only twenty-eight individuals. Four tapes are Talbot's. Probably the originals of what we saw."

"Where the hell are the rest of them?" Enrique asked, confronting Crenshaw. "There must be hundreds more. Where are they?"

"This is all of them," Crenshaw said. "There are forty-eight—"

"Bullshit," Enrique said flatly.

"Think about it," he said. "What's the benefit of continually taping a specific client? There isn't any."

"What about the other guests who have stayed in the bungalows over the years?" Enrique demanded. "Where are their tapes?"

"The vast majority we didn't bother to tape— You going to let me answer or not?"

Enrique remained silent, glowering.

"Mr. Slater," Crenshaw continued, "was very selective. He knew he was engaged in a high-risk endeavor. He only pressured individuals who he was certain wouldn't go to the authorities and would be of use to him. That's another reason he restricted the number of tapings. To minimize the risk that a video might be misplaced or stolen, perhaps find its way to the authorities."

Enrique squinted at him, trying to determine if Crenshaw was lying. "Bullshit," he announced again, making his decision.

But I saw the logic of what Crenshaw was saying. I said, "I noticed there's no tape marked with General Baldwin's name."

"No," Crenshaw said. "To avoid confusion, Mr. Slater only marked the tapes with the people he was targeting. Their partners are referenced in the ledger. It's in the safe."

Simon reached inside it.

I said to Crenshaw, "You're telling me Slater never targeted General Baldwin for blackmail?"

"Not to my knowledge. Mr. Slater's criterion for videotaping someone was whether they could be politically useful."

"Slater threatened General Baldwin with the tape last night."

Crenshaw shrugged, cinching his robe tight around him. "I wouldn't know about that."

Amanda asked, "What about money?"

Crenshaw's brow wrinkled.

"Money," she repeated. "Surely Mr. Slater blackmailed people for money."

"He didn't," Crenshaw said. "Mr. Slater only sought influence. Power."

"Like controlling the president of the United States."

Crenshaw was silent.

"He's lying," Enrique said. "There have to be more tapes. Look at the size of this place. It cost millions. He's lying."

"There are only forty-eight tapes," Simon said.

He was staring into a green ledger. He shook his head and closed it. He had the same expression of deep sadness that we'd noticed at the Days Inn.

"What is it?" Amanda asked. "What did you see?"

"A name."

"Whose name?"

Instead of a reply, Simon told Crenshaw to play the Harris tape.

Crenshaw walked over to TV cabinet and inserted the video into the VCR. Stepping back, he said to Simon. "The remote is on the desk, Lieutenant."

As Simon picked it up, Crenshaw gave him a tiny smile. "You really didn't know?"

"I didn't want to know," Simon said.

He extended the remote and stood frozen. As if with great effort, his thumb slowly depressed a button. Seconds later, we realized why he was reluctant to view this video.

When the image appeared, Amanda gave a little gasp and my knees almost buckled. We'd mentally braced ourselves for several scenarios, all involving Congressman Harris. Nothing prepared us for seeing two nude women interlocked in each others arms. Even though their faces were shielded by a wild mass of hair, we knew who they had to be. One was a tall and black, the other a slender blonde.

"I can't believe it," Amanda said. "I can't."

But we had to believe it because the blonde woman brushed aside her hair and we found ourselves staring at the face of Teresa Harris.

★45★

No one spoke. We couldn't.

A voice in my head told me it couldn't be true. Slater had been a TV producer. He must have staged this somehow, altered the image with some kind of special effects trick. The bright and beautiful Teresa Harris wouldn't be involved in a lesbian affair with her personal assistant.

But of course it wasn't a trick. In our hearts, we knew we were staring at reality. Teresa Harris and her assistant were not only lovers.

They were killers.

I rubbed my face hard, thinking I should have at least considered this possibility. The reason I hadn't was because I'd focused on the obvious. I'd assumed the killers had been men. Women don't kill in such a brutal fashion. They don't torture people to death. Certainly not their own nephew. They don't.

My mind shifted back to the clues that had been there all along. Subtle, but they were there.

The height disparity between the killers, one tall and the other much shorter.

The closeness of the killers to Talbot; why he let them into the house.

Major Tenpas's statement to me: *Major Coller is separating from the Air Force . . . He's going to work as an administrative assistant for Mrs. Harris.*

The absence of an alibi; Teresa Harris *hadn't* campaigned with her husband in Pennsylvania.

Simon's comment to Amanda: *I want so much to be wrong. Can you understand that?*

And Harris's admonition to the Secret Service agent: *You've already screwed up enough for one day, Hassall.* That singular comment should have been a huge red flag. Hassall's job was protection. His screwup must have been that he'd failed in that duty.

And lost his charge, Teresa Harris.

No, I should have known. The clues were there, if I'd only paid attention. Even now, I still had difficulty believing what I was viewing on the screen. How could this stunningly beautiful woman kill all those—

I frowned. Coller's murder? How could she have pulled off Coller's murder?

I asked Simon if Teresa Harris was an expert marksman.

"Exceptionally so," he said. "It was her discipline in the Olympics."

"Excuse me?" Amanda said. "She was a cross-country skier."

"Not exactly," Simon said. "She competed in the biathlon."

Which meant Teresa Harris had spent years shooting at targets with a rifle. "Jesus," Amanda said.

Coupled with the church janitor's description of the killers, this fact explained why Simon had harbored suspicions of Teresa Harris. What it *didn't* explain was how someone could be in two places at once.

I said to him, "So how did she manage Coller's killing? We saw her and her assistant . . ."

"Abigail Gillette."

"Board the helicopter. Teresa Harris couldn't have driven to Talbot's apartment in time to murder him. Not from Harris's home."

"Perhaps the helicopter dropped off the women en route."

"She ditched her Secret Service security a *second* time?" Preposterous. Agent Hassall would never allow himself to be burned twice.

Simon passed on a response. He didn't seem concerned about explaining away this inconsistency. I wondered why, since it had bothered him a great deal, back at the rectory.

"A man," Amanda said, highlighting another problem. "Officer Hannity seemed convinced the person in the car was a man."

"From the height," Simon said. "That's why he concluded the driver was male."

"So what are you saying? You think *Gillette* was the person in the car?"

Another diffident shrug. Simon making it clear he had no desire to discuss this.

A warning bell chimed in my head. Yet again, his behavior indicated he was withholding information—

"Here it comes," Crenshaw announced. "You don't want to miss it. Mrs. Harris has *varied* sexual tastes."

We all looked at him. He was focused on the screen, his eyes shiny. He murmured, "Such a shame. He was such a good looking man."

Amanda said, "Mrs. Harris is *bi*sexual?"

Crenshaw didn't answer her. He was fixated on the television.

On screen, we saw the women sit up and look toward the foot of the bed, at something or someone off camera. Teresa Harris pouted seductively and flashed a kittenish smile. Her assistant, Abigail Gillette, began motioning insistently. Both women giggled. They kissed on the lips and looked again toward the person—apparently the unseen man—who was in the room. The women smiled provocatively and cupped their hands in a slutty, come-on gesture, urging the man to join them.

We glimpsed an arm at the lower edge of the screen. A man's arm. Teresa Harris pulled on his hand and the man tumbled between the women. He was nude except for his briefs. The women playfully pounced on him. Teresa Harris pressed her face down upon his, gave him a violent kiss and rubbed his crotch.

"Who is he?" Enrique said. "Can anyone tell?"

There were arms and legs everywhere. Teresa Harris's face and hair completely covered the man's. He struggled to free himself, but she continued to cling to him, her mouth pressed against his lips. I should be disgusted by what I was watching, but I couldn't turn away. Teresa Harris had been an athlete. Her body was lithe and spectacular. She exuded a primal, animalistic sexuality.

It was exciting to watch.

Seconds later, Teresa Harris released her grip on the man and pushed away. And that's when we finally saw his face.

Simon's only reaction was a low hiss of disapproval. Because of the ledger, he'd known what to expect. The rest of us were slack jawed, reeling. We never considered that the male lover would be this particular man. It was unthinkable. Gay men don't have sex with women. And they certainly don't have sex with female family members.

But on screen, that was precisely what was happening.

Teresa Harris wet her lips and buried her face in the crotch of her nephew, Franklin Talbot.

As the sex act continued, Talbot looked awkward and uncomfortable. His eyes floated around the room, looking everywhere, but at his aunt. It was obvious he wasn't enjoying himself.

So what the hell was he doing there?

Abigail Gillette joined in and both women worked on Talbot. It soon became apparent he was responding physically. The deviancy was too much. One by one, we turned away from the television. First Amanda, Enrique, and me. Crenshaw remained riveted on the screen, his breathing labored. It creeped me out.

Amanda glared disgustedly at Crenshaw. To Simon, she said, "I think we know how it ends."

No reaction. Simon was looking at the screen with a distracted expression. Not so much watching as thinking, trying to understand.

Amanda said impatiently, "Anytime, Simon."

That remark got through and he raised the remote. When the tape kept running, we looked to him quizzically. He was staring past us, toward the doorway. For an instant, I detected what appeared to be an expression of relief. But that didn't make sense because of what Simon said next.

"Put the gun down," he ordered.

Crenshaw gave a strangled cry and the rest of us spun around.

Him?

★ 46 ★

General Sam Baldwin's tall frame filled the doorway, a small automatic in his hand. He wore tan slacks, cordovan loafers, and a navy sports coat embroidered with his family crest. Despite his preppy attire, he looked like hell. His lean face appeared puffy and haggard and there were dark bags under his eyes. Focusing on me, he said, "I'm sorry, Marty. I have to do this."

My shock gave way to cold rage. "You fucking son of a bitch. You were part of it, all along. You used me."

"Marty . . . Marty . . ." Sam shook his head dismissively. "You're something. You really are. I thought you were supposed to be a bright detective."

"Coller," I said. "You killed Coller. It had to be you. It couldn't be anyone else."

The head shaking stopped. "You're fucking crazy."

"They threatened to release the tape unless you took out Coller. So you did it. Blew him away. You couldn't have it get out that a Baldwin was anything but a perfect soldier. After all, what would your father think when he realized his own son was—"

"Don't," he said. "Don't say it."

I looked right at him, saw his shame.

"Gay," I announced loudly. "You're gay, Sam. Everyone here knows it. Pretty soon, the entire country will know it. Guess what? No one's going to give a damn who you slept with. You're a murderer. A goddamn murderer who—"

"Shut the hell up, Marty."

"You going to shoot us all? Forget it. One of us will take you out. It was all for nothing, Sam. Ironic, huh? People are going to remember the Baldwin name, all right. Not because you're gay, but because—"

"I said shut up."

I'd pushed him too far. His temper kicked in and he looked as mad as I'd ever seen him. His lip was curled into a snarl and he was shaking with rage. He pointed the gun at me and for an instant, I thought he was going to shoot me. "You goddamn son of a bitch. You have no right. You don't understand—"

The bullet.

I kept waiting for the impact of the bullet. My only chance to go for my gun. I reached down, hoping Sam kept talking long enough—

"Stop!"

We both froze, looking to Simon. He was glaring at us. Beside him, I noticed Amanda had placed her fingers on her weapon, ready to take Sam out if that proved necessary.

But Enrique's hand wasn't anywhere near his holster. And he appeared completely relaxed. That threw me. Enrique was was usually the one who was spring-loaded to react first and ask question later. It was as if he didn't understand the threat Sam posed—

"Stop it, both of you," Simon said. He swung around to me. "You're mistaken. General Baldwin killed no one."

I stared at him as if he was certifiable. "Simon, it had to

be him. Teresa Harris couldn't have killed Coller. We know it wasn't Colonel Kelly. That leaves only—"

"It wasn't General Baldwin."

I pointed to my ear. "And *this?* You said the shooter was trying to miss me, us. That only makes sense if the shooter was Sam."

"You're wrong, Martin. It wasn't him. The general is here only because I asked him to come."

"Huh?"

Simon nodded to Crenshaw, who was cowering behind the desk. "General Baldwin might have been of use in gaining access to the grounds, had Mr. Crenshaw not co-operated."

My eyes were on Sam. He was nodding, his anger dropping below the homicidal level.

This was all coming in too fast for me to understand. Before I could voice my next question, Amanda beat me to it. "What about the *gun?* Why does General Baldwin have a gun?"

Simon had no answer. He told Sam to put his gun down.

"Sorry, Lieutenant," Sam said, keeping his weapon level. "It's insurance."

"For?"

"I can't allow you to destroy more lives. Franklin wouldn't have wanted that. It's why they killed him. He was going to expose all this." He looked right at the tapes on the desk.

His message was clear. A tense silence filled the room. We watched Simon, knowing he couldn't agree.

"I take it," he said, "that you intend to destroy the tapes."

"Not all of them, Lieutenant. I realize you need the ones on Major Talbot and Mrs. Harris to prove your case. You keep those; I destroy the rest and the ledger." He glanced at the computer on Crenshaw's desk. "I also erase the membership list stored on there."

"If I refuse . . ."

Sam shifted his gun until it was aimed at Simon's chest. "I'm not asking, Lieutenant."

Again my eyes went to Enrique, who still appeared calm. It made no sense. Simon was being threatened. Why wouldn't he display some concern or at least—

And then the reason came to me in a sudden moment of clarity.

Simon's gaze rose from Sam's gun to his face. "You're destroying evidence, General. It will make proving the case more difficult."

"You'll have the crucial tapes and my testimony. Once you apply the pressure, those involved will crack. It's already worked with Crenshaw. Slater will do the same thing. That bastard doesn't want to go down for five murders. You'll get your conviction, Lieutenant. I promise you."

Simon looked conflicted. He obviously didn't want to agree to Sam's terms. At least that's how I read him until I detected something on Enrique's face that shouldn't have been there. It was the suggestion of a smile.

My suspicion evolved into a certainty.

By now, Amanda had also noticed Enrique's reaction. She was frowning, cycling through explanations. Her eyebrows crawled up when she got a hit. She became aware of me watching her and our eyes met. A tacit question.

Would Simon arrange this, Marty?

My head dipped. As a cop, it would have been difficult for him to explain why he'd willingly destroyed evidence. The operative word was, willingly. Now he could put the blame on Sam, with no one the wiser.

Ethics 101, according to Simon. He had no desire to destroy innocent people's reputations and now he wouldn't have to.

Amanda didn't appear angry over Simon's deception. I wasn't either. We both realized that he'd kept us in the dark in order to protect us, should his ruse ever come to light.

Simon made a big show of conveying his reluctance to give in. He shifted between a series of unhappy grimaces and regretful head shakes. Finally, he threw up his hands, as if being forced to concede.

"You win, General."

Sam wasn't much of a thespian. He nodded stiffly and swung the gun around to Crenshaw. "David, do you keep copies of the tapes stored anywhere else but here?"

Crenshaw fixated on the barrel. He tried to speak and coughed instead. "No."

"If you're lying . . ."

"I'm not. The only copies that exist are ones Mr. Slater sent to the individuals."

"He doesn't have any copies of his own?"

"No. He only makes them when he needs them."

Sam raised the gun to his head. "I don't believe you."

Crenshaw's body spasmed in panic. "Why the hell would I lie?"

Sam contemplated Crenshaw's trembling form. "How many computers contain memberships rosters?"

"Mine and Sally's. My secretary's. That's her desk outside." Crenshaw couldn't get the words out fast enough.

"No central database?"

"Too risky. Anyone who worked here could download the information, so Mr. Slater—"

Sam abruptly turned away from Crenshaw and asked, "Who's good with computers?"

"I am," Amanda said, after a moment.

"Here." Sam passed her a CD-ROM he'd slipped from his jacket.

She read the label. It was a program to scramble the data stored on hard drives. She sat down at Crenshaw's computer and inserted the CD.

Sam dug out car keys from his pocket and tossed them to Enrique. "The green Caddy. There's a bag containing lighter fluid, in the back seat. Get it."

"First," Simon said, "I'd like him to remove the tapes we're keeping."

"Fine."

While Simon retrieved the Harris tape from the VCR, Enrique gathered the four Talbot videos from the desk. I never believed Sam would allow Enrique to walk out with the video of him and Talbot.

But as Enrique departed with the tapes, Sam never said a word.

He eased into a chair, the gun still trained on us. I thought this part was overdone, but I understood why he was doing it. He wanted to make it look good.

"How long will it take?" he asked Amanda.

"A few minutes to upload the program in each computer, General. Another thirty minutes or so to scramble all the files."

By the time she finished uploading the program on the secretary's computer, Enrique had returned and we'd placed the remaining videotapes in a cardboard box.

"Let's go boys and girls," Sam said.

The bar had an enormous stone fireplace, one that actually burned wood.

Under Sam's watchful eye, Enrique layered the videos on

top of several logs. After dousing the tapes with lighter fluid, he set them ablaze and moved aside. Sam came forward and stared into the smoky flames. Facing us, we saw his shoulders sag and tension escape his body. This had been important to him, something he'd been compelled to do.

"This was Franklin's goal," he said quietly. "Before exposing what was going on, he wanted to force Slater to turn over the tapes to us. To prevent anyone else from being hurt."

We all nodded our understanding.

Simon said, "Now tell us everything you know, General."

"There's one more thing I have to do. It'll only take a second."

Stepping around us, Sam walked over to Crenshaw. He gave him a big smile right up until the moment he punched him flush in the jaw. Crenshaw dropped in a heap, out before he hit the floor. Sam stood over his still form, watching the blood ooze from a cut in Crenshaw's lip. "He's lucky I didn't kill him."

"Do you believe he was aware of the murders?" Simon asked.

"No. Crenshaw's weak. Slater knew he wouldn't have the stomach for it." He passed his gun to Simon. "I'm ready, Lieutenant. You want to do this back in the office?"

"Please."

Sam made a couple of false starts, as if he wanted to say something to me. Unable to voice the words, he left the room.

As we followed him out, Simon said to me, "I misjudged him. He's a good man. He deserves our respect."

His way of telling me I should consider apologizing first.

★

Simon wanted to get Sam's account on tape, so while Enrique revived Crenshaw and helped him to his suite upstairs, I went out to the limo and retrieved the small cassette recorder.

Returning to the office, I found everyone except Enrique seated in the waiting area of the anteroom. Since all the chairs were taken, I set the recorder on the coffee table and stood against the wall, near where Sam was sitting.

His eyes remained fixed straight ahead, ignoring me. Several uncomfortable seconds passed, as I tried to figure out how to break the ice. When nothing came to mind, I went with the way I felt.

"I'm sorry, Sam. About everything."

At first nothing. Then Sam's head tilted up and I saw the beginnings of a smile. "That makes two of us," he said with feeling.

"Look, a lot of the stuff I said—"

"We both made mistakes. Said things we shouldn't."

"So we're okay?"

His smiled widened. "We're getting there."

For a moment, the years disappeared and we were back at Virginia Tech. Two young men filled with the hope and promise of the future that awaited us. It was an image I wanted to preserve.

But when I blinked, I'd returned to the present and the reality of what we were facing.

Sam squeezed my arm and something caught in my throat. At the start of the case, I'd hoped to keep him out of it, but that wouldn't happen now. He would be our chief witness, which meant the world would soon learn that a Baldwin was gay. The reaction would be swift. Some would empathize and understand, but most wouldn't. He would be the butt of jokes, his family ridiculed.

It wasn't right. Sam had served his country honorably. He didn't deserve this.

But the ugly lesson we'd both learned was that life wasn't fair.

"Clayter Lake?" he said quietly.

"Just say when."

When Enrique entered the room, Simon immediately started the tape. "Whenever you're ready, General . . ."

★47★

Sam spoke in slow, measured words, aware of the significance of what he was saying.

"Teresa Harris was into sex. Any kind of sex. It was a sickness with her. Men, women, it didn't matter. Boys too. Franklin was eleven when she first molested him. It freaked him out. His parents were barely in the ground and here was his aunt doing these things to him. Franklin begged her to stop, but she wouldn't. He didn't know what to do, who to turn to. She said no one would listen to him if he told, and he believed her. She was this important woman and he was only a kid. So he kept his mouth shut and took the abuse for almost a year. Until he was twelve.

"That's when he ran away the first time. It wasn't only the sex he was running away from, it was also the control she had over him. By then, Teresa had gotten into his head. She could make him do almost anything. Sick stuff. He considered suicide. Thought about it all the time. Twelve years old and he was going to kill himself. Jesus, I thought I had it tough, being different. But when I think about what Franklin went through . . . what it must of been like . . ."

Sam blinked hard, trailing off. He turned away until he

regained his composure. "Anyway, he stayed gone for almost a month. Then he got busted for shoplifting and was sent home; Teresa punished him. He never told me what she did, but it was bad. Franklin shook like a leaf when he mentioned this part. After a couple months, he took off again. This time when he was returned, his uncle shipped him off to military school. He'd had it with Franklin and wanted to get rid of him. Little did Congressman Harris know, he was saving Franklin's life. Teresa couldn't get to him when he was at school. A Catholic priest there also helped. Franklin was suicidal when he arrived and the priest spent months counseling him. The priest tried to convince him to report his aunt, but Franklin never would. Like I said, Teresa had this control over him. Even when he got older, he could never say no to her. I couldn't understand it, but . . . hell, you saw the tape. She still had this power over him. Sick fucking bitch."

He shook his head angrily. We waited for him to continue and when he didn't, Amanda said, "Maybe I missed something, General, but Major Talbot *was* gay, right?"

A nod. "It was something he discovered in school. Part of it, most it, must have been reaction to the abuse. A kind of defense mechanism. For a while, he hated women."

Now came the dicey part. I had to bring it up because of what I'd seen on the tape. I said, "He seemed to perform with her physically. Mrs. Harris."

"And only her," Sam said. "She was the one woman who could arouse him. Go figure."

I couldn't. I doubted anyone could.

Simon asked, "Was Father Carlacci the school priest?"

Sam nodded, his voice thick. "He was a good man. A saint. And that crazy bitch killed him."

At this remark, Simon's face hardened. A reflection of his

own hate simmering below the surface. "You're certain Mrs. Harris was responsible?"

"I know she killed Talbot. She and that black woman. Her assistant."

"How do you know, General?"

Sam measured Simon with a long look. "Easy. I saw them."

Amanda and I stared at him, but Simon showed no reaction. He calmly leaned forward and slid the tape recorder closer to Sam.

"Go on, General."

Sam had been on his way to the Pentagon athletic club when Talbot called him on his cell phone. It was around 4 P.M. Talbot told Sam that a car was slowly driving by his house. Talbot was convinced it was Slater's people. He was frightened. Could Sam please come?

Sam rushed right over without notifying his office. When he arrived, he noticed a car rolling up the front drive. Initially, he was also convinced it had to be Slater's people. Then he saw two women get out.

Teresa Harris and Abigail Gillette.

Sam said, "I asked Franklin over the intercom to let me in. He said it would be better if he talked to his aunt alone. He said it would be okay. She would never hurt him. I blame myself. I knew what she was like. I knew what she was capable of. But I let him talk me into leaving. Walking away. I should have insisted he let me in. If I had, Franklin would still be . . . but I left. I *left* and . . . and they killed him. Butchered him like an animal."

He stared at his big hands, his face etched with guilt.

"It wasn't your fault," I said. "You couldn't have known."

"I was there, Marty. *I was there.*"

Sam was determined to bear responsibility for Talbot's death. Because of my own demons, I knew that nothing I could say could remove that burden. Sam would have to do that on his own . . . if he could.

He sagged back heavily in his chair, saying over and over, "I was there . . . I was there . . ." We let him talk, get it out. At some point, he closed his eyes, as if overcome by the burden pressing down upon him. I was worried for him. He was on edge, close to coming apart. Ideally, it would be better if we left, questioned him at a later date. But that wasn't an option. Five people were dead and we had to know the truth.

Simon asked Sam about the motive, the reason behind the killings. Sam didn't answer. He lay there with his eyes closed. He could have been asleep, but we knew he wasn't.

Simon prompted, "General?"

Sam's eyes fluttered open. "I told you. Franklin was going to expose the blackmail operation."

"We need to know the details. How it all began."

He reluctantly sat up, looking at Simon. "It began with a phone call . . ."

As Sam laid everything out, the remaining pieces of the puzzle came together. Not every space was filled, but what we didn't know, we could guess at.

Last year, Slater made a call to Teresa Harris. He informed her he had a videotape of her and Talbot—the one we'd viewed—and threatened to release it unless Teresa convinced her husband to hire him as campaign manager. Teresa resisted. She asked Talbot to negotiate with Slater, see if he would take money instead.

Slater wouldn't. He wanted to manage the Harris campaign and would accept nothing less. In the end, Teresa Harris surrendered to Slater's demands and convinced her husband to hire him.

Initially, she despised Slater, for the hold he had on her. But because of the campaign's spectacular success, her attitude soon changed. She came to realize that Slater *was* a brilliant political strategist. Moreover, she began to accept the fact that she *needed* him to achieve her dream of becoming first lady. An alliance was formed, a pact between two ruthlessly ambitious people who would do almost anything to succeed. With every primary win, they became increasingly convinced they would succeed. They believed nothing could stop them.

They forgot about Talbot.

He was the one person who knew of the alliance between Teresa and Slater. Once Congressman Harris became president, Talbot realized Slater would try and control him, through his influence over Teresa. That was the reason for the two-for-one candidacy. Slater wanted Teresa to have political clout in her own right, because she was the source of his power.

Years of military schooling coupled with his deepening Catholic faith had changed Talbot. Once a troubled youth, he'd evolved into a young man with an uncompromising ethical and moral center. To him, it was unconscionable that a blackmailer might actually control the next president of the United States. He told his aunt he couldn't agree to this. He begged her to reconsider.

She promised she would.

The next day Talbot received his own call from Slater, telling him to keep his mouth shut. That same afternoon, a tape arrived. Several days later, another video was delivered.

Slater wasn't screwing around; he was going to make sure Talbot behaved. For a while, his tactics worked and Talbot, stung by his aunt's betrayal, was cowed into silence.

As time passed, Talbot's resolve gradually stiffened. Despite his fears, he knew he was the only one who could stop Slater. But he also agonized how to accomplish this without destroying his aunt.

It came down to control. The control she held over him. While he hated her, he also loved her at some level.

For months, his feelings for his aunt kept him from revealing what he knew. He held out hope that perhaps Harris wouldn't win his party's nomination. As the primary victories piled up, that hope dimmed and Talbot realized he couldn't wait any longer. He had to act.

So he did by confiding in Sam, Major Coller, and Father Carlacci, informing them of his intentions and enlisting their help.

"What he wanted from Major Coller and me," Sam explained, "was help in doing what I did today. Destroying the tapes and membership lists. Also, he wanted us to support his assertions that Slater was a blackmailer. We were the obvious choices; we were his partners on the two tapes Slater had sent. Father Carlacci provided moral support. He was Franklin's conscience. Whenever Franklin wavered, the father reminded him — Go ahead, Lieutenant."

Simon edged forward as if to ask a question. When he voiced it, Amanda and I winced. This was something we'd wondered about, but hadn't had the nerve to ask.

"General," Simon said, "did it bother you that Major Talbot had other partners?"

Sam sighed. "Sure it did. But that was the reality of our lives. Because of our professions, we could never have an exclusive relationship. It was too dangerous for our careers.

We rarely got together more than once or twice a month." He shrugged. "He was a young man; he had needs."

"But he tried not to . . . stray?"

Sam seemed to smile. "He tried hard. Hated himself when he did. You saw his bedroom . . ." He waited for Simon's nod. "He understood homosexuality was a mortal sin. He knew he was going to Hell, for what he was." Sam paused, his voice turning quiet. "I hope that's not true."

Simon was silent. He was too much of a Catholic to voice reassurance if he believed it was false.

Changing the subject, I asked Sam to expand on something he'd alluded to earlier.

"By coming forward," I said, "Major Talbot realized he was going to destroy his military career. Everyone would know he was gay . . ."

"Right. Sure."

"What about Major Coller? He would also be exposed—"

"Coller never agreed," Sam said. "He had a lot to lose because he was separating from the Air Force to work for Teresa Harris. Once the scandal broke, he knew the Harrises would be dead politically and he'd be out of a job." His eyes held mine, knowing where I was going with this. When he spoke, I heard his sadness. "The answer to your next question is no, Marty. I also told Franklin no. I couldn't come forward. I asked him to destroy the tape of us."

It was a stunningly candid admission and explained Sam's overwhelming sense of guilt.

I said, "And the reason you're allowing us to keep that tape . . ."

"There has to be a tape of someone who can testify to being blackmailed. Teresa Harris certainly won't admit it and everyone else is dead." He shrugged. "Besides, it doesn't really matter anyway. It's all going to come out in the end.

And you know what, Marty? I don't give a damn. I'm tired of living a lie. I'm tired of being scared and hiding in the shadows. I don't care what people think any more. I really don't."

Sam sounded as if he genuinely believed what he was saying. Was he rationalizing to make the inevitable more palatable? Only he knew for sure, but the conviction in his voice told me he wasn't.

"I'm glad for you, Sam."

"Don't be. I should have done this years earlier. If I had . . ."

He didn't complete the thought.

I asked my remaining question now: Did Sam know the extent of Congressman Harris's role in the murders?

"I might be wrong," he replied, "but I suspect he was in the dark. It was something we discussed earlier. According to Franklin, his uncle was a straight arrow—"

"We?" I said.

"Oh, the lieutenant and me." He glanced at Simon. "Over the phone, we discussed the congressman. I told him Franklin never implicated him. That's damned suggestive, since there was certainly no love lost between him and his uncle. If Congressman Harris was involved, Franklin would have said something."

Simon was nodding. I said to him, "Come off it. Harris had to know. Maybe not about the murder, but about the blackmail."

"How?" he said.

"What do mean how?"

"How? If Mrs. Harris didn't tell him, how would he know?"

"Talbot," I said. "What if Talbot told him?"

"He didn't."

The conviction in his voice irritated me. I said sarcastically, "And you know this because . . ."

"Would Congressman Harris have continued to give Talbot a million dollars a year, if he knew his nephew had slept with his wife? Would you?"

"I . . . well . . ." As I hunted for a response, Amanda and Enrique shook their heads. They knew this was an argument I was going to lose.

"Fine," I said, surrendering. "So maybe it wasn't Talbot." Simon tried not to smile . . . and failed.

"Anyway," Sam said. "The lieutenant said he'd check."

I was curious how Simon intended to pull this off. But I was still annoyed with him and didn't want to give him the satisfaction of me having to ask.

Focusing on Sam, Amanda asked, "What about Major Coller, sir? We know he's the one who betrayed Major Talbot—"

"He *what?*"

She seemed puzzled by Sam's surprise. "Betrayed Major Talbot, General. He also planted a gun on Colonel Kelly to incriminate him for the priests' murders. You didn't know, sir?"

"Why would he?" Simon said. "I never told him."

"Jesus," Sam said. "I knew he was an ambitious little prick, but—" He broke off with an angry head shake.

Amanda said, "So you wouldn't have an idea who might have killed him, sir?"

Sam seem to tense at the question. Before he could respond, Simon said, "We still can't rule out Mrs. Harris or the possibility that Ms. Gillette is also a marksman."

Amanda eyed him dubiously, mirroring my sentiment. Since we couldn't completely discount either scenario, neither of us pursued the matter. Once we ran a background check on Gillette and interviewed Secret Service agent Hassall, we'd be able to narrow down the shooter's identity. If neither Harris nor Gillette had the opportunity to kill Coller—and in Gillette's case, the marksmanship expertise—then we were looking for a fourth person.

"Anything more, Amanda?" Simon asked.

She shook her head. When Simon looked to me, I told him I had no questions.

Smiling at Sam, Simon clicked off the tape recorder. "Thank you, General. You've been most cooperative."

"Glad to help, Lieutenant." Sam's tone indicated anything but.

Simon and Amanda rose. Sam watched them, but chose to remain seated. He seemed in no hurry to leave. As everyone edged toward the door, he reluctantly stood. With a sigh, he said to me, "Now comes the hard part."

"The hard part?" I said.

"I'm going to Blacksburg to tell my parents."

★48★

Enrique, Simon, and Amanda quickly left the room, sensing Sam wanted to talk to me privately. As we trailed them into the corridor, Sam remained quiet, preoccupied by his thoughts. Walking beside him, I could almost feel his dread over what he was about to do.

"Will your father understand?" I asked.

"No one in my family will."

"Once they get over the shock, they'll come around. Just give them time."

"They're *Baldwins*, Marty." As if that summed everything up.

It didn't for me. I pointed out that he was still his father's son.

"That's the problem. I *am* his son. That's precisely why he won't understand." Seeing my frown, he said, "You still don't get it, Marty? How about telling me how *you* would react."

"Excuse me."

"If you were in their position. If Emily came to you and said she was . . . different."

"She's my daughter," I said. "I'd try and be supportive and—"

"Would it bother you?"

I hesitated.

He abruptly swung around and faced me. "*Exactly*. It's not something you'd want. Sure, you'd try and accept it, but it would eat at you. You'd feel embarrassed; you wouldn't know what to tell friends and family. It would feel like the death of all the things you'd hope and want for her. You'd drive yourself crazy, trying to figure out what made her that way. Was it your fault? Were you responsible? At some point, you'd start blaming her, that this was somehow a choice she was making. Don't shake your head, Marty. I've seen this play out too many times."

"She's my daughter," I insisted. "No matter what, I'm always going to love her—"

"And my parents might still love me. But the point I'm trying to make is that they'll never understand or accept me. They'd always consider my lifestyle a perversity, a violation of a fundamental law of nature. Men aren't supposed to be attracted to men. Period."

His eyes were riveted on me, challenging me to respond. I didn't even try. As much as I didn't want to admit it, I realized what he was saying was true. It would be hard for me to truly accept having a gay child.

Perhaps even impossible.

But that still wouldn't change the fact that I would always love my daughter. That's another inviolate law of nature.

When I told him this, Sam said, "Then Emily is lucky. That's something I can't count on. That's why I said my parents *might* still love me. The thing is, I don't know. You probably think I'm exaggerating, but I'm not. I have a cousin who's an alcoholic. The family got him into rehab a number of times, but he could never shake it. Five years ago, he killed a couple kids in a DWI. When he got out of prison, he was ostracized by the family. Emily is a lucky girl and not only because you're her father. She's damned lucky she wasn't born a Baldwin."

And with that pronouncement, he turned and continued down the hallway.

Entering the lobby, we detected signs of life. Two older men in jogging clothes were talking to the woman at the reception desk. One of the men appraised us with a look that lasted a couple beats too long. Ignoring him, I glanced out the glass doors and saw Simon, Amanda, and Enrique waiting beside the limo.

I said to Sam, "I could go with you, if you like."

His face softened even as he shook off the offer. "Thanks, Marty, but I've got to do this alone."

"It's a long drive. You might need company."

We'd arrived at the doors and as Sam opened one, he said, "How about I call you when I get back? We could get together for a beer."

"Sure. Whatever."

Stepping into the brightness of the morning sun, we both knew he wasn't going to call anytime soon. But he would eventually. I'd made the offer and he realized I'd be there for him, when he needed me.

I suppose that's the reason Sam became emotional when we shook hands at his car. Despite our recent difficulties, we managed to mend our friendship before it was irretrievably broken. In the scheme of things, that might not seem like a big deal, but it was to us. For a four-year period, we'd been the closest persons in each other's lives. You don't sever a connection like that without a fight.

And we were fighting hard.

As he drove away, Sam kept waving until he disappeared behind the trees. When I was sure he couldn't see me any longer, I lowered my hand. To be honest, I was relieved I didn't have to accompany him on the drive. I was dead on my feet. I just wanted to go home, have a heart-to-heart with my daughter about her escapade last night and go to bed. That was my game plan when I went over to the limo. Just go home and get some sleep.

I never counted on Simon.

"We're going to Blacksburg *now?*" I said.

This was the announcement Amanda had blindsided me with, the moment I'd strolled up. She was scowling as she said it. She had no desire to make this trip and I damn sure didn't either. She jerked a thumb at Simon. "Talk to him. It's not my idea."

It dawned on me why Simon wanted to do this. But I thought he was crazy to think we could pull it off. I said to him, "You can't just walk up and throw the cuffs on Mrs. Harris. You're going to have to present your evidence to the DA. Have him lay out a case and obtain a warrant. Without one, you'll never get past the Secret Service. Even then, you're probably going to need their approval—"

"*Time*, Martin," he said. "That will take time."

"So what? The DA has enough evidence to indict. So it takes a month or two or three? What's the hurry?"

His smooth face contemplated me. "Think about it, Martin. Think about what happens if we wait."

I frowned, my eyes going to Amanda and Enrique. Both had blank expressions. Neither had a clue what Simon was intimating. I said to him, "What? You worried about Colonel Kelly sitting in jail? You know the DA will order his release once he sees the evidence—"

And then I saw the problem. Enrique and Amanda began nodding; they'd figured it too. "Oh, shit," I said. "The primaries."

"Yes," Simon said. "Within weeks, Congressman Harris will have enough votes to win his party's nomination. If we wait, the entire process will be in turmoil. It's better to do this now. Get it out in the open."

Amanda gave me a knowing look. It wasn't necessary. My tired brain was still working well enough for me to grasp the significance of what Simon had just said.

"Hell," I said to him, "you're not planning to arrest Mrs. Harris, are you?"

He shrugged. "If the opportunity presents itself—"

"You're going there because of the press. You're going to make an announcement, publicly accuse Teresa Harris of murder. Once that happens, it doesn't matter how long a formal murder charge takes. The Harrises' poll numbers will plummet. In a week, they won't even be able to get elected dogcatcher."

Simon was silent, looking at me. We noticed a hint of a smile.

"Your reporter friend," Amanda said, following up with a possibility I hadn't considered. "He going to be there? You going to maybe give him the tape with Harris and Talbot?"

Simon's smile disappeared. He signaled the discussion was over by opening the right limo passenger door. "Mrs. Harris's speech is at eleven. I don't want to be late."

That was close enough to a yes. We also understood that Simon's actions had little to do with his professed desire to prevent chaos in the upcoming election. What really motivated him was a much more human instinct. He hated Teresa Harris and wanted to destroy her.

Couldn't fault him for that.

As Amanda and I settled into the back of the limo, Simon watched me take out my cell phone. He asked me if I intended to call General Hinkle.

"Yeah. Let him know that we cracked the case."

"Call him later."

"Why?"

"It could cause problems. It's better if you wait."

"What kind of problems?"

Simon wouldn't say anything more.

" 'Night, Marty."

Amanda smiled sleepily. She and I were lying across from each other on the seats alongside the limo. The drive to Blacksburg would take four hours and unlike our trip to the club, we had no illusions about remaining awake.

I smiled back. "Night."

She closed her eyes and within seconds, I heard a steady breathing. My eyes went to her big engagement ring and I shook my head.

"You'll never know unless you ask," Simon said softly.

Looking to the rear, I saw him watching me. "What if she says no?"

"Then you will know."

I nodded and closed my eyes. We were several miles from the compound, winding though the countryside. As I waited for sleep, my thoughts turned from Amanda to my daughter. I reminded myself to call her later. I also thought about Sam and the torment he was going through. If he didn't contact me in a few days, I would phone him. Despite his bleak assessment of his family's reaction, I was convinced they would accept him eventually. Until they did, he would need someone to confide in and by default, that responsibility fell to me.

As I drifted off, a question floated up to me. If Simon had intended to go to Blacksburg, why hadn't he mentioned it sooner, so I could have ridden over with Sam?

The limo accelerated as it merged onto the highway. From somewhere in the darkness, I heard a voice call to me. I was irritated. I wanted to sleep.

A hand shook me. "Marty, wake up. Marty . . ."

"Go away. Leave me alone."

More shaking. Insistent. "We're almost there, Marty."

I opened my eyes, wincing at the bright sunlight. Amanda was leaning over me. I sat up and saw a sign affixed to a stone wall.

WELCOME TO VIRGINIA POLYTECHNIC INSTITUTE AND STATE UNIVERSITY it said.

★49★

There can't be many universities larger than Virginia Tech. Set on twenty-six hundred sprawling acres, the school included something like a hundred buildings, a sixty-five-thousand-seat football stadium, and its own airport. We were cruising along South Main, toward the academic center of the campus. About a half mile ahead, I could make out the green of the mall and the quadrangle of buildings that housed the corp of cadets—my home for four years.

"When did you graduate?" Amanda asked.

She and I were wiping our faces with Perrier-moistened napkins. A waste of designer water, but it wasn't like we had a choice unless we wanted to go alcoholic. Other than Perrier, the limo's fridge was stocked with beer and wine.

"Geez, you're that old, huh?" Amanda said, when I told her.

As if she didn't know.

Enrique asked, "Anybody know where we're going?"

Simon was on the phone, checking with someone. I said, "Probably Burruss Hall. When you come up to the mall, make a left and head toward the drill field." Burruss was the central administration building and had a large auditorium, where most of the speakers made their presentations.

"It's Burruss," Simon announced, cupping the mouthpiece. "How long until we arrive?"

"Five minutes," I said.

He relayed the information into the phone and punched off.

"Was that Agent Hassall?" Amanda asked him. She was reapplying her makeup. This was a first. In the past, I'd never known her to *carry* makeup, much less use it.

"I spoke to Hassall earlier," Simon replied.

She looked at him.

"When you were asleep," he added.

Not the answer she wanted, so she kept staring at him.

He sighed. "I was speaking to a friend of mine."

"He got a name?"

He avoided answering her by looking out the window.

Of course Amanda and I realized the person on the phone had to be the reporter, Eric Olson. Simon didn't want to reveal his name because of the reason I'd alluded to earlier. Since leaking information to a reporter broke about a hundred department regulations and was borderline illegal, he was protecting us and himself. What we didn't know, we couldn't testify to.

The flap for the trash was tucked under a seat. After shoving the napkin through it, I checked my watch. A shade past eleven. Mrs. Harris would be starting her speech. "The next left," I told Enrique.

We cruised past the mall. A smattering of students were lounging on the grass, studying or bagging rays. Rolling under the war memorial archway, we continued right around the parade field loop. Most of the buildings were formidable, turn-of-century structures constructed of Hokie stone, mined from nearby quarries. I pointed Enrique to a massive brownish gray building, fronted by two flagpoles and a circular drive. "That's Burruss."

"No kidding."

Reporters were by the building's entrance. About a hundred yards ahead, we saw the telltale fleet of press vehicles.

"What are the reporters doing outside?" Amanda asked. "Congressman Harris said yesterday he wanted the speech to be covered."

"The murder," I said. "He probably reconsidered and doesn't want to deal with questions about the murder."

Enrique pulled in front of Burruss Hall. The moment we stopped, the press descended the stairs and surrounded us. This rock-star treatment was getting old.

"Wait, Martin."

I'd been about to open a door. Glancing back, I saw Simon reach into a compartment and remove a videotape.

Amanda said, "Is that smart? Giving Olson your only copy?"

"It can be reproduced within minutes." Simon was referring to the highspeed dubbing machines that were standard equipment in television vans.

Nodding to the reporters, I said, "Not going to be easy to slip Olson the tape with them hanging around."

Simon shrugged, unconcerned. After he wedged the tape in his waistband, he covered it with his jacket, then stepped outside. Immediately, he was bombarded with questions. Amanda and I followed Simon out the same door and we forced our way through the crowd and up the stairs toward the building entrance. As we walked, I looked for Olson, didn't see him.

As we approached the double doors, one opened and a

large black man in a suit appeared, ordering the reporters back. To us, he said, "Lieutenant Santos?"

At Simon's nod, the man stepped aside to let us inside.

We were in the large foyer with two curved marble staircases rising to the second floor. The man had a spy-guy earpiece—Secret Service. A second agent stood at a table with two metal-detecting wands.

"IDs?" the black agent said.

After studying each one, he handed them back. Since we were members of the law enforcement brotherhood, we didn't get the wand treatment.

"Follow me," the agent ordered.

He was the strong, silent type, with an emphasis on silent. He never said a word as he led us up one of the staircases. I casually mentioned I'd heard there was a problem with Mrs. Harris's security yesterday. The agent looked at me and kept on walking.

"In fact," I said, "I heard they lost her for four or five hours."

This time he didn't even bother with a look.

We reached the second floor. Before us was a lounge area and beyond, the doors of the auditorium. They should have been closed, but instead most stood open and we could see that the house lights were on. The place appeared to be packed and we could hear a buzz emanating from the audience, as they conversed among themselves.

Amanda and I checked our watches. Simon, I noticed, didn't. Amanda said to the agent, "Wasn't Mrs. Harris supposed to speak at eleven?"

"Yes."

His only response. He made a sharp left toward a hallway, which I knew led to a series of administration offices and eventually descended to an access for the stage.

Simon said, "I need to freshen up."

I said, "You should have tried some Perrier."

He appeared less than amused. I told him the restrooms were just ahead. I added, "I've got to go too."

He froze me with a look. It took me a second to understand what the problem was. When we came to the restrooms, Simon and Amanda disappeared through their respective doors, while I remained in the hallway with the agent.

Noticing his frown, I said, "Bladder's bigger than I thought."

No reaction. Apparently, Simon wasn't the only one without a sense of humor.

As the agent and I watched the walls, I wondered how Olson had managed to get in the building. It had to be that certain reporters had been allowed to cover the speech. The ones who promised to behave.

Amanda alighted from her restroom first, followed by Simon a few seconds later. I cocked an eyebrow at him. He ignored it and the question that came with it.

As he went past me, I brushed against him. That generated a glower from Simon; he knew why I'd done it. I didn't care. He'd forced my hand and I wanted to know whether he still had the tape.

He didn't.

The hallway seemed to go on forever. In actuality, it's something like seventy meters and change. I only knew this because, as a freshman cadet, I was required to measure *all* the hallways in Burruss. One of those hazing pranks that seemed senseless then, but looking back, I realized it had been crucial in my development as a military officer.

Uh-huh.

We continued past more offices. Since it was the week-end, they were unoccupied. As we walked, I lagged behind, firing glances toward the restroom. After a dozen steps, I saw a man emerge. It wasn't Olson or anyone I'd ever seen be-fore. The man was pushing forty, small and bookish, and wore black-framed glasses that seemed too large for his head.

He also carried a briefcase.

When he noticed me looking, he quickly walked away in the opposite direction.

What are you up to, Simon?

Prior to reaching the stairs that descended toward the stage entrance, the agent turned into a spacious office with an el-egant reception area. Two tense-faced twenty-somethings were pacing circles in the carpet, talking into cell phones. Several others sat at desks, clicking frantically on laptops. No one looked more than thirty. Campaign staffers out to change the world.

"In there," the agent said, pointing us to a door marked "Conference Room."

As our escort departed, we headed for the door. From within, we could hear the loud voices of an argument. A man was saying he thought the speech should be canceled. Someone—a woman—interrupted him. It sounded like Teresa Harris and she was clearly furious.

"I *spoke* to General Murdock," she said. "He's under a lot of pressure. Half the members of Congress and the presi-dent have called him to reconsider. The VFW has launched a letter-writing campaign against him. We wait and we can kiss his endorsement good-bye. Rollie, what are we running against conservatives?"

"Under thirty percent according to the latest Gallup,"

Roland Slater said. "And conservatives vote. They go to the polls. If we can't raise our unfavorables by at least three points, we could still lose the general election."

"That settles it," Teresa Harris said. "I'm giving the speech."

"Honey," a third man, who was obviously Congressman Harris, said. "Agent Hassall is right to be cautious. We shouldn't compromise security because—"

"Garrison, let me worry about that. I'm making the speech, not you."

"Mrs. Harris," Hassall said. "A door was breached. There's no telling who might—"

"I don't give a damn. *I want General Murdock's fucking endorsement.*"

We waited a few seconds. There was only silence.

Simon knocked.

Filing inside, we saw six people standing around a conference table. Four we'd previously identified: Teresa Harris, Congressman Harris, Slater, and Agent Hassall. The fifth person was Hassall's sidekick from last night, Agent Coleman, and the sixth, another guy with an earpiece. No one looked happy, but I knew that wasn't our fault.

Yet.

Teresa Harris dismissed us with a cryptic glance and returned her attention to Hassall. "I'm going on stage now. I'll shorten my speech. Once General Murdock gives us the endorsement, we'll leave. That's the best I can do. If you can't protect me for twenty minutes from some imagined threat—" Her face went glacial when Hassall started to speak. "Not a word. You *told* me those doors are often breached by students as a prank. You *said* it happens dozens of times each year. Is that true or not?"

I realized what doors she was referring to. And Teresa Harris was right. They were broken into all the time.

Hassall said, "According to Dr. Peters, that's true, but—"

"Peters should damn well know. He's the president of the university, for Christ's sake. Now get out of here, Hassall. You're giving me a headache."

Hassall's face reddened. He looked to Congressman Harris, seeking support. For a moment, it seemed as if Harris was on the verge of doing so. But when he saw his wife glaring at him, the man who would be president reconsidered and remained silent.

Congressman Harris's reaction was telling. Yesterday, when I'd met the two of them, I'd assumed he was the one who called the shots in their relationship. Now I realized it was the other way around.

Teresa Harris said to Hassall, "I told you to *leave*."

Without a word, the emasculated agent turned away from her and departed the room.

"You too, gentlemen," Teresa said. "Wait outside. Go."

Coleman and the third agent followed their supervisor out.

Addressing her husband, Teresa said, "I want Hassall replaced."

"Let's not be hasty. He's only doing his—"

"*Tomorrow*, Garrison. He's disrespectful and incompetent. I won't put up with him. I simply won't."

Congressman Harris sighed, nodding.

Watching Teresa Harris, I found it inconceivable that she was the same person who had been so distraught over viewing her nephew's body. Everything about her manner, from the tilt of her beautiful head to the arrogant set of her perfectly formed jaw, projected a sense of innate superiority and open disdain. Up to this moment, I still had difficulty believing that she'd carried out the murders with her own hands, but now there was no doubt. This was a ruthless calculating woman, who was capable of anything.

A total bitch.

Her eyes went to a television mounted on a wall. It was on a closed circuit and showed the center of the stage. Angled behind an empty podium, we saw a single row of chairs. Perhaps a dozen. Some were occupied—I recognized the university president and the dean—but most weren't. Teresa asked Slater how long it would take to get everyone to return.

"I told them to remain nearby until we made a decision."

"All right. Let's do it. Coming, Garrison?"

"In a minute."

As Teresa Harris and Slater walked past us to the door, she said, "Where the hell is Abigail? Those stage lights can be brutal. I'll need my makeup retouched."

"She went to find somewhere quiet to make calls," Slater said. "I'll have Donna run her down. Have you decided what to cut from the speech?"

"Social Security and universal health care—"

"Perfect. These kids don't care about medical coverage. They think they'll live forever. Go after the president's economic policies hard. Particulary the rising unemployment. That's the one thing these kids understand. Jobs. A lot of them will be graduating and if we frighten them . . ."

"I know what I'm doing, Rollie."

"Hey, hey. Relax. I'm only *reminding* you. . . ."

They continued into the outer office. Amanda was frowning, as I was. We wondered why Simon hadn't said anything. We watched Slater and Teresa Harris disappear into the hallway, Agent Coleman in tow.

Still, Simon said nothing. He seemed content to stand quietly, looking at Congressman Harris.

"I understand," Harris said to him, "that you're here to brief me on the case against Colonel Kelly."

"Yes, Mr. Congressman."

"By the way, nice work, Lieutenant. I knew he was responsible. Sorry, I had to pull strings, but it all came out in the end. No hard feelings, huh?"

"None, Mr. Congressman."

Simon was smiling. It was a pleasant smile and seemed distinctly out of place. I saw Amanda stiffen slightly. Like me, she sensed this meant Simon was getting ready to drop the bomb.

I folded my arms and prepared for the explosion.

Except the explosion never materialized. Rather than going nuclear, Simon tossed out what amounted to little more than a stun grenade. He said, "Tell me about the club, Mr. Congressman."

"Club?" Harris frowned. "What club?"

"The one northwest of Manassas. It's in the country about thirty miles away. You don't know of it?"

"Should I?"

"It's where the videotapes were made, sir."

"Videotapes? The ones Franklin had?"

"Don't you know, sir?"

"No, I don't." Harris was getting irritated. He seemed to have no idea what Simon was talking about. "What the hell is this, Lieutenant? I thought you were here to *brief* me on the evidence against Colonel Kelly."

"I'm getting to that, sir."

A woman stuck her head in the door. "Congressman, we

need to leave now if you want to be on stage before the introductions."

"Christ." To Simon, he said, "Well, you better do it damn quick, Lieutenant. I'm a busy man. When I return, I expect answers, not questions. You understand me?"

"I understand, sir."

"Let's go Tanya." Harris hurried from the room, gathering several aides as he went. The Secret Service agent I hadn't recognized followed the group, talking on a radio.

Amanda murmured, "He really didn't know, did he?"

"No," Simon said.

This was why he'd danced around the club and the videotapes: to judge Harris's reaction and determine whether Sam's assessment of his innocence was correct. From what we saw, it was. I wondered why Simon wanted to clear this up now. It didn't really prove anything. Harris's guilt or innocence would come out later, once a more comprehensive investigation was completed.

Before I could ask Simon about this, he said, "Excuse me for a moment."

"Where are you going?" Amanda asked.

Simon slipped out of the conference room. He looked suddenly anxious about something. Pausing in the outer office, he took out his cell phone and contemplated it. Shaking his head, he returned it to his jacket, stepped over to a desk, snatched up a receiver.

Amanda said, "What was that all about? He didn't want to use his own phone."

"I wish I knew."

Reacting to something in my voice, she said, "Spill it. What's bugging you?"

After I told her about the man I saw leaving the restroom, she said, "Maybe it was a television reporter Simon gave the tape to. When you think about it, that makes more sense anyway."

"The guy didn't strike me as a reporter. He looked more like a businessman or an accountant. He had a briefcase."

"Sure. He needed the case to hide the tape. Besides, who else could he be, if he wasn't a reporter?"

Which was precisely the problem. He couldn't be anyone but a reporter.

Could he?

Simon was still talking on the phone. Glancing at the television, I saw various dignitaries beginning to take their seats on the stage. General Murdock was sitting on the very end, opposite the podium. A burly man with red hair appeared and eased down beside him.

I realized I recognized him. It was Senator Tobias Hansen. Like General Murdock, he'd also been blackmailed by Slater. Hansen's presence here puzzled me because he was the conservative senator who had previously endorsed Congressman Harris. Was he here to ratchet up the pressure on General Murdock, ensure he went through with his—

Another man appeared. He strode rapidly across the stage toward Senator Hansen. He leaned over and spoke to him. Only I was mistaken. He was speaking to *both* men.

Senator Hansen *and* General Murdock.

My mind kicked into overdrive. I tried to decipher what I was seeing, but couldn't even come close. One thing I did know for certain was that Amanda was wrong. This man sure as hell wasn't—

"Marty . . ."

Amanda was reading my face. She sighed. "What's the problem now?"

"Simon."

"Simon?"

"Something doesn't smell right. Take a look at the man who is—" I stopped. Simon was reentering the office. His expression was relaxed, his earlier anxiety gone.

"Who is the man with the glasses?" I asked him.

His face went blank. "Man with glasses?"

I pointed to the television. "The guy talking to Senator Hansen and General Murdock." As I said this, the man with the glasses turned and hurried from the stage.

Simon said, "I don't know. I've never seen him—"

"You passed him the tape in the restroom."

Amanda said, *"That's* the guy?"

Simon went still, staring at me. Most people who get caught in a lie go on the defensive. Not Simon. His face darkened and he became angry. He snapped, "This doesn't concern you, Martin."

"The hell it doesn't. Something's going on here. Something between you and Senator Hansen and General Murdock—"

"Forget about this. It's for your own good."

There was an ominous quality in his voice. Amanda picked up on it too. "My God, Simon. What have you done? What *is* going on?"

A long silence. I would have bet a month's pay he would never answer her, but he surprised me.

"I did what was necessary," he said.

The blood drained from Amanda's face. She knew Simon and knew the significance of these words. *I did what was necessary.*

An instant later, we heard what sounded like a scream.

★50★

The scream was faint, muffled. It sounded as if it came from a room some distance away. The scream was followed by sounds of hysterical crying. We looked out the door into the main office. The remaining aides were rising to their feet, their faces quizzical. Then we saw expressions of growing alarm as they hurried into the hallway. Amanda ran after them, with me on her heels. Racing out the door, I looked back at Simon.

He was walking.

I swore. It was starting.

Amanda and I sprinted down the hall. We were running away from the stage, toward the entrance to the auditorium. We could still hear the crying. Ahead, I saw the aides duck into an office. One that should have been empty.

That's when I knew who it was. Who it had to be.

She went to find someplace quiet to make calls.

As we ran, I kept looking for Secret Service, but didn't see any. Harris wasn't the president yet and would have a reduced security complement. Not more than eight or ten agents. And they would be manning the building's entrances, or on the stage or inside the auditorium.

They wouldn't be here.

Amanda and I darted inside the office. The cries abruptly quieted. We found ourselves in another large reception area, private offices toward the back. In the far corner, we saw an open door, the aides we'd been following cluttered around it. They parted to reveal a young man clutching a sobbing woman.

"Get back," Amanda ordered, running up. "Police."

The aides drifted aside. All wore expressions of horror. The man and the woman walked past us. She was young, no more than twenty-one or -two. Amanda and I went into the office and saw the victim immediately.

It was Abigail Gillette.

The big, muscular woman was lying on the floor in front of the desk, her chest matted with blood from several deep stab wounds. It only took a glance to see she was dead. Looking at her, I felt a complete absence of emotion. No regret, no sympathy, no pity.

Nothing.

Amanda rose after checking her carotid artery. "Still warm. Couldn't have happened long ago."

I nodded.

She looked to me. "What do we do?"

She was asking whether we should follow Simon's advice, let this play out. For a moment, I was tempted to say yes. Just say yes and do nothing. It was more than because I felt Abigail Gillette deserved to die. Much more.

I knew who was responsible for her death.

When I revealed his name to Amanda, she said, "That's impossible. He wouldn't have time. We just got here ourselves."

"It's him. It has to be him because of the door. The one that was breached. Only he would know."

"Huh?"

When I explained, I saw her nod her acceptance. "Coller," she said. "He's the one who killed Coller."

"Yes."

"Simon lied to us. He knew all along."

"Yes."

She shook her head. "But the rest of it. It's crazy. You really think there's a chance he will—"

"He broke the door for a reason."

Her eyes held mine. "So what are you going to do?" she asked again.

I was still conflicted. I wasn't aware I'd responded until I heard myself say the words.

"We're police officers," I said quietly.

Reluctance and disappointment registered on her face. Not the answer she'd been hoping for.

But as I hurried from the room, she was right behind me.

Simon was entering the outer office as we ran up. He said, "Abigail Gillette?"

I looked right at him. "Like you didn't fucking know."

His jaw knotted. Grabbing me hard by the elbow, he leaned close and whispered harshly. "You're being foolish. Your interference will only cause trouble. It's all arranged."

"What's all arranged?"

"I'm not at liberty to say. It's not my decision."

"*Not your decision?* Whose the hell is it?"

He said nothing.

"God*dammit*, Simon—"

"People of influence. Do not interfere."

"You talking about Senator Hansen, right? Who else? General Murdock?"

Another silence. I saw his frustration. This was a reflection of our divergent moral outlooks. He believed the end justified the means; I didn't.

He abruptly stepped away from me and said stiffly, "I'll notify the Secret Service."

He went down the hallway, toward the stage. Still walking.

It was the long way. At Simon's pace, it would take him over a minute to raise the alarm, which was his intention. That suggested that whatever was about to happen was going to happen soon.

"This way is quicker," I said to Amanda. "There will be Secret Service guarding the auditorium entrance."

I broke into a jog. After about five yards, I realized I was alone. Turning, I saw Amanda standing in the middle of the hall, shaking her head.

"Damn you," she said. "*Damn* you."

She began to run after me.

I sprinted up to the auditorium. The doors were closed, indicating the presentation had started. As I gripped a handle, I heard Amanda's footsteps behind me. I yanked open a door and we ducked inside, pausing to let our eyes adjust to the darkness.

On stage, Dr. Peters, the university president, was at the podium, introducing Mrs. Harris. She remained off to his side, taking in his glowing words with apparent modesty. On the chairs behind the podium, we saw her husband sitting in the center, Slater in his customary position to Harris's right.

"There," Amanda whispered.

She gestured to the left. An agent was standing on the other side of the projection booth. It was Coleman. I gave him an urgent wave. He disappeared behind the booth, making his way toward us. Two more agents stood alongside the right wall of the auditorium—one about midway, one near the bottom—monitoring the audience.

"And now without further ado," Dr. Peters said, "I'd like to introduce the next first lady of the United States of America, Teresa Harris."

The auditorium erupted in enthusiastic applause. Teresa Harris stepped up to the podium. Behind me, a voice whispered, "What's the problem?"

People seated nearby watched us curiously. Their faces were all young. Taking Coleman by an arm, I drew him back a few steps. "Something's going to happen, but I don't know what. We just found Abigail Gillette—"

"What the hell?"

This came from Amanda. At the same instant, a rumble of surprise rose from the audience. A man in the back row said loudly, "My God, is that who I think it is?"

Then a woman squealed: "It's *her*. It's really her."

Turning, I saw Teresa Harris standing at the podium, beginning her speech. Behind her, images danced across the curtains at the rear of the stage. Because of the creases in the curtains, the images had a wavy, almost ghostly quality. It could have been a movie that had been inadvertently started, but we realized it wasn't.

Someone was playing the video of Teresa Harris and Abigail Gillette having sex with Major Talbot.

Teresa Harris continued her speech, oblivious to what was going on behind her. Finally, she heard the gasps and titters and broke off, frowning. Hundreds of hands rose up, pointing.

"Oh, *fuck*—"

Coleman rushed past me and tried to open the door to the projection booth. He began to pound on it. "Terry, what's going on in there? Terry, open up. Dammit—"

At that instant, it happened. Like everyone else, I'd been watching Teresa Harris, waiting to see her reaction to the video. She was slowly pivoting, eyes crawling up the curtains. That's when I noticed a sudden movement over to her right. On one of the chairs where the dignitaries were sitting.

Shifting my gaze, I saw Slater buck violently and clutch at his chest. He had a confused expression.

Then he slowly toppled forward, his hands falling away, and we saw the blood.

★ 51 ★

The silence was deafening. Everyone was confused, unable to comprehend what they were seeing. Then one of the dignitaries jumped from his chair and shouted, "My God, he's been shot." Pandemonium immediately followed. People rose from their seats, shouting and screaming. Those seated in the rear clawed over one another and raced toward the exits. They were upon us within seconds. Amanda and I pushed our way through the panicked mass, fighting to keep our eyes fixated on the stage.

We saw agents rush out from the wings toward Teresa Harris and her husband. In her case, they were too late. The next bullet struck Teresa in the head, tearing away a part of her scalp. A third shot struck her in the shoulder, spinning her as she fell. We saw the blood and gore, but heard no gunfire. It was like watching a movie with the sound turned off. I turned to the projection booth. Through the little window in the front, I glimpsed a rifle barrel.

It disappeared.

A hand struck me in the chest and I winced. Someone began pulling on me from behind. Amanda shouted, "This way or we'll get trampled."

I followed her lead and we moved back, crouching

against the front of the booth. Peeking around the corner, I saw that Coleman was no longer knocking on the door. Instead he was pressed against it, trying to avoid people who were running by. On stage, agents shielded Congressman Harris with their bodies, dragging him to safety. As I watched this frantic scene play out, I finally understood Simon's questions to Congressman Harris and his subsequent phone call—the one he'd been hesitant to make on his cellular.

Simon would have wanted to be certain there was no mistake as to the congressman's guilt. He would also have wanted to ensure the call would not be traced to his phone.

"Look, Marty," Amanda said.

She pointed to the left edge of the stage. At two men who were staring at the body of Teresa Harris. There was no panic or fear on their faces . . . and certainly nothing approaching remorse.

Moments later, General Murdock and Senator Hansen disappeared into the wings.

Amanda said, "You called it . . ."

I nodded.

"Wonder who else was involved?"

I passed on a response; she was musing aloud. We continued to stare down at the two bodies, lying still on the stage.

Amanda said, "I wish I could say I felt badly about this . . ."

"I don't."

Her eyes widened in surprise.

"I don't," I repeated.

It wasn't a lie. Once again, I hadn't seen the complete picture. If I had, I would have realized there was no other logical way for this to have ended. He couldn't have handled testifying and a trial. He certainly couldn't have tolerated the shame of going to prison. In his mind, this was the only option.

The crowd was beginning to thin, most of the people having escaped. The two agents I'd noticed earlier were working their way up behind it, coming toward the booth. More fanned out behind them. It wouldn't be long now and I wanted a chance to say good-bye.

"I'm going to try and get into the booth," I said to Amanda, rising from my crouch.

She looked at me and I saw a glimmer of understanding. "You could be too late. We wouldn't have heard the shot."

I spoke into the opening of the booth, which was just above my head. "It's Marty. I'm coming in."

There was no response.

I went around to the side door anyway.

"What the *fuck* are you doing?"

Coleman slapped my hand away as I reached for the door knob. His mouth was bleeding, his eyes a little wild. He had his pistol out and was waving it in my direction.

"I'm going inside."

"The hell you are. We got an agent in there. He could be hurt or worse. Not to mention at least one more hostage. Either the projectionist or—"

I tried the nob and was surprised when it turned.

"Goddammit," Coleman roared. "I'm warning you. Step away or—"

The door to the booth suddenly opened and an elderly man with fearful eyes tentatively emerged. He stopped after a single step and looked at Coleman and me. In a wavering voice, he asked, "One of you Collins?"

"I am."

"He'll let you in. No one else, or the agent dies."

I glanced at Coleman.

He hesitated. "Fine. Be my guest. It's your funeral."

I motioned the old man forward, then slipped by him and closed the door behind me.

"Hello, Marty," a voice said.

"Hello, Sam."

★ 52 ★

The booth was cramped, not much larger than a prison cell. Sam was sitting on the floor, across from the door, looking up at me. He wore his class A military uniform, his stars glittering on his shoulders, a dizzying array of medals on his chest. In his big hands, he held a civilian version of the M-16, affixed with a silencer. I tried to recall if I'd ever seen it in his collection, but couldn't remember. He had so many guns.

He gave me a tired smile, shifting the barrel from the door. "So you figured it, huh?"

"It couldn't be anyone else."

"No lectures, Marty. It was meant to end like this. Call it fate. Call it anything you want. They were coming here. The one place where I could pull this thing off. Besides, once I killed that double-crossing son of a bitch Coller, I was committed. There was no going back. Sorry about the ear. That was one tough shot."

"You could have killed me."

He grinned. "Have a little faith. I wouldn't have fired if I thought I'd miss."

"Uh-huh. Mind telling me why you were driving Talbot's M5?"

His grin faded into a somber line. "It was a gift. Franklin bought it for me. I told him I couldn't accept it, but he insisted I drive it for a few days." His expression turned wistful at some private memory. "Franklin was always doing that. Surprising me with gifts."

I didn't ask Sam what the car was doing in the Pentagon lot; the answer was obvious. Knowing the vehicle had been spotted by Officer Hannity, he'd ditched it there, figuring it wouldn't be noticed for at least a day.

And that's all Sam needed. A day.

My eyes fell on an unconscious man in a suit, lying face-down a few feet from Sam. His hands were bound with duct tape, an ugly wound visible on his scalp.

"I'm sorry about that," Sam said, "but it couldn't be helped."

"He needs medical attention."

"Take him when you leave."

There was a chilling finality to that statement. I wasn't ready to say good-bye quite yet and sensed Sam wasn't either. He'd allowed me in here for a reason and I waited for him to bring it up. When he didn't say anything, I asked him how he managed to gain access into the booth.

He shrugged. "The uniform. One of the perks of being a general is that no one questions you. I told one of the agents that the projectionist was an old friend, from when I was a student here. I said I just wanted to say hello. What I didn't figure on was that they'd have another agent inside."

"You smuggled the rifle through the steam tunnels?" This was what tipped me off that it must have been Sam who killed Abigail Gillette. Only someone who had gone to school here would be familiar with the labyrinth of steam tunnels that snaked below the campus.

"Yeah. Brought it in that." He indicated a large briefcase

sitting beside him. "A couple of hours ago. Right after I flew in."

This was how Sam had beat us here. He'd flown himself, landing at the airport on campus.

I said, "And Abigail Gillette?"

He looked surprised. "You know about her already?"

I told him we'd found her body.

"Got a little lucky with her," he said. "Call it a bonus. When I planned all this, she was the one person I never counted on getting. I didn't see how I could. She wouldn't be on stage like Teresa Harris and Slater. But once I had everything ready, I had a few minutes, so I went by the offices where the Harris people were setting up. Someone told me she'd stepped out to make some calls. They didn't know where. I walked around until I found her. After that . . ." His eyes went cold. "She got off easy. Died quick. They all did. Not like Franklin."

He stared into space, gone for a moment. Abruptly, he said, "Hell, you can't have everything. So what if they didn't suffer? They're dead and that's all that matters."

"What about General Murdock and Senator Hansen?" I asked. "What are their roles in this?"

Sam squinted. "What makes you think they're involved at all?"

I went over to the VCR machine and removed the tape. "A guy who works for Senator Hansen gave you this."

He was silent, measuring me. "Lieutenant Santos say that?"

"I got this on my own."

He appeared relieved, probably because Simon hadn't broken a confidence.

"The way I figure it," I said, "is that at least three people knew what you were going to do. I understand why Senator

Hansen and General Murdock signed on; they were being blackmailed by Slater. What I don't know was why you needed them. You could have pulled off the killings on your own. Why tell them?" I waited to see if Sam had a response. He didn't.

I went on, "Simon's involvement also confuses me. How did he get wind of what you intended? Was it in your phone conversation with him? It must have been. After he confronted you with the fact that you'd killed Coller, you must have said something which made him believe you were going to finish the job. Or maybe he guessed. Knowing Simon, he might have even asked you straight out if—"

"No," Sam said.

"No? Simon didn't ask—"

"No, I'm not going to tell you a damn thing. Quit playing cop, huh. It's over. Does it really matter who did what, Marty? Does it?"

I hesitated and shook my head. Holding up the video, I said, "At least clear this up. You could have taken this when you were at the club. The reason you didn't—"

"It had to look good. Couldn't have you and Major Gardner wondering why I'd needed the key piece of evidence against Teresa Harris. You might have put two and two together, tried to stop me." He paused, looking at me. "So? Would you have tried to stop me, Marty?"

I looked right back at him. "I did try, Sam."

He winked. "That's my boy. You always were too straight for your own good."

Outside the door, we could hear voices. Someone was saying this was a hostage situation and was asking for SWAT.

Sam's expression softened. "Looks like our time's almost up."

I nodded, not trusting myself to speak.

"Do me a favor, Marty. I wrote a couple letters. One to my son Ryan and one to my folks. Ryan's a strong kid; he'll get through this. I don't know about my folks. If you can, I'd like their letter delivered today. What I did will be all over the news soon. It's important that they understand why. It will be easier on them if they do."

"Sure," I managed over the lump in my throat. "Where are the letters?"

When he told me, I tried not to appear surprised. This transaction must have occurred when I went to get the tape recorder from the limo.

After I slipped the video into my waistband, Sam helped me drag the agent toward the door. The man moaned, a sign he was coming to.

Sam held out his hand and we shook. It was a lingering handshake, neither of us in any hurry to let go. When I released my grip, I had the fantasy of knocking the rifle from Sam's hand and overpowering him.

"Don't do anything stupid, Marty," Sam said, reading my body language. "You'll only delay the inevitable. I have to do this. He's scared. I can't leave him there alone."

I was confused by this comment. Then Sam explained what he meant. He spoke of how terrified Major Talbot was of being in Hell.

"I hope he's not there. But if he is, I've got to be with him. You understand what I'm saying, Marty. I'm not crazy. It's just something I have to do."

"I understand." And for the first time, I realized I truly did.

"Good-bye, Sam."

"Good-bye, Marty."

As I reached for the door, Sam was smiling. He appeared

completely relaxed, as if he didn't have a care in the world. It was an act. He was doing it for my benefit, to make it easier on me. In actuality, it made it even harder. If Talbot had been terrified of what awaited him in the afterlife, I knew Sam must be also.

"It's Agent Collins," I shouted. "I'm coming out."

I opened the door to find at least a half dozen guns pointed
at me. No one moved until I dragged the groaning agent
clear and the door closed behind me. Several people rushed
forward. Among the faces, I saw Coleman and Amanda, but
no Simon or Agent Hassall.

"He's alive," Coleman said. "Terry's alive."

"Let go, Collins," another agent said. "We've got him.
Where the fuck are the EMTs?"

"Outside," someone else replied. "I just talked to Hassall.
We're to keep everyone outside the building. Local cops too."

"No SWAT?" Coleman said. "Who's supposed to get that
pyscho general out of there? *Us?* Hell, he's got us out-
gunned. Whose bright-ass idea is that?"

"Relax, Barry. Someone's flying out to handle the extrac-
tion. Our job is to secure the scene until they arrive. Give
me a hand."

The agents moved away, carrying their injured comrade.
I turned to Amanda. "No local police?"

"It's going to be a federal show." She punctuated the
statement with a look that was more than suggestive.
"What's the status on General Baldwin?"

Several agents crowded around, waiting for my response.

Before I replied, I pictured how long it would take Sam to act. Not more than a minute or two. Once he gathered up his courage, he would place the rifle barrel beneath his chin and slowly squeeze the—

I flinched, looking at the projection booth. It was as if I'd heard the silent shot, though that was impossible.

"I think he's dead," I told Amanda.

"*Think?*" an agent asked.

"He was going to commit suicide."

"Great," he grunted. "Now all one of us has to do is stick our head in the window and hope to hell we don't catch a bullet . . ."

The emotion of the moment caught up to me and I'd turned away to wipe the wetness from my eyes. I never made it because I found myself confronted by the determined face of the black agent who'd escorted us into the building.

"Come with me," he ordered.

He was too big to argue with, so Amanda and I fell into step behind him. She whispered, "It's okay, Marty. He was your friend. It's nothing to be ashamed of."

I still waited until none of the agents was looking before I wiped my eyes.

Déjà vu.

Once again, the agent deposited us in the office we'd been in only fifteen minutes earlier. Pointing us to chairs across from the conference room, he said, "Someone will talk to you shortly."

Six whole words. He was practicing. I said, "Lieutenant Santos?"

True to form, he pulled his disappearing act and slipped out the door.

In contrast to the frenzied activity that had greeted us when we'd first arrived, the room was quiet, the campaign staff long since cleared out. Other than Amanda and me, the only other person present was a stern looking female agent, who was seated near the conference room. Occasionally, voices filtered out, the words too low to be decipherable.

Amanda said to the woman, "Is Lieutenant Santos in there?"

A nod.

"You know how much longer it will be?"

Head shake.

"Who is with him?"

A shrug.

Another dazzling conversationalist. I took out my cell phone.

"No calls," the agent said.

"Why?"

"I was told not to allow you to make calls."

"It's personal. It's to my daughter."

"No calls."

I stood, putting away my phone. "I need to use the restroom."

"You'll have to leave the phone," she said, extending her hand.

She was smarter than she looked. I sighed and handed her the phone.

Shortly after I returned from the restroom, Agent Hassall stepped from the conference room, scowling. Ignoring Amanda and me, he said to the female agent, "Pass the word we'll be moving out when the choppers arrive. Probably within the hour."

She produced a radio from beneath her coat. "Who's replacing us, Chief?"

"Edith, just make the damn call." Hassall left the office, walking quickly.

"Asshole," Edith mouthed, keying the radio.

"Interesting," Amanda murmured

The conference room door was open and we could see five people seated around the table. Senator Tobias Hansen sat at the head, facing us. To his right were General Murdock, Simon, and the man with the glasses, who had a laptop, a small printer, and a neat stack of papers arranged before him. The person Amanda and I were interested in was the person sitting to Hansen's left.

Congressman Harris appeared to age five years since we'd last seen him. His face was drawn and pale and he blinked constantly as if under great stress. Initially, I concluded he was suffering from the shock of seeing his wife brutally murdered in front of him, then realized he was staring at a folder on the table.

No one in the room was speaking. The other four men were fixated on Harris, as if anticipating a response. But Harris remained silent, looking at the folder.

Sitting back, he shook his head. "I'm sorry, gentlemen. I need time. This is too much to assimilate. I can't make a decision until—"

"Get the tape," Hansen ordered.

Simon left the conference room and came over to Amanda and me. By then, I was holding out the tape to him. As he took it, I asked him what was going on.

"A negotiation." He returned to the conference and closed the door.

"What?" Amanda asked, noticing my frown.

"I wonder how Simon knew I had the tape."

"Easy. He knew you went into the booth and assumed you'd get it."

I nodded slowly. "Unless maybe Sam called Simon after I left."

"You think a guy who's about to commit suicide would stop to make a phone call?"

Point taken; it was a stretch.

Under her breath, she said, "At least this explains why they're keeping out the local cops."

"Because of the coverup," I said.

This was an eventuality Amanda and I should have seen coming. By definition, a homicidal would-be first lady who specialized in kinky sex with her nephew and subsequently murdered him was a monumental scandal. Add in her dramatic assassination by a vengeful general officer, the homosexual and blackmail angles, the ties between the club and prominent government officials and celebrities, the attempt by Slater to corrupt the presidency—and you were talking about a scandal of historically epic proportions. One that would almost certainly shake the public's faith in the electoral process, destroy countless reputations, and damage America's credibility throughout the world. This latter consideration was by the far the most important. With the ongoing war on terrorism and the occupation of Iraq, the last thing America needed was to be likened to some Third World dictatorship.

A coverup?

Hell, it was a given. The more that could be swept under the rug, the better for all parties concerned. It occurred to me that this must be why Sam had revealed his plans to Senator Hansen and General Murdock. So they could be here to protect his interests when he was gone.

For the next forty minutes, Amanda and I sat, cooling our heels. For a tenth of that time, we had a whispered discussion, as I related my conversation with Sam. Afterward, we kicked back and played stare and silence with Edith.

And that woman could stare.

"You hear it?" Amanda said.

I nodded. The beat of approaching chopper rotor blades. There were at least two machines, perhaps more. They chattered toward the rear of the building and we heard the engines wind down.

"FBI Emergency Response?" Amanda asked.

"Be my guess."

Edith's radio squawked. Hassall told her to expect to leave in ten minutes. Seconds later, the conference room door opened and Simon exited, motioning Amanda and me to follow. Before he shut the door, we glimpsed our friend with the glasses, punching away at the laptop.

Simon led us to a corner of the room, out of earshot of the female agent. With a tight smile, he said, "It's finished. I'll have to remain for the press conference, but your presence won't be required. You can leave with Enrique and I'll arrange—"

"What *exactly* is finished?" Amanda asked.

"The press statement. Once a few details are resolved, it will be released. It will be somewhat sanitized, but that was unavoidable. To satisfy the parties, concessions had to be made."

The ubiquitous C word. Amanda jumped on it, saying, "Define 'concessions.'"

Simon hesitated. "I can tell you that some aspects will be . . . disappointing. Don't dwell upon them. It will only make you angry. The outcome is the best that can be achieved under the circumstances."

Amanda grimaced, realizing what he was really telling us. Somehow, the official version of the murders would tone down Teresa Harris's role. As I mulled this over, I decided I could live with a shading of the truth, as long as Sam got the same treatment.

But when I asked this question of Simon, his only response was to say that Sam got what he wanted.

I pressed, "So there will be no mention he was a homosexual?"

"Not directly, but it will certainly be implied."

"You said he got what he wanted."

"He did. He wanted a public acknowledgment that he and Major Talbot had great affection for each other."

"But that makes no—"

I broke off because I realized it *did* make sense. It made perfect sense. Sam had been tired of living a lie and wanted people to know.

Now they would.

I said to Simon, "I understand you have some letters . . ."

Walking Amanda and me to the door, Simon asked us to attend to a final loose end and we said we would. As we shook hands, he told us we'd both done our jobs well. He also apologized for not being more forthcoming over his arrangement with Sam.

"In some respects, Martin," he said, "you share some of the blame. If you'll recall, you told me you didn't want to know if I intended anything . . . untoward."

Simon was alibiing; he wouldn't have come clean, regardless of what I'd said. I let his comments go for the simple reason that I was glad I hadn't known. Sure, it was a cop-out, but the truth was it was a decision I'm not sure I could have made.

A spur of the moment judgment was one thing, but if I'd had the time to think everything through, would I have stopped Sam from killing Teresa Harris? I probably would have tried; it's the way I'm conditioned. But deep down, I realized it was a decision I might have regretted. No, I'm glad Simon never told me . . . unlike Amanda.

"Next time," she said to him, "how about keeping me in the loop?"

"It was an oversight. I intended to tell you, but there never was a good time." He said it as if he expected her to believe him.

"Uh-huh."

The conference door opened and the man with glasses peered out. "Lieutenant Santos, we're almost ready . . ."

"Coming." To us, Simon said, "The reporters are restricted to the front of the building, where the press conference will take place. I've told Enrique to meet you around back. It goes unsaid that the events which transpired can never be repeated. Amanda, give me your keys, I'll have your car delivered in the morning. It will save you a trip."

Amanda couldn't hand over her keys fast enough.

I said to Simon, "What about General Hinkle?"

"He'll be briefed."

"And Colonel Kelly?"

"We're in the process of arranging his release." He was smiling. "Relax, Martin. Your job is finished. Go home and get some rest."

After patting me on the back, he returned to the conference room. As the door closed, I saw Congressman Harris slumped in his chair, staring vacantly into space.

"I feel sorry for him," Amanda said. "He was almost the president."

"Almost."

As Amanda and I walked out into the hallway, she said, "Isn't the exit the other way, Marty?"

★54★

I had an obligation to Sam's parents. They had a right to know whether their son had completed his final act.

Approaching the auditorium, we saw armed men in black uniforms rush up the stairs. Two carried collapsible stretchers. They moved with military precision, communicating with hand gestures. Several raced past us, heading the way we'd come. One detached and came over to inspect our flip top IDs. We noticed his uniform was completely unmarked, no insignias of any kind.

The man returned our IDs. "You'll have to leave the building immediately."

"I need to confirm the status of the shooter," I said. "He's in the projection—"

"I'm sorry, you'll have to leave." His weapon inched up fractionally.

Amanda and I weren't crazy enough to argue. We smoothly about-faced and went down the stairs to the first floor. She said, "They might not be FBI."

I nodded.

"Delta Force?"

"They'd have some kind of insignia." I added, "My guess is they're a special unit of the FBI."

We continued down a hallway toward the rear exit, encountering more black-garbed Rambo types who again checked us out. Passing through the double doors onto a stone landing, we were greeted by the sight of three military Blackhawk helicopters parked on an expanse of lawn. In the distance, large crowds watched from behind a barricade of police vehicles. The sheer number of people made you stop and look; there were thousands. Closer in, the police had set up a second perimeter around the building.

"The Virginia Tech connection," Amanda said, surveying the scene. "Remember, when I mentioned it last night . . ."

"I remember." Uniformed officers on the sidewalk below motioned to us and we started down the steps.

Amanda said, "I know it's all a coincidence. You said General Baldwin called it fate. Whatever term you use, it's damned convenient, the way everything worked out."

"You going somewhere with this?"

"Take those helicopters. I don't understand how they got here so—"

"IDs?" a cop demanded, the moment we reached the bottom of the stairs.

He and his partner scrutinized our identification. They were expecting us, since one pointed to Simon's limo parked along the sidewalk. Enrique was leaning against the driver's door, waving.

Walking toward him, I said to Amanda, "The helicopters?"

"How'd they get here so fast? There's no base nearby. If they are FBI, that means they flew from Quantico. That's at least an hour flying time, not counting alert and mobilization. Yet they showed up in what, forty-five minutes? The only way that could happen is if they were already airborne—"

"Stop," I said.

She looked at me.

I said, "You don't want to go there. You know you don't."

"Marty, someone with real clout had to be in on this thing from the beginning. Someone above Senator Hansen. It might have even been someone in the White—"

"Don't say it. Don't even think it."

We walked without speaking for a few steps.

"You know," she said, "the government is capable of doing something like this. You're naive to believe they wouldn't."

So I was naive.

Dead man walking.

That was my conclusion when I saw Enrique. He looked completely wasted. He could barely stand upright and his eyes had more red lines than a AAA road map. Ignoring his protests, I told him to get in the back with Amanda and I would drive. It was a prudent move. Halfway through Amanda's account of the shooting, he began nodding off. Within minutes of her description of the climax, he was asleep.

Sam's parents lived on several acres twenty minutes southwest of Blacksburg. When I called to tell them I was coming by, Sam's mother sounded thrilled to hear from me.

"Why, it's been years, Marty. What's the occasion?"

I told her the truth; I had to drop off something from Sam.

My intent was to get to their place before the press conference began, so they could read the letter before they heard the dirt about Sam. Three miles after we left the campus, that goal went out the window.

"It's starting," Amanda said.

Checking the rearview mirror, I saw her watching the TV. She gave me a play-by-play, saying, "Simon and Senator Hansen are coming down the steps outside Buurrus Hall. I don't see Congressman Harris or General Murdock. Simon and Hansen are walking up to a podium. Hansen's introducing Simon. The senator is going to read the statement."

I heard the words faintly. "Mind turning up the volume?"

"Oh, sure."

In a somber baritone, Senator Hansen announced the deaths of Teresa Harris, the wife of presidential hopeful Garrison Harris; Roland Slater, her husband's campaign manager; Abigail Gillette, an aide to Mrs. Harris; and Major General Samuel Baldwin. He went on to say that Mrs. Harris and Mr. Slater were shot during a speech she was giving at Virginia Tech University, while Ms. Gillette was killed in a separate incident, the victim of a stabbing. After identifying Major General Samuel Baldwin as the shooter who subsequently committed suicide—I had my confirmation—Hansen expanded on Baldwin's motive for the murders. Citing new evidence unearthed by Lieutenant Santos, Senator Hansen stated that Mr. Slater and Ms. Gillette—and not Colonel Kelly who had been charged earlier—murdered Mrs. Harris's nephew, Major Franklin Talbot, and four other individuals in an attempt to prevent Major Talbot from revealing an affair that Mrs. Harris and Major Talbot were having.

At this bombshell, there was a flurry of questions from reporters.

In the limo, the reaction of Amanda and me was diametrically opposite. We were silent, too disgusted to speak.

Finally, I heard her say bitterly, "They're giving her a pass. She's a murderer and they're giving her a pass. I can't believe it."

Neither could I. Toning down Teresa Harris's role was one thing, but *this*—I felt angry enough to tell Amanda to turn off the television.

Instead, I kept listening.

When the questions died down, Senator Hansen explained that General Baldwin's motive for the killings was revenge. While Hansen never used the word homosexual, he might as well have. Characterizing the bond that existed between General Baldwin and Major Talbot as longstanding and extremely close, the senator concluded that a grief-stricken General Baldwin had acted to avenge the death of someone whom he cared for deeply.

"In his grief," Hansen said, "the general wasn't thinking clearly. While he correctly determined that Mr. Slater and Ms. Gillette were responsible for Major Talbot's death, he tragically mistook the role of Mrs. Harris. Based on Lieutenant Santos's investigation, I can state unequivocally that neither Mrs. Harris nor her husband had any involvement in the murder of their nephew. The blame for Major Talbot's death and the four others rests solely at the feet of Mr. Slater and Ms. Gillette. Many of you have heard of the videotape that was shown by General Baldwin prior to the shootings. There is no denying that Mrs. Harris was a flawed human being. Despite her faults, she was someone who loved this country and had dedicated herself to its service. If you must judge her, do it in totality of her life, weighing the good with the bad. I also ask you to remember Congressman Harris in your prayers. He is as much a victim as those innocents who perished. At some future date, the congressman will announce the status of his campaign. That's all I have, ladies and gentlemen. There will be no questions—"

Amanda turned down the volume, looking more resigned than angry. In the mirror, I saw her watching me.

She said, "Simon warned us. I guess we shouldn't be surprised."

"No . . ."

"And they kept the club out of it."

I nodded.

"Guess you can't have someone who was almost in the White House turn out to be a multiple murderer."

"Apparently not."

She kept looking at me. "You're still upset."

"Very."

"General Baldwin?"

"Damn right. People will think he killed Teresa Harris without cause. I can't believe Simon went along with it."

"What choice did he have? He was ordered to go along."

I eyed her in the mirror. "Simon had a choice. He let them use his name to justify the conclusions. He had a choice."

She was forming a response when her phone rang. Checking the caller ID, she said, "Speak of the devil . . ."

Into the mouthpiece: "Hello, Simon. Yes. We saw it. Oh, yeah. He's plenty pissed. Huh?" She squinted, listening. "Okay, I'll tell him."

Clicking off, she said to me, "He knows you're angry. He says he had to endorse the statement about Mrs. Harris because it was the only way to get something General Baldwin wanted. He said there was an unforseen problem in the initial arrangements and that someday you would understand."

I tapped the brakes. "Problem? What kind of problem?"

"That's all he would say. Is that the Baldwin house?"

I nodded and turned into the driveway of a large ranch-style home.

*

It had been less than ten minutes since the press conference ended. As I walked up to the front door, I held out hope that maybe Sam's parents hadn't heard yet.

But when no one answered the bell, I knew they had.

I kept fingering the buzzer. Finally, an attractive, silver-haired woman opened the door. She blinked at me through misting tears, dabbing her eyes with a tissue.

"Marty," Sam's mother said. "I . . . we . . . we can't really talk to—"

"I only came here to give you a letter from Sam." I held it out to her.

Her face went blank, as if she was confused by what I'd said. She gazed dully at the letter. "Sam?"

I nodded.

As she reached for it, a voice called out sharply, "No, Loretta. Don't take it."

Mrs. Baldwin jerked her hand away, startled. Looking past her, I saw a lean, graying figure standing in the middle of a carpeted living room. Except for the hair, General Samuel Baldwin III was a dead ringer for his son.

I said, "General, it was Sam's last wish. He wanted you to read it."

"We're not interested, Marty. Please take the letter and leave."

I stared at him in disbelief. "Sir, I'm only asking you to—"

"We have no son," the general said. "Not any more. Now leave us alone. Please."

He turned his back on me and ducked through a sliding door onto a covered porch. When he disappeared from view, I looked at Mrs. Baldwin. She was staring at the letter in my hand, tears rolling down her cheeks.

"I'm sorry, Marty."

She shut the door in my face.

★

I tried. I'd done what I could. I should respect their wishes and leave.

But as I stepped away, I felt myself getting angry. Sam was their son and he was dead. All his life, he had done what they wanted. What the entire family wanted. He'd been a good son, the perfect Baldwin. They owed him the courtesy of reading his letter.

They didn't have to understand what was in it.

They didn't have to accept his explanations or his motives.

They could even toss the letter in the trash, for all I cared.

As long as they read it first.

I returned to the door and rang the bell. There was no answer. I slowly walked around the side of the house, scanning the windows for movement. No one appeared. As I approached the screened-in porch, I saw the solitary figure of the general, seated in a high-backed chair. His body was angled away from me and I could tell he was staring out across the backyard.

I started to call out to him, when I noticed his head bend forward. He began rocking back and forth, saying Sam's name, softly at first, then gradually louder. His voice shook with pain and anguish, as he called out for his dead son. After a while, the general broke down and buried his face in his hands.

I stood there frozen, my eyes dropping to the letter in my hand. As I slowly backed away, I pocketed it, feeling ashamed.

Someday the general would read the letter . . . when he was ready.

★

On the way home, I had one more stop to make. It wasn't something I'd planned, but we were in the vicinity and it seemed a fitting way to attend to the loose end that Simon had mentioned.

After I parked the limo along the side of the road, Amanda and I went down a dirt embankment and stood for a while, gazing out across the dark blue waters of Clayter Lake. Toward the opposite shore where the campground was located, we saw a ski-boat full of young men, towing a skier.

Amanda asked, "How many times did you and General Baldwin come here?"

"Fifty, sixty." I shrugged.

"Been back since you graduated?"

It took me a few moments to realized I hadn't. "No."

The skier wiped out spectacularly. His buddies in the boat were pointing at him and laughing.

"Must have been fun," Amanda said.

I smiled at the memories. "It was."

Over to the right, we saw another ski-boat coming our way. "Better do it now," Amanda urged, "before they get too close."

Using both hands, she offered up the stack of four videos. One by one, I flung them as hard as I could, far out into the water. After the last one splashed in, I watched the sunlight dance off the spreading ripples.

"You thinking about General Baldwin?" Amanda asked.

"Yeah. He should have told his father the truth."

"About his homosexuality?"

I nodded. "Sam died believing his father would have rejected him. I think Sam was wrong."

"Fear of rejection," she said quietly, "is a powerful deterrent. It keeps a lot of people from doing things they should."

Her eyes held mine; inviting a response.

"And saying things," I replied.

A tired smile. "C'mon. Let's go, Marty."

As she turned to leave, I said it. Those three little words I'd wanted to tell her for years. Timing is everything and mine couldn't have been worse. At that moment, the ski-boat roared by close to shore, drowning me out. It must have drowned me out, because Amanda continued up the embankment without looking back.

Not even once.

★55★

It was hard to believe I'd been gone only twenty-four hours. It felt more like a week. If time is judged by the intensity of one's experiences, it could easily have been a month.

The sun perched like an orange ball on the horizon as I turned down the long gravel drive toward the rustic farmhouse my parents left to me when they moved to Florida. Since Dad had been a crop duster, the house included twenty acres and a grass airstrip that doubled as my front yard. Amanda lived in a modest brick one-story several hundred yards behind me, on a couple acres she'd sweet-talked my Dad into selling her.

Dad liked Amanda . . . a lot.

Approaching my house, I saw my daughter Emily step out onto the front porch, and throw up a tentative wave. I'd phoned earlier, telling her when to expect me.

"What are you going to say to her?" Amanda asked.

I read the concern in her voice. "Relax, I won't overreact."

"Since when?"

Ouch.

I continued down the road toward Amanda's. As I came

to a stop, she shook Enrique, who was still sleeping. He groaned and rolled over.

"I'll wake him later," I said. "There's something I want to say to you."

Her eyes crawled up to mine, as if she sensed what was coming.

"I'll walk you to the door." I gave her a smile and reached for the latch.

"I heard you, Marty," she whispered.

It took me a second. I twisted around and stared at her. "I see." After a beat, I heard myself say, "Bob? You're still going to marry him?"

"This has nothing to do with him. It's about you."

"Me?"

"This isn't the time for you to make this kind of decision. You're hurting. You're emotionally vulnerable. One of your closest friends died and you were almost killed. You're only doing this because—"

"I love you. I know I love you." The words came out easily this time.

Amanda's eyes caressed mine. "Why now, Marty? After all this time, why now?"

"I wasn't . . . ready before." It sounded lame, but it was the truth. It had always been the truth.

"And you're suddenly ready now? Today? This minute?"

"Yes."

She studied me without speaking. "Tell me," she said softly, "if Sam hadn't died, if I wasn't engaged, would you still be telling me this?"

The yes was on the tip of my tongue, but I couldn't lie to her. "I don't know. I hope so."

She smiled sadly. "You still aren't ready, Marty. You know it and I know it."

My left hand was curled on the seat back. She glanced at my wedding band and shook her head. Opening the door, she paused, looking at me. "In some respects, it's better this way. I could never have been sure. I always would have felt I forced you into it."

"Forced me how?"

But she'd climbed from the limo and closed the door. I watched her slowly walk toward her house.

"She means the movie," a voice said suddenly.

I spun around, saw Enrique ease upright. He blinked at me sleepily. "You know you're crazy if you let her get away."

"Tell me something I don't know."

He crawled up to the fridge, took out a beer and killed about a third of it. Stretching back, he gave me a long look. "You want to know about the movie?"

"Please."

Instead of talking about the *Sleepless in Seattle* connection, he first explained about Bob. Afterwards, I felt relieved and extremely foolish.

I knew Bob well.

Enrique passed on my offer of dinner, saying he needed to get back. As he drove off, I turned to my daughter who was standing beside me on the porch. She looked at me anxiously, waiting for the shoe to drop.

I smiled away her concerns. "It's almost time for dinner, honey. Tell Mrs. Anuncio I'll be down in ten minutes."

Getting cleaned up was only one of the things I felt compelled to do. After grabbing a quick shower, I dressed in front of my bureau and spoke to Nicole's picture. It was a test; I had to know whether I really was ready. When I finished saying what I had to say, I stood there for several minutes, waiting for the guilt to come.

It never did.

During dinner, Emily continually shot me furtive looks and squirmed in her chair. I made small talk, asking her about school, the dance, her studies . . . everything except what happened last night. She responded like a prisoner of war under interrogation, suspicious of every question and volunteering nothing. It didn't make for great dinner conversation, but at least I didn't have to deal with her hormonal, teenage princess attitude.

After dessert, I made a drink and announced I was going out onto the porch. Emily watched me leave with a look of astonishment. I heard her talking to Mrs. Anuncio, asking what was wrong with me. Sliding into my battered rocking chair, I barely swallowed my first sip before Mrs. A's stocky frame materialized before me. She bluntly asked whether I was going to "poonish" Emily.

Her English was improving. I told her I didn't think I was.

"Why change? Always, you punish."

"That's not true."

"True. You soldier. No change."

Logic I wasn't sure I understood. I sighed, "Well, I'm not going to punish her now."

Mrs. A withdrew, grumbling. I heard her say the word "loco." She was mistaken. I wasn't crazy; I was scared. Sam had scared me.

As I nursed my drink and contemplated the dark, I thought about how fearful Sam had been of sharing his secret with his family. They were the one group in the world he should have felt he could trust. Since Emily and I were all we had, it terrified me that she might feel that way about me. Was it wrong not to punish her for drinking? Probably.

But right now, I couldn't bring myself to do anything else.

Rocking slowly, I replayed the events of the past twenty-four hours. I thought about the ambition that could drive a beautiful and talented woman to kill her own nephew. I thought about her husband and how he'd almost reached the pinnacle of power, only to be brought down by her treachery. I thought about the twists of fate, which led to the death of the innocents at the rectory and the guilty in the auditorium. Finally, I thought about Sam and the tragedy of a life defined by fear. Not only the fear of being found out, but also the fear of not measuring up to his legacy. At times, the combined pressure must have been unbearable.

At least that was over for him now. Sam was through being afraid.

Gazing at the stars, I raised my glass in a silent toast to him. As I did, I noticed Emily framed in the doorway.

"Something wrong, Em?"

"I can't take it, Dad. Shout. Yell. Do *something*."

"Why?" I asked mildly.

"*I got drunk.*"

"Did you intend to get drunk?"

"No. I mean I knew the punch tasted funny—"

"Will you do it again?"

Her pretty face twisted into an exaggerated scowl. "No way. It was disgusting. I was sooo sick."

"It seems to me you've learned your lesson."

Her face untwisted, pausing at a suspicious squint. "That's it?"

"That's it."

"You're not going to restrict me or anything?"

"Nope." I tried to reassure her with a smile.

Apparently, it wasn't reassuring enough. She promptly deposited herself in the chair beside me. "Dad, why are you doing this? Why are you letting me off so easy?"

I almost didn't tell her the truth. Then it occurred to me I wasn't giving her enough credit. She was thirteen, more adult than child.

So I told her about Sam. Our history together, the secret he kept. I told her everything except the part about the killings.

"He believed his parents would be ashamed of him?" she said.

I nodded.

She got quiet, thinking this over. "It's kinda sad, isn't it?"

"Very."

Her big eyes focused uncertainly on me. "Would you ever be ashamed of me, Dad?"

Something wrenched inside me. "Never, honey. You're my proudest achievement. Nothing you could do will ever take that away. You know that, right?"

A nod. She shifted in her chair, biting her lip. "Dad, there's something I need to tell you."

"Anything."

Twice she started to speak, but held back. She avoided my gaze and I could see she had her guilty look. I asked gently, "Does this have to do with the party last night?"

"No. It's something else. It . . . it's sort of a confession . . ."

"*Sleepless in Seattle.*"

Her eyes popped wide. "You *know*?"

I nodded.

She jumped excitedly from her chair. "Amanda. She must have told you. It must have worked. I knew it would 'cause—"

"Not so fast, Em. Nothing's been decided yet."

Her brow furrowed in confusion and disappointment. "Don't you like her?"

"Very much."

"She likes you."

"I know."

"Then I don't understand."

I sighed. "We're adults, honey. Silly adults who don't know any—"

I stopped when I saw Emily's eyes darted past me. When her face lit up, I realized who it was even before I turned around.

"Hello, Bob," Amanda said.

★56★

When Emily saw *Sleepless in Seattle* on HBO last month, her romantic teenage mind latched onto the idea of orchestrating her own matchmaking attempt. Emily concluded that the only way to stir me to action was to make me jealous. Enter the very fictitious and extremely wealthy fiancé Bob, a name Emily had chosen as an ironic little joke, since Robert was my middle name.

In my defense, the reason I never made the connection was because no one had ever called me Robert or Bob in my life. Hell, I barely even knew I had a middle name.

An excuse Enrique never came close to buying.

"It won't flush, Marty. We were dropping hints all over the place."

"Just tell me the rest of it," I said irritably.

So Enrique told me that Simon endorsed the deception, but Amanda wanted no part of it. She had no desire to trick me into coming around. Even after Simon shelled out for the monster engagement ring, it took him several more weeks to convince her to play along.

"Look," Enrique said, "I'm not sure why I'm even telling you all this, except that I think you two are both nuts. If you like each other so much, why can't you get together? How hard can it be?"

"You have an hour?"

Rising from our chairs, Emily and I watched Amanda slowly make her way up the porch steps. She said to me, "Enrique called. Said you two had a talk. I decided I should explain."

I nodded, deducing as much.

Flashing Emily a tired smile, she asked, "So what's the verdict? Need me to ask the judge for an appeal?"

When Emily told her of my decision, Amanda appraised me coolly. "My, my. No bread and water for thirty days?"

"Only for the second offense."

Emily kept grinning, anticipating the proverbial happy ending. What she didn't seem to realize was that this wasn't a movie and we weren't standing on the top of the Empire State Building.

I said, "Uh, Em. Do you mind if—"

"I'm gone, Dad." She practically skipped toward the door. "If you want me to turn off the lights—"

I shot her a blistering look.

She winked at Amanda. "Dad's okay. He's a little slow because he hasn't had much prac—"

"*Emily.*"

She giggled, disappearing into house.

My ears burned. Facing Amanda, I said awkwardly, "Have a seat. I'll get you a drink—"

She shook me off. "I only came over to tell you . . . to apologize. I never really wanted to do it. That's why I tried to decline the investigation, made everything so . . . difficult."

"If it helps, I'm glad the way things turned out. Being with you made me realize how much I—"

"Don't say it, Marty. I'm pretty fragile at the moment. I understand you think you love me."

"I do love you. Very much."

She sighed. "What I said earlier still goes. Why now? Why are you willing to admit your feelings now?"

"Because I'm ready to put the past behind me." I held out my left hand to prove it.

She stared at my ring finger, unable to comprehend what she was seeing. "It's . . . gone."

"It's gone."

"Marty, don't do this unless you're sure. I can't compete with Nicole. I won't compete with her. I couldn't handle it if you—"

"You won't have to compete. I loved Nicole, but she's dead. She died five years ago."

She appeared shocked by my statement. An understandable reaction. She never heard me admit this so bluntly before.

"She's dead," I repeated, "and we're alive. We have a right to be happy."

She shook her head, still unwilling to accept what I was saying. I moved toward her. "I love you, Amanda. I've loved you for a long time."

She stared at me, her eyes glistening. "Marty, I've waited so long. I never thought . . . I never allowed myself to believe . . ."

"Believe it. I'm asking you to believe it."

I drew her to me, felt her tremble in my arms. She kept asking me if I was sure and I said I'd never been so certain about anything in my life. Afterward, we stood clinging to each other and I felt her tears on my shirt. Finally, she tilted her head to me and as I leaned down to kiss her, the porch lights went out.

What took you so long, Emily?

★ Epilogue ★

ONE YEAR LATER

I had no choice, Martin. It was the only way to get something General Baldwin wanted.

For a long time, Simon's justification for whitewashing Teresa Harris's role in the murders bothered me. No matter how hard I pressed him, he would only repeat his remark about unforeseen problems in the initial arrangements. "Someday, you will understand, Martin."

But someday never came. As the months passed and the shooting faded from the headlines, I gradually forgot about his comments and the case. To be honest, I wanted to forget, so I wouldn't have to think about how much I missed Sam.

That all changed a year later, when I found the letter in my mailbox.

It arrived in a plain white envelope. Other than my typed name and address, nothing else was written on it. The absence of a stamp indicated someone had placed it in my mailbox. Inside the envelope was a single piece of paper, with two typed lines. When I read them, I thought it was a joke. It had to be a joke.

Then I remembered my talk with Sam's mother.

A few days after the shootings, she'd phoned me, apologizing for the rudeness of her husband and asking if I still had Sam's letter. When I said I did, I heard the relief in her voice. After I promised to FedEx it to her, she thanked me for being such a good friend to Sam. She told me his funeral would be held the following week in a secret location, with only close family attending. In light of the circumstances, her husband felt it was better that way. She hoped I understood and I said I did.

What I didn't understand was what she told me next; Sam had been cremated. Knowing their family was devout Catholic, I mentioned my surprise over this.

"It was Sam's wish, Marty. He made it clear he wanted to be cremated."

"I see."

But at the time, I didn't see. Now, as I stared at the letter in my hand, I was thinking about the cremation and the secret funeral and Simon's remark about unforseen problems. It was all beginning to make sense now.

"I'm afraid of Hell," the first line read.

And below: "Clayter Lake."

I arrived at the lake around four in the afternoon. It was a beautiful spring day, clear and cool, and as I drove around the campground, I could see it was only about a quarter full. Rounding a bend, I came to a familiar rock outcropping and glanced at a nearby campsite, where a shiny new Toyota Land Cruiser was parked. Through the trees, I could make out a domed tent and a bobbing ski boat.

Pulling in behind the Toyota, I followed a rocky path toward the tent. As I passed through the trees, I saw a man in a wet suit standing in knee-deep water, bending over the boat. He appeared to be quite tall and had long, shoulder-length brown hair.

I said tentatively, "Sam?"

The man glanced up, frowning. His face was hidden by a neatly trimmed beard. "Who is Sam, Mister?"

I squinted at the man. "A friend of mine. I was supposed to meet him here."

The man shrugged, stepping out of the water. "Must be at another site. My name's Caldwell. Stephen Caldwell."

It had to be Sam; it was his voice. But the beard held me in check. I couldn't be absolutely certain if—

The man's face spread into smile. He began to laugh.

I said, "You son of a bitch."

"It was worth it. But whatever you do, don't call me Sam. He's dead, remember? Sam Baldwin is dead."

He laughed harder and harder, as if he'd pulled a joke on the entire world.

When you think about it, I guess he did.

POCKET BOOKS
PROUDLY PRESENTS

The Commander
Patrick A. Davis

Available in paperback November 2004
from Pocket Books

Turn the page for a preview of
The Commander. . . .

Ray appeared in the doorway. "Chung-hee thinks we should talk," he said quietly.

I shrugged.

"Mind if I come in?"

I hesitated, then waved him to a chair.

After he sat, he gave me a long look. "For the last time, I didn't know General Muller screwed you on your OPR."

OPR stood for the annual officer performance report. I'd been passed over for lieutenant colonel because, in my most recent one, General Muller had marked "nonconcur" in the promotion block.

"Ray," I said wearily, "we've been through this. You're his exec. You processed the evaluation—"

"Damn right. And when I passed it to him,

Muller said he *would* recommend promotion. How was I supposed to know that the son of a bitch was lying? I was as surprised as you were when you didn't get picked up for light bird."

"Uh-huh," I said dryly.

"Cut me some slack, huh? If I'd known, don't you think I would have told you?"

"Maybe. Unless you were ordered not to."

His face hardened. "You're way out of line, Burt. You know I'd never have gone along with something like—"

"What about my wedding?"

Ray grimaced, but said nothing. He had no response, and we both knew it. Ray had promised to come to the ceremony but never showed. Later, he'd called to apologize, explaining that General Muller had suggested it wouldn't look good for his executive officer to attend.

"Jesus, Burt, what was I supposed to do?" Ray had said. "The son of a bitch practically ordered me not to go."

I'd told him I understood, that it was okay. But of course it wasn't okay. I was hurt. From then on, I knew our friendship would only go so far.

Ray eased into a chair with an apologetic

smile. "We've been friends for a long time. Let's not let it end like this."

I appraised him, trying to determine whether he was sincere or just talking. Because with Ray, I couldn't tell anymore.

"Aw, hell," he said, rubbing a hand over his face. "You're right. I know I push too hard, trying to make rank. Over the years, I must have told myself a hundred times to ease up, but it's not that easy to . . . to just turn things off. And it's cost me big time. First Linda and the kids . . ." He focused on me. "And now maybe you."

Linda was his ex-wife. She'd gamely hung on for five years, trying to get Ray to put her and their twin sons, Michael and James, somewhere on his list of priorities. I remembered her phone call to me a week before she left him. They'd had a fight about his working another weekend, and Linda was crying. She said she couldn't take the neglect anymore and asked me whether I thought he would ever change. I was torn about how to respond, but figured I owed her the truth. Besides, I wasn't telling her anything she didn't already know.

"He won't," I'd said.

Their divorce became final a year later,

shortly before Ray came to Korea. In the past fourteen months, he's flown back twice to see his sons. He'd planned on another visit recently, but had abruptly canceled it without explanation.

Ray was staring at me, his expression subdued. As if he sensed my thoughts, he said, "She recently got remarried, you know."

"Linda?"

A nod. "A college professor. That's why I didn't fly out to see the kids. I couldn't have handled seeing him there. With them."

"I'm sorry, Ray."

"Yeah . . ." He stared at his hands.

Seeing his pain, I felt a wave of sympathy. Even though he hadn't been much of a husband or father, he'd loved Linda and his boys deeply.

Looking up, he said, "Burt, I'd really like to square things between us—"

"We're square."

"You sure?"

"Like a box." I gave him a faint smile. "Anyway, Chung-hee thinks I overreacted. Maybe she's right. I always knew getting passed over was a possibility, but when it actually happened—" I stopped. The cell phone in Ray's jacket was chirping.

He answered it, listened for perhaps ten seconds, then said curtly, "I'll call you back in five minutes, sir." He eyed me uneasily as he hung up. "That concerned you . . . whether you'd agreed to help."

I shook my head. "Tell General Muller—"

"That was Ambassador Gregson."

I frowned, my curiosity rising. I'd gotten to know Ambassador Gregson from a case I'd worked on last year involving an Air Force major assigned to the American embassy in Seoul. It turned out the guy was a junkie who had been selling classified information to North Korean operatives to support his drug habit. I asked, "Why would Gregson care whether I'm involved—"

Ray abruptly stood and went to the door.

After he shut it, he returned, speaking quickly. "Burt, what I can tell you is this thing is damned serious. The Korean government, the State Department, the American military, everyone is jumping through hoops, trying to figure out how to handle the situation. The current plan is to keep the press out of it until an investigation can be conducted to determine who is responsible. The Koreans will have the lead, but Ambassador Gregson wants an American to monitor the investigation and protect U.S. interests. You must have impressed Gregson on that embassy investigation because he personally called General Muller and ordered him to assign you to this thing. When Muller told him you'd resigned from the service, Gregson went ballistic. He calmed down when I told him you still lived in the area and might be available. Officially, you'll be a contract civilian assigned to the embassy security detail. Gregson's already having the paperwork ginned up for your signature." Ray stepped toward me with an expectant look. "So how about it?"

"Jesus," I murmured. Ray had spit everything out so fast that I was having trouble taking it all in. "We're not talking a murder investigation, are we?" Because with all the high-level interest, I was thinking it had to be something with a major political connection, possibly another espionage case involving a high-ranking diplomat or—

"First things first. You in?"

I paused, uncomfortable with rushing into a decision before knowing the facts. But I knew Ray wouldn't give me anything more. "I'm in."

Ray grinned and asked for my fax number as

he thumbed the redial on his cell phone. After a brief conversation with Ambassador Gregson, he made a second call to General Muller. By the time he hung up, my fax machine on the table was clicking away. I went over to it, and Ray joined me.

"Your contract with the embassy," he said to me.

I nodded. "Let's hear the rest of it."

"It's a murder."

"Okay . . ."

"A bar girl from one of the clubs. Her body was found a couple of hours ago in her apartment after someone anonymously called the Osan security police emergency line to report an injured woman. The Security Police dispatcher said the voice was heavily muffled, but it was definitely made by a man." He paused. "An American."

I felt a chill. No wonder the State Department and the Korean government were running scared. This would be the third major PR hit against the U.S. military in less than a year. The first, the shocking revelation that during the Korean War, American GIs had intentionally gunned down fleeing civilians, had generated a swell of anti-American sentiment among the Korean public. The U.S. government tried to temper the outrage by calling for a full inquiry and promising restitution to the victims. For almost six months, the policy seemed to work. The protests died away, and the clamor for an American troop withdrawal faded.

Then three GIs got liquored up and gang-raped a fourteen-year-old girl. In the ensuing riots, a block of Seoul was burned to the ground and forty-two protestors, mostly college students, were killed by the Korean military. With emotions still raw, there would be no telling the extent of the carnage when the word got out that an American soldier had now murdered a Korean.

"Son of a bitch," I murmured.

Ray nodded grimly. "And that's not the worst of it. The brutality of the killing is particularly scary. If that aspect ever became public—"

"How brutal?"

The fax machine had gone silent, and Ray was plucking the pages from the tray. After a quick look, he passed them over. "Sign the last page and fax it back. Then we'll run over to the murder scene." He frowned at my head shake. "There a problem?"

I told him I needed to go home and change first, explaining that Korean detectives always wore suits and I was going to be out of place in a pullover shirt and khaki slacks. He was gazing at me skeptically when I finished.

"It's important, Ray. They might take my dress as a sign of disrespect."

"You're actually serious?"

I nodded. Ray's ignorance of Korean customs didn't surprise me. Other than an occasional shopping trip to the Ville, he rarely left the confines of the base.

Ray checked his watch. "There's no time, Burt. Investigation's already started. General Muller ordered me to get you there ASAP."

The lap-dog image popped into my head again, but I refrained from comment. I quickly read through the contract.

It was for thirty days and listed my job title as a security consultant. I'd be paid a little over seven thousand dollars, the monthly salary of a GS-13—the Civil Service rank—equivalent to a lieutenant colonel. There wasn't anything in the fine print that I couldn't live with, so I grabbed a pen when I got to the last page.

"By the way," Ray said, "the girl was disemboweled."

I froze, holding the pen over the signature block. Seconds passed. I didn't move.

"I know," Ray said. "That really shook me too."

But the horror of the crime didn't disturb me as much as what it suggested about my role. I slowly straightened, setting down the pen. "Why does Ambassador Gregson really want me on this case?"

Ray seemed puzzled. "I told you. You'd impressed him."

"Bullshit. The case against the major was cut-and-dried."

He shrugged. "Well, that's what Gregson told—What are you doing now?"

I'd stepped around him and was reaching for the phone on my desk. I said, "Gregson needs to understand I won't cover anything up. If an American turns out to be the killer, then I'm obliged to—"

"Oh, come on, Burt. Don't you think Gregson knows that? His concern . . . the State Department's concern . . . is that the ROKs don't pin this on some American without cause." ROK stood for Republic of Korea; it was a common term to describe the South Koreans.

I gave Ray a dubious look. He was suggesting a possible frame job. To me that was the last thing the Koreans would do because of all the turmoil it would cause.

"You're forgetting," Ray went on, "the push for reunification. A lot of ROK officials would love to see Uncle Sam tossed out because they think it will speed up the process."

I paused, holding up the phone. Ray had a point, but I still thought I should—

"Trust me on this, Burt," Ray said. "You're wasting your time calling. Ambassador Gregson personally assured me he's only after the truth."

I couldn't help but wonder if maybe Ray had a reason for not wanting me to talk to Gregson. But that's crazy. Why should Ray mind if—

"Anyway," Ray added, "Ambassador Gregson won't be in now. He's already left for a meeting with President Rhee and the ROK cabinet. How about I call Gregson at home tonight? Express your concerns? Okay?"

I nodded, hanging up the phone. "A couple of things I'll need. I don't have a military ID to get on the base."

"Way ahead of you. General Muller has instructed the security police to allow your entry."

"Fine. I'd also like someone from the OSI office assisting me."

"It's being arranged. That woman investigator you're so high on, Lieutenant Torres, will meet you at the scene."

I nodded my approval. Despite her relative inexperience, I considered Susan Torres the most competent investigator on the OSI staff.

"Anything else?" Ray asked.

I thought, then shook my head. It took me another minute to sign and fax the acceptance page to the embassy. I grabbed a notepad, my dog-eared Korean-English dictionary, and a couple of pens from the desk and went over to a small storage closet by the safe. Next to Chung-hee's raincoat hung a blue corduroy sports jacket that had seen better days. I slipped it on and joined Ray, who was holding open the door.

Following him out into the short hallway, I said, "I assume I'll report my findings to Ambassador Gregson."

"Nope. To me."

"Oh?"

He pulled up at the staircase and faced me. "Both Gregson and General Muller feel it will be more efficient for me to act as a liaison. Not that I agree. Hell, I think it'd be easier for you to talk to them directly."

So did I. But at least this explained why Ray hadn't wanted me to call.

He gave a suggestive cough as he eyed my

coat. "Uh, Burt, about your jacket. You might want to reconsider wearing something—"

"Don't go there, Ray."

He grinned, about-faced, and we went down the steps.

Join top authors for the ultimate cruise experience. Spend 7 days in the Western Caribbean aboard the luxurious *Carnival Elation*. Start in Galveston, TX, and visit Progreso, Cozumel, and Belize. Enjoy all this with a ship full of authors, entertainers, and book lovers on the **"Get Caught Reading at Sea Cruise"** October 17–24, 2004.

Mail in this coupon with proof of purchase* by September 1, 2004 to receive $250 per person off the regular **"Get Caught Reading at Sea Cruise"** price. One coupon per person required to receive $250 discount, subject to availability. Offer valid in the U.S.A. Void where prohibited. Sponsors not responsible for lost, late, illegible, postage due, or misdirected mail. Limit 1 per customer.

For further details call **1-877-ADV-NTGE** or visit **www.GetCaughtReadingatSea.com**

PRICES STARTING AT $749 PER PERSON WITH COUPON!

If you liked *A Slow Walk to Hell*, you'll love Patrick Davis's other bestselling paperback, *A Long Day for Dying*.

*Proof of purchase is original sales receipt with the book purchased circled. (No copies allowed.)

Carnival
The Most Popular Cruise Line in the World.

GET $250 OFF

Name   (Please Print)

Address   Apt. No.

City   State   Zip

Email Address

See Following Page for Terms and Conditions.

For booking form and complete information, go to www.GetCaughtReadingatSea.com or call 1-877-ADV-NTGE.

09630

Carnival Elation

7 Day Exotic Western Caribbean Itinerary

DAY	PORT	ARRIVE	DEPART
Sun	Galveston		4:00 P.M.
Mon	"Fun Day" at Sea		
Tue	Progreso/Merida	8:00 A.M.	4:00 P.M.
Wed	Cozumel	9:00 A.M.	5:00 P.M.
Thu	Belize	8:00 A.M.	6:00 P.M.
Fri	"Fun Day" at Sea		
Sat	"Fun Day" at Sea		
Sun	Galveston	8:00 A.M.	

TERMS AND CONDITIONS

PAYMENT SCHEDULE:
50% due upon booking
Full and final payment due by July 26, 2004

Acceptable forms of payment are Visa, MasterCard, American Express, Discover and checks. The cardholder must be one of the passengers traveling. A fee of $25 will apply for all returned checks. Check payments must be made payable to **Advantage International, LLC and sent to: Advantage International, LLC, 195 North Harbor Drive, Suite 4206, Chicago, IL 60601**

CHANGE/CANCELLATION:
Notice of change/cancellation must be made in writing to Advantage International, LLC.

Change:
Changes in cabin category may be requested and can result in increased rate and penalties. A name change is permitted 60 days or more prior to departure and will incur a penalty of $50 per name change. Deviation from the group schedule and package is a cancellation.

Cancellation:

181 days or more prior to departure	$250 per person
121 - 180 days or more prior to departure	50% of the package price
120 - 61 days prior to departure	75% of the package price
60 days or less prior to departure	100% of the package price (nonrefundable)

US and Canadian citizens are required to present a valid passport or the original birth certificate and state issued photo ID (drivers license). All other nationalities must contact the consulate of the various ports that are visited for verification of documentation.

<u>We strongly recommend trip cancellation insurance!</u>

For further details call 1-877-ADV-NTGE or visit www.GetCaughtReadingatSea.com

---

For booking form and complete information
go to **www.getcaughtreadingatsea.com** or call **1-877-ADV-NTGE**

Complete coupon and booking form and mail both to:
**Advantage International, LLC,
195 North Harbor Drive, Suite 4206, Chicago, IL 60601**